BROKEN GROUND

Also by John Keeble

Crab Canon
Mine (with Ransom Jeffery)
Yellowfish

BROKEN GROUND

John Keeble

Harper & Row, Publishers, New York
Cambridge, Philadelphia, San Francisco
London, Mexico City, São Paulo, Singapore, Sydney

Excerpts from this work have appeared in *Willow Springs* #16 (1985), Cheney, Washington, and in *Rolling Stock* #11 (1986), Boulder, Colorado. Certain material has been drawn from Colonel John C. Frémont's *Exploring Expedition in the Rocky Mountains* (1849), originally published by George Derby and Company, Buffalo, New York; Captain James Colnett's *The Journal of Captain James Colnett Aboard the Argonaut from April 16, 1789 to November 3, 1791*, The Champlain Society, Toronto, Ontario; and from Dr. Loon's "Tusk Shell, Gold Dollar, Pulp Note, and Weed: Four Principles of Economy in the Six Rivers/Humboldt Bay Region," which appeared in *Reinhabiting a Separate Country; a Bioregional Anthology of Northern California*, edited by Peter Berg (1978), Planet Drum Foundation, San Francisco. Passages from Hector Zeta's *Manifesto for Spirits* are quoted from manuscript with the permission of the author.

A hardcover edition of this book was published in 1987 by Harper & Row, Publishers.

First PERENNIAL LIBRARY edition published 1989.

Library of Congress Cataloging-in-Publication Data

Keeble, John, 1944–
  Broken ground.
  I. Title.
[PS3561.E3B7 1989]   813'.54   88-45616
ISBN 0-06-091523-4 (pbk.)

89 90 90 91 92 93 FG 10 9 8 7 6 5 4 3 2 1

For the refugee
in retreat . . .

Grateful acknowledgment is made to the John Simon Guggenheim Memorial Foundation and to Eastern Washington University for support given as the book was composed. I owe also an inexpressible debt to my brother, Paul, for sharing with me his knowledge of architecture and construction, for taking me into the "field," and for putting me in touch with his friends and associates in the construction trade. These in turn, and especially Chris Green, gave freely of their knowledge. For their advice and counsel with the manuscript, I wish to thank, as always, my wife, Claire; my editor, Ted Solotaroff; and my friends Michelle Huneven and Fred Newberry.

BROKEN
GROUND

Chapter One

*The line between life and death is as translucent as the sac that bounds
the bulging innards of the jackrabbit.*

Hector Zeta,
Manifesto for Spirits

The midnight-blue pickup stopped at the curb in front of Gus and Jewel
Lafleur's house. Henry Lafleur slid out of the cab to the pavement. On
the pickup door was a plastic stick-on sign that said CUSTOM EXCAVATION.
Under the words a phone number had been struck out with a stripe of
black paint.

Lafleur stepped up onto the grass and then to the sidewalk, which had
been fractured by the root systems of the big maple trees that lined the
street. The trees were just leafing out. Evening light slanted against the
trunks and spidery limbs and it glinted on the power lines. The neighborhood was an old one in Portland, Oregon, and the years had obscured the
geometry of the street, sidewalks, power poles, and of the kit houses set
back just so on the lots.

Lafleur turned onto Gus and Jewel's walkway. The stem tips of the
almond tree that stood in the center of the yard had swelled, and beneath
the tree a webwork of new green peeped through the pale of last year's
grass. The plywood ramp that he'd built over the steps thudded softly
under his boots. A huge azalea leaned ominously into the porch. Along

1

the rail stood a row of pots in which Jewel had started her geraniums. The deck was dark gray, the wall of the house was a lighter gray, and the trim was white. A swinging divan with blue cushions hung from the ceiling, and for just an instant he saw the apparitions of three children sitting there, swinging. He paused for a moment before the doorway, deeply inhaling the fragrance of cooking food. He pulled back the screen, knocked lightly, and pushed the door open.

Jewel met him just inside, embraced him, and then leaned back, holding firmly onto his arms and smiling. She had a striking face, strong chin and cheeks, sharp eyes, and leathery, profoundly wrinkled skin. Lafleur smiled back, then glanced over her shoulder at Gus, his father, who was asleep in a reclining chair. Jewel moved to the chair and gently raised its back, making the old man fold in the middle. She held one leg against Gus's knees so that he wouldn't slide onto the floor. Gus awakened and stared blankly outward. Jewel bent and straightened him up. "Hank's here," she said. Slowly, Gus focused on his son, and then executed the half-inch movement of his head that Lafleur knew as the remnant of his father's habitual friendly greeting from the old days. Now the pale skin of the face did not move and the eyes seemed bleached. Lafleur asked his father how he was. Gus nodded again, and grunted softly: "Ugh."

Lafleur followed Jewel into the kitchen, where the fragrance grew dense—beef, bread, and vegetables. He murmured with pleasure. Jewel smiled at him. Her black hair was lined with silver. She had kept it long and let it hang in a loose rope down her back when she was home. Lafleur admired Jewel. It was not easy to be widowed, then to marry another man and a few years later have him become helpless. As he looked at her and received her warmth, his eyes welled with tears. This had been happening to him lately.

Jewel picked up a pot from the stove, strained the steaming liquid into the sink, then dumped the contents—broccoli—into a bowl. The strong scent was like a garden, like black earth, like leaves after a hard rain. She turned and set the pot down lightly on the counter. Her suppleness, the strength in her hands, and her hair belied her age.

Lafleur carried the vegetables to the dining room, then the meat. He moved into the living room and stopped near his father, who still wore his old khaki trousers and plaid shirt, but whose body, like his nod, was a vestige of what it had been. The clothes were baggy. The ankles going into the worn slippers looked like sticks. He'd had a stroke and it had shocked his face into stillness and turned his skin white as porcelain. His silver hair was sparse and wispy. Lafleur feared for his ghostly father, for the stymied life in him.

Jewel rolled the wheelchair into the living room. The two of them

2

maneuvered Gus into it. Jewel held Gus by hugging him full about the body and Lafleur steadied the operation by holding Gus's elbows. Once again, Lafleur was appalled by how light his father was, how limp and doll-like. As he wheeled his father to the table, he gazed down at the kidney-colored blotches that showed through the fine hair. Jewel came along with the catheter bag.

"Did somebody called Clinton U find you?" she asked.

Lafleur looked at her. "You?"

Jewel laughed softly and gestured with the bag, making the liquid slosh against the plastic walls. "I did the same thing. U as in T, U, V. Chinese, I guess."

"Who is U?" he said. His mind knotted on the nonsense of the question.

As Jewel bent to attach the bag to the side of the wheelchair, her hair slid over her shoulder and touched the floor. She checked the connection between the tube and the bag, then straightened up, brushed back her hair, and said, "I don't know." Lafleur nudged the wheelchair close to the table. Gus sat there still as a stone. Jewel sat down. Lafleur sat across from her. Between them rested the steaming bowls of broccoli, carrots, mashed potatoes, a fresh loaf of bread, a salad of blanched spinach and egg, and the beef dish—a feast.

The stewed meat smelled of garlic, sage, and bay. The herbs, Jewel would say, were there to combat the drugs Gus had to use, and his lack of activity. The garlic cleansed his system, the bay aided digestion, the sage mollified the midnight sweats. She'd told Lafleur that sometimes she would wake up at night and hear Gus moaning and feel his side of the bed drenched with perspiration. It was as if he came alive in his dreams where nobody could see him, she'd said.

Jewel was of the old school, a farmgirl from Nevada who had survived thirty years in the Multnomah County Auditor's Office. Arcane things appeared from her stores—blackberry root, nettle, and wormwood, or birch leaves to purify Gus's blood. With these armaments she waged war against her husband's infirmity. The linen cloth she'd spread across the table, the white Austrian china with its delicately painted rosebuds, and the glittering chandelier above their heads were also among the weapons. The table setting appeared and the chandelier was lit whenever guests came so she could show Gus that some things in life were still fine. Lafleur always handled the china cautiously. Along with the chandelier, it was an heirloom. Jewel had children of her own, a son in Minneapolis and a daughter in San Diego, and Lafleur sensed a perhaps angry orbit there and felt a vague guilt for what had befallen Jewel as a member of his family.

He said grace.

Then Jewel said, "I thought he was a salesman at first, but his suit was too expensive. He came in a Cadillac and had a ring with a stone big enough to choke on. He had glasses thick as bottle bottoms. He asked how your father was. He said he'd been trying to reach you on a business matter. I was sure you knew each other."

"Never heard of the guy," Lafleur said, then smiling, he added, "U."

She looked relieved. "I told him you had no phone, that he should catch you at work." She placed dollops of food on Gus's plate, then looked across at Lafleur again. Her face shuddered. It was a stirring as of leaves by the wings of a small bird. "Eat," she said.

He served himself. Jewel held a spoonful of potato in front of Gus. Gus opened his mouth and she put the potato in. Gus's eyes grew wider as he chewed. Jewel served herself. Lafleur slipped his fork under a chunk of broccoli. He stopped for a moment and inhaled deeply, inwardly marking his appreciation for the one homecooked meal he got during the week. It was a second, flashing prayer, one of gratitude for Jewel's generosity. He ate the broccoli, then said, "What's wrong?"

When Jewel sighed, Lafleur's eyes darted to his father. "No, Hank," she said, meaning it was not Gus, that he was fine, or the same at least. She looked straight at Lafleur with her luminous gray eyes. "It's Ned Blaylock," she said. "He's putting the squeeze on us."

Lafleur set down his fork. Jewel went on. She told him that his father's company, the old partnership of forty years between Gus and Blaylock, had been taking losses and that Blaylock was applying his father's interest to offset the shortfall. He was expanding from excavation to general contracting, she said, though he and Gus had been planning that before Gus's stroke, or had been fighting over it. Lafleur knew about that, that each old man had tried to outdo the other by hatching one new scheme after another, but he'd had too many of his own troubles at the time to pay close attention.

Jewel touched the edge of her plate with her fingertips and said that now Blaylock wouldn't stop, or slow down, or listen. He'd fortified the gap left by Gus. He wouldn't give her figures. He wouldn't answer her questions. He hardly acknowledged her existence.

When Jewel paused, Lafleur said, "But he has to."

"Supposedly."

"You've got power of attorney."

"I'm a woman. To a man like that, do you know what that means?" Jewel said. Lafleur squinted at her, not speaking. He guessed he knew. "To a man like that," Jewel said, "power of attorney means you'd damn well better go out and hire the best one you can find."

Lafleur remembered his father's periodic anger with Blaylock, and the

4

bitter conversations at the dinner table, the anxiety Blaylock sometimes caused in his mother. He remembered Blaylock's drinking habits and being afraid of Blaylock himself when he was little, and just now as he stared at the spears of light Jewel's chandelier cast against the ceiling, a haunting from his boyhood flashed through his mind: the giant of a man seen usually back in a dim corner of the shop, or bent into a piece of machinery with a flashlight in his mouth and the neck of a pint bottle sticking out of the back pocket of his grimy coveralls.

Blaylock was a mechanic, which was how he and Gus had come together. The two young men, a diesel mechanic, a good one, and a heavy-equipment operator, another good one, had joined forces after the war to make a company. Blaylock ran the equipment yard that through the years came to surround his big house down on the river, twenty miles south of Portland. He'd rarely spoken to Lafleur, the boy, who sometimes went up to the yard with his father from their house, which was less than a mile down the road from Blaylock's place. Lafleur remembered the few times Blaylock had, the man coming near and grasping his arm, bending down from above as he told the boy to stay away from something, or to get over there—to *watch out!*

Once Lafleur had been in a dozer cab, pretending to operate the controls. He heard Blaylock shout. When he looked across the yard, he saw the man darkening the doorway of a shop. The boy—Hank—started to climb out of the cab, but Blaylock shouted again, "Get off that!" As he slipped to the ground, Hank looked back and saw the big man striding toward him. He ran across the yard, heading for the front where he had left his father, but Blaylock cut him off at the side of the house and backed him into a corner. He grabbed Hank's shoulder and forced him down to the mud. Blaylock had a monkey wrench in one hand. Hank saw the wrench rising.

He saw the wrench glint above the man's shoulder. The man stared venomously at him and bent down, tightening the grip on his shoulder. Hank writhed in pain and shrank from the man's nearness, from the stink of sweat and of sweet, overpowering breath, and from the wrench poised against the sky, but suddenly Blaylock released him and straightened up, rocking slowly. He looked at his wrench. Hank didn't move. He hardly breathed. "It's you," Blaylock said, meaning Hank, his partner's son, but looking at his wrench. "You," Blaylock said, drawing the wrench close to his face and addressing it, or addressing the large, bruised, oil-smeared slab of meat that held the wrench, the hand—Lafleur thought now—the mark of the man in all things: levering and hoisting, bullying heavy articles and winching them out, and though big and blunt-fingered, capable of delicate nurselike maneuvers with needle valves and gaskets and with tweezers

5

picking out particles of steel from a cylinder, and of calibrating by touch the foot pounds applied to a turned-down bolt.

Blaylock had stared at his hand as if amazed, as if it, drawn from his essential being, had just issued him an astonishing ultimatum, then he dropped his hand to his side and wheeled away. He tottered, steadied himself, and lumbered off. Hank gulped for air and pulled himself up. The man weaved. He was drunk. Hank had understood that, frightened as he was. Blaylock's hands swung at his sides and the wrench glimmered, then his body tilted through the doorway of the shop and disappeared in the darkness.

Hank began to shiver. He went out front to where his father was chaining down a bulldozer on a trailer. Wiry and darkened by working in the sun, his father cranked the chains snug with a hand-operated winch, hooked the chain, then sprang to the ground and tousled the boy's hair with his hand as he passed by. It was as if nothing were wrong. When Hank got home his mother asked about his trousers, lightly touching the mud-caked knees, but he made an excuse. That night he had a dream that would become a recurring nightmare. In it were points in space that expanded into fathomless planes and then shrank again. The planes never intersected. The points never touched. He was in the dream, marooned. He could not move from one geometrical figure to the next. He could be tiny as a dot or swell to ghastly proportions. The dream was barren. It overwhelmed him with its disconnectedness.

From then on, Hank kept close to his father at Blaylock's place. He observed how his father dealt with the man—circumspectly and crisply. So far as he knew, exchange between the two consisted entirely of externals, the data of their business: equipment, what was ready and what was not, what was needed where and for how long, what needed to be loaded and when, what needed repair, what drivers they would have to hire. The boy knew vaguely that more had to pass between the two—contract bids, taxes, money, moments of friendship, even—but he didn't see that. What he saw was that his father was not afraid, that his father's crispness became formal when Blaylock was drinking, that the formality kept Blaylock out in the light, and that was what the boy eventually learned from the event—the uses of formality, distance, and circumspection.

Lafleur lowered his gaze to Jewel. "He's still drinking?"

Jewel was leaning toward Gus, spooning potato into his mouth. She tipped up the spoon and dragged it under Gus's lip in order to strip off the remains, as with a baby. "He's got his faculties, all right," she said, "if that's what you mean."

"It's hard to believe he's in that deep a hole, then."

"He has work, but he's showing a loss. He has a new machine."

"You bet." Since his separation from his wife, Lafleur had been holing up in his father's toolshed at the old family place just past Blaylock's big pink house. In his trips up and down the road, Lafleur had glimpsed the snout of the new acquisition, an earth-moving machine, a monster parked behind the house. "The LeTourneau," he said. "He wouldn't be able to touch that thing if he weren't solvent."

"How much would it have cost?"

Lafleur shrugged. "It's used. Even so, probably a couple hundred grand."

Jewel looked down at her plate and sighed, then looked up. "Your dad can't make up a loss."

"Why should he?"

Jewel's voice rose. "How's he to make up a loss? Look at him."

"Hey," Lafleur said softly, reaching across and touching her hand.

"I'm sorry." She eased a spoonful of beef into Gus's mouth.

"He has his interest," Lafleur said. He felt something childlike in him, like a cry rising in his throat. At the same time he felt a deep, adult despair—more trouble, another tangle.

"Yes," Jewel said, "but we used to get money every month from the company. Now we get debit statements. He's upset about it," she said, glancing at Gus.

Lafleur looked, too. The old man's once leathery, calloused hands lay on the wheelchair arms like two dead fish. His eyes were milky. It was true that he'd improved. A couple of months ago he hadn't been able to sit at the table. Now he could manage a few steps with his canes and he could even speak after a fashion—the guttural growls and grunts that Jewel translated for him. Maybe there was hope. Maybe there was none. Lafleur didn't know. Gus's jaw worked slowly and beef juice trickled from the corners of his mouth. Jewel dabbed at him with a napkin. Lafleur didn't know what to hope for with his father; for Jewel he hoped for some relief from the care, certainly, but for his father he didn't know at all—for minimal motor control or for complete recovery, for ambulation, for fluid speech, for laughter, for renewed, dynamic life, for a miracle, or for an easy passage in his sleep. "He knows?" Lafleur said.

"Yes," Jewel said. "Blaylock's got a major project on line. They were planning to expand before your dad's stroke. Actually, they'd set up the purchase of that machine, too." Lafleur nodded. He knew that. "Now Blaylock's gone ahead, but the company's going into the red," Jewel said.

"I thought their credit was set in bedrock. You're not saying that Blaylock's deliberately scuttling the company."

"No."

Lafleur cut off a piece of meat and ate it. "They say you have to spend money to make it," he said, although that whole gambit, what he had watched wear his father down as the company grew—talking to bankers and playing with the books, running loans against contract commissions, liquidating inventories, dodging deadlines, laying off help and taking it on, going into hock for supplies—was one reason why he had kept his distance from the partnership.

"Sure," Jewel said. "But maybe not so much. Not so fast. Blaylock won't leave anything alone." Her voice was rising again. "Either people move where he wants them or he beats them down. He's just an old man loaded up with sex and fear."

Despite himself, Lafleur chuckled. "That's quite a picture."

Jewel took a deep breath and smiled weakly back at him. "He's got an accountant writing the books so he can absorb your dad's interest."

"He can't do that."

"It increases the company losses on paper. The more the company loses, the more of your dad's interest Ned absorbs. Now he's about to finance this new project. He's figured out how to squeeze water from a stone."

"It's a scam."

"Of course, Hank. Good heavens."

"I'd get that legal advice."

"I've talked to Louis," she said. "He says he could put a stop to it, but that it'd be better for us to come to terms with Ned. Louis tried to get your dad and Ned to divide their interest and put themselves on salary years ago so this kind of thing couldn't happen. It's a mess, Hank. Louis says he could probably force Ned to liquidate, but it might take forever. He says it would be best just to use legal action as a threat." She fed Gus another spoonful of beef, then turned back. She held the spoon poised above her plate. "Otherwise, there might not be much left. And it would hurt your dad. Hank, we're practically broke."

Alarmed, Lafleur straightened up in his chair and glanced at his father—bony nose and slowly working jaw. The old man blinked. "I wish you'd told me this sooner," he said, and at the same time he thought, But I should have known, I should have asked months ago. I'm an idiot.

"You have your troubles," Jewel said, looking directly at him. She held him with her eyes, and the exchange of their gaze grew long and searching. Something began to heave between them, something exquisite and frightful, a phantom that contained the complexity of his regard for her: she was in the position of his mother, but was not his mother; she was familiar to him through his knowing her and obliquely familiar through her mate, his father, and yet she was a stranger to him. He felt drawn into a flickering world of mortality which, though they were strangers in the blood, they shared quite explicitly. It was like a complicated algebra made up of corporeal and once-corporeal bodies:

His infirm father. Her husband.

His dead mother, whose shoes she filled. And her dead husband, his ghost on her back almost like Lafleur's own near-dead father.

His children, including one who had died—her step-grandchildren.

His estranged wife, Penny—her stepdaughter-in-law. And her friend, too. Penny came to visit more often than he did.

And himself, beset with such algebra: the idiot.

He looked into Jewel's clear gray eyes and traded with her on a subliminal, almost sexual level. He felt overpowered as if by sorcery. He had a glimmering of something coming, but he couldn't name it. He looked away, wondering, What now, where's this going? . . . Then she said, "Ned's charging your dad for the loss of his services. He says he'll stop if your dad puts something back into the company."

Quite calmly—his calm surprised him—Lafleur replied, "And that's the squeeze?"

"That's the pinch. The squeeze is general. This is quite specific."

"I see."

"He has a point in a way," she said. She turned and gazed at Gus for a moment, touching base with him, then to Lafleur she said, "Obviously your dad isn't working."

"But he has the interest, the investment, the years put in to make that company float." Lafleur paused, hearing his own voice rising. "Without him Blaylock would be nowhere."

Jewel's body visibly gathered itself. "Yes."

"I'm sorry," he said. "God, I'm sorry you have to go through all this."

"I know, Hank."

"I'll talk to Blaylock. If we have to, we'll dig up some money somehow until we get it straightened out."

She gave him a worried look, then they were quiet for a moment. They ate. Forks clinked on plates and Gus gurgled softly as he swallowed. Liquid trickled into his catheter bag. Lafleur served himself seconds on meat, potatoes, and bread. Jewel smiled, pleased to see him eat well.

She got up to fetch the coffee. He watched as she passed into the kitchen, her body erect. She held it so against the world. He ate and looked around the dining room, at the cracks in the spackled ceiling. A hutch stood against the opposite wall and on its shelves were knickknacks from both Jewel's and his father and mother's past—ceramic and stone figurines, vases, centennial plates. Among them were articles from Quebec—religious items and French glassware. The artifacts of two long lives brought together late had bred in here with muted passion. Everything

9

in the room, and in the living room and kitchen, was clean and pure as snow, but old and worn.

The house had been toiled over, the yard outside was kept up, and three times a week Jewel had to get Gus out into the car and to the hospital for therapy and back again, and otherwise care for the old man, haggle with the insurance company, balance the checkbook, take the trouble over the last several months to treat him—Lafleur—with kid gloves because of his difficulties, and to counsel Penny, and somehow through all of that maintain her sanity and even the slightly forbidding quality of her strength. On the wall to Lafleur's right hung the household crucifix, glittering in the descending slant of light from the windows at his left.

At his back hung photographs of his family together and then the two children separately. Without looking, he could envision the two—the professional, retouched portraits in which his children, Tricia and Andy, had fixed smiles, gleaming teeth, and angelic, unreal-looking skin. They were quite unlike the kids he'd dropped off across town a couple of hours ago—today, Saturday, his day with them.

When he'd arrived at their place early this morning, the drape in the living-room window flicked back and the edge of a long form appeared: Penny, with whom he no longer came face to face. The kids came out, darting across the lawn. As they clambered inside the cab, the drape swung back and settled.

He tended to indulge the children on Saturdays—the races, the zoo, the movies, the museum—and to handle them as fragile articles. He loathed that part of himself, his remorse, which made it hard for him to treat them as themselves. Today, they'd eaten at Wendy's, gone to see *The Temple of Doom,* and as it was a fine, rare, early-spring day, they played Frisbee and fed bread to the ducks in the park. The parkwise ducks, the mallards and pintails, widgeons, shovelers, mergansers, and redheads bunched up near the bank, and then some came out of the water. Andy, who was six, tossed handfuls to one side and the other. The ducks crowded after the morsels and teemed around Andy's ankles. Tricia, who was eleven, moved off and stared pensively across the pond. Lafleur gazed with her. A pair of whistling swans patrolled the far rushes, their heads imperious and erect, their bills perfectly parallel to the surface of the water.

When he returned the children, the front door opened as if driven by an automaton. The children's arms and heads glistened in the sunlight as they ran back to the porch. Like sprites they vanished into the zone he could no longer touch, what seemed like a spectral region made half of recollection and half of what had come to twist darkly in his imagination. He had sat still in his pickup for a moment, saddened, and feeling then, too, like an idiot.

There was a third picture on the wall behind him, an enlarged family snapshot in which he might have seen himself and Penny, and a healthy Gus standing with his arm around Jewel, and three children in front, including the small figure of Nicole. That picture captured the whole, horrifying gap in Lafleur's life. He glanced up at Gus. Gus blinked and curled his lip. He looked crazed. Jewel returned, carrying the coffeepot. "What about the river property?" Lafleur said. "You two have that free and clear."

"Sell it?" she said as she poured coffee, first into his cup, then hers, then into an insulated mug for Gus. Gus had a startled expression. She added milk to Gus's mug. "And just let the company go down the drain?" she said.

Gus lurched and tried to speak. His mouth twisted. "Naw!" he said. It came out a soft, high moan that sounded like the caw of a distant crow. His arms shook as he tried to bring his body forward. He struggled to say more, but Jewel sat down and spoke for him.

"No," she said. "He has that for you and your kids."

"But we don't need that," Lafleur said, addressing his father, and at the same time thinking, Don't you see? Everything's come apart. It's all different, now. He turned to Jewel and said, "But you do. Use some of it to make whatever arrangements you have to with the partnership and keep the rest. You need it."

Gus's arms had stopped shaking and he held himself erect. His eyes were bright and moist. His set face had the vestige of the look it always took on when he made flat refusals. He spoke again. It sounded just like a big crow flying away over the trees. "Naw!" he cried.

"Careful," Jewel said. Gently, she let her hand rest over Gus's on the arm of the wheelchair. "He won't sell the house and property and he doesn't want you to, either. He feels the same way about the company. It's the future. He needs the future he spent his life working for. I need him to have a future."

Gus, apparently satisfied with what Jewel had said, looked at Lafleur with glossy eyes. "Something has to give," Lafleur said.

Jewel looked down and stroked the handle of her coffee cup. Then she looked up and said, "He can put you in."

"In?"

"Not money. Not ours and not yours, Hank, not what none of us has. You."

"Work for him?"

"With him."

"I see," he said, but he thought, Of course. It was obvious. The room was still. He became aware of the refrigerator humming way back in the kitchen.

"I'm sorry. I hate to do this to you." She nodded at Gus. "It's his idea."

He looked at Gus. The acuteness still edged the old man's eyes, and he had a knowing smile on his lips, or held what Lafleur took to be that smile, a kind of half-controlled smirk now, but poking through, as if from behind a fog of uncooperative musculature, the exact self-satisfied smile his father had always presented in ticklish situations. Lafleur felt aggrieved, seeing the old smile, and he almost felt like laughing.

Jewel said, "We understand that you want no part of the company."

"You do?" She'd put it much more definitely than he'd ever thought it.

"But we'd like to know how you feel about it now."

"Oh?" He was a little taken aback by Jewel's approach. He felt his surprise in his face and in his eyes, which skittered away from her and back and away again, to Gus, to the opposite wall. Then his eyes stopped. He felt his face becoming calm. He grew absorbed by thought.

There'd never been serious breaches between himself and his father, but simply a divergence of ways. His ambition—when he had it, when he felt more collected than he'd felt for some time—was different, both more limited and more speculative, perhaps, than his father's. Gus had his roots in another age. He was a monumentalist, the son of a half-Montagnais Indian woman and a French Canadian. Gus's father, who'd been dead twenty years before Lafleur's birth, had ventured west to British Columbia as one of the last of the *engagés* of the then-foundering Canadian fur trade. He became a *disengagé* by ripping up his papers and fleeing south to Oregon, where he worked as a logger. He returned to Quebec, married a woman thirty years younger than himself, had four children, left for Oregon again, returned, and in his old age had one more child, Gus, and then died. What happened to Gus then, where his mother took him, what she did with him, taught him, told him, or what happened to the older children, was a mystery. Lafleur had the idea that his father was ashamed of her. There were stories there, Lafleur had thought, which if told might have explained things. It was another obscurity.

Lafleur, too, had been born in Quebec, in a small town up north near Quebec City. Once, when he was very young, his mother had taken him by train to Montreal to meet his grandmother. He remembered the city and the line of tall, decrepit tenements where his grandmother lived. He remembered going into one, a shadowy place that smelled of mildew. He seemed to remember that his grandmother was pleased to see him, but could remember nothing she'd said. He remembered how she looked sitting in a kitchen chair—a tough old bird with a hatchet face and dark, sharp eyes. She held herself straight as a post. He'd been five or six then. He remembered the torn linoleum floor and a wooden sink. The next year his mother had told him that his grandmother was dead.

Jewel's sinewy hand still lay over Gus's frail one on the arm of the wheelchair. There was a certain form of female stalwartness, Lafleur thought, that came in old age, something hard and erect in certain women that showed through after the years had worn down the flesh and compliance and convention.

Jewel glanced up and caught him searching her face. "It's an idea, that's all."

"I understand."

"If you want to consider it all, you should take some time," she said. Gus struggled to grip his coffee mug and she turned to help him. She supported the bottom of the mug while the old man awkwardly squeezed the sides. Together, they lifted and he drank. Coffee flowed around his mouth and down his shirt. Jewel took the mug away and dabbed at him with the napkin. Gus smirked as if amused by his incapacities.

Lafleur wondered about his father, who'd come all the way back across the continent to the very place, Oregon, where Lafleur's grandfather had been. He wondered what tales had impelled the son to come, or what tales taken through the mother to her son, or what osmosis of tales, or perhaps what lack of them, or even what renunciation of the mother. There was spite there, maybe, a revenge against poverty. Lafleur didn't know. All he remembered was the talk between his mother and father before they left for Oregon. He'd been eight, then. The hopeful talk went on for months and Oregon was implanted in his mind as a place of riches, where big fish leaped out of the rivers into baskets and berries hung through the kitchen windows. There were trees as big around as houses, and when they were cut down new trees sprouted instantly out of the old trunks. The trees were immortal. There was gold in the creek beds and mountains where winter went on all year round and valleys where there was never any winter. The seasons were divided differently in Oregon. They would live in a valley where anything would grow whenever it was needed, where the air was sweet and deer wandered up onto the back porches, begging to be eaten for dinner.

Lafleur thought that there was another algebra in this, one that included an irrational integer, an obscurantism derived from too much hardship, too much darkness, too much silence, too much dreaming.

He'd known all along that it would please his father to see him come into the excavation company, although his father had never pressed the point. That was assumed, the lack of pressure, the choice left to the son, which was finally a most exacting form of pressure, and way back in college Lafleur had struck an inward bargain by taking degrees in architecture and structural engineering. After school he'd been with the Army Construction Engineers. He did a tour in Vietnam, where he worked on dikes and bridges mainly, designing them on the spot to be thrown up. For a short time he had been transferred to the Combat Engineers for whom he "read" existing designs and earth forms in enemy territory and composed demolition instructions. He'd been in the midst of the action, but somehow nestled safely as if in the eye of a hurricane. Except for a few instances, his days were filled with machines, drawings, and maps. He was cut off from the actual slaughter.

He'd spent the last few months of his hitch assigned to Army Intelligence in Alaska. There, he'd "read" photographic evidence taken by satellite over hostile territories, or so he presumed—Russia, Mongolia, North Korea, Afghanistan, Cambodia, maybe China. He didn't really know. He had only the faintest notion of what he was doing in Alaska. He was mustered out a captain and moved to Myrtle Point in downstate Oregon, where Penny and their first child, Tricia, had been living with her parents while he was gone. He found work. They had their second child and then, drawn as if by tropism, they moved back up to Portland, and he went to work as an excavation foreman for Zymanski's contracting firm—not his father's company. He began moonlighting with the backhoe, truck, and dozer he'd bought, thinking that someday he could have his own small company. In fact he'd come a step nearer to his father and Blaylock. It was like the very gradual, ineluctable closing of a jaw, his father's hopes and the resistance of Lafleur's nature, and his submerged expectation that someday he would defer to his father's hopes after all. Lafleur thought all this not in so many words, but in images: his grandmother in the rickety chair, the Oregon deer, the bridges and dikes in the jungle, the white Alaska night, the nameplate stuck to the door of his pickup with the phone number struck out. The images carried a cargo that he couldn't fully grasp.

Everyone at the table had been silent for several minutes. The atmosphere of the room had become heavy with their thinking. Lafleur glanced at Gus and saw the vestige of the amused, self-satisfied smile that Gus had always assumed in ticklish situations. The old man looked like a clown. Lafleur felt his own face quickening. He wondered if Gus was thinking that his son had been flushed from cover at last. "Has Louis heard about this?" Lafleur asked Jewel.

She gave him a sheepish look. "He didn't foresee any particular legal difficulties, if that's what you mean."

"And Blaylock would allow it?"

"We think he's too greedy not to."

Gus lurched sideways in his chair and looked up, clinging feebly to the arms, and said, "Yaw!" His affirmative word sounded almost exactly like the negative, and more than anything else it sounded like a solitary crow going away over the trees and down around the bend in a river.

Lafleur smiled. He felt his smile like a smirk, faint and self-satisfied and bemused just like the smile that had slipped back onto his father's face. "He says that? That Blaylock's too greedy not to?"

Jewel smiled, making a beak out of her lips. "He would."

"Of course he would," Lafleur said, considering that this was the way with the dead and infirm, that their power transpired to those nearest them, that in a way personal power—including the power of parents and even of lost generations over children—was immortal. He wondered if the name for his irrational integer was death.

Carefully, he placed his knife and fork next to each other on his plate and looked up. There was a curious air of levity at the table, as if the bemused, anxious smiling were there to mask something awful. "Okay," he said.

"Okay?"

"Okay," he repeated. He felt bedazzled. "I'll do it."

Jewel inhaled and seemed to grow larger in her chair. Her eyes brightened and looked young in her old face, and in response Lafleur felt his eyes welling again. She said, "When that man Clinton U came here I thought you were making another deal."

"No, I don't know him. And I should have thought of this myself," Lafleur said. Then he asked, "What kind of project is it?"

"Blaylock's? I'm not sure. Maybe a government project."

"Do you know where?"

"Southeast Oregon."

Lafleur thought about that. "Out there it'd probably have to be a government job," he said, thinking about the place—the desert. "A lot of money. Lots of concrete, I bet," he said, thinking about government design, about tearing open the sand and rock and pouring concrete in the desert, about the trucks and their loads made vulnerable by the heat, about how fast the concrete would set up.

"You're going to talk to Ned?" Jewel said.

"And Louis," he said. Despite himself, even he had begun to feel a little tickle of greed. "I want Louis right behind me if I need him." The sunlight came through the window at a low slant and hit the chandelier, overwhelming the electric bulbs, but wildly activating the prisms. Small, rainbow-hued shafts of light glittered all across the ceiling and over the hutch and knickknacks on the opposite wall, and down to the passageway. It was like an elongated flower spraying its parts through the room. Lafleur thought about concrete, the slaked surfaces in the dry, desert air. "Government," he said.

Chapter Two

It was May, the second Saturday in May.

Lafleur would be able to name it months later as a beginning of sorts, although he didn't really believe in beginnings any more than he believed in endings. Maybe he believed in intersections as if bodies in space appeared from the gloom and sank toward one another, incandescent, and in rare instances adhered together and thickened to make something massy like a nodule on a stalk. But how such an occurrence was caused he had no idea. Nor could he say how it should be marked except as an illusion, a "functional" beginning . . . by a signature on a piece of paper, a photograph in a wedding album, a tiny footprint on a birth certificate, or an old mudprint, some seed, or mineralized egg. And for him, what encounters marked the "beginnings" in his short life—mother, step-mother, estranged wife, daughter, son, dead second daughter, infirm fa-ther, work, war. . . . He glanced back over his shoulder as he thought this as if to see his entanglement, the strands that clung to him, heavy as rope, endless, twisting and snarling in his trail.

What he saw, truly, was the inside of the toolshed, grown dark and littered. He'd just returned from his father and Jewel's place. He'd made a pot of coffee, fed his dog, then hunkered down next to the doorway of the shed in a patch of sun. He straightened his head and arched his back, pressing his shoulders against the clapboard. The shed stood between the river and the house his parents had built when he was a boy. The dog, Jones, was a Labrador retriever, a road waif that had adopted him several months ago. His coffee, one of his few luxuries, he made strong from freshly ground beans. He held the mug before his nose, inhaling the pungent steam as he looked up from under his eyebrows at the old family house. It was a rental, now. It had an elevated deck and pale-blue window sills. The cedar siding had begun to gray. He should bleach and refinish it.

In the old days, the shed at his back had been a place of fragrance—wood shavings, solvent, oil, and the flinty odor from the honing wheel. It had been a place where plans were studied and modified and tools kept as the house was built. As a boy of nine or ten, he'd looked up at the emerging house from this very spot: concrete foundation, studwork, the skeleton of the roof, then the raiment, skirting and stairway, plywood, the deck, siding, windows, roofing, the stone chimney. For a time the shed had been the germinating cell from which everything emanated. When he was eleven he and his parents moved into the house. He had a bedroom window from which he should have been able to see the shed, but only a patch of the shed's metal roof could be picked out, and sometimes on overcast days even it took on the precise coloration of air. The rest of the shed, hidden by a screen of ferns and blackberry bushes or camouflaged by age and weather to match the surrounding foliage, was quite invisible. He had considered that a great mystery.

When he'd been troubled, night after night when he was fourteen, after his mother died, he sat at the window and looked with longing down toward the old nearly invisible place of calm. Now that window was dark in the shadows. Looking at it and remembering filled Lafleur with longing, and he thought this a mystery, too, the transduction of the boy's longing into the more complicated, less acute, more chronic, and more comical longing of a tangled-up man.

Lafleur lowered his eyes to the dog, Jones. She had a crippled leg and a congenital overbite so extreme that she could not eat out of a dish. Her way was to tip the dish and spill the contents, then eat the food off the ground. She grunted as she ate. She had a fixation on her dishes. She carried them around, buried them, and slept with them. She had a stash of the chewed-up remains of five or six plastic dishes in a small open pit at the base of a blackberry bush. Lafleur had chained an aluminum dish to a timber, but she'd mangled the light metal until it came loose from the clasp. Then he tried a ten-pound cast-iron pot he'd found, thinking it might be heavy enough to discourage her, but he caught her carting it off, her neck muscles bulging with the weight of it as she stumbled drunkenly through the weeds. Now he chained the dog so that he could retrieve the pot when she was finished. He had tried simply pouring the food on the ground, too, but Jones refused to eat it. Not only did she covet her dishes, but she also attached a ritual to them.

The cast-iron pot lay on its side. Jones lunged at the heap of food, then lifted her head to chew with her back teeth. She wagged her tail and gazed at him with her golden eyes. Her shiny black coat rippled as she moved.

Behind her stood his pickup truck. Its deep-blue hood hazily reflected the clear sky and the leaves and white limbs of the cottonwoods that lined the drive. A fly, trapped in a Coke bottle on the ground next to Lafleur, buzzed noisily. The cottonwoods rattled in the evening breeze. From the other side of the blackberry bushes he heard hoofbeats. There was a stable over there below the house, and a horse, a chestnut mare owned by the Goods, the people renting the house. For a moment the hoofbeats went fast enough to be two horses. Jones looked up, raising her ears and sniffing the air. The hoofbeats stopped. Lafleur could hear the river down below the shed, the soft, never-ending whisper of the water eating at the bank. His pickup's engine ticked as it cooled from the thirty-mile drive down from Portland.

He took a sip of coffee. Soon he would walk over to the Goods' place and use their telephone to call Ned Blaylock. For the moment he didn't move, but hunkered there and thought about Blaylock, whom he remembered even with some amusement now, and sardonically, as the perpetrator of his childhood nightmare: the hulking, forbidding man, a black welder's skullcap perpetually on his head, the hump of bone like a bolthead high under the inflamed skin of his nose, the sagging flesh of his face, and the whites of his eyes the color of rust. He thought about Jewel and his father, and about his mother, who back when he was fourteen had been brought home from the hospital because the doctors gave her no hope. She had brain cancer. The chemotherapy made her bones shatter. He remembered vividly how she had looked, skeletal and frail, her eyes and cheeks sunken, and he remembered the smell of her body rotting from the inside. It was as if she had already been buried, then unearthed to die again. In ten days she was gone. He remembered how, when he was younger, she never failed to kiss him goodnight, and how her dark hair fell across his face, how it smelled of the ground, and how that earthy darkness of her affection, her essence to him, seemed finally to merge with the shadow cast by her death. He thought about the house and his mother's happiness with it for three years. He thought about the shed at his back. He could almost feel the density and confusion in the narrow room, that darkness pressing against the root of his spine.

The shed was loaded with old things and his things—his cot and bedding, his hotplate and tiny black-and-white television, a small woodburner he had moved in, and what of his personal articles he'd brought down as the night or two he had originally planned to stay back in November stretched into months. He thought it astounding that it was May already. It was a patch of rare evening May sun he was sitting in, and he supposed that the buzzing fly had hatched in the incubating May warmth of that Coke bottle, out of the mud and decayed bodies of last year's trapped flies at the bottom. Broken-down deck chairs were stored in the shed, and tools and supplies left over from thirty years ago when the house had been finished: nails, bolts, and screws placed in jars, bits of Sheetrock and plywood, excess plumbing and electrical parts, bundles of copper pipe, coils of wire. His old Huffy bicycle hung from the ceiling.

What was left in the shed had been neatly organized by his father several times, but gradually the layering-on of years' worth of things for which there was no better place, and of dust, bird, and rodent remains, had gained sway. Now Lafleur's things had stacked up on the benches and floor. Sometimes, when he dug down through the debris to the original layer, he found things that made time buckle back: the very lumber crayon he remembered drawing with as a boy, his mother's old hair dryer, a butane burner he remembered his father using to heat steel strapping, and his father's Thompson pistol with interchangeable .45 and .410 barrels, a combination heavy-duty persuader and light-duty snake gun. He'd completely forgotten about the pistol. There was a holster for it somewhere. He'd spent an evening rubbing off the dots of rust with steel wool and oiling the gun until it gleamed, then returned it to the molded cushions in the hardwood case. Illegal because of the short shotgun barrel, the gun was probably a collector's item. He guessed it had become his.

Jones sat facing him and swept her tail back and forth in the dirt. She'd finished eating. In a moment she would bark, demanding to be released from her chain. If Lafleur looked directly at her, she would certainly bark. He looked up toward the house through the ferns and blackberry bushes. The bushes had hard pale-green berries. Besides refurbishing the house for his father and Jewel, he should clean up the shed. At the least, he should trim the trees along the drive and repair the Goods' mailbox before it fell off its stand. He'd become a derelict, almost, disconnected from nearly everything but the rudiments of daily routine and living off the tailings of a previous, more opulent life. His mail went to his father and Jewel and he scarcely looked at it. Most of his meals came out of cans and were contemptuous of nutrition. He got his drinking water from a hose that ran from the stock hydrant at the Goods' stable. He showered at work once or twice a week. He smelled. His toilet here consisted of a canvas outhouse with a ten-gallon can behind the shed. He had to cart the can up to an R-V park to empty it. It was a scatological comedy he engaged in every two weeks, surreptitiously slopping his personal sewage into a public tank and driving around town all day with the stinking can in the back of his pickup.

A horse whinny broke the evening air. It sounded like brass, like a rooster measuring the distance between the toolshed and the Goods' place. Jones barked and whined in response, and curled back her upper lip, displaying her truncated lower jaw, and then let out a string of annoyed, high-pitched barks that rattled in Lafleur's ears. He tossed out his coffee dregs and stood. The dog quivered with excitement as he walked to her. She grabbed up her ten-pound pot and trotted in circles, limping heavily on her bad leg. One front foot twisted crazily sideways, but she could act lame or not as she chose, it seemed. Lafleur considered her a model of adaptation. Adroitly, she jumped her chain each time she went around.

When he reached her, she dropped the pot and nuzzled his crotch, leaving a smear of dog food. The horse whinnied again. Lafleur unclasped the dog's chain and she took off, not limping at all. She crashed through a small opening in the wall of blackberry bushes, heading for the stable. He heard horse hooves thudding rapidly. It was an evening ritual between the dog and mare. He heard a woman shout, which was another ritual: Mrs. Good shouting at his dog. In a moment he heard Jones thrashing in the shallows. He heard ducks quacking. A pair of mallards flew overhead, their wings whistling. Lafleur admired the ducks, their missile-like bodies and deep-set wings, their acceleration. They disappeared into the trees, weaving magnificently.

He set the pot in the doorway of the shed, then moved to the bed of his pickup, where he had groceries—a loaf of bread, canned chili and ravioli, beer, toilet paper, cookies, a fresh sack of dog biscuits, and a two-pound box of dehydrated milk. He looked up the road toward Ned Blaylock's place. Through the trees he could pick out a dot of gray roof near the bend in the road, that was all, but he'd given the place another hard look as he passed this evening: the big pink house set back from the road, the metal roofs of the shops gleaming out back, around the yard a fence made of yellow poles and chain link, and equipment everywhere, in every corner and nearly engulfing the house. Machinery leaned against trees and had torn through the steel fabric to the ditch next to the county road. The disrepair of the equipment increased the farther it was from the house, so that what Lafleur saw best as he drove by was the leading edge of confusion: heaps of iron, wheels, booms, tangled cables, buckets, plows, disemboweled engines, and thrusting through it all the wild blackberry bushes that refused to be daunted by leaking fuel and oil, or even by the gouging at their immense, tangled root systems. For weeks Lafleur had been picking things out as he passed: the wheel hub of a Mack truck, the tracks of a Caterpillar crawler, the engine block of a Case, even the familiar blade of a grader on which he'd ridden with his father years ago; and today the disarray had played a trick with him. Despite his childhood experience with Blaylock, despite the outrage he shared with Jewel, he was also as old now himself as Blaylock had been in the days of the monkey wrench, haunted by a sense of his own error and of knowing too much about human frailty, and he had discovered in himself a curious, circumspect, wary, and sardonic affection for the old despised one. Maybe it was Gus's method with Blaylock, passing over to Lafleur now, or maybe the prospect of having to work with the man. Maybe it was just the junk.

He liked that junk. Occasionally over the last several months he had seen direct evidence of Blaylock's presence, but never the man himself—sometimes a curl of exhaust coming from a running engine out back, and once the tail section of a pink Continental vanishing behind a descending garage door. Blaylock was too old, maybe, or too busy reconnoitering the carcass of the partnership to keep close charge of his machinery, and too much a pack rat to ship the irreparable out for salvage. Lafleur understood. He had the pack rat in himself, the impulse to allow his nest to become complex. One never knew when one would find just the part one needed in a junkyard, or at least a part that could be used, or maybe a part one had not even thought of wanting but which one wanted in its being found. One might need those things: bolts and clamps, a bit of iron rail or a piece out of a track, a length of hosing, copper tubing, a bearing or seal, a carburetor needle, or maybe a whole transmission to mate to an engine.

He rested his elbows on the edge of the pickup bed and thought about wanting. He thought about wanting and not knowing what one wanted. He thought about need. He thought about yielding. He thought about giving in to the fibers of attachment made out of DNA and memory and time that bound him to his father. He thought about his life, which seemed like a junkyard. He thought about fishing, which was one of the few things he knew that gave the kind of pleasure looking for something in a junkyard could give, and forgetting what one was looking for and getting lost in the yard, just dreaming and looking for whatever one might feasibly want, and slowly finding what one needed that way.

He moved. He picked up his groceries, carried them into the shed, and set them on a bench. He went back for Jones's pot in the doorway. Bending for the pot, he heard the fly again. He wedged the Coke bottle loose from the mud and turned it upside down. The fly dropped out, took off, banged into the wall and staggered in midair, then flew out of sight over the shed. Lafleur went back in and set the pot on the bench, shoving other articles aside. He switched on his gooseneck lamp. Just behind it was a blackberry bush. The roots had cracked the concrete floor and driven up a stalk between the wall and bench. Its leaves clung to a small, dusty window. The lamp cast a pool of light on the filthy floor and seeped to the profound heaps under the benches: cartons and jars, bundles, all manner of things compressing under their own weight. Too much junk here. Or enough junk, maybe, for him to have enjoyed if he had not felt entrenched in it. His cot was piled with soiled clothes. In a corner his tools were scattered and next to them was the small woodburner he'd kept himself warm with during winter. The dangerously cockeyed stove pipe vanished through a hole he had cut in the wall.

Outside, the sun was about to set. Through the doorway he could see the earth blackened by long shadows. He heard another whinny, a long bloodcurdling shriek. Jones came in and looked up at him, puckering her snout, then she sat and dragged herself toward him by her front paws, wiping her rump on the floor. She probably had worms. He went out and strode across the clearing, then pushed through the blackberry bushes and ferns, following the route of his hose. Jones came after him. The house stood to his right. Below, a donkey was in the corral along with the Goods' chestnut mare. Lafleur paused, looking. Mrs. Good and her daughter stood watching the animals. The mare trotted around the corral along the inside of the fence, her flanks darkened with sweat. The donkey, a big one, was an obscure color, not black exactly and not quite gray. It followed the mare. The two came around Lafleur's side of the corral. It was too much for Jones, who charged, barking wildly. The mare shied. The donkey danced sideways. Mrs. Good wheeled to shout at the dog, but Lafleur, moving to the corral, beat her to it: "Jones!"

He stopped next to Mrs. Good and she looked at him out of the corners of her painted eyes. She was chewing on a matchstick. The donkey followed the mare across the corral, then the two began to circle again. The mare had a gash on her flank. The animals passed under the shade of the cottonwoods at the far side of the corral. Coming out of the shade and into the low slanting sunlight, the donkey changed from black to a steam color with russet in it. The donkey was the color of dark tea, deep and changeable according to the play of light. "A donkey?" Lafleur said.

Mrs. Good took her matchstick out of her mouth and stroked the side of her nose with its flattened end. "We're making a mule."

"A mule," Lafleur said. He looked from her to the animals, then back again, wondering—Why? "Mind if I use your phone?" he said. He disliked troubling the Goods for their telephone. He disliked the trouble Jones gave them. Actually, he rather disliked the Goods themselves, wife, daughter, and husband, a rug salesman who never seemed to be home. He especially disliked the way Mrs. Good seemed to regard him—as the landlord. It made him feel like a target.

"Feel free," she said. She was a solid woman who looked as though she had been inflated inside her pants and white cowboy shirt. She had red hair and plucked black eyebrows. The daughter, who stood on the other side of Mrs. Good, leaned forward and peered at Lafleur.

"Is Al up there?" he said.

Mrs. Good grinned at him, holding the matchstick between two front teeth. "Hell, no."

The mare and donkey came around again and the donkey pushed the mare against the fence and bit at her head. The fence creaked and Lafleur instinctively stepped back. The mare snorted and spun, bent her head down. The donkey slipped behind and tried to mount her, but the mare broke free and pranced along the fence again. Jones leaned against Lafleur's leg. Puffs of clouds had begun to drift in. The earth in the corral was churned up and black, and the leaves on the cottonwoods and bushes and the rocks down near the river gleamed in the light. Over the river, visible through a clear space beyond the corral, an evening mist had begun to gather. A narrow, cocoon-like cloud floated above the river. Near the bank a sand spit extended into the water and a blue heron stood at the far edge, waiting for fish.

Nicole!

This was another reason he disliked troubling the Goods. The shed, so long as he stuck to the beaten path between it and his pickup, protected him from this view. Nicole had been playing on that spit with Andy. Tricia had been there, watching the two younger ones. They had a bucket and were dipping it into the water, catching minnows. Lafleur and Penny had been down at the back of the toolshed, barbecuing chicken. They had come out from Portland for a weekend picnic, as they often used to do. The children had been schooled against the river, which in its heart had tremendous force. He remembered checking on the young ones there. Nicole was squatting with the bucket, her brown limbs dark against a yellow bathing suit. He saw her there now and felt a wrenching, and tried to force out the image. He gazed at the heron, then turned when Mrs. Good spoke: "That mare's a twitch."

He glanced past Mrs. Good at her daughter, who was watching the animals intently. The girl was about seventeen and built not unlike her mother, but more tightly, closer to the bud, a distillation of the mother. He caught himself running his eyes down the girl's body. "That's a big donkey," he said.

"He's a mean damn Abyssinian jack," Mrs. Good said.

Lafleur smiled. He didn't think this procedure was right. He thought it would be a better arrangement to have a jenny and a stud horse to make a mule, or a cage at least and straps, or some such rigging. He wondered if Mrs. Good had any idea what she was doing. "Seems a little rough," he said.

"We had him shipped up from Redding, California," Mrs. Good said. She leaned toward him and thrust out her chin and tongued her matchstick to the corner of her mouth. "Got here yesterday. If this takes, the mule's going to be worth a bundle, you bet."

As she spoke, the donkey went for the mare's neck, but the mare came back, rearing and pawing at the donkey's head. Lafleur and the two women stared. The donkey went up with the mare and bounced a hoof off her head, but the mare went under him, biting at his chest, and nearly toppled him. He came down on her sideways. His leg muscles bulged and he bit at her neck and tried to work around to her hindquarters. Lafleur felt his leg muscles tightening. The mare jumped out and whinnied. The hair on Lafleur's neck prickled. The mare had cuts on her head now. The donkey spun and kicked her in the flank. The thud of it resounded and echoed back from the house. The donkey kicked her again and she bounced against the fence. The fence creaked and sagged. Jones nuzzled Lafleur's leg and he pushed her away. He found himself breathing heavily. The mare and donkey began to circle more quickly, blowing and kicking up chunks of mud. Their hooves thocked. Lafleur felt their warmth as they passed. Their sweat smelled pungent.

He looked down at the heron. It had its toes in the water, its neck outstretched, and its bill tilted downward, as is the way of herons in waiting. For as long as he could remember that sand spit had been there, though it changed its shape annually, and its elevation, and sometimes its position because of the flux of the changing banks and big river that surrounded it. Herons had fished from the spit, too, for as long as he could remember. He had played on the spit as a boy, and had fished from it, just as his children played on it when the family came down. He remembered what he wished not to remember, what came at him whenever it wanted to, and came with the force of a dream: himself bending over chicken pieces on the grill, and hearing cries, the voices of the girls, Tricia near them and Nicole's remote-sounding voice, and hearing Penny next to him suddenly gasping, then screaming—"Nicole!"—and himself straightening up, turning, knowing instantly that something was terribly wrong, and looking and seeing her out in the water, out in the current, and himself not moving, freezing, disbelieving, trying to get himself to move, then moving at last, finding himself right on Penny's heels. He remembered Penny's skirt and hair, askew and wildly fluttering, and her shrieking as she ran—"The tree! The tree!"—pointing at a dead cedar that had fallen into the far side of the river at a bend Nicole was headed for.

He'd seen Nicole's face coming up and going down, and her hands thrashing. She knew how to swim, but not in that fast, roiling water, not strongly enough for that. Her yellow bathing suit bobbed. At the spit he looked down into Tricia and Andy's stunned, wide eyes, and into Penny's face, sharp and agonized, then back down the river at Nicole. She bobbed past the tree. Penny waded into the water, and he broke into a run along the bank, crashing through the shrubs and stumbling on the rocks. He stopped to strip off his shirt, then ran again, then stopped and pulled off his trousers and shoes, and went in, swimming, though he was not a strong swimmer. He hoped to swim strongly enough to ride the current and catch her, but moving into the current, feeling its pull, he marveled at it and despaired, and heard Penny's voice behind him, from the bank, he thought, a thin wailing whipped around by the breeze—*"Nicole! Nicole!"* He'd seen her in front of him, the yellow spot bobbing crazily up and down and rolling in the mud-colored river, grown small, going around a bend, and he rushed around the bend, driven by the wild, inexorable current, turning head over heels in the water, then he glimpsed her again, the yellow dot still precisely the same distance ahead of him, small and lightweight. His limbs were going dead, and without thinking to do this, or willing it, he'd moved out of the heart of the current nearer the shore where the water had less force. He flailed and raised his head to look. She was gone.

He barely got back to the bank himself, half-drowned and vomiting, and racked with guilt—for letting the children play on the spit, for his inattention, for not acting faster, for not being a better swimmer, and— knowing this now—for not staying in the center of the river. And Penny, who had been fighting her way along the bank with Andy and Tricia, when she reached him stopped in her tracks and her face wrenched with horror at the truth. Nicole was gone, snatched away from her. Her one hand twisted in Tricia's hair. She sank to her knees and clutched at Tricia, and moaned, "Not in that cold."

Tricia looked up at her father. Andy, standing to one side, looked up. The children's eyes grew huge in their faces until it seemed they would blow out into the sky. Lafleur's knees buckled and he went down, sobbing uncontrollably. "Alone," Penny wept. "So lonely for a child. It's no way," and that night, a mother still, clinging to a mother's sense of a child's welfare even in death, she would say, "Not that way, it's no way for a young one to die, not Nicole, not taken like that in the cold, alone. Not without me!" She sat up straight in the bed and tore at her hair.

They'd called the fire department. The river was searched, but the body was never recovered. Nicole was utterly gone. She'd been sucked down to Portland, maybe, or was tangled in the locks, or dragged out to sea, or devoured, or atomized into water. That death was what Lafleur and Penny had always between them. Together they were gripped by that cold.

The mare and donkey circled the corral. He felt them and heard them blow air as they passed. He gazed at the heron. It was as if it were the same heron he had seen as a boy on the spit, an unchanged element in

25

all the years, an intaglio, something as permanent as death incised through the skin of time, a masquerade of death dressed in baby blue, the exact and strange essence of time. The heron's long neck folded toward its body and unfolded again and swayed gracefully. It tipped its head to the side and froze, watching. Lafleur watched it. It was just the blue heron he was watching. He instructed himself in that: to watch, to be unafraid.

If one watched a heron closely when it caught a fish, one could sometimes see the head come up with the fish sideways in the beak, and then see the heron flip the fish acrobatically in the air, then swallow it headfirst. It was a good trick. Lafleur watched, thinking the bird was about to stab for a fish. The heron did not move. If one looked away for an instant, he knew, the heron might catch a fish. Or it might vanish altogether.

"She's about to accept him," Mrs. Good said.

He turned. "Oh?"

Mrs. Good grinned. "You bet."

He looked into the corral. The donkey appeared almost small next to the mare. He was wiry, long in the legs, high in the withers and straight in the back. He moved like silk, like a killer, and his tea color rippled as he moved in and out of the deepening shadows. Lafleur glanced at the heron. It hadn't moved. Its long legs, blue body, and extended head were poised against the silver cocoon of mist. It looked like a picture on a coin. The sky was turning pink. He looked back at the donkey. The donkey held his head low, his ears flat, and had an almost disconsolate expression. He looked sullen like a Spanish dancer, straight and tensed like one who is about to handle his partner brutally. The mare playfully bumped her hindquarters up against the donkey, then she slowed. The donkey slowed. There was a moment in which they were moving but seemed to have stopped, a lucid moment like a long inhalation of air in which their strength visibly gathered. Suddenly, the donkey lunged and bit into the mare's neck. The mare whinnied and stopped. Mrs. Good made a rattling sound in her throat. Standing there with the two women became too much for Lafleur's sense of propriety.

"I should just let myself in?" he said.

"Huh?" Mrs. Good said without looking at him. "In?"

"To use the phone," he said.

"Oh, that," Mrs. Good said. Her rattle enlarged to a chuckle. "I guess you know the way." The donkey pawed at the mare's back and moved adroitly around her on his hind legs. Lafleur turned away. The daughter glanced up at him as he passed. Her eyes were wide and glassy as if she had been stunned. He walked up to the house and climbed the steps to the deck. Jones followed. He went inside to the kitchen. The black telephone hung on the wall near the sink, where his mother had wanted it to be. He located the phone book and searched for Blaylock's number. When he found it he put his finger on the name and paused.

Jones sat on the deck, peering in the window at him. Mrs. Good was no longer at the corral, but her daughter stood there. He leaned over the counter and looked down and to one side of the house for Mrs. Good. She was nowhere to be seen. The girl looked small, and the mare and donkey looked small at the extreme end of the corral. They stood facing each other. Their heads overlapped. The coitus had stilled them. The heron had vanished from the spit. The twilight air had turned pink. The cocoon of mist above the river was pink. The trunks and limbs of trees on the opposite bank were faintly visible through the mist and made it look crenelated like a sheepskin. The surface of the river was like smoked glass. A dark beam floated into sight from behind the trees, cruised by, then vanished.

During the winter floods, it was not uncommon to see entire trees hurtle down. If they caught on the bank or on rock, they heaved like matchsticks. He had seen shattered boats, stoves, and parts of car bodies kept off the bottom by the speed of the water, and turkeys, pigs, and sheep, bloated cow carcasses dancing on the surface like balloons. Once, he'd seen a herd of Holsteins, one black-and-white cow after another, bouncing by. Exquisite, chaotic, and horrifying, the river was full of its trade with the earth. It was a sometimes macabre telemetry of everything upstream. It brought things by and sometimes it snatched them away.

He looked over in the direction of his toolshed, which was now utterly invisible. He looked back down at the phone book. The number was right there. He caught sight of a figure in the corner of his eye, and turned. Mrs. Good stood in the doorway to the living room. She looked directly back at him and her eyes widened invitingly. Her hands hung at her sides and her red lips, without the matchstick now, were parted. Her abdomen swelled as she inhaled. Lafleur's breath jumped. He sank into the pit of his late, protracted abstinence. He was suddenly filled with desire, but he caught himself, thinking: *No, no, not with you.* He passed his eyes down her body, then turned away. His hand shook as he dialed the number.

The telephone rang at the other end. He looked down at the churned-up, blackened earth inside the corral, at the motionless animals, at the girl. A gust of wind made the girl's hair flutter and flipped up her shirt, baring the hollow of her back. He heard Mrs. Good's footsteps going away. He considered himself an idiot for having allowed himself to step into that situation, and an idiot for not capitalizing on it, and also an idiot for being tempted to do so. He made himself think about this other thing—the desert, and what he still assumed was a government project.

A voice came on and snarled at him: "Yeah?"

Chapter Three

Four days later Lafleur stood knocking at the door of the pink-and-gray house. The door swung open and Ned Blaylock appeared. He had the greasy welder's skullcap on his head and a cigar in his mouth just as in the old days, but his skin was pallid and he'd put on weight. He leaned forward, making Lafleur lean back, and he peered out toward the drive and past the machinery stockpile toward the road as if checking to be sure nobody else was out there, then he held the door open and told Lafleur to come in. Lafleur stepped inside. The door sucked shut behind him. He followed Blaylock gingerly, unsure of his footing. The living room was in near darkness. No lamps were on and the drapes were drawn. What light there was seeped in around the drapes from the overcast sky outside. The chairs and couch, he made out, were covered with sheets, and the air of the place had the brackish reek of cats.

They moved down a hall and past the kitchen. Lafleur saw a bent figure flit by the stove and vanish through a doorway like the tentacle of something withdrawn. He remembered that. Blaylock's wife was never glimpsed except in retreat. On the stove a pot of liquid was boiling. Blaylock opened a door at the end of the hall and went into a room. Lafleur followed. In the center of the room stood a desk, and on the desk a lit gooseneck lamp, a pile of papers, an old-fashioned adding machine, a half-full bottle of Scotch. The window blinds were pulled. There was a single bed at one wall, the blankets on it in a heap, and along the edges of the room were shadow and chaos, piles of papers and manuals, clothing and cartons in the murky darkness. Blaylock apparently lived in here. A scampering thing caught Lafleur's eye, a cat-sized creature that flitted into sight, then dissolved back into the darkness. Blaylock moaned as he eased into a chair behind the desk, then motioned at another chair. Lafleur picked up a shirt from the chair and held it uncertainly. Blaylock lit his cigar. Lafleur dropped the shirt on a carton and sat, stretching out his legs.

Blaylock slouched down in his chair and stared into the smoke that flattened against his desk. His voice rumbled. "Brenneman called me."

Lafleur had talked to the lawyer Louis Brenneman, too, once on Monday, then again after Louis had contacted Blaylock. Louis had told Lafleur that he thought the excavation company was treading water, leasing out just enough equipment and doing enough work to stay afloat, that Blaylock was starving the company while he fooled with the books and waited for the government bid to clear. He had said that he thought Blaylock had something else running on the side, another interest, maybe another company. Louis was checking into it. Lafleur went right to the point. "We have to be straight with each other. Otherwise it won't work, me taking up Dad's part."

Without moving his body, Blaylock rolled his eyes to look at him. Lafleur felt the eyes holding him, but there was no sharpness in them, no edge. There was just gloom in the eyes. "You're not him," Blaylock said.

Lafleur said, "That's true enough."

"I don't need the money," Blaylock said. "Let's get that straight. It's as a kindness that I agree to anything."

Lafleur saw how things would be—confrontational and deceptive. "But I'm not going to work for your kindness," he said. "That way's too loose for me."

"Fine." The word sounded like a threat. Blaylock had not moved, not anything, body nor eyes. He held the cigar poised in front of his lips.

"I'll need an inventory of equipment and help, so I know what we're doing," Lafleur said.

"You," Blaylock said. "You need to know what the hell you're doing. I know what I'm doing."

"Which is?"

Something in Blaylock's dark, bumpy face almost moved. It looked like a toad's body. "Sitting pretty," he said.

Lafleur set his hands lightly on his knees. "Uh huh."

"You can do the hiring," Blaylock said.

"And the equipment?"

"It's there."

Lafleur looked away to the one window in the room, or at the blind that covered it, pale with the light that came silver through the clouds. It might be drizzling out there by now. It had been threatening to start all day, and once it began, he knew it could sock them in for a week or more. He thought of the machine parked just outside the window, the LeTourneau. He thought about how much his father would have liked to drive it. He visualized the machine standing almost as high as the house, its eight-foot wheels, its cargo bed stretching the length of the house and protruding into the trees, the high, armored, insectlike snout of the engine compartment. He turned back to Blaylock. "I'll hire the help. That's fine. But I have to get a complete equipment inventory. Otherwise, it's no good."

Blaylock lowered his eyes and gazed in the vicinity of Lafleur's knees. "I don't need the money," he said.

Lafleur went on. "And I'll be on the payroll as field supervisor, and the rest of it, salaries and the division of interest into shares just the way Louis has discussed with you." He stopped for a moment and studied Blaylock, who had not moved. "And I want the buy-back clause."

The toad in Blaylock's face expanded, then ebbed. "What's that? Brenneman didn't say anything about that."

"Bullshit," Lafleur said.

Blaylock did not move.

"You have to let him go through the books, too, and see this bid you've floated," Lafleur said.

"Brenneman?"

"That's right."

"Buy back what?"

Lafleur knew that Louis had spelled it out to Blaylock, that Blaylock was toying with him, but he told him again: "My father's interest until it's back up to where it was. In his name and at value, what it's worth now, not what it was worth before you started starving the company."

"If I wanted money, son, I could sell the goddamned company."

Lafleur marked that—the third time Blaylock had said he didn't need money. He said, "Then you'd have it locked up in escrow by a court order."

To Lafleur's surprise, Blaylock smiled, then laughed. The laugh emerged from his chest, dark and velvety, and when it came out it seemed disconnected. The eyes were dead. Suddenly Blaylock jerked open a desk drawer. Things rattled. "Like a drink?"

Lafleur eased back a little in his chair and took a breath. "Why not?" Blaylock removed two glasses from the drawer, then a rag with which he dug at the insides of the glasses. Lafleur was glad that the room was too obscure for him to get a good look at the rag, or at the glasses, for that matter, which probably had the grime of the house in them, the dust adhering to liver-colored whiskey stains in the bottoms. Blaylock poured the whiskey. A large gray cat leaped out of the darkness and landed noiselessly on the desk, startling Lafleur. The cat walked sinuously, rubbing up against Blaylock's elbow. Blaylock guided one glass across the desk. Lafleur leaned over and took it.

Blaylock sipped at his whiskey and stroked the cat's neck with two fingers. "Who fixes the price of the interest?" he said.

"We need an accountant. Louis and an accountant would do that."

"I've got an accountant."

Lafleur took a sip. The cat rolled onto its back, extended its legs, and gazed upside down at Lafleur with its yellow eyes. Slowly, Blaylock stroked the cat's belly. The warmth of the whiskey suffused Lafleur's throat. Tasting its sharpness on his tongue, and feeling it quickly in his blood, he found himself wanting to go deeply into the conflict. Carefully he positioned the glass on his knee. "But I don't trust your accountant, Ned," he said.

Blaylock took his cigar out of his mouth and set it in an ashtray that was made out of a cut-off piston. He drank half his whiskey, set the glass down gently, and stared at Lafleur. He kept stroking the cat's belly, his thick fingers moving to and fro in the silvery fur. "Let me tell you something," he said. "Sorry as I am about Gus's condition, I'm not doing this for him, the jackass. It's survival of the fittest out here and he didn't make it."

Lafleur looked away quickly, feeling heat in his eyes and acid in his throat. He remembered the monkey wrench poised in the air, and how Blaylock had looked at it as if startled by the wayward powers of his own hand. Lafleur thought about the utter chaos that would have engulfed Blaylock if he had actually struck his partner's son, about how there must have been a margin within Blaylock finally not crossed. Lafleur had never told his parents about the incident, out of the fear, perhaps—not under-stood, but felt—of provoking his parents' rage. Old enough then to have felt his capacity to trigger that rage, yet not old enough to comprehend it, he'd kept it secret in his weird, barren, mathematical nightmare.

He thought of the powers of children, not just of his powers when he was a boy, but of his children's powers, too, for absorbing shock, and of the resilient powers of children in general. He thought of the intractability of adults, especially of those locked into obsessive pacts with themselves, of the force of adult rage. He thought of his own present brittleness. He counseled himself to be patient. He told himself that Blaylock was an old bear, cranky, clumsy, omnivorous. Thinking this way, Lafleur came out on the other side of his anger, and he felt a curious, almost inquisitorial attraction to Blaylock again, this junk hoarder, this loathsome man to whose foulness he would probably end up coming as near as to that of a bed partner.

He was staring at the window blind. It had begun to rain. He could hear it whispering against the eaves. When he turned back to the desk, Blay-lock was tickling the cat's abdomen, making the cat kick at his wrist with its hind legs. Blaylock looked up and laughed again. It was the same laugh, a dark, elongated chuckle. "You've got your lawyer and I've got my accountant," he said. "That makes us even."

"We've made our compromises with you," Lafleur said. "No more."

That seemed to stop Blaylock for a moment. He picked up his glass and finished off his whiskey, then his face jerked and he looked at Lafleur with his dead eyes. "We've got a bid out," he said.

"I heard."

"If we get it you'll have to supervise. But it's on my say-so." Blaylock reached back, grunting heavily as his thick body twisted. He pulled out a three-foot cardboard tube, then stopped, holding the tube up in the air. "Do you understand? It's my say-so. Nobody else's. Not yours, not yet, no matter how free a hand you think you want. And not Clinton U's say-so, neither."

"U?" Lafleur said.

Blaylock gazed at him and in the gaze—in the lifeless eyes and heavily folded flaps of skin below the chin, the jaw that despite the flab of flesh looked powerful enough to shake something to death, and the bony, darkened nose and broad face formed by trouble, work, predation, and whiskey—was a steadiness, perhaps the only steadiness Blaylock knew, that of distrust. Lafleur understood. "You can call him off," Blaylock said.

Something kept Lafleur from saying that U had tried to contact him. Instead, he said, "I don't know Clinton U."

Blaylock kept looking, distrusting and measuring. "Maybe not," he said. He extended the end of the tube toward Lafleur.

Lafleur took it. "Blueprints?"

"Preliminaries. Keep them." Blaylock picked up his cigar and relit it. "We should be moving on it in a week, so get ready."

Lafleur placed his half-empty glass on the edge of the desk and caught Blaylock eying it. He thought Blaylock was going to pick it up and finish off the whiskey, but instead he slopped a little more into his own glass from the bottle. Lafleur set the end of the tube on the floor and balanced it with his fingertips. There was a muffled thumping sound from the direction of the hallway at Lafleur's back. It was Blaylock's wife, he guessed, chopping at something on a block in the kitchen. Lafleur asked, "Who is Clinton U?"

"Another fucking lawyer."

"Why should I know him?"

"Maybe they want you on this project."

"Me?" Lafleur said. "Who?"

"The owners," Blaylock said, barely moving his lips. "U represents them."

"Why?" Lafleur said. Blaylock stared at him. Outside, the rain hissed. "Why me?" Lafleur said.

Blaylock held his blank, brute gaze. "Fuck, I don't know," he said. Lafleur gazed back, measuring Blaylock.

"But you can't get the whole picture, especially of what you don't know, of what's not coming into the picture, or of how much there is of what you'll never know in a damn afternoon, or in a week, or in a year. You got to break in."

That was true enough, Lafleur thought, but it was also an evasion. "You mean you told them I might be coming on the project."

Blaylock blinked slowly. "Maybe."

"Maybe what?"

"Maybe you would."

"Okay," Lafleur said. "Okay," he repeated, still not understanding. He let it lie. He turned the tube up to the light and looked at the label. It had one word printed on it—ROME. He had an absurd image of ground littered with shattered wine bottles, and hordes of cats in the shadows, torn parasols, monkeys climbing through thick vines that draped the crumbling walls of a ruin, and a blue, exotic Mediterranean sky. "A little out of the way, isn't it?"

"Oregon. Rome, Oregon," Blaylock said. "Ever been there?"

Lafleur shrugged. "Desert."

"Yeah."

"It's a government project, right?"

"A prison."

"Ah," Lafleur said, pausing. "It's what—a county facility?"

"Hell, no," Blaylock said. "It's a sixty-million-dollar project."

Lafleur turned the tube in his fingers, hefting it. It was heavy. It made him a little afraid. "You've got the excavation contract?"

"No, son," Blaylock said. "We've got the whole ball of wax."

"Ah," Lafleur said, startled.

Blaylock smiled and blew a thick cloud of smoke. The smoke twisted under the lamp like a snake, then spread and floated above the cat. Blaylock's head hung in the smoke above the cat, whose golden irises looked like O-rings around its pupils. Blaylock's smile deepened to a grimace. "I'm doing this for your mother and for Jewel. Not for you and not for that old fart. Don't you ever forget that."

Lafleur stared in amazement. He set the end of the tube back onto the floor and ran his fingers lightly down to its center. Blaylock leered. His head looked disembodied as if it were hanging from the ceiling by a rope. "It's the ladies," Blaylock said. "They suffer. God knows mine does." He laughed eerily, then said, "Gus and me planned this expansion for three years, then he folded up just when we were ready to move. Now he's whining. Now I've got all the ducks out in the water and he wants to deal Henry in. Okay. Let's see if Henry can cut the mustard."

Lafleur didn't speak. He revolved the tube slowly in his fingers. He was angry, but as fast as his anger grew it dissipated into a functional anger, not real, exactly. It made him feel dry. His mouth was dry with anger. His chest felt hollow with a lack of anger. He understood now why Blaylock was starving the company, why Gus was so anxious to insert his son into the company. Everything was pitched to a fundamental shift the old ones had devised. He imagined his father beside Blaylock, the one taken to the edge of death, burned clean and dry and all that remained in the shell the pure dust of his life, and the other, in fair if abused health, walking, talking, an obese, dangerous spirit. Outside, the rain hissed. The gray cat nuzzled Blaylock's chin and purred while Blaylock caressed its throat with his fingertips. Then he extended his hand across the desk. "Partners?" he said. Lafleur did not move for a moment, wondering how long he could live with anger that was not real, with emotion that was to be traded like coin, with this new kind of complicity. Blaylock leered at him again, widening his dead eyes until they looked like two fried eggs.

Chapter Four

Trade is at once the most carnal and abstract of human activities. Look hard at trade and all the animals creep out of its abstraction.

Hector Zeta,
Manifesto for Spirits

A fancy, glittering place on the fifteenth floor of a downtown building, Louis Brenneman's office had thick carpeting and stainless-steel furniture. The walls were white. It had a bank of rain-spattered plate-glass windows that looked out on the city, which was dusky under the gray sky. The accountant was there, Julia Rose, whom Louis had hired for Lafleur and Blaylock. Blaylock had become malleable on that issue. The accountant was thirty or so, pretty and tired-looking. The tiredness gave her the appearance of fragility. She sat to one side, caged in a fancy chrome-plated chair with black Naugahyde cushions. A slender briefcase, exactly the same auburn as her hair, stood on the carpet at her side.

Louis was in his fifties, soft-skinned, well-fed, and aggressive. He told Lafleur that he'd found out that Blaylock had cloned the excavation company. When Lafleur asked what he meant, Louis said, "Cloned it. Duplicated it. He's shrunk one and started another just like it. And . . ." Louis leaned heavily over his glass desk top, "he's using the same stock for both, the same equipment."

"Can he do that?"

Louis chuckled. "He is doing it."

"On paper, Louis. Can he do it?"

"Is it legal? Not exactly, not when somebody else owns part of the property. It's murky. The equipment's more than half his right now. His partner's an absentee. It's a hell of a deal, actually, very slick. It's illegal only if somebody calls him on it. If nobody calls him . . ." Louis's voice trailed off and he shrugged.

Lafleur didn't share Louis's admiration for the adventure. "So?" he said.

"You've called him," Louis said. He nodded at Julia Rose. "We've got the figures here, the new contracts. He's agreed to sign."

"Hell, Louis, I mean what do you advise?"

"You're in pretty deep to be asking for advice."

Lafleur ran his palms along the slippery steel arms of his chair. "Is he trying to hide the duplicate company, or does he figure I'll know about it?" It was important to Lafleur that he understand what Blaylock willingly divulged and what he did not.

Louis shook his head. "He didn't try to hide it."

"What happens to the duplicate?"

Louis smiled. "Just what I asked him. He says he'll diversify it into concrete or something, and divest it of excavation."

Lafleur looked down and smiled despite himself. "Often, concrete is what you pour into holes."

"Even I figured that out," Louis said, chuckling. "He may want to merge them. If he does, he has to have your agreement, and you've got first option on up to fifty percent."

"Fine," Lafleur said, though he doubted he'd want to be drawn any deeper into these financial convolutions, dense, it seemed, as brain. "And the property? The equipment in the old partnership? The tools?"

"Everything goes back. He owes you, or you and Gus, for the use of equipment in the past year. We'll set that against the losses the company's taken, which will help, even if it still doesn't quite make you come out ahead."

"Then he has the old partnership, which we're in arrears to him for, and the other company, too. It's hard for him to lose."

"Damn near impossible," Louis said. "And he has more. He's a rich man. He's got interests in about six other outfits. For a dirty old mechanic he's awfully slick." Louis glanced at Julia Rose and smiled at her. "He left grease smudges all over the papers." Lafleur looked at Julia. She stirred in her chair and smiled faintly back at him. "Look," Louis said. "You can still sue him, which would supplement my income for a few years, but what you'd get wouldn't hold a candle to what Gus put in the company."

He wrestled loose the knot in his tie and undid the top button of his shirt. "Personally, I think you're going to be a lot better off going ahead and gaining some ground on him. You see? It's tactics, that's all. Legally, sure, you've probably got him cold right now, but financially your position isn't strong, not if you want to make a living and support your family and get ahead and get that income going back to Gus and Jewel." Louis held out his hands. "So?"

"And that's what Ned's gambling on," Lafleur said.

"What? That you won't take him to court?"

"Yes."

"Are you considering it?"

"No."

"Of course not. He's not gambling. If you go to court everybody loses. We'd have to be morons not to figure that out and he knows it. He's set it up beautifully. He may look like a slug, but in there somewhere is an intelligent sonofabitch."

"Okay," Lafleur said. He knew that Blaylock was crafty, but he'd never exactly considered him intelligent. He thought about that and let it stretch way back to the beginnings. It put things in a different light. The man his father had hooked up with years ago was an intelligent sonofabitch.

"Best of all is to dig in and make a go of it, though you're certainly going to have to mix it up with him once in a while," Louis said. "To tell you the truth, I think Blaylock wants you in."

"Seems like he was counting on it," Lafleur said.

"Sure," Louis said, smiling faintly. "He gets you in there to run that company for him, which he knows you can do . . . will do. The fact that you've come to me, had me check it all out, hired an accountant, everything you've done is telling him that when you take a job on you do it right. He knows who you are, for Christ's sake." Louis leaned back, making his calibrated stainless-steel swivel chair click. He put his hands behind his head and stared at the ceiling. "That's another thing," he said. He looked at Lafleur out of the corners of his eyes. "Gus was in on this, the changeover in the company."

"Yeah."

"Have you asked him about it?"

Lafleur frowned. He felt a quizzical and mystified expression pinch his face. He'd been over to see Gus and Jewel several times in the last week. He didn't know what went on in his father's head, or what half of the croaks that came out of the old one's mouth meant, or if Jewel really knew, either. "He can't talk," he said.

"I see," Louis said softly. He lowered his chair and leaned on the desk again. "They were getting on. They were moving toward general contracting. More management and less labor for them. More money. It's logical."

"This new contract is a general contract."

"Right," Louis said.

"It'd probably be a good idea to make damn sure that contract's been written by the partnership."

Louis stared at him for an instant, then picked up a pen and wrote himself a note. He glanced over at Julia and said, "We'll double-check it." He leaned back and stroked his belly. "It's just laying there, Hank."

"I know."

"And that bothers you."

Lafleur grunted and looked down at the carpet.

Louis chuckled resonantly, then said, "You can make it work. If you decide to pull out later, that'll work too. The only way this can fail, financially speaking, is if the whole ship goes down."

"And that's the bottom line?"

"In private partnerships like this there is no bottom line, not until everybody's kicked off or the sole survivor sells off the leavings. Look, I know what the situation is. Julia knows." He tipped his head toward her. "We'll watch it."

"Good." Lafleur had finally got what he wanted most from Louis: a judgment call, a voice from the outside that echoed some of his own conclusions, and by that mounted a triangulation—the lines from Louis's perspective and from Lafleur's converging upon the obscure point, Blaylock. The conjoining of perspectives established angulation and defined the field. It was a survey.

"I haven't told you anything you didn't know, right?" Louis said.

"The duplicate company. The other six he has an interest in. I wondered. I figured he had something running on the side, but I didn't know for a fact."

"Do you want me to check them out?"

"You're offering?"

Louis smiled. "For you, fifty bucks an hour."

Lafleur pulled a scrap of paper from his shirt pocket and wrote: H. Lafleur, P.O. Box 19, Rome, Oregon. He passed it across the desk.

Louis looked at it, then up at Lafleur, and laughed softly. "You've already got an address out there?"

"Yeah."

"You're as slick as your partner."

"No," he said, although it was true that things had been moving fast in the last two weeks. He'd given notice at work, and the bid on the project in Rome—a tiny place on the other side of the mountains, deep in the southeastern Oregon desert—was virtually finalized. He'd been in touch with a man named Victor Sabat, the owner's representative for the project. He'd called yesterday from a booth on a street corner, in the rain at dusk, and he got through first to a woman with a crisp, professional manner that jarred with his mental image of the barren, wind-scoured place. The connection was clear, exact even, and the woman sounded like a television announcer. By the time she passed him on to Victor Sabat, Lafleur had conjured up a whole imaginary, meticulously turned-out person perched behind a desk to go with the smooth voice.

At first, Sabat was chatty about payment schedules, Lafleur's arrival time, Lafleur's lodging, and about a host of details concerning the project. Lafleur bent over the counter in the booth and made copious, confused notes on tiny slips of paper. He didn't understand who was funding the construction. His set of plans had no government stamps, but instead the name of a corporation called International Data. When he asked about that Sabat abruptly become terse: "It's a storage facility."

"Storage?" Lafleur had said. "I understood a prison."

"Yes," the voice said. "Storage."

Lafleur said, "It is a public institution."

The voice turned ice-cold: "We'll fill you in as soon as you get here."

He'd pocketed his slips of paper and ducked through the rain to his pickup. By the time he got back to the toolshed, his paranoia had a grip on him. He shoved the clutter off a bench, spread out the plans, and worked through them. There was no question but that it was a prison design: the concrete, the walls reinforced with steel mesh, the security fence imbedded in more concrete, the razor wire, the controlled traffic patterns, the emphasis upon visibility, the observation decks, and the sheaves in the plans devoted to state-of-the-art electronics: lights on, lights off, lock-ins, lockouts, lockdowns, lights and outlets triggered in phases, electrified security grids, computerized electric eyes, and laser-operated alarm systems. He wondered if he had violated decorum with Sabat, somehow, or if it was just a question of semantics, of euphemism . . . *storage*.

He had a box of books and among them a dictionary, which he dragged out. He blew off the dust and came backward in it, seeking his bearings through the definitions that now, in Louis's office, he remembered this way:

Storage:
A supply, put in safekeeping.
A place for storing goods.
The components of a computer designed to accept, store, and recall information.
Prison:

A place for confinement.

From the Latin *prehensio*, as with the tail of a monkey adapted for seizing or grasping by wrapping around something.

Penitentiary:

A place for persons convicted of serious crimes.

For penance.

Latin *poena*, penal, punishment, pain, penance a sacrament for sin.

The words had spooked him in the toolshed, which pooled with darkness at its edges and under the benches. A bristling blackberry limb drooped over the bench and swayed in the breeze. The stove pipe hummed. A tree rubbed against an eave, and the hairy, excrement-encrusted tail of a monkey looped down and twisted like a snake. He jerked back. The monkey tail vanished, and something strange came out of the words, then, the phantom, and out of Sabat's tone of voice on the phone another phantom. The two phantoms intertwined and encircled Lafleur:

The project was corporate.

But beyond the obvious, he didn't understand what that meant.

Here in the fancy office the same prehensile tail seemed about to twist at him, but he forced himself back out into the light, saying, "Not slick at all. If you ask me, I'm pretty damn knobby." Louis chuckled. Julia smiled. Lafleur said, "I wanted to hear this from you, that's all. Thank you."

"Sure," Louis said.

Lafleur remembered that he had a letter from Sabat in his pocket. He found it, ripped off the letterhead, which had both the Rome address on it and a Los Angeles address and the name of the client company, International Data. On this he wrote the name Clinton U, and underlined Sabat's name. He passed it to Louis. "If you run into anything concerning that company or those two guys, let me know, too." Louis took the scrap and looked at it, then placed it on top of the other scrap of paper. Lafleur said, "This project's a prison."

Louis nodded. "Right. Big."

"I think it's a private project, though."

Louis was unfazed. "They're doing that."

"It bothers me that I didn't know out front, that Ned didn't tell me, avoided telling me, I think."

"Call him on it."

"Yeah. It still might bother me. I don't want to be Blaylock's or anybody else's Trojan Horse."

"No," Louis said. His face steadied and he gazed directly at Lafleur, as if he were searching for what went on beneath the surface. Then he said, "Investigation's not my bag, really."

"I know. It's just in case you bump into something. The question is . . ." Lafleur stopped cold, uncertain as to what question he meant. He changed tack and said, "They're talking about incentives, too. For supervising."

"That's good," Louis said.

"Maybe, but for what? I'd rather just be paid for the work."

Louis smiled. "Do you want to be your dad's Trojan Horse? Is that it?"

"I don't mind that."

Louis murmured, then said, "Yes, you would, if that's all it turned out to be. You should be your own Trojan Horse."

"Maybe," Lafleur said. His mind locked up on a picture of himself hidden inside himself disguised as an ostentatious gift.

"Do you have enough doubts to not sign the papers?"

"No."

Louis stood up. "Maybe it's pre-nuptial jitters."

"Maybe."

Louis went out to dictate a letter, leaving Lafleur with Julia Rose. The two of them moved to a table against a wall. She popped open her auburn-colored briefcase, removed a sheaf of papers and began showing him totals: what the company owned, what it owed and on what, what it owed Lafleur and his father, what they owed it, how much cash would pass to his father and Jewel. There were investments. There would be a bank note, a huge one with balloon payments to finance the Rome project, that cast everything into arrears. The tip of Julia's pencil trembled as she guided it down the columns to the totals.

It was just the woman's fatigue, Lafleur supposed, that made her hand do that, but he wondered what caused the fatigue: young children at home, excessive hours spent trying to get ahead, personal trouble. . . . In a few minutes Louis returned and plopped down in the swivel chair behind his desk. He revolved the chair and tipped it back. It clicked. Lafleur glanced back and forth between him and the papers. Louis had removed his coat and rolled up the sleeves of his white shirt. He picked his nose and stared contemplatively out his windows at a highrise that was going up a couple of blocks away. When Lafleur had first come in he'd looked at the twenty-story concrete slab. There was a crane poised on top and to the side a second crane mounted on its own derrick, scaffolding all up and down the slab, plastic sheeting to aid in curing the freshly poured concrete, and wet, everything wet and glossy under the dark gray sky. Tattered swathes of sheeting that had been used to close in the girders during winter fluttered from the sides of the slabs. Tiny men worked on

41

top. Union carpenters and welders in yellow slickers dotted the scaffolding, where they built new forms and took down the old and worked on the weld plates. There were more men on the ground, where cement trucks steadily came and went, emptying their loads into the canisters that the cranes raised and lowered.

Louis no doubt knew what the building was for, who was financing it, what zoning regulations and political resistance had been battled and overcome in order to break the ground in the first place. Maybe that was what he thought of as he watched it go up—his world interlacing with what he saw—while Lafleur in one glance had read in an intricately interfaced schedule of work, of deliveries and routing slips, of change orders, of labor hired and released according to stages. He saw the weather slowing everything down, and the danger—in the height, in the slick surfaces—and a labyrinth of specifications, numbers, dates, and personalities compelled into a pattern. He watched Julia's pencil and tried to concentrate on the numbers she recited. He half listened to her, half dreamed. He became lulled by her soft voice and nearly hypnotized by her wavering pencil tip. She wore a sharp-smelling perfume. Then he realized that the voice had stopped and that the pencil no longer followed the columns. He felt her gazing at him. She had finished.

"I see," he said, looking back at her.

The gaze between them grew searching, the meeting of their eyes deepening to contact. Her eyes, streaked in the whites, took him in, and for an instant the female creature that was in there behind the fatigue, the worn voice, and the numbers touched him, and triggered his desire for a woman, his ache.

Louis swiveled his chair around abruptly and landed with his elbows on his desk. "Ready?" he said.

"I don't think there's any question about the new project being written from inside the partnership," Julia said.

"Ah," Lafleur said. "Good."

She passed a pen to him, brushing his fingers. He began signing the papers, sheet after sheet. Some of the totals were affixed to years: fifteen, twenty, thirty. In thirty years he'd be pushing seventy. He came to a sheet that listed his equipment: backhoe, bulldozer, and dump truck, even his pickup truck, and valued them at $110,000, of which he owed over $70,000. The same bank still held the titles, but under a different account number now, tucked into the numberings for *Blaylock and Lafleur, Incorporated.* He stopped there, alarmed, holding the pen poised above the paper. He was about to sign away his dream of going independent, of skimming the waters of finance with a streamlined outfit (and of returning to his children in the evening), of staying light and solvent day to day (and

42

of being with his woman at night, their feet touching between the sheets, the blankets pulled up to their chins, the moon hanging in the window).

Suddenly, the idea that anything had ever been his seemed foolish—not the machines he'd carried like the image of a woman, not those machines he'd internalized: bearing, ball joint, armature, shaft, bucket, blade and track. He had dreamed them, how they moved and yielded, how they drew him and how they resisted, as he might dream a woman. All this was about to pass away and leave him in the shadowland of uncertain, functional possession and endlessly shifting numbers that he would wear always, irritating and hot like a set of Mormon underwear.

He stared at the list of machines. The print fuzzed in his vision. He wished not to see the numbers, not to understand them. His personal debt would be plowed into the company. What he had paid on his machinery would be set against a much greater indebtedness. He would be in debt to the company in which he was a partner. He would be in debt to himself. What had been his would be the company's, and paying off the debt would not be an alternative. The only way he would ever be free was to sell his indebtedness, his share, or to liquidate. He would never see the titles to his machines, and never own half the company, not any more than he could bend over and eat his liver out of his own belly.

He felt the silence around him, Julia and Louis looking at him. He didn't raise his head but signed the sheet, and he felt a cold knot in his belly, then almost frantically he signed again and again to the right of the red X marks. He finished and looked up at Julia. She tapped the papers into a neat stack. Her face smiled at him. She placed the ballpoint in the center of the top sheet. He felt his body going rigid. He felt the way Mrs. Good's Abyssinian jackass had looked.

Julia turned her head and looked toward Louis. Lafleur didn't move, though he understood that her gesture was meant to refer him to Louis. He rejected her act of deference. Louis was either looking at him or he and Julia were exchanging a look of concern. It occurred to Lafleur that besides manipulating numbers the purpose of an accountant was to try to keep clients at a distance from the totals that had the air of finality to them, and then to defer obligations. Julia was trying to escape him. He stared furiously at her. She didn't respond. He thought that one should also keep one's distance from accountants, and not ever jostle their masks, because they were in a class along with lawyers, doctors, priests, insurance agents, and morticians, those who service death in its various aspects. He wondered if what wore Julia Rose down was always having to keep her eye on her escape route while she tended the portals to other people's horrors.

Chapter Five

The next day he sat in his backhoe. Rain dotted the windshield and slid down to the rubber molding on the outside. The backhoe, which he'd just driven up into the bed of his dump truck, growled beneath him. He was at Zymanski's warehouse, loading his equipment—which was no longer his. He would take the equipment to the Rome project tonight. Phil Grimes, a heavy-equipment operator and an old friend, was to transport the LeTourneau. Lafleur had to finish here, then stop at the toolshed to pick up his dog and clothes, and be at Blaylock's by eight o'clock to meet Phil.

His truck was a recalcitrant starter in the wet and he'd left it running, too, as he loaded. The backhoe had its vibration and it took up the vibration that came through the steel bed of the truck, up through the bed mounts on the frame from the trembling diesel engine. Lafleur was eating a cheese sandwich that he'd bought from a machine. The height he was at gave him a westward view of Swan Island, an industrial park, of the docks on the Willamette, and to the southwest of downtown Portland. A cloud cover stretched from the Coast Mountains over the city, and the low area from Swan Island to downtown looked like a pool of darkness filled with tiny candles. It was raining gently.

He bit off a chunk of sandwich and looked out the right-hand window at the warehouse, an old brick building painted gray. A man in uniform walked by the front of it. He'd seen that one a few minutes ago, a figure too big, much too tall, and too young to be the watchman Lafleur knew, Dave Petra, an old man with hunched shoulders. But then Dave appeared from the side of the building, climbed the steps onto the loading dock, and went inside to the offices. He shambled behind windows. The other man came back around from the other side of the warehouse and moved to the end of a line of equipment that stretched from the corner of the warehouse behind Lafleur's truck to the street. He had a watchful air and a light step for such a big man.

When Dave came back along the windows inside the warehouse, the other one vanished behind the equipment. Dave stepped out onto the loading dock and glanced up toward Lafleur, then moved down the steps and headed off in the opposite direction from where the other one had gone, back around the building. It was the second time Lafleur had seen that tonight, the two men prowling in a kind of extended dance, always missing each other. It seemed odd.

He stuffed the last of the sandwich in his mouth, pulled on his gloves, pushed open the door, climbed down, and walked to the edge of the truck bed. The backhoe's arm angled upward and the toothed bucket hung like a dislocated mandible over his head. His trailer and Caterpillar bulldozer, still loaded from his last job, stood in Zymanski's line of machines. His truck stood out in the open with its bed cocked up a foot and bridged to the ground by the two steel ramps that he had used to load the backhoe. The backhoe was a good-sized one, a Case 280B, and the truck was a Mack ten-yard rig, but not even the two of them together seemed particularly big because of their company in the line of machinery: bulldozers, earthmovers, cranes, semi-trailers and tractors, lowboys and more dump trucks. They were a prehistoric-looking bunch, mammoth animals, queerly appendaged and heavily armored. He gazed tenderly down the line as if to bid the machines farewell, and looking in the direction of the street he saw the big man again, across the street, standing under the awning of a used-furniture shop. A flickering red neon light played on the man's figure and rainwater streamed from the edge of the awning. Lafleur guessed Zymanski had hired a second watchman, but he couldn't make out why the man was over there. The figure did not move.

Lafleur turned back into the bed of his truck, crouched over the first of four chains, and fastened it to the undercarriage of the backhoe. He moved around, fastening the other three chains. Each time he bent, a rivulet of water slid from the hood of his slicker. It had been raining all day. His gloves were soaked. His shirt collar and socks were wet, the cuffs of his trousers were wet, and the moisture had wicked up to his knees. Quickly, he worked around the backhoe the second time, securing the chains to eyelets welded to the corners of the truck bed. The fourth chain hung up, jarring his shoulder when he jerked it. A link had caught sideways in the eyelet. He shook the chain loose and tugged again. It ran through and he kept it coming until it played out. He hung on to it, feeling his fingers going numb from handling the cold metal, and went down to his knees and peered behind the wheel of the backhoe to check the hook at that end. It was fine, still turned against the tension. He felt that someone was behind him, watching, coming near. Spooked, he froze, then slowly pulled out from under the backhoe and looked around. There was no one. He stepped up on the backhoe and looked over the truck's side panel to where he'd seen the man under the awning. The man was gone.

Lafleur went to the end of the bed and looked up and down the lot, then craned his neck and looked along the side of the truck. There was no one in sight—just the yard, machinery, warehouse, and across the street flickering neon signs and darkened shops, and everywhere the steady drizzle in the half-light. He ducked back into the truck bed. It was the running engines, he thought, that had spooked him, so surrounded him with noise that he conjured a presence out of his inability to hear. It was like the itch on an amputee's toe. It was absence, filling itself with emanation. He grabbed the chain, braced himself against the side of the bed, and tugged. Another link came through. He hooked the chain onto itself, then stepped over it and climbed up the side of the backhoe, entered the compartment, sat, and swiveled the seat so that he faced the bucket. He used the controls to raise the bucket, then made the light-colored articulated arm do a probing acrobatic in the gray air. The arm straightened, telescoped, folded, and the bucket came down neatly until its heel nearly touched the truck bed. He lowered the pods, the four flat steel disks mounted to hydraulic retractors on the insides of the wheels. He used the pods to lift the tractor, taking weight off the wheels and slack out of the chains, then he swung the door open and looked down at the chains. They were tight enough to play a tune on. He lowered the tractor slightly on the pods to ease up on the tension. He dropped the bucket to the bed, making the ninth point for the machine to rest on, to hold it steady on the trip across the mountains. He switched the backhoe off and climbed out, then jumped out of the truck bed to the asphalt. He picked up the end of each of the ramps, slid them under the backhoe, and climbed back into the truck to mount the tailgate, looking again as he moved, scanning the yard.

Heavy, the tailgate took everything he had to move it from where he had leaned it against the side panel. He slid the tailgate into position and lifted one end into the slot, then the other, grunting, feeling with satisfaction the pull of the cartilage in his knees and the thunk as the tailgate pivot fell into the second slot. It felt good to be engrossed with the manipulation of mechanical objects.

He clamped the gate shut, then eased down. He went around to the cab of the truck, climbed in, lowered the bed, backed the truck up and let it coast gently into the trailer hitch. It hit the mark and slid to, thumping resonantly. He got out, dropped the pins into the hitch and attached the safety chains between the trailer and truck, got back in the cab and pulled the trailer out of line and parked near the street. A car passed, illuminating cones of raindrops in the gray with its headlights. The truck engine idled and the windshield wipers slapped rhythmically.

He looked down at his toolbox on the floor of the passenger side and rapidly ran its contents through his mind. He had a steel case in the back of the truck, too, which held the heavier items: grease guns, filters, hosing, jacks, large tools, more chain, cable, spare parts. . . . He had his extra three-quarter-yard bucket in the back, and six ten-gallon cans of oil, two five-gallon grease cans. He was ready. His watch said ten after seven. It was time. He switched off the wipers. Rain dotted the windshield. He opened the door, stepped down to the ground, and headed for the warehouse to check his locker one last time.

At about thirty feet the idling truck became a pocket of noise behind him. He felt as though he had walked through a wall. The sun had dropped beneath the cloud cover. It shone laterally through the slit between clouds and distant mountains. The rain kept falling, but everything gleamed. The evening had taken on an unreal, luminous quality. He searched the yard for Dave Petra, for the big man. He looked between the machines to his right as he passed them. He saw no one. The puddles in the asphalt were a-quiver with light and had oily, coiling rainbows in them.

He climbed onto the loading dock and went into the office. Dave was not in here. Lafleur moved to a pasageway that led to the shop and peered through the opening. Heavy tools lined the walls—jacks, bench presses, welding equipment, metal lathes—and in the dock nearest him stood a D-14 International tractor, disemboweled of its engine. The engine sat on the floor, a pig of a thing. A hook and chain hung from a rolling winch mounted on a track on a beam above the D-14. In the stillness it was a lethal-looking place. He called the watchman's name: "Dave?" His voice echoed in the cavernous room.

No one answered. Puzzled, Lafleur squinted. He turned back into the office and walked to his locker, opened it, and squatted.

An old sweater lay wadded in a corner. Scattered bits of things that had fallen out of his pockets over the several years littered the bottom. He scooped them out and looked: scraps of paper, tickets torn in half, a broken jackknife, pennies, paper clips, and a small, hard piece of clay. Junk. He picked up the clay. It was a head with protruding ears, agape mouth, and deep eye sockets, something slightly hideous made by one of his children, but he couldn't remember by which child, or when, or why he had carried it here. He turned the head slowly in his fingers, then put it in his shirt pocket. He put the pennies in his pocket and dumped the rest of the debris in a wastebasket, picked up his sweater, stood, swung the locker door shut with his knee, and moved back to the front door.

He went out onto the dock, stopped, and looked for Dave Petra. Usually Dave came out to talk to him when he loaded equipment after hours. The sun had sunk deeper and whitened light reflected off the bottoms of the clouds. He glanced over at his truck and trailer, which were waiting right next to the street. The truck rumbled. He snaked his eyes back along the line of huge, protuberant machinery, then he moved down the steps and started across the lot.

He felt cold under his slicker from being in the warm building. The air began to reverberate as he neared his truck. He looked around, across the street, even back over his shoulder, seeing no one. He went around the trailer, scrutinizing his load as he passed, checking it again, and walked to the cab. He had his foot on the step-up and the door half open when he saw a thick shape loom out from the front of the truck. The shape, a man, scurried under him. Startled, Lafleur froze. The man came up from beneath Lafleur, grabbed his belt, and thrust him into the cab. Quickly, Lafleur bent his leg up and kicked, and felt his bootheel strike, but there was another one inside the cab, who grabbed his coat and dragged him in, actually lifted and turned him and sat him down on the seat. The one outside got into the cab, jerked the door shut, slid over and pushed against Lafleur. Lafleur found himself wedged between the two of them. He had his foot caught behind the shift lever. He couldn't move. He smelled the men's wet clothing. The one on his left was bent over, rubbing his forehead through the black ski mask he wore pulled down to his neck.

"Caught you one, did he?" the one on the right said. He, too, wore a black ski mask. He was big. He had a big frame and a head like a huge black blot, but his voice came out sweet-sounding.

"Shit," the one on the left said. "The sucker kicked me." Then suddenly he turned on Lafleur, wildly punching Lafleur's chest and face.

"Easy," the big one said. Lafleur had raised his arms to ward off the blows. He drew up one knee to try to shove the man off him. His other foot was still caught and he felt his ankle wrench. He heard himself shout. It sounded like someone else shouting, then he felt the big one lean over him, felt himself smothered by the body and pressed back into the seat, and he glimpsed the big one's arm move by and gently shove the man on the left away. "Easy," the big one said.

"Okay," the man on the left said. He slid back next to Lafleur, shoving against him. "Okay."

"We thought we'd lost you when you first pulled this thing out to the street," the big one said. The voice still sounded sweet.

Lafleur hadn't been hurt by the attack, just shaken. His foot was still caught and his blood was pounding. "Get out of my truck," he said.

He felt the man on his left quivering. On his right, the big one's jaw worked slowly underneath the mask, then he said, "He wants us out of his truck. It's so nice and dry in here. Plenty of room, too." The man on the left chuckled.

Lafleur tried to think what they wanted, or what he could give them. He tried to remember what he had on the floor, wondering if there was something loose down there that he could use as a weapon, but what had been so clear in his mind a few minutes ago, exactly what equipment he had packed, and where, had become a muddle. By pressing their bodies against him, the two men had him in a helpless position. When he shifted his leg slightly to disengage his trapped foot, the body on his right turned, then suddenly the movement became fast and inescapable like a tree, tipping, then rushing for the earth. He saw the fist coming at him, and the blow exploded in his face and banged his head against the back window. Everything went black.

When he opened his eyes he saw the windshield as a blur, wet and glistening. He felt the bodies next to him, the one on the left quivering as if with excitement. The two had their heads down. The one on the right was chewing something. The mask moved rhythmically at his cheek. When Lafleur stirred he spat and said, "There, now." Lafleur's head throbbed. He touched his face, felt it. Through the windshield he saw a car go by, lighting up the street.

He looked at the big man out of the corners of his eyes. "What do you want?"

"Good," the big one said. He raised one hand and put something through the hole in his mask, and resumed chewing. "Much better," he said.

"Money?" Lafleur said. "Do you want money?" The two didn't speak. "I'm going to take out my wallet," Lafleur said, "and put it up on the dash. Take what you want."

Neither of the men spoke, but the one on the left abruptly stopped quivering and Lafleur thought, Addicts, they're addicts, they want the cash. He moved gingerly, reached back for his wallet. He had to wedge his hand between himself and the one on his left to get at it. He eased it out, set it on the dashboard, and the one on the left jerked forward, snatched up the wallet, then bent down again, and rifled the contents. "There's two hundred dollars," Lafleur said. He watched as bits of paper—his receipts and the notes on bits of paper—scattered to the floor. The man dropped the wallet and made a fan out of the bills and held them near the dashboard lights. The big man on the right turned his head slightly to look and Lafleur caught a glimpse of the pale skin around his eyes. The man on the left put the bills in his pocket, then squeezed back against Lafleur. "Now," Lafleur said. "I don't know who you are. Leave me."

"Full of ideas, isn't he?" the big man said softly.

The man on the left chuckled.

The big man spat again, then said, "It's a cage out there."

Lafleur sat still, watching the big man's head. He was thinking that he needed to watch, to not appear to be a victim, even to try to talk. He closed his eyes and opened them. He felt groggy.

"They sent me to check on you," the big man said. The man on the left laughed. "You've got to steel yourself before you go out there."

"Okay," Lafleur said.

"Wherever you're going," the big man said. He laughed. It came out as a rapid wheezing, then he paused, drew his breath, and said, "Okay, he says. Okay what?" The man on the left laughed. It sounded like a cackle. Lafleur could feel the two bodies rocking gently with laughter, and he thought, These two aren't simply out of control, they're crazy. "It's all a cage," the big man said, almost whispering. "I've spent my whole life in a cage. Life is hard."

"I'm sorry," Lafleur said.

"Sorry?" the big man said. "You don't know me." The man on the left had begun to quiver again, then he pulled away from Lafleur, and Lafleur thought, Maybe they're going now. But the one on the left stopped. Lafleur sensed expectation in his position, then realized that the man wasn't leaving, but just getting out of the way. For an instant, a terrible, accepting sense of calm descended upon Lafleur. "You don't know what my life is like. Who do you think you are?" the big man said, and Lafleur saw the big, oval head bow, and then felt the huge body turning again, coming at him. Desperately, he tried to twist free, but the one on the left knocked him back. Lafleur raised his hands. The fist crashed through them, striking him on the forehead, and then again he took another crushing blow to the side of the head, and he smelled the big man near him, the strong odor of wet wool and something in his breath, rancid and faintly salty. The man hit him a third time. Lafleur's skull rattled against the window. As he passed out he felt another blow and it seemed almost soft, a cushion for him to lay his head on as he went under.

When he awakened he found himself half stretched out on the seat. Confused, he tried to raise himself. His foot was stuck. He disengaged it and turned it to test his ankle. He remembered that detail, the ankle. It was all right. He heard a car swish by. He tried to pull himself up by the dashboard, but couldn't do it. He fell back on the seat. His head pounded.

He stared at the ceiling of the cab. He remembered the two men, then realized that he was alone. He felt a tremendous wave of relief. Groggy, he passed out again.

Then he came to, his thoughts clearer. He eased upright and hung on to the steering wheel. His head knifed with pain. The truck was still running, trembling. Down below, the lights of Portland stretched as far as the eye could see. He thought of Phil Grimes waiting for him at Blaylock's and he tried to read his watch, but couldn't make it out. He thought—*Blaylock!* In his mind, he saw Blaylock's pitted face. He wanted to blame Blaylock for this. He straightened, pressed the clutch down, pulled the shift lever, and grasped the wheel. He eased the truck out into the street. Behind him, the trailer clanked. A car honked. Its horn wailed and changed tone as it passed. He drove on, fighting sleep.

Chapter Six

He awoke in his own bed. He knew that by how it felt and by the place in the ceiling directly above him, by the way the faint light from the hallway darkened at a scoop in the spackling.

He was in his clothes. His boots were off. He moved his toes and felt the stiff grain of his wool socks. He ran his hands along a nylon quilt, then reached out and touched the wall behind the pillow. For a moment he felt a powerful sense of well-being, an almost sexual pleasure. It was the quilt and something to do with the wall, the familiar smell of the woman left on the quilt and the feel of the wall on the other side of which his children slept, and also the penumbral glow from the nightlight placed in the hall so the children could find their way to the bathroom. It made the hall safe from their imaginations. It made him feel safe. He rolled toward the wall at the side of the bed, seeking out of an old habit to touch the naked hip of the woman. He had a peculiar sense of his weight turning, a buoyancy in the bedsprings granted by the absence of the other body, the lack of counterweight, and then it came to him again, but quite differently: he was in his bed.

Startled, he sat up, then buckled with pain and reached for his head. His head was bandaged.

A portion of it came back to him—waking up sprawled on the seat of his truck, dragging himself upright by the steering wheel.

Presumably he had then driven here—home. He didn't remember that. He remembered thinking he would try to make it down to Blaylock's place to meet Phil.

Vaguely he remembered finding himself half-conscious at the wheel with the door open and Penny standing on the step and her arm, white as bleached bone, reaching to turn off the truck. He remembered the truck going off, the sound of it gone like something dropped through a chute to the center of the earth, and the headlights going off, and Penny's face, white in the night at his side.

He remembered what she had said, annoyed: "What do you think you're doing here?" Then alarmed: "What happened?"

He remembered being walked to the house and steered inside. He remembered Penny tugging on him, leading him into the bathroom. He remembered catching a glimpse of his face in the mirror, his swollen cheek and the blood spidering down his jaw. She sat him down on the toilet seat. She washed his face and head and applied ointment to his wound. He remembered her wanting to take him to the hospital and himself refusing. He remembered her ear sticking out from behind her hair as she reached around to the back of his head. One soft breast had crushed against his shoulder. Her breath had been as familiar as the smell of the quilt.

He slid his legs out from under the covers and touched his feet to the floor. He stood. His head reeled and he felt himself swaying. He closed his eyes for a moment, then opened them and moved alongside the bed. His boots stood on the floor. He sat on the foot of the bed and pulled them on. His head pounded as he bent to tie the laces. He straightened, closed his eyes again, and had a vision of bills fanned out near the dashboard lights. He reached for his wallet. It was gone. He was chilled. He stood, moved, and turned down the hall. He felt like a sleepwalker. He stopped at the children's ajar door and looked in. They lay under the blankets on the two beds, one very small shape—Andy—and the other longer—Tricia.

He couldn't see their faces, only their narrow, absolutely still bodies under the covers. They looked dead. The chill of fear ran deep into his blood and he heard a distant howl—*Nicole!*—then details came at him, but slowly at first and clumsily like beetles dragging themselves out from the dark. He remembered being bumped into the truck by one man, then grabbed by the other. He remembered the darkness of the cab, the blunt, masked heads, the bodies pressing against him, the blows to his face, the one man talking, something about a cage . . . and now he wondered, *Why?*

He remembered wishing to blame Blaylock, and now felt himself wishing it again out of an obscure anger, a resentment. He heard Andy and Tricia breathing, the tender rise and fall of their breath, and felt easy for them, for their safety, and he ached for their loss—their sister, himself.

He moved to the kitchen. The fluorescent light in the stove panel was on and he saw the time—five-thirty. He looked at his watch. It said the same thing exactly and he stared at it in confusion because he didn't know what it meant. He glanced around. The linoleum floor shone dimly. The stainless-steel coffeepot stood where it had always stood on the counter.

Next to it was the yogurt maker, then the can opener. Those things were just as they should have been, but other things were different: a new soap dish next to the sink, new towels, a new blender to replace the old one that had to have its buttons struck with the butt of a screwdriver to make it work, a microwave oven, a new cloth on the old table. The old kitchen knives were stuck into a new holder. He looked through stunned eyes and for a moment everything seemed to be a figment. A thought gripped him: He was the figment. He was dead. He was a passing spirit. He rocked back on his heels and felt tempted to yield to the world of such thinking, which was religion, steamy and psychic, and which tapped out its own crooked and powerful telemetry. He caught himself just there on the edge of an abyss and touched the tile of the counter, then made his legs carry him into the living room, where he found Penny curled up under a blanket on the couch. He stood over her. He felt cold. She opened her eyes and looked up at him with a startled expression.

"Damn curious," he said.

"Where are you going?"

"To work, I guess," he said. The words activated his brain and he thought: That's right, the job in Rome.

Penny stretched. Her rib cage and hip rose under the blanket. Her bare feet appeared from beneath the hem. "What happened?"

"Somebody beat the shit out of me."

"Who?"

He couldn't answer that.

"You've got a nasty bump," she said.

"Bump?" He touched the bandage on his head. Pressing lightly, he felt the tenderness on the right side of his forehead, then his jaw, the back of his head. "Yes," he said.

Against the dark blanket, Penny's arms looked white. Her face was white. Her eyes were dark as holes. Her voice was clear. "You were out cold. How you managed to drive here is beyond me. Were you at Zymanski's?"

"Yes. Loading up."

"You should see a doctor." He looked away. At the end of the couch stood a dressmaker's dummy draped with cloth. Penny was a seamstress and designer. She and a friend had opened up a custom shop downtown. Thick and headless, the dummy looked like a stump with a sheet drawn over it in the shadowy light. Behind the dummy were drapes, drawn to cover the window. She probed him softly with his name: "Hank?" He turned to her. He didn't want to see a doctor. She pulled herself up so that the small of her back rested against the arm of the couch. She raised her knees under the blanket and drew the blanket up to her shoulders. He thought that she had lost weight.

"There were two. They were like junkies." Saying that, he thought it to be true—nothing to do with Blaylock. "I guess they were just junkies."

"Oh, Hank," she said.

"They took cash," he said, and he went on to tell her about the big man vanishing and reappearing, how the big man seemed to be playing cat-and-mouse with the watchman, how the other man came out from the front of his truck, how the big one was in there, how they wore black ski masks, how they held him and beat him, how they seemed crazy like junkies, how the one on his left had the shakes, how they took two hundred dollars cash and left him. When he finished he was weak. He closed his eyes and felt the room tipping to and fro.

"Sit down," she said.

He did. He sat down in an easy chair across from the couch. "I'm glad I had the cash," he said, and then as he went on he heard the fright moving into his voice: "They were pissed when I asked them to get out of my truck. Can you believe it? My truck." He heard a whisper within him—*not yours*—which subtly increased his fright. "If I hadn't had the cash, I don't know what they would've done."

"You need to see a doctor," she said. "No doubt you have a concussion." Her voice was husky and motherly. He wanted to yield, to sit next to the warmth of her body. He looked sideways past the dressmaker's dummy at the window drapes, and took a deep, shuddering breath. Reddened morning light seeped around the edges of the rust-colored drapery. "I'll drive you downtown," she said.

He didn't want to see a doctor. "You heard about the partnership?" he asked.

"Yes, Hank," she said, smiling faintly.

He smiled, too, faintly, for he knew that she knew his way of playing tricks, such as changing the subject, whenever the question of his visiting a doctor came up. "It'll mean more money in the long run, I guess," he said. Since he and Penny were not talking, he'd asked Jewel to explain the partnership to her, but now they were here talking, and without rancor, too. She looked directly at him and her face grew alert. It seemed extraordinary to Lafleur that she was there, and for a moment it seemed as though the months of not talking had not happened, or the trouble before that, or as if they had entered the imbroglio as into the heart of the woods and come out again, but separately, on their separate adventures, out through the thinning trees to the other side where they met, where everything was different. They were going on, now, like old partners sojourning in the bright air who in the dark clarity of their memory recalled all the old things that were so utterly changed. He grew hopeful. "I'm sorry," he said abruptly.

"Sorry?"

"I didn't mean to come here."

"No," she said. "I know." They held one another's eyes and the very air in the room seemed to grow taut as a drumhead. It became too much to bear and they both looked away at once.

He stared back at the drapery and felt himself filled with despair. "Don't tell Jewel about this, me getting beat up. She doesn't need another worry."

"No," Penny said.

"I'm just glad I didn't end up at her place."

"Yes."

"I'm all right."

"You should report it to the police." When he didn't respond at first, she added, "You have to."

"Dave," he said. "Dave Petra, the watchman. I don't know what happened to him. He was there, then he wasn't."

"You have to go to the police."

"All right. Yes," he said, glancing at her, then he turned his head and looked into the kitchen and thought about how he'd felt like a dead spirit. It seemed silly, now, the whole thing a figment of his imagination that had retracted into a very small and very heavy bundle like a bullet. "I probably came here out of habit," he said.

"You were hurt."

He paused, then said, "I guess I'd better get out of here before the kids wake up."

"I guess."

"It would confuse them."

"Probably," she said.

They were speaking guardedly now. He shifted forward in his chair as if preparing to leave, and he made a weak joke: "Unless I went out and got myself hit on the head every night until they were used to me turning up."

Penny sat up straight. He thought she was about to speak. He feared what she would say. His body tensed. She said nothing, but looked at him with a hooded expression, then leaned back. That bodily gesture formalized her position, but exerted the opposite effect upon him. Her formality denied him, and yet she looked sensuous, the long neck, the thin, bare arms coming out of the short-sleeved nightgown. She looked as familiar as earth—flesh, bone, and breath. His desire rose within him and at the same time he considered the years he had stitched into that female body, the quirks he'd acquired to match its quirks. Her body and his and the desire between them were like weatherbeaten bushes grown together to look like one deformed bush that sent out branches in strange directions to protect itself.

Between them they had the pure, hot desire of the old days, and the wear, and also the grief, which waxed wantonly in the cold. For weeks after Nicole's death, he and Penny had lain side by side in bed at night, two felled trees with grief between them like a chasm of snow. They touched hands or toes. They talked across the chasm. Their conversations were repetitious. They misunderstood each other in the same ways again and again. Even when each of them used exactly the same words and meant practically the same thing, they seemed to be moving farther and farther apart.

He would plead with her by saying that somehow they had to get back to the business of living, that that was the only way anything would ever have meaning for them again.

I'm not ready, she would say. I had her in me. She was part of me, my very body. And now she's gone.

You have to get a grip on yourself, he would say. Both of us do. Somehow we have to steer ourselves away from the trouble. We can do that.

No, she would say. I can't solve it by thinking. I have to wait. A death is the end of a presence. You can't just decide to repair it. Don't you see!

But we have to find a way to heal the loss, he would say.

Not me, she would say. Not find it. The body, she would say . . . and then invariably she would pause, balancing herself, and she would think of how he was fixed on the body that had never been found, the body that was out there in the water somewhere, in the Willamette, the Columbia, or the Pacific, and which had not completed the circuit for him by making palpable the end of its life. By this time, whether or not Nicole's body was found meant little to her, but he seemed to need that palpability to complete Nicole's life, and to feed . . . to feed what? His hopefulness? Sometimes she would complete her sentence even though she was sure he wouldn't understand it: I'm waiting. The body goes its own way.

Most of the time she didn't complete it. Sometimes when they reached just that juncture, she would merely yield to his sexual need, the strength of urge she sometimes envied in a man, even though she knew it made him feel as if he had come into a house that had its doors ajar but in which there was never anybody at home. She felt like that house, empty but for the stranger in it, and the night he'd left they had done that, and a while afterward he sat up in bed and stared through the doorway into the hall, and he said he didn't understand what was wrong, that maybe he should go out and sleep in his father's toolshed for a couple of nights so they could have some time to think. He was weeping. He was trying to reach her. He wanted her to tell him not to go, but she lay still on her back, terrified, utterly incapable of finding words, and slowly growing cold, cold with outrage that he could so misunderstand her and abandon her when she

57

needed him. He left. When his form turned in the hallway, he looked like a stranger.

Now, seated across from him on the couch, she saw his need in the almost invisible glimmerings of his soft brown eyes and still face—the face bruised and bandaged, but nevertheless the same handsome, dark, slightly pockmarked, strong-featured face she admired for its composure and resented for what it hid. She had seen him responding to her with his need. She'd seen it in the way he leaned forward and put his hands on his knees as if to prepare to stand up and go, but equally prepared, she thought, to lie with her on the couch, which she would probably have allowed. She still loved him in a way he didn't understand. It was only that her body wouldn't accept him until he allowed her to become herself in his presence, until he became himself, until he understood that Nicole's death was not his death to fix and patch up, until he understood that her grief was not his, until he stopped his insufferable thinking and allowed his body to find its own way. Penny rocked forward and gazed at the carpet on the floor.

Lafleur's contemplation quickened when she moved. He thought of the old times before the drowning. He thought of her bare legs levering against his legs, of her breasts dipping to brush his chest, of the mole on her left side, of her long fingers. He thought of the way she had of pausing and balancing herself in the midst of lovemaking. He thought of her abdomen pressing against his, of how her ribs, back, and buttocks felt under his fingers. He looked at her. Bent forward, her head bowed, the blanket spreading downward from her shoulders, and the tops of her breasts visible above the loosely gathered gown, she had taken the position of a penitent. His desire changed into a haunting and then everything froze: Penny, the couch, the dimly lit room, rug, walls, drapes, and the headless dummy. Abruptly he stood up and said, "What happened to my coat?"

"In the hall closet."

He went to the closet, found his rain slicker and felt for the keys in the pocket. His wallet was there. He took it out and unfolded it. They had taken the money, that was all, and left his credit cards and photos. He placed the wallet in his hip pocket. He could hear Tricia and Andy talking softly in their room. He returned to the living room, holding his slicker by the collar. Light from the kitchen windows caught Penny's face, accentuated the bone, and deepened the shadows in her eye sockets. He paused. The space between them was tremulous with the unspoken. He heard a muffled giggle from down the hall.

"I forgot to tell you that Phil Grimes called last night," she said. She looked up.

"Here?"

"He said he'd tried everywhere else. He said he'd tried Jewel. He's gone on ahead."

"That's one less thing for me to worry about," he said, smiling faintly. His head ached. "Where Phil is, I mean."

"He said he would call after he got there. I told him you were hurt."

"I'll call ahead. If he gets you, tell him I'm coming."

"Jewel will call to find out what's going on."

They'd become like husband and wife, making arrangements, naming the bases to be touched. Their adherence to the daily thing seemed merciless. "For God's sake, don't tell her," he said.

"No."

"Tell her I'm fine. Tell her I'll call from the site."

She inhaled deeply. "All right."

He looked down and said, "Thank you." He heard footsteps in the hall, then the bathroom door clicking shut. Afraid, he said, "I'd better go." A groping look passed between them. "Thank you," he repeated. She didn't speak. He went toward the front door, touching the dressmaker's dummy with his fingertips as he passed it. He felt like an idiot. Of all the times he'd felt idiotic, it had never come as strongly as it did just then. This place, he thought, and that woman were the fount of his idiocy. He glanced back. Penny had not moved. She stared blankly into the space before her.

He walked out into the soft Portland air and across the street to his truck. The elbow of his backhoe's armature stuck above the sides of the truck bed and the bulldozer crouched like a pig on the trailer. He climbed into the cab and started the engine. The sound washed over him. He pulled out and headed downtown to the police station, where he reported the robbery and beating and waited while an officer filled out forms. He had to tell the story twice. They said they would check on the watchman, Dave Petra. They wanted him to go back with them to the scene of the crime, but he resisted, saying he was late already. "Besides," he said, "the scene of the crime is portable. It's parked outside." It was barely seven o'clock, and the nightshift was still on duty. Two drunks sat on a bench with their heads between their knees, and a lunatic mouthed inaudible screams from within the soundproof holding pen at the far end of the room. The officer asked if anyone else had been in the truck cab lately. "Not for a long time," Lafleur said, remembering how sometimes one of the children, or even Penny, used to ride with him on short runs. The officer glanced alertly at him, then touched his arm and asked if he was all right. "Sure," Lafleur said.

He waited again while two officers prowled around the inside of his cab.

They dusted for prints. Lafleur walked several blocks down to a cash machine to get more money. There was morning fog, growing radiant in the sunlight. He called Rome from a phone booth to let them know he was coming. Again he got the woman with the impeccable voice. He called Zymanski's to ask about Dave Petra. The graveyard watchman told him Dave hadn't said anything about a robbery. Lafleur set the receiver on its hooks and stood for a moment, puzzled. He walked back to the station. The police said they would let him know of any developments, and he left, jigsawing along the streets to the freeway, which took him over the river, across town, and then southward on an upgrade. The fog dwindled.

He drove with one hand on the wheel, the other resting on the shift lever. He felt more than listened for the raw roar of the truck's engine, for the vibration of the suspension and wheels, and for the load, the weight of the trailer on the hitch, for how weight bore up on the swivel when he took a curve. The motion and manipulation of the truck, and the taking in of data, touching the wheel and shift knob, those palpable tools of leverage, began to clear his head. The rain had stopped during the night, but the pavement was wet. His tires hummed and hissed.

At Multnomah Boulevard he hit the half-mile downgrade and let the truck ride up to seventy for the sake of the coming mile-and-a-half grade. On the grade he geared down and had slowed to forty-five by the time he reached the crest. He passed the Lake Oswego exit, the Ethan Allen funeral home—an excessively imposing place with a line of pillars in front. It was set in manicured grounds and designed in the federal style, like the back of a nickel. His mother was there in the adjoining cemetery. Gus had reserved a plot. Nicole had a plaque. He passed an industrial park. The warehouses looked ghostly against the backdrop of forest. He crossed the Tualatin River, eased back up to seventy, and entered the flat of the rural valley.

The sun glinted horizontally at his mirrors. The moisture on the pavement lifted in steamy curls. Again he crossed the Willamette, then geared down for the off-ramp, took it, and headed west toward his place. He drove seven miles on a paved road through the seed fields. Dense mist hung above the ground. He drove into the woods. The mist draped the tree trunks. He turned onto the gravel road, drove another half mile, and unconsciously began to ease up on the accelerator as he approached Blaylock's place. He saw pink, an expanse of wall shining like fluorescence through the fog, then bits of equipment, dark shovels, booms, and engine compartments sticking through the fog. As he neared he saw the tangled saplings and blackberry bushes, and the equipment in greater detail, and the looming pink house with its shades drawn, everywhere the shadow and damp and diaphanous white shrouding of fog the same color exactly as the metal roofs of the outbuildings in back. What he saw was how he felt, his mind in a shimmering ground fog with the shapes inexactly perceived. This was where he should have been twelve hours ago. His hand rested on the shift lever. The LeTourneau was gone. His truck slid slowly by. He discovered that he'd been holding his breath.

He let air out and accelerated. The trailer boomed as the hitch took up slack. The silver, fog-draped woods slithered by, then he slowed again for the toolshed. Alder branches strummed the ribs of his truck as he turned into the drive. The fog deepened. The front of his shed became obscurely visible. Jones leaped out of the fog and balanced on her hind legs, making him jerk with surprise. The taut chain held her up like a man. A blue heron sailed over the shed with its wings spread, braking for the shallows at the edge of the river. Jones stayed there like an ape with a flat dog head. Her front paws wagged eagerly and her tongue flapped at the side of her misshapen snout.

Chapter Seven

The great Basin stretches from southeastern Oregon southward through Nevada and inland southern California nearly to Arizona, and eastward across Nevada into Utah. Cut off from the sea, it is actually a series of basins that drain into one another. The evaporation rate exceeds ten inches a month, more than a hundred times the average rainfall.

In the old days, the people ate roots, seeds, piñon nuts, and grass, any plant that gave nourishment, and rabbits, squirrels, insects, worms, birds, lizards, every form of animal. They collected fish at the annual runs on the few waterways that entered the basin. This was their trade, interior and stable. Goods came in occasionally, but rarely went out. "Almost like plants," wrote Colonel Fremont, "these people seemed to have adapted themselves to the soil and to be growing on what the immediate locality afforded."

They were like air ferns, economical to the extreme. They lived the lateral existence of gatherers, attuned to natural detail. Their skin was like the sand, moistened by blood. Even today, most of the small towns are like tiny conductive densenings on vast circuit board, while the big towns, Reno, Las Vegas, and Salt Lake City, soak up money and religion for their densely inward games of chance.

Hector Zeta,
Manifesto for Spirits

Lafleur loaded up his personal articles at the toolshed, changed his clothes, and pulled out. To Rome, he took the route out of the valley and through the mountains by way of Corvallis, Lebanon, Waterloo, Foster, Sweet Home, and Cascadia to Sisters, the last town low on the eastern slope of the Cascade Range and named after the mountains, the snow-capped Three Sisters. The mountain country was cool and dense, a tangle of waterways, rock, and woods. The winding roadway made the driving intense. He pulled off not far beyond Santiam Pass to let his brakes cool. Jones jumped out from the seat, grunting heavily when she hit the ground.

He looked at his dozer, secure in its chocks, and stepped up on the truck bumper to check the backhoe. The chains were snug. He circled the rig, kicking tires, then stopped, leaned against the front bumper, and stared out at a charcoal-colored lava flow ringed sparsely with ponderosa pines. The conversation with Penny this morning and the robbery at Zymanski's last night seemed like figments, small as cocoons and heavy and elusive as mercury. He needed to bathe. He could smell his own odor coming through his shirt.

A magpie dropped out of a pine and jumped across the lava flow near the road. A second magpie scolded from the tree. Jones pissed on the rock. It was clear that this was the eastern side of the summit: dry earth and desiccated rock, twisted ponderosas, bright sky, bright black-and-white scavenger birds. One magpie made the needles at the ends of the limbs quiver as it jumped and cawed at the other's stiff-legged tour—looking for what, he wondered: seeds, granules, moth wings, larvae, mouse feces, bits of animal hide? Jones crapped, and when she left it, the bird hopped over and pecked at the pile. Jones looked back at the bird. The bird in the tree jumped and cawed. It sounded like a crow, like Gus trying to laugh.

Lafleur helped the dog into the truck, got in himself, and drove down from the mountains with surprising quickness to Sisters. The town was dressed up for the tourist trade. It had harmonized facades on its buildings and was organized, he imagined, to circulate bills of small denomination with great rapidity. A place of scrubbing, wiping, and arduous quickness, clean fingernails and shiny shoes and an infinity of price tags, Sisters sold curiosities along with the hamburgers, milkshakes, and fishing tackle: postcards, decals, signs, "Back Off!" mud flaps, dancing "Fuck You" fingers to mount in the rear windows of cars, bumper stickers that ranged from scatology to moral advice, something for everyone, toy guns, pocket knives, paperweights, ashtrays, polished rocks on chains, Indian head-dresses made out of turkey feathers, scorpion and rattler tails mounted in clear plastic blocks, pornographic playing cards, coffee mugs with obscene slogans, crystal balls with naked women inside them, crucifixes, Saint Christopher statuettes, Day-Glo condoms, and rubber monster masks. It was a gateway, a complicated, thousand-headed creature of prey crouched at the verge of mountain and desert. Lafleur drove through.

Soon the three mountains rose from the flat on his right, white and looming. As he continued, they stood in his rearview mirrors, gradually growing smaller and more distinct. The Three Sisters became a measure of his progress. The pines were a measure. Back at the summit, the firs, cedars, spruces, and white pines had given way to yellow pulpwood, the ponderosas. Outside Sisters, the ponderosas dwindled. Water-starved, they grew scraggly and jackish, then they gave ground to the small piñon pines. When the piñons vanished it was just sand and scrub. He had slipped into the northwestern edge of the Great Basin. The aching in his head was a measure, too. It had spread down from his neck to his shoulders, slowly softened and enlarged like a web. Jones had her snout on his leg.

He would pass through two towns of size before reaching Rome, first Bend and then, better than a hundred miles later, Burns, those two dispersal centers where the sun would glint off the plastic and sheet metal of new construction. Otherwise, the tiny towns perched alongside the highway measured the hugeness of space, and his progress into something like nothingness . . . scrub, barren sand, harsh sun, and mountains in the distance, the three white ones quivering in his mirrors for miles, and the lower blue-colored ridges to the north and south like remote islands at sea, and the tiny towns that looked precisely like what they were and, he supposed, had been from the start: combination fuel sources, post offices, spare way stations for travelers—the faintly marked indices of a tenuous economy spread thinly across space.

The three white mountains occupied his mirrors, then they were lost in accordance with the long, slow rise and fall of the road. He would think they were gone, then they would come back again, surprising him with their whiteness, miles away, well after he had passed through Bend. Back and forth the mountains went. Long after they were gone for good he thought they must still return to his mirrors. They were there, all right, behind him somewhere, as luminous as memory.

Each little town consisted of two or three wind-scoured buildings, sometimes one, and had small mutilations of shed and fence, piles of metal, and had nurtured, usually, a few scorched trees. Sometimes there was just the one bleached, lonesome building standing against the waste. His road map gave them names: Tumalo, Millican, Brothers, Hampton, Riley, Hines, Lawen, Crane, Princeton, and Burns Junction on the way to Rome. He peered out at these places as he passed. Jones sat up and pressed her warm body against his. He pushed her off. She licked him in the face. He jerked and shoved her away. She snaked back to rest her snout on his leg again and left a widening patch of drool on his trousers.

The steering wheel trembled and the truck and trailer jolted rhythmically over the seams in the pavement. The engine roared softly. So straight was the highway and so monotonous the landscape it began to seem as if he were not there, hardly driving, hardly needing to touch the wheel. He wondered about the desolation of living in such a place. He made up sad, barely ambulatory lives: going to the hydrant outside, going to the cupboard for food, the husband and wife brushing shoulders, and the two of them staring across the table at each other with hollow eyes, wondering what to do, going to bed to make love, maybe, for a transfusion of entanglement, breath, and wet, and coming back out lightheaded and wondering what to do next, waiting for something to happen, a telephone call, a change in the weather, a breeze, a cloud, anything, or children watching the road, wondering what would happen if one of those vehicles that sped by, such as his, were to stop and pull in. He imagined such lives as he drove. It was his desolation he pondered, however. It was the half-crazed longing he had but only faintly understood in himself to be utterly empty, to scorch out his troubles and aching. Miles into the desert, beyond Burns, he passed under a line of high-tension wires mounted on derricks. Startled, he looked to his left, northward. A file of derricks strung together by gleaming cables extended to the distant hills. Metal glittered up there at the outer reach of visibility. Feed lines that he could not see dropped from the derricks to the ground. The Bonneville Power Administration had claimed an alley out of nothingness and filled it with high voltage.

A half hour later he was startled again by a Pacific Northwest Bell transmitting station: a low building, a tower made out of girders, steel guy lines tracing triangles in the air, and mounted on the tower four satellite receivers. The tower and cable and dish receivers shone in the sun. He cruised by at seventy-five. The transmitting station grew suddenly huge as he neared it and stuttered brilliantly in his eyes as he passed. He blinked and held the image in the back of his head, that thing that caught and sent on the voices from the airwaves through here—*nowhere*—to somewhere else.

He went through Crane, a slightly larger town than the others because of the station, he guessed, though with its line of square houses and dirty yards it still looked lonesome enough. His head felt big, but as he looked out at the desert his thinking tightened. His lassitude began to narrow toward the more alert melancholy of the good stranger. Maybe it was the vastness of the desert that did it to him, the barrenness of rock and sand growing insistent, and the way it refused to define itself as he roared through it, and something about the corporations—Bonneville Power, Pacific Northwest Bell—their extraneousness and their inevitability. The monoliths had left their tracings here, and his paranoia was stirred. He sharpened up. He was in transit as a loosely strung-together collection of disparate parts, truck and trailer joined by a hitch and loaded with cable and chain, a backhoe, bulldozer, cans, clothing, tools, dog, and tangled-up, stinking, earthbound man—on his way to scratch up the ground himself.

He rubbed Jones's ear, digging his fingers into the cartilage. The dog squirmed with gratitude. The cab reeked of dog and sweat. His shirt was stuck to the seat. He had a growing sense of the desert's abstractness, huge and undefining, which gave it the character of God. As he remembered, it was country near here for which the MX missiles on tracks had been proposed. Maybe it was a perfect place for a prison, too. He thought of the blueprints: housing unit and support building, gymnasium, industry building, high-security cells, shakedown rooms, contact and noncontact visiting areas, towers and control rooms, playing fields, and the cages and fences, fences upon fences, fences with razor wire, electrified fences . . . *the monkey's tail.* Growing apprehensive and a little wild as he neared his destination, he thought that he had entered one of those Biblical testing grounds he'd learned about in catechism classes, the tortuous wildernesses: Beer-sheba, Jeshimon, Shur, Paran, Negeb, or Zin. He wondered if he'd been longing for such emptiness, for a scorching. He almost felt as though he were at last entering the actual, barren, geometrical, overwhelming nightmare of his boyhood.

Rome was a three-building town. He pulled off onto the shoulder, dug his directions out of his hip pocket, and spread the moist paper out over the dashboard, studied it, then looked across the highway at the gravel road he was to take. It passed by one of the buildings, an old house freshly painted white that did multiple duty, it appeared, as a café, gas station, and post office. Its whiteness was brilliant in the early-evening sun. A bleached American flag hung dead in the air above the doorway. To his right was a second café, a rundown stucco affair. It sold gas, too. Out back were locust trees and a series of jerrybuilt pens. He saw a calf and a donkey, then a large sow dragged herself into view. The place had beer signs in its windows.

He could see the third building in his mirrors. It was a mobile home set off from the highway a half mile back. As he had passed it he had seen a sign advertising automotive parts and stones: geodes, agate, petrified wood. A small wrecking yard surrounded the mobile home. In his mirrors he saw the heat shimmering above the car bodies. Two pickups were parked in front of the café on his right. A car was parked at the café on the other side of the highway, but he saw no one, not a soul. Just ahead was a startling swatch of deep green, an irrigated alfalfa field, then a bridge that spanned the Owyhee River, and beyond the bridge and stretching into the distance along the far side of the riverbed was a line of pale-green limestone cliffs.

He glanced to the right at the beer signs in the windows of the second café. He was tempted to go get a cold six-pack, but he put his rig in gear and pulled across the highway onto the gravel road. Dust mushroomed behind him and his trailer clanked in the potholes. He passed irrigated fields and counted a dozen or more widely spaced farms, low wooden frame houses with attics, wooden barns, and the machinery in antic rows—protruding levers and perforated tractor seats and cockeyed wheels—alongside the outbuildings, the new closer to the buildings than the old, and the old closer by natural selection than the ruined. It was the river, the irrigation source flashing down at the bottoms of the fields to his right, that made the farms possible. After several miles of following his directions, making two turns and taking one fork to the right, he crossed a cattle guard and passed a sign that said BUREAU OF LAND MAN-AGEMENT. Federal land. Abruptly, there were no more farms.

He drove on. All along the gravel road jackrabbits had been killed by passing vehicles. Some of the bodies were fresh. Some were dry and flat. Back by the farms the road was littered with them, but here they became occasional. They were a measure of traffic. He saw a herd of mule deer running away from the road. They jumped a fence one after another, fifteen or more of them, their bodies going up and coming down, shining in the light like a snake sliding over a stick. They ran across a field, descended, darkened, and vanished into an arroyo. The road swung away from the river and wove through sedimentary formations—tall, weird shapes, eroded and hollowed out, leaning precipitously. The jackrabbit bodies became rare. A hawk crouched over one at the roadside, then as the truck bore down the hawk spread its wings and flew straight up with entrails dangling from its beak.

He was angling nearer the pale-green cliffs again. He passed a well-drilling operation, a dark derrick poised high in the sky. Two men were there. He passed a big field grown wild with alfalfa, oats, and thigh-deep weeds. The field was marked with Day-Glo-pink survey flags. That was the site. As the road swung right, he saw more of the field. It crested and sloped downward. At the crest stood Phil Grimes's tractor and lowboy trailer, and next to them the LeTourneau, and then down low on the slope he saw a ranchstead—a metal building, old barn, rock silo, outbuildings, and a house. Just past the house lay the river, curled against the base of the cliffs. He geared down and took a hard right toward the ranchstead. He leaned forward and peered expectantly over the dash. Jones peered with him. The trailer tugged and clanked on the rough roadway. He turned into the ranchstead and circled, passing first a pair of loaded semi-trailers with yellow tarps drawn tight over their cargoes, then an ancient crawler tractor, a pickup, a silver Mercedes-Benz sportscar, a low-slung outbuilding, the barn, a string of small outbuildings joined by corrals. In the spaces between the outbuildings he glimpsed the overgrown field, sloping upward now, and the fluttering markers. He stopped in front of the house. A dense cloud of dust billowed over the hood of the truck. No one was in sight. He switched off the engine and climbed down.

Jones followed him. She squatted. The sharp scent of dog urine rose on the dry air. He moved around the front of his truck. The blazing sun hung at thirty degrees. From the distance he heard the drilling operation—the running engine and clanking of pipe. Jones rolled in the dirt, nuzzling it and happily kicking her legs. Lafleur looked down at the Owyhee River, which was hardly more than fifty paces from the house, its surface smooth and oily-looking. The dust his rig had raised had blown across the river, and now drifted slowly up the face of the limestone cliffs. He followed the dust with his eyes, tipping his head, and tried to gauge the cliffs' height—two hundred feet, maybe more. Looking made his head hurt. He told Jones to stay and headed for the house. He reached around and picked his damp shirt away from his back. He heard the clanking of drilling pipe more distinctly. The noise came at him from two directions—from the corner of the field and also reverberating off the cliffs. The porch of the house had a new board nailed in amongst the old ones and it moaned when he stepped on it. He had his fist poised to knock on the screen door when he heard voices.

He heard a woman say, "Where do you get off?"

He heard a man say, "No, no. When do I get on?"

He heard the woman say, "Try climbing out of the ditch first."

The man's bright, coiling laugh made Lafleur arch his back and bring his hand down.

"I need help out of the ditch," the man said. "I need a hand."

"Not from me," the woman said.

"Who else?" the man said, chuckling. The voices, the man's elastic tenor and the woman's silken alto, Lafleur recognized as the ones he had spoken with by telephone.

"Listen," the woman said. "Slippery is one thing. Screwing a guy like Smythe is still one thing. But this business with that soldier of fortune, as you call him, is another thing altogether."

"Not your concern," the man said.

"It wasn't," she said, "until that personnel file popped up on the screen."

"Forget it."

"For all you know that guy's a killer. Somebody's going to end up with him in their face. Then what?"

There was a pause, a profound silence from the house, and Lafleur rocked back without moving his feet. He wanted to get out of there, but he was afraid that if he moved the board would creak again. He thought about trying, anyway. He thought that if it creaked and the pair inside heard it, he could change direction and come up to the door and knock as if he had just arrived. Maybe he could just jump clear. Or maybe, he thought, he should take his chances and knock right now. Maybe they wouldn't know what he'd heard.

He raised his arm and held it up indecisively. A movement at a window on the side of the house caught his eye. It was a woman, bending over. The light played on her naked loin, side, and arm. Her hair glistened. Lafleur's arm lowered as if under its own power, and he whispered to himself, "Holy shit."

"He's not," the man said in a low voice, "but you got to figure somebody like that's always going to be around."

"Not around me."

There was another, shorter pause, then the man said, "We need a demilitarized zone. A place where we can be ourselves. One would think it'd be the bedroom."

"You're changing the subject," the woman said.

"Or certainly the bed," the man said, his voice filled with mockery.

"Bull," the woman said.

"Beds. We've got two of them for God's sake. If one doesn't work, we could try the other," the man said.

The woman straightened up. She was thin and tall and dusky-looking behind the screen. Lafleur's breath caught in his throat. She drew a blouse over her head, wriggled into it, then stepped out of sight. Her words emerged muffled as if she were leaning into a closet. "There's the barn. Maybe you could get stirrups on one of those pigs."

There was another pause. Lafleur stared fiercely at the screen door in front of him. Whatever the conversation was about besides seduction—files, beds, pigs, a soldier of fortune who might be a killer—he had no idea and didn't want to know, but a strange thing had happened to him: While his sympathies were unquestionably with the woman, his body had been gripped by a craving wantonness. He found himself picturing the woman bent into a dark closet, her naked buttocks out in the light. He detested having been carried across the barrier to voyeurism, and yet he was definitely there, alone, helpless. An animal tingling filled his limbs. He imagined sliding his hands from the woman's pelvis to the bowl of her belly, and bending to press his mouth against her neck.

He stiffened when he heard footsteps. The footsteps stopped. He glanced at the window and back through the screen door, but saw no one. The woman spoke, her voice angry and clear. "You don't get what you want whenever you want it, not with me. Not now. Not every damn time I take a shower."

Lafleur thought: Of course, the shower. They'd been in the bathroom when he rolled in and neither one of them had bothered to look out the window. They had no idea he was here, but then he thought: *Here.*

And he wondered: *Where?*

. . . standing on the porch of an old ranchstead that was tucked into federal land, a sloping field full of survey flags on the other side of the house, out in the barren, high desert, alone here, seized by carnality.

He shifted his weight uneasily. The porch creaked. He froze.

"I guess I'll just have to learn how to surprise you," the man said. He sounded as if he were about to spring.

"There've been too many surprises, already," the woman said. "You're a surprise."

The man said, "Then I'd better find a way to take surprise into a new dimension," and then he laughed again. Because of the tone of his voice, and because of the sound of the laugh twisting toward cruelty, Lafleur expected to hear something crash in reprisal, a vase or boot thrown. That is a formidable woman, he thought. He heard the footsteps, then nothing, and then again the footsteps, coming near. Quickly, he reached out and knocked, making the screen door rattle violently. A figure appeared through the screen, a paleness growing larger. The door swung open and a man came out, a round man with a belly and a round brown face like a Buddha. He had small dark eyes. He squinted at Lafleur. "Yes?"

"Hank Lafleur."

"Of course," the man said. He stuck out his hand, which Lafleur took. The man introduced himself as Victor Sabat. "Vic," he added. He glanced at the truck, then back at Lafleur. "I thought I heard something." Lafleur frowned. Sabat grinned, revealing teeth and blue gums. He crinkled his skin all the way up to his forehead, and leaned forward and nodded briskly as if encouraging Lafleur to join in on a joke. Lafleur leaned back. Sabat was short and massively built in the shoulders and torso, but soft, as his palm had been soft, pudgy, and warm. He had tanned, spindly arms and wore beige cords, a white polo shirt, and a large gold ring on his finger. He scrutinized Lafleur's head.

Lafleur reached up and touched the bandage on his forehead. "Had a little trouble."

Sabat's grin vanished. "So I heard."

"I'm fine."

The grin returned to Sabat's face. He was older than Lafleur had anticipated, perhaps fifty. As he grinned he turned his body and hunched up as if to subordinate himself, and yet he addressed Lafleur directly with his sharp, dark eyes. By his bodily presence he made Lafleur feel at ease, which if he had thought about it a moment ago would have been the last thing he might have expected from this one, who proposed taking surprise into a new dimension, who kept, conceivably, a killer on his payroll. The man's eyes, however, turned from one thing to the next as if to coldly tick them off in an inner ledger. "You didn't find Phil?" he asked.

"No, I came here first."

Sabat moved to the edge of the porch and gazed up toward the outbuildings. Over to the left, but hidden behind the barn, was Phil's equipment, and farther along in the same direction the well-drilling operation. Sabat passed his hand slowly across his belly and brought it to rest at his belt buckle. Then he pointed. "That one's the bunkhouse." He meant the low-slung building across from the barn. "You and Phil will be in there." A light breeze blew by them. Lafleur smelled pig shit. "We're going to have you and Phil down for dinner," Sabat said. "At about eight?" Lafleur understood that he was being told to find his own way to his room and that Sabat wanted to go back inside. He had losses in there, Lafleur supposed, that he wanted to recoup. "Then we need to talk," Sabat said. "I'm sure you have questions."

"Sure, I've got questions." Lafleur was put off. He looked over at his dog, a lump of shiny darkness lying in the deep shade under the truck.

"I promise to fill you in," Sabat said.

Lafleur turned back to him and nodded.

"Ned Blaylock tells me you're going to be very good," Sabat said, and his eyes flicked to Lafleur's bandages again, then to the doorway, out toward the truck, and back to Lafleur. His eyes rested and widened, and his mouth opened. He had a gold incisor on the lower left side. Lafleur felt himself being keenly measured. He shifted his feet. The porch creaked deeply. He looked down at the new board that had been fitted in snugly amongst the old ones. The new board was scuffed, blond, and sappy. The old ones were gray and patinaed by wear and weather. He felt Sabat waiting. He was waiting, too, composing his own response to being measured while not speaking or looking at the man. It was a moment, a hiatus, in which an unspoken transmission passed from one man to the other, something made of fog, a shimmering, osmotic inquiry. The house was silent. Lafleur looked at the river, then at the rock promontories above the river and at the gently mounded earth between them, the sand as if airbrushed to a sheen and tight like skin over the bones of the earth. The river came through like a dark vein. He glanced back at his truck.

"Your dog?" Sabat said.

"Uh huh," Lafleur said. "A problem?"

"No, of course not," Sabat said, grinning. "Here?"

Lafleur looked down, then up again, and said, "Until dinner, then."

"Yes," Sabat said. He moved quickly across the porch and opened the door. He hung there for a moment, rising buoyantly on the balls of his feet, and grinned again at Lafleur with his rubbery face, and said, "You can meet Iris, too." It was a deft stroke that threw Lafleur off-balance. Sabat held his grin. His tongue tip was poised in the center of his mouth. The lines of his brow were angled upward. The smile invited Lafleur to smile back. Lafleur obliged by curling his lip. Sabat went in. The screen door's spring sang as it compressed and the door thudded softly against the jamb. Lafleur was left with his curled lip as he watched the cream-colored shape dwindle, then vanish inside the lair like a lion in a zoo. He wondered how long the grin remained fixed to Sabat's face, and how it looked to the woman in there, or what replaced the grin as the man neared her.

"Iris," Lafleur said to himself.

Chapter Eight

It took him three trips to carry his suitcase and cartons to the bunkhouse. It was an old bunkhouse that had been made over on the inside. Phil was nowhere in sight, but Lafleur found the room they'd been given. Located at the end across from the barn, it had new double-paned storm windows and white curtains, a new door, new tongue-and-groove paneling on the walls, and a fresh coat of white paint on the floor. They had steel beds, a desk, chairs, and two dressers. Phil had claimed the bed near the wall. It was made up, the cover drawn tight in military style. There was a small refrigerator at the foot of Phil's bed and on the floor a set of barbells.

Lafleur went back to the truck for the sack of dog food. In the space between the sheds and barn he could see the derrick of the well-drilling rig at the most distant corner of the surveyed field, a dark tower of pipe and couplings. He smelled pigs, too, each time he passed the sheds, but couldn't see them. The smell vanished as he moved into the shadow of the barn, which was huge. Swallows darted in and out of the barn's eaves and swooped crazily through the air. He went into the bunkhouse as into a doll house, shiny and quaint, and set the dog-food sack on the floor. He opened a side door and peered down the hall. At the far end of it, steam issued from a doorway. He moved toward it. There were several smaller rooms off the hall where other workers would stay later, Lafleur supposed. There was a laundry room. When he reached the ajar bathroom door, he eased it open. Phil was there in his shorts and T-shirt, bent over the sink with his back to the door, shaving.

Lafleur stepped inside. Hot water rushed into the sink and threw up a cloud of steam. The bathroom, too, had been refurbished—new fixtures and plumbing, toilet stalls, a stainless-steel counter around the sink, and gleaming white tile, everything slick with condensation. Lafleur saw Phil eying him in the mirror. Phil grunted and raised his eyebrows. His black hair shone and his long mustache drooped into the lather. Short and burly, about the size of Sabat, he had powerful, hairy arms and legs. He shaved the front of his neck and clear around to the back. He rinsed his razor, punched off the tap, and buried his face in a towel. His face came out as he turned, beaming and ruddy as a rose. He grabbed Lafleur and hugged him, lifting him off the floor, then he set Lafleur down, stepped back, and said, "You look like shit."

Lafleur murmured and glanced at the mirror. He looked bad, all right, even desperate—bandaged head, tangled hair, haggard face, dirty shirt. He was embarrassed. He decided he would shower first, then unload his equipment.

Phil pulled on his trousers. "Penny told me to watch out for you," he said. He reached for a white shirt that hung near the door. "Did you meet the boss?" Lafleur nodded and felt bewilderment coming on his face. "Right," Phil said, eying him narrowly. "My feelings exactly."

They walked down the hall to the room, where Lafleur rummaged through his cartons, separating the clean clothes from the soiled. He stuffed the soiled clothes back into a box. When he looked up he caught Phil gazing at him with a concerned expression.

"What happened?" Phil asked.

"Junkies. They mugged me."

"Shit."

"Yeah." Lafleur turned away and walked back to the bathroom, undressed, stepped into the shower, and worked up a thick lather. Then he stood under the stream and swayed to and fro. His body loosened. He turned the tap as hot as he could stand. Pools of dark water formed on the floor of the stall. He washed himself again, and lathered and rinsed his hair twice, moving his fingers gingerly around the tender places on his head. He lathered his body for the third time. He turned off the hot tap and stood in the cold, gasping for breath. His head pulsed heavily and his skin tingled. He stepped out, dressed, shaved, and replaced his bandages with smaller ones. He peered at himself in the mirror. It was just himself there and nobody else, rough-looking, but the same familiar face with its spooked-looking eyes.

He returned to the room and found Phil sweeping. Jones had dug up an old bone from somewhere and she lay on the floor between the beds, gnawing at it. Phil eyed the dog as he bent to sweep his pile into a dust pan. Lafleur leaned over his bed, extracted his shirts from the heap and went to hang them up. He pushed them apart from Phil's array of clothing, half of which were wrapped in cleaners' plastic bags. Lafleur hung up his one pair of dress slacks and put his shoes underneath them.

Phil had three pairs of boots in the closet. He was an experienced bachelor and, as Lafleur recalled, liked to have things neat, and he dressed for work almost as he was dressed tonight—clean trousers, clean shirt, shiny boots. He was crouched beside his tiny refrigerator, just then, peering into it.

Lafleur went back to the bed, picked up his underwear, and stuffed it into a lower drawer of his dresser. He set his suitcase on the bed and opened it. A bottle of aftershave lotion had broken and the suitcase reeked. He had notepads in there, which were soaked. He had broken down his 30.06 rifle and packed it in the suitcase along with his father's old Thompson pistol in the hardwood case. It was not his habit to carry guns. He set them on the bed and stared at them for a moment, the case, the dark stock of the 30.06, and the rifle barrel glinting against the bed pad. They looked strange to him, dangerous. He put his bathroom supplies into the top dresser drawer. He put his first-aid kit there, and then he picked up the suitcase and dumped the remainder of its contents into the drawer. He stopped there, staring at the drawer's contents: besides the first-aid kit and toiletries, he had the notepads and several pens, a carpenter's pencil, a cold chisel, his folded Buck knife, an old Rolleiflex camera, wooden matches, a screwdriver, six boxes of 30.06 shells, a box of .410 shells and one of .45s, a magnifying glass, an address book, several magazines, an old bottle of Penny's face cream, ChapStick, a bottle of vitamin E, bootlaces, pictures of his children, the clay head made by one of them, and a mostly used, dirty roll of Scotch tape. Most of the things had been poured from a shoebox that he had kept in the shed to store what he considered his valuables.

He saw an empty key case in there, an old Boy Scout merit badge, a spool of fishing line, and one of Penny's sewing kits. He glanced over at Phil's toiletries neatly arranged on top of his dresser, flanks of them— bottles, brushes, tubes, packets, shaving equipment, and a mirror. He remembered that he had a mirror. He found it in one of the cartons, wiped it with his sleeve, set it on the dresser, and looked over at Phil, who was standing beside his barbells, watching.

Phil was holding two cans of beer. He frowned. He had a steam iron on his dresser, too, and a bottle of distilled water. He'd brought his own blankets, sheets, and a pillow. Lafleur picked up the broken bottle of aftershave lotion, turned it in his fingertips, and flipped it into the suitcase. It landed with a thump.

Phil's eyes jerked to the suitcase. The bone cracked sharply as Jones bit into it. Phil's eyes went to her, and then back to Lafleur. "Are you all right?"

"Yeah," Lafleur said. The care in the question made him feel vulnerable.

"Like a beer?" Phil said.

"You bet." Lafleur took the can from Phil and gulped at it. The effervescence rose straight to his sinuses.

"The dog," Phil said.

"I know."

"Maybe we don't need a dog in here."

"No problem," Lafleur said.

"I don't mind sharing with you. I'm pleased to share with you, and I guess I can share the head with half a dozen other clowns so long as they don't piss all over the seat, but I'd just as soon not have a dog in here."

"Okay. She sleeps outside." Lafleur set his suitcase on the floor, thinking that bits from the broken bottle would probably fall through the hole mice had eaten out next to the hinge, and that he would cut his feet getting out of bed in the morning. He flipped the suitcase over, then set the Thompson pistol up next to the mirror, sat on the bed, and screwed the rifle barrel into the stock, thinking *Guns*.

"He's slobbering on the floor," Phil said.

"She," Lafleur said. "It's all right. She goes out."

"I can't sleep with a dog farting all night long and chewing on a bone."

Lafleur looked down at Jones. It was some kind of small skull she'd dragged in—jackrabbit, perhaps. The bones crunched now as she chewed on them. "Okay."

"First thing I know he'll be climbing in bed with me," Phil said. "Dogs like me, damn it."

"Okay," Lafleur said.

"It's okay with you?" Phil said.

"Shit, yes," Lafleur said. He went out and called Jones. The dog came, carrying the bone and limping profoundly. Phil followed. The sun was descending rapidly. They walked to the truck and climbed in. Lafleur started the engine. The truck and trailer raised a cloud of dust as he wheeled them around in the lot. He eyed the windows and door of the house as they passed. He saw no one.

"Guns," Phil said.

"I know," Lafleur said. "I guess it's a reaction."

"The mugging?"

"You bet." He drove up the road, cut across the ridge of the slope, and stopped in front of Phil's equipment. Phil climbed out. Lafleur waited. Dust billowed over the front of the cab. He heard the dozer's pony engine start up, then the diesel. He felt the dozer backing off the trailer, the shuddering sent through the trailer, hitch, and truck carriage. Phil parked the dozer next to the LeTourneau. Lafleur backed in next to Phil's rig and Phil unhitched the trailer from the truck. Lafleur heard chain clink, then

76

the deeper clank of the stand being set. Phil shouted and Lafleur pulled his truck out, then climbed down from the cab. They unloaded the backhoe and parked it next to the dozer. By the time they had finished fooling with the chains, unloading the ramps, the large tool box and lubrication cans, and had remounted the tailgate, Lafleur's head was pounding. He got in the truck, parked it, switched it off, and closed his eyes. His head swam in the silence, and an undulating incandescence snaked through his brain. He remembered the two men pressing against him in the cab, the shaking of the one on his left and the physical power of the one on his right. When he opened his eyes he was staring at the ranchhouse, the river, the high green cliffs.

He climbed out and joined Phil in front of the equipment, which they had in two groups: the LeTourneau, and the dwarfed-looking backhoe, dozer, dump truck, and a rusted tank truck all in line and ready for work, then the trailer and Phil's lowboy hauling rig off to the side. The noise from the well drilling rattled in the air, and Lafleur looked over to his right at the tall rack and pipes tipped up at the back end of a heavy truck, sticking above the slope, dark against the sky. The rig was perhaps two hundred yards away from them. "Junkies, huh?"

"Yeah. They took two hundred bucks." A wave of rage passed through Lafleur. "You must have called Penny back."

Phil nodded. "The boss didn't bother to let me know you'd called in here until an hour ago."

"Maybe he was busy."

Phil snorted. "The woman?"

"Maybe." Lafleur smiled faintly. "Is there somebody around here called Smythe?"

"Got me."

They fell quiet, standing there, facing the ranchstead. The sun was setting and the air had turned bright pink. The sands were almost red. The late spring growth, still green, looked black. The distant mountains to the south were purple, and the sheer limestone cliffs just east of the house seemed a darker shade of green than they'd been a couple of minutes ago. In the sky the color had deepened to crimson and floating in it were long black clouds like rips. The hue of everything changed every minute. There was no holding on to it, Lafleur thought. There was only being in it. The Owyhee River made a dark cut in the land to match the rips in the sky.

"Boy," Lafleur said.

"Yeah," Phil said.

The slope on this side of the river was gradual and the ranch followed it upward: first, the house, above that the bunkhouse, and running between them but just to the south of the bunkhouse a row of small outbuildings with pens, the large gambrel-roofed barn, and off from it, a rock silo. Above the barn, nearest to where they stood, was a corral and then the new metal building—something added recently for storage, Lafleur guessed. Its stainless-steel roof reflected red sky and a black cloud.

In the corral two horses stood end to end so that they looked like the silhouette of a monster with a head facing each direction. There was movement in one of the lower corrals and Lafleur strained to make it out—sheep. He saw pigs in another corral. "There's pigs down there," he said.

"Don't ask me why," Phil said.

Farther south of everything, running alongside the river and up from it, was the construction site. The river flowed north like the Willamette. Lafleur took in the scene, broke it down, and re-formed its components. The ranch had been arranged east to west to take advantage of the river, to put as much as possible of the field—now the weedy construction site dotted with Day-Glo-pink survey flags—near the river for irrigation and, he supposed, to compensate for the shortage of sunlight in the canyon. What appeared to be a closed aqueduct emerged from the river and passed along the far end of the site, up the slope toward the well-drilling operation. It was a scene on the verge of violent change.

Over by the drilling trucks, two men, stick figures, moved to and fro. Lafleur looked at his watch. "Seven," he said.

"We've got an hour," Phil said.

They moved toward the well drillers. They walked into the racket— running engine and the crash of twenty-foot sections of ten-inch pipe, which just then were being hoisted by a boom from one truck to a holding rack on the drilling rig. They stopped to watch. One driller climbed up the side of the drilling rig and used a pry bar to lever five lengths of pipe into a cradle. The other driller operated the control box from the ground. He made the boom lift and swing clear. No water was being pumped just then, but there were signs of it everywhere. The trucks and equipment were wet and there was a long cut in the sand where the water had flowed downhill from the hole. The driller with the pry bar jumped clear and the other one flipped the switch that hoisted the cradle to a vertical position next to the derrick. Once up, it turned, then snapped into position, and a set of knuckle clamps gripped one length of pipe, lifted it out, and held it directly above the drilling line. At the top of the derrick, a revolving bell dropped and twirled onto the pipe. The clamps retracted. The driller with the pry bar greased the male threads at the bottom of the pipe, then the bell lowered the pipe and spun it onto a coupling at the top section of the pipe in the line. Ready, the fresh length of pipe was secured at both ends by female fittings.

The driller at the controls switched on the compressor. There was a pause as the compressor hissed, then water blew out of the hole, sending a fine milk-colored spray over everything—trucks, drillers, Phil, and Lafleur. The driller drove the line up and down inside the hole as the compressor blasted out the bottom. He let the line drop. The engine throttled down. The bit grabbed and ground, revolving the line slowly, slowly sinking deeper as water poured out the top of the hole. The two drillers looked like father and son. They were burly and curly-haired like satyrs and had contented, dirty faces. The one at the controls was the older and slightly the shorter of the two. He pulled a pad out of his back pocket and wrote on it. The younger one took a shovel to the heap of ground-up rock that lay around the hole and made a dam, then entered a length of pipe into it. Dirty water poured out the end of the pipe. He held a bucket to the end of the pipe, filling it, timing the flow with his watch.

The older one came over and stood between Phil and Lafleur. "She's coming!" he said in a half shout. He leaned toward Lafleur and spoke in a twangy voice that cut through the noise. He said they had nearly eighty gallons a minute. They were over six hundred feet down, he said. They would try for a hundred gallons a minute, but would stop at eight hundred or if they hit granite. He looked up at the dark-blue and bright-crimson-striped sky, then down again. "If you hit granite that's the end of the ride," he said. "Dry as bone she rips up the bits."

He gazed expectantly at Lafleur. Lafleur raised his eyebrows. "It's always chancy," the driller said. "You're the ramrod, ain'tcha?"

Lafleur nodded.

The driller grabbed Lafleur's hand and wrung it, and said, "Backstop. Name's Backstop."

"Backstop?" Lafleur said.

"And my boy," the man said proudly, gesturing at the younger driller. He worked back through his notepad, then, and told Lafleur what they had drilled through—sand and clay leaf and more sand and basalt and clay again and more basalt—and how much water they had struck at each interval and what kind of casing they would use, what kind of bit they were using and how they would have liked to change bits, but didn't want to pull the six hundred feet of pipe to put another one on. The recitation was almost pedantic. The man's notes were thickly scrawled on the page.

Lafleur asked how much sand they'd gone through before hitting rock.

"What's that?" the driller said.

"Sand!"

"Sand?"

"At the top. How much?" Lafleur shouted.

The driller leafed back through his notebook, his blunt fingers fumbling with the pages. "Four and a half feet," he said. Lafleur winced. The driller asked, "Excavation?" Lafleur nodded. "Might be even shallower down close to the river," the driller said, then he smiled. "Might be deeper, too. Who knows? Only thing for sure is that you'll hit rock, and P.D.Q., too. This is the desert."

Desert, Lafleur thought.

The line bounced and suddenly sank a foot or two. The driller walked over to the makeshift dam and scrutinized the water, then stood and watched the rig again, gauging the bottom six hundred feet down, Lafleur guessed, by the way the bit telegraphed its action through the pipe to the derrick. The driller reached for the control box and flipped a switch. A floodlamp came on, illuminating the back of the drilling truck, dark with grit and grease, littered with tools. The sand, the dam, the pipe that spouted water, and the slowly revolving drilling line fell under the light. The younger driller rested his chin against his shovel handle. The older one returned to Lafleur and Phil. "Sand pocket," he said. "If we get a lot of sand we're in trouble. Have to screen it off in a well this big, you betcha. Pull everything and drop a screen. Heard old Abe Kasanian is doing your blasting."

Puzzled, Lafleur shrugged.

"Rock," the driller said. "Abe's been fighting this thing at the County Commission from the start. He wanted to take them to court, but he couldn't get enough help."

Lafleur didn't speak. He glanced at Phil, who was transfixed by the slowly revolving line.

"Me, I don't mind," the driller said. "You got to put the criminals somewhere. I'm proud to do my part and I don't mind the work, either. A criminal breaks out of here, where's he gonna go? They come to my place, I'll shoot their knees off, by God. That boy down there is smooth." The driller tilted his head toward the house. "He turned around and offered Abe a job. How do you like that?"

Lafleur nodded and watched the line, allowing himself to become transfixed, too. The driller fell silent. Lafleur remembered a tale he'd heard as a boy about somebody's cousin or uncle, a relative of a boy he'd known vaguely from up the road. The equipment they'd used back then was more primitive than what he saw here, but basically the same—heavy, coarsely mechanical, dangerous. There'd been more winching and less hydraulics, most likely. While they were pulling a line out of a well the young man had caught his coat on the bell just when they were lifting a section, and it took him up and crushed his skull against the crown of the derrick. He remembered the look on the face of the boy he knew who'd told him the tale, the wide eyes and the eagerness, the pleasure in being able to tell it. He remembered wondering about that—what struck him now as a form of cannibalism. He remembered the words "crushed his skull." He remembered thinking about the weight of such equipment, and about the lethal weight of the equipment his father ran. He thought about the weight of the equipment these drillers here operated. He thought about the danger, the exposed moving parts as in a tractor out of the forties. He wondered how much six hundred feet of ten-inch pipe weighed. He thought about how deep the hole was and about trying to control a bit six hundred feet away in the narrow darkness. He pictured the dead youth hanging from the top of the derrick, raglike against the sky, and his imagination veered toward his own children, Tricia and Andy, for whom he feared because he was apart from them. One never knew. Things came out of nowhere. He had a horrifying vision of Andy lying in the street, hit by a car. He had a sudden, irrational urge to go right down to the ranchhouse and call Penny to ask if the kids were all right.

He dug his thumbs in behind his belt and looked down at his boots. The toes were scuffed and muddy. He told himself to get a grip on himself. He straightened, leaned toward the driller, and asked if the geological report had been accurate.

"Who?" the driller said.

"Was it accurate?"

"Accurate?" the driller said.

"The geological report!"

The driller smiled knowingly. "We witched her."

He strutted over to the rig. The top of the line was just four feet aboveground, and the two men set about adding another length of pipe. The line caught on the clamp, the bell spun off the pipe and sailed up the derrick. The knuckle clamps inserted another pipe. The younger driller greased the threads, and once the bell had spun on the fresh pipe, he gave the pipe a hard jerk with a two-foot pipe wrench. The line drove up and down in the hole. Water blasted into the air. The line resumed drilling. Water poured out the top of the hole, into the dam, out the end of the pipe, and in a stream downhill toward the river.

The older driller came back, vigorously knocking the water out of his hair with his fingers. "She sure squirts," he said. He stood next to Lafleur. "Geological reports don't tell much," he said. "Once you've drilled a few holes in a place, you know as much as you're gonna." He gestured at the other driller. "He witched it. Welding rods. He got the touch from his mama." Lafleur wished the man were joking, but he wasn't. "We should get a hundred gallons at seven hundred feet if we don't hit granite or sand. But you never know," the driller said. "You could have a good well, then

81

have her go dry on you. A lot of wells went dry after Saint Helens blew, all the way over to Utah."

"Oh?" Lafleur said.

"Business is up," the driller said. "The Lord watereth the hills from his chambers. He knows. Only Him. He's preparing us. That's where Abe Kasanian is dead wrong. You got to take what you can out of what's given, you betcha."

Lafleur glanced at Phil. Phil's eyes cut back and he grinned. The driller walked over to his pickup and bent into the cab. He pulled out and crammed a small newspaper into his hip pocket as he moved into the light beneath the derrick. He reached for the control box and switched off the drill, stopping the line about four feet aboveground again. Metal clanked heavily. The driller climbed up the side of the rig and switched off the engine. It coughed and died, and then an immense silence swelled around the men. The driller returned and pushed the newspaper at Lafleur. It was a copy of *Watchtower.* The driller leaned near Lafleur and pointed at the headline that said WORLDWIDE QUAKES MEAN END IS NEAR. "See what I mean?" the driller said.

In the driller's nearness, Lafleur could smell him—sweat, crushed stone, and water—and he could hear his breathing. He felt an odd bodily unanimity with the man. For a moment he envied the driller the comfort of his God. "Thanks," Lafleur said, gesturing with the newspaper.

"You can have it," the driller said.

"Thanks," Lafleur said, taking a step back. He folded the newspaper lengthwise and put it under his arm.

The driller stepped forward. "The Lord's here to help us," he said.

"Yes," Lafleur said. He had understood that the driller's God was strong on economics prior to the final end.

"He loves us," the driller said.

"Yes," Lafleur said.

"All of us," the driller said. "You, too."

"Yes," Lafleur said. He stepped back. "I hope so."

"We got to do His bidding, that's all," the driller said, stepping forward.

"Yes," Lafleur said, thinking, What the hell? He glanced over at the son, the younger Backstop, who looked stunned. His eyes were glazed. He knew exactly what was going on, and he looked like he'd switched himself off until it was over. In the corner of his eye, Lafleur saw Phil easing away. He moved to follow.

"The Lord won't bend," the driller said. He touched Lafleur's arm. "Either you get your reward or you don't." He searched Lafleur's eyes, but seeing his failure there, he settled back on his heels and looked down.

When his face lifted again it was smiling and hard, and his voice came out with the edge on it that he used to cut through the noise of machinery: "We'll probably finish up here in the morning."

"Yes," Lafleur said, nodding as he shifted to join Phil.

"You'll have all the water you need," the driller said. "Put up a tank and you can flush a thousand toilets." He cackled.

Lafleur waved awkwardly and walked along next to Phil. The two of them went around the rig and cut back toward the site. Lafleur glanced back once and saw the Backstops standing side by side at the edge of the pool of light. The younger one raised his hand.

"He thought he had a bite on you," Phil said.

Lafleur grunted.

"Religion," Phil said.

"Strong on religion," Lafleur said. "I must look like a mark."

"Naw. Did you hear what he said about her squirting?"

Lafleur chuckled and looked up. The combination of the man's ardor and foolishness made Lafleur feel sad. The sky was sensuous. The radiant clouds were the color of blood. He looked down across the slope as they walked. He heard the drillers tossing tools onto the steel floor of the rig. The shadowy layout of the ranch—enclosures within enclosures set according to the necessities of sun, river, and earth—was a code to the lives formerly passed here.

"It takes all kinds," Phil said.

They pulled up in front of their equipment and paused, looking down. Jones appeared from near the horse corral and ran up the slope toward them. In the twilight she looked like a dark, spinning thing. When she arrived, Lafleur bent to scratch her ear, but recoiled. She smelled like shit. She nuzzled his leg. He pushed her off. She sat in front of them, looking down with her ears perked up—smelling horses, sheep, and pigs, most likely, conjuring up dog images of the bodies that went with the scents, and savoring her meal of shit. Lafleur looked over at the site. The marker sticks looked like pegs on a cribbage board. He had a code in his mind for the project taken from the plans, and as he gazed at the site, the actual earth swelled through his mental diagrams. He even began to feel the stirrings of an excitement for the promise of work, for the solitude and strangeness of the place.

"Looks like the silo and some of that fencing has to come out," he said.

"You're in charge."

"Have you seen the plans?"

"Nope."

"We'd better look first thing in the morning."

The two horses walked single file along the edge of the corral, then

83

turned and headed toward the barn. Jones stood up. The horses stopped at the barn, waiting to be let in, perhaps. Lafleur looked toward the house. In the lot just across from it were a new pickup, the silver sportscar, which in the rarefied light looked exactly the same color as the weathered boards of the bunkhouse and barn, the old crawler tractor with the boom, and the two loaded semi-trailers. Yellow tarps were drawn over the loads and held snug with straps. The yellow was brilliant and the black straps looked sharp as seams.

"I guess that's cement on those trailers," Lafleur said.

"Right."

"I guess we'll have a plant in here next week."

A pickup truck approached from the well. As it passed the two Backstops solemnly raised their hands. The pickup went down between the bunkhouse and barn, past the house, then turned up the road. Another pickup was coming down the road. Dust billowed as the trucks passed each other. The dust grew more and more irradiated the higher it rose in the sky. Lafleur and Phil started down toward the bunkhouse.

"Did you see Blaylock while you were waiting for me?"

"He came out."

The light was changing rapidly now. Everything previously shadowed had turned black. The cliffs across the river were black. The river was black and shiny-looking. The roof of the metal building looked like a black mirror. It reflected the black clouds and red sky. The dust their boots kicked up as they walked had a dark iridescence. The pickup that had been coming down the road had stopped in front of the house.

"He said it wasn't like you to be late," Phil said.

"Yeah?" Lafleur felt Phil's attention riveted on him. He felt the danger of being near someone who cared for him, who could see into him, whom he could trust. He was grateful for Phil's presence, but at the same time he felt vulnerable. His voice came out huskily. "I think I'm a little punchy."

"Shit, yes," Phil said. "You've got call."

They walked through a patch of sagebrush. The twigs hissed against their trousers. They reached the metal building and walked through a pocket of warmth that radiated from it. They came abreast of the corral. Jones ducked under the bottom rail and trotted toward the horses. The horses took off, galloped along the fenceline, then turned back toward the barn. Jones chased them, yipping with excitement. The horses stopped at the barn again. Jones stopped. She had a new ritual. "Whose horses?" Lafleur said.

"The lady's, I guess. Hell, I don't know. There's a lady. Wait until you see her."

"Pretty?"

"Built like a rebar."

Lafleur smiled.

"Walks like somebody broke off a bottle in her butt."

Lafleur winced. They walked along the side of the bunkhouse and out in front of it, where they could see the pickup that had driven down the hill. It had a crumpled fender and a bumper that twisted up at one end in a crazy salute. Two children stood in the back, hanging on to the stock rack and peering over the top of the cab. A man, a woman, and two more children were inside. The man was speaking to the woman. His head jerked. She got out and walked around the front of the truck, passing before the headlights. Her black hair hung to her shoulderblades. She wore a long skirt. The man said something to her through his window. She turned and said something back. Lafleur thought they were arguing, but then they began to laugh, all of them, woman, man, and children. The air rang with laughter. Lafleur and Phil grinned at each other. The woman walked to the house.

"That ain't her," Phil said.

This woman walked like a cat, her footsteps low and smooth. She went into the house without knocking and closed the screen door softly. The man turned the pickup around and drove off, spitting gravel from his rear tires. The two children in the back clung like lizards to the shaking stock rack as he turned again and roared up the hill. "Who is she?" Lafleur said.

Phil shook his head. "Got me."

Gravel popped as the pickup went along the road above the ranchstead. Children's voices could be heard calling. The voices grew thin. They sounded like distant saxophones crying back and forth, delicately measuring the space in the canyon. In a moment the sound vanished. It was nearly dark. The earth and sky were the same color exactly, a luminous gray, and they gave Lafleur the sensation of floating between two identical planes. Swallows darted and swooped in the air. He and Phil walked toward the glowing yellow light on the ranchhouse porch. A glittering nimbus of moths fluttered around the yellow light that was designed to repel them. The window through which Lafleur had heard voices was black. A din rose from beyond the house, a pulsing noise made as if by a thousand tiny wailing voices.

"Jesus, what's that?" Lafleur said.

"Frogs," Phil said.

The two of them brushed elbows. They walked in step like soldiers. The din grew louder. The porch creaked deeply as they moved up onto it.

Chapter Nine

ADDENDA:
Sheet B-7, f) Trenching, Support Bldg., Generator Rm. to Housing
Unit: See ADD, Sht. E-9, Generator Rm., Plan Y, s; & ADD, sht. Q-13,
Industries Bldg., Lower Level "Pit" Plan T.

Lafleur looked, leafing forward through the pages of the Addenda,
which was clipped onto the back board of the binder that held the Project
Manual. He found it and read:

Sheet E-9, Support Bldg., Generator Rm., Plan Y, s) Change the load
on Item #3 to 114 KW, increase the feeder to 3 #2/0, 1 #6G, 1½"
C, increase the breaker in Panel "M" to a 3P-1 75A. Upgrade outlet
cable to #00 weatherized. See Plan D, a; Plan Y, s; ADD Sheets M-23
and M-14, d.

He had already checked the blueprints for what he wanted, a trench.
That was where he'd begun. All he wanted was one short trench between
the Housing Unit and Support Building. He was on his knees at the side
of his bed with the binder before him, and above that he had the blueprints, which stretched nearly the length of the bed, open to Plan Y.
Doubtfully, he leafed forward again in the forty-odd pages of the Addenda
until he reached the M headings:

Sheet M-14, d) Water Heater WH-2, #24, Storage Room, Housing
Unit: Recirculating pumps for domestic water shall be Type RC-1
typical of (2). Recirc. piping completing a loop between the water heater
and storage tank shall be 1-inch in size.

Sheet M-23, Housing Unit, Plan D a & c) Kitchen: Delete 140'
hot water, connect to main 120' F hot water service at point main ser-

vice drops thru Mechanical Rm. (#14) floor. Note trenching from Generator Rm., Plan Y, s. Provide shut-off valve at branch tie-in. See ADD B-y, f.

He glanced up at Plan Y. The trench he wanted wasn't there. He went back and checked the listings for Sheet B-7, f, just to make sure he'd looked in the right place. He had. What did it mean?

He returned to the listing for Sheet E-9, which was where B-7, f had directed him. The trench was absent from the plans, it seemed, although the error had apparently been caught by someone, hence the note on trenching (B-y, f). The gesture begun to correct it, however, had not been completed, so that what Lafleur was left with was a circle dense with numbers and data—Panel "M," #00 cable, 3 #2/0, 1 #6G feeder. The cross-reference spun around the flaw like a whirlpool in the plans. When he checked ADD, sht. Q-13 he found that ten heavy 220 multicables were also to be routed through the same nonexistent, or quasi-existent, trench to the "pit" in the Industries Building, which was strange in itself—that so much power was being piped into that particular space. He let that go. He pushed back from the bed, and tried to concentrate on the one thing, the trench.

Actually, there should have been two trenches there, since the Addenda suggested that both power and water lines were to be run. To put both of those in one trench was usually forbidden, especially one with those 220 lines in it. One did not want to be digging to find a leak in the water system and hit power lines in the process. Lafleur told himself to keep a grip on that fact. He didn't even need to dig the trench now, and certainly didn't need to fill it with anything. They'd begun to excavate and grade. The surveyors had come out and he wanted them to flag the trenches. That was all. He'd happened upon the error while he and Phil were talking with the surveyors, then he'd come up to the bunkhouse to check the full set of plans. The others were waiting for him out there, Phil killing time and the two surveyors setting their sight lines—their transits targeted above the earth, through the clear, midmorning air. It was Lafleur's fourth day on the job.

The error raised the likelihood of others, and Lafleur felt intimidated: *service drops, branch tie-in, loop, feeder, water heater WH-2, #24.* He was neither an electrician nor a plumber. It was his obligation to oversee, he told himself, not to know all those parts and numbers, but he had to wonder what would happen if he was standing there between the water heater and storage tank, if he found himself with the length of pipe and a recirculating pump.

How would the installation and loop be executed?

Even familiar as he was with the construction trade in general and capable, presumably, of extemporizing on the but dimly understood, there would be jobs that would leave him completely in the dark, jobs that would require another quite different level of expertise, some alien jargon, some wilderness of knowledge . . . and then the numbers, the blinding brilliance of the numbers, the obscurity of the worlds the numbers brightly bridged, the darkness of the doubt beneath the bridging, and the flimsiness of the bridgework itself. The item numbers made a vast puzzle, strange and secret as glossolalia: specification numbers, tolerance numbers, numbers with letters in them to increase the holding capacity of integers, numbers crunched in upon themselves, numbers with slashes, dashes, and curious characters, numbers one had to read word by word and symbol by symbol *(increase the feeder to three number two slash zero comma space one number six upper-case G comma space one and one-half inches space upper-case C stop)*, numbers listed in thick catalogues and parts directories on microfilms or disks, and the parts themselves stored in lots or on shelves, shelves upon shelves in outlets all across the land and overseas, numbers of interchangeable and mated parts that might or might not be listed in synchrony with one another. And people standing at counters, and cashiers capable of messing up a receipt at any moment so that one could receive the right part and think it was the wrong part, and requisition agents and shipping clerks misplacing tags, truckers receiving the wrong carton or unloading the right one in the wrong place, computer operators striking a lower-case *c* instead of an upper-case *c*, and so opening the path to chaos, and receiving clerks, Lord knows what all, jaded, pissed-off, or just plain incapable, and telephone receptionists taking down those numbers spoken to them, their eyes narrowing toward sleep and their minds turning elsewhere to something less ephemeral, to a meal, maybe, or to sex. It was as if, since science had discovered the atomic and subatomic worlds, the outward world, or the daily world of construction, at least, had been reinvented to equal the subatomic in detail and sheer mind-locking quantity. Lafleur found himself sucked into a dark metaphor as if into a bomb.

He looked up, then, remembering that it was impossible to mount a project of this scale without error, that the trick was to learn to live with error, to catch errors before they burrowed too deeply into structure. Uncaught errors compounded themselves and created labyrinths within labyrinths.

He leaned forward and flicked the edge of the Addenda, making the pages riffle back to the beginning, then closed the binder that held the Project Manual. He stood, rolled up the plans, and carried all his papers out the door into the full, bright sunlight. A lizard flicked out of sight as he passed. He walked by the barn and heard horses moving inside, the hooves on the floor and wood creaking from weight cast against it. He heard a light voice, too, urging the horses on—Iris.

He passed the end of the barn and started around the corral. On the other side of the corral, the stone silo stood solidly against the sky. Swallows darted in and out of the vent holes at its top. A good forty feet tall, and built out of the same cut limestone that had been used for the foundations of the bunkhouse, the sheds, the house, and the barn, the silo was the dominant feature on the ranch. The stonework was impressive for the sheer quantity of it, for the placing of it in the round. The walls tipped inward ever so slightly. One wanted weight bearing in upon structure. That was an imperative.

He heard the horses shifting and turning behind the sliding door. He passed between the top of the corral and the metal building. Straight before him, he saw the two masons working on the wellhouse. The drillers, satisfied with just over ninety gallons per minute, had capped the well and left the site three days ago. Phil had excavated a foundation trench for the wellhouse, and now the masons were laying concrete block. They had it up out of the trench already. One wall made a jagged line that bristled with rebars.

The stainless-steel metal building flashed and reflected the corral and barn, and then Lafleur saw himself in it, walking along in his khaki work clothes. A small white bandage stood out against his black hair. His face and arms had burned dark already. He heard a thump, turned, and saw Iris pushing the big barn door along on its rollers. The door boomed softly when it hit the chocks. Iris—tall, angular, and nimble—vanished into the darkness within, and two horses, a white and a black, stepped gingerly out into the light.

Lafleur saw Jones first as a dark slit coming through the narrow passageway between the silo and the corner of the corral, then she became a hurtling, snarling ball of black. She broke into the corral and charged the barn door. The horses whirled and burst out into the corral. Lafleur could barely see the dog in the dust, but her frenzied barking punctuated the pounding hooves. He shouted and saw her stop. Iris stepped into the doorway of the barn and raised her arms to keep the galloping horses from going back inside. They shied and circled the corral, blowing as they slowed. Their heads swung gracefully up and down and they nickered softly. Jones stalked them. Lafleur shouted again. The dog's ears went back and she lay down.

Lafleur moved around the corral toward the silo. He glimpsed the machinery down below—LeTourneau, bulldozer, and compacter—and Phil awaiting him, and the two surveyors in their Day-Glo caps. As he neared the silo he felt the heat radiating from the stone. The corral was a haze of dust. He watched Iris's long legs draw her jeans taut as she pushed the barn door shut. She moved in his direction, stopping to turn on a hydrant. Water blasted from the spigot into a stock tank. "I'm sorry," he said. Iris brushed her hair back from her forehead, and her gaze—green eyes, fixed and steady as stone—peered into him.

It was the same searching look she'd given him three nights before when he'd first met her in the glassed-in porch behind the house—that, the dining area, had been added on to the house, and the high-tech kitchen, the computer-equipped office, the entire interior had been made over for Sabat. As soon as Lafleur and Phil had stepped up on the porch, Sabat thrust open the door and led them into the kitchen, where the other woman, the one from the pickup with the twisted bumper, was cutting vegetables over a fire-engine-red sink. Sabat introduced them to her— Diane. She turned and smiled faintly. She was Indian. She wore a man's flannel shirt with yellow in it and an orange skirt. Her dark eyes and tawny complexion gathered up the jarring colors of her clothes and the sink and put them at peace.

As Sabat led them out to the dining area, he told Lafleur and Phil that Diane was the cook. "But not tonight," he said. "I cooked tonight." He grinned at them, revealing teeth and gums and crinkling his skin up to his hairline, then gave them a drink and abandoned them there in squeaky rattan chairs that faced a table set for four. The room had glass on three sides. The floor, like the kitchen floor, was newly tiled. Spanning the ceiling were wooden beams mortised into the previously existing wall, and Lafleur had thought about that—the additions to an old house that had had neither dining nor sitting room. He imagined the old residents, a farm family with noisy kids, probably, who ate and socialized in the kitchen— work-weary mother and dusty father coming in from the fields to the food steaming on an old stove. It made an alien image. What surrounded was insistently adult and urban, the chairs too lightly built to take the weight of fatigued bodies falling into them, and too much shine in the kitchen for the aching hand that dragged and deposited the heavy pots, for the body too weary to chase down every spot and spill, or for the dust that flew off clothes, and here in the new room too many windows, built too low to the floor, too fancy, too dangerous to trust to heavy boots and children.

"Money, huh?" Phil had said softly.

"Seems like it. Project money."

"Somebody's got money to fucking burn."

Diane brought in a soup tureen and a dish of bread, which she set on the table. She had the set, studied smile of one who wishes not to be

90

noticed. She went out and Sabat came in with Iris. Lafleur rose and found that the drink had gone straight to his head. The room rocked. He took the woman's hand when Sabat introduced her, or she let hers lie in his, cool and still as a blade, and he received her gaze—steady, probing—and he shied because of its pressure, because of the libidinous thing he had lodged in himself from having seen her naked. Embarrassed, he glanced away and found Sabat edging almost between them. "Iris is the field architect," Sabat said to Lafleur. "So you two will need to get along." Shorter than either Lafleur or Iris, Sabat seemed to be balancing them with his rubbery face.

In the three days of seeing her in passing, then, and now as she moved near him at the corral, she seemed different from the professional woman he'd first met. It was the same angular, tanned face, but less meticulously prepared. It was the same lithe body, but wearing jeans, boots, and a white, western-cut shirt, not the cream-colored skirt and dark, formal sleeveless blouse. The body was less imperious, less reserved, less angry perhaps, and more in contact with things—the hydrant she had opened, the top rail of the corral that she grasped. He liked her.

"They'll get used to each other," she said, referring to the horses and dog and speaking in the same low but more gently modulated voice.

The black horse walked toward them and the white moved toward Jones. Jones, obedient for once, hadn't budged. "I hope so," Lafleur said, "but that dog likes to do the same damn thing over and over again."

She smiled. "Like people."

The water overflowed the stock tank. It beaded up and rode the parched earth. Iris stepped back to turn off the hydrant. He watched her shirt draw tight against her back as she pushed the lever down. When she straightened and gazed into the sky, shielding her eyes with one hand, he looked, too. There was a bright speck out there in the distant sky, and the faint buzz of an engine.

"Clint's coming in," she said.

It took Lafleur a moment to understand. "Clinton U?"

Iris nodded. "Met him yet?"

"No."

Iris leaned against the fence. The black horse drank from the tank. Its lip spread as it sucked water. It smelled of dust and sweat. Iris reached out and patted its shoulder. The white horse had stopped near Jones. Both of the horses looked expensive—long-legged and full in the chest. Veins stuck out like cords in their necks. The white lowered its head toward Jones in a graceful, ponderous motion like a stalk bending from the weight of its seed. Jones leaped up, quivering with excitement, and barked. The white jerked back. The black lifted its head out of the tank, spraying a glittering fan of drops. The two horses moved toward each other and stopped. The white rested her head over the black's neck. Jones stared at them.

"The dog likes horses to run," Lafleur said.

"They're pretty calm," Iris said. "Sometimes Jim can get feisty, but not usually."

"The black?"

"He's proud cut."

"Just enough to hurt his pride?"

Iris smiled and looked back into the sky. The drone of the plane's engine was louder and the contours of the wings and fuselage had become visible. A primitive earthen runway ran parallel to the road above the construction site. A plane had flown in yesterday with the surveyors. "Vic and Clint fly back out tonight with the survey team," she said.

Lafleur knew about the surveyors flying out, but not the rest of it. He skittered his eyes from Iris to the dog, to the affectionate horses, back to Iris again and hungrily up the body sectioned by the rails of the corral—boots, abdomen, chest, and then the face, the eyes. He sensed Sabat's presence here, his power, the quixotic energy that seemed capable of entering everything. He had to keep himself from turning around to see if Sabat was coming up on them from behind.

Once the four of them had settled at the dinner table three nights ago, Sabat had become impressive. He gestured broadly with his knife, poured wine, offered helpings, and kept up a virtuoso patter made out of light stuff that skimmed over surfaces like hot-air balloons: his boat in Sausalito, his collection of maritime art, the coyotes that cried at night out here, the deer and jackrabbits, the character down the road, Smythe, from whom he'd bought the quail they were eating, as well as the pigs and sheep in the pens, which were to be slaughtered for a barbecue later.

. . . *pigs* . . . Lafleur had thought, remembering the conversation overhead through the window.

And he'd marked the name—*Smythe*—who'd been subjected to one kind of scam.

He stayed alert for mention of the other one—*the soldier of fortune.*

Sabat had a subtle, intimidating form of intelligence that attracted data and glibly redistributed it in conversation. Every subject drew arcane attachments. He was charming, but just behind the charm, Lafleur saw, instruments of leverage were fully in play. Iris said little. Phil eventually gave up trying to say anything at all, and instead devoted his attention to the food on his plate—quail, new potatoes, buttered carrots, and cauliflower with a lemon sauce. Sabat described Iris's duties. He said that she operated the computer, that the blueprints were on computer, that she was in charge of quality control for the company and would be checking the construction, that any questions about the plans should be routed through her. He used that word, *routed*, and put his elbows on the table, snapped a quail bone in half and sucked noisily at the marrow, then went on, saying that Iris handled all the supply bids and shipments, and maintained contact with the design architects in Reno and the company offices in Alameda.

Lafleur had marked that, too: *Reno, Alameda.*

He had watched with misgiving the growing hardness in Iris's face as Sabat—her boyfriend, husband, or what?—spoke of her as if she were not there. "She's brilliant," Sabat had said, fixing Lafleur with his small eyes. It came out sounding condescending and Iris had set her fork carefully on her plate, straightened up in her chair and gazed past Lafleur's shoulder out the window into the darkness. Darkness entered her face. To Lafleur, the formidable woman he'd overheard through the window—*beds, pigs, stirrups*—and the equally formidable but much cooler one across the table from him, had seemed two small pieces of a whole, the bulk of which remained at large. Sabat, on the other hand, had seemed to be of a piece—expansive, aggressive, and bright, a talker and probably a troublemaker, an egotist, a liar, and yet a transparent liar, one who might quickly smile and admit his egotism and lies, a juggler who kept more balls in play than one could count.

At the corral, the air suddenly pulsed with the roaring airplane engine. The plane, a Cessna prop-jet, bore down rapidly on the house, then banked radically and flashed close to the cliffs. Its shadow chased it. The startled horses danced around the corral. Jones revolved, watching them. The Cessna jumped upward as if jerked by a string, then leveled, steadied its wings, throttled down, and circled the landing strip. Its image sped across the roof of the metal building. It dipped and fell from sight behind the crest of the slope. Its brakes whined. A long dust cloud drifted upward. Lafleur shifted the rolled-up blueprints from one shoulder to the other and turned back to Iris. "I've got a problem with the plans."

"Already?" The horses had stopped near her. She stroked the black's nose. Jealous, the white nickered and nuzzled her. She shoved its head away, then leaned back into the hollow between its shoulder and ribs and gazed straight at Lafleur. "Do you want to run through it?"

"I think I've got it patched together for the time being. I have to get those surveyors out of here." The smell of the corral was sweet—horse sweat, manure, the wet earth at the tank, and the dust that filled the air.

"It's just the trenching, but it's tricky. We need to take a hard look at it."

"I've got time now."

This was a professional exchange. He'd shown her courtesy by presenting the problem to her. In return, she was giving him rope to go his way. "My guess is you'll want to put it up on the computer."

"Tonight?"

"Fine." His unspoken response was anything but professional. Desire flickered through his body.

Abruptly, he pulled away and swung around the silo, the webwork of pale green rock and gray mortar. He touched it as he passed and, as if administering a corrective to his yearning, he thought about how the silo had probably been built without plans or transits, but with a mental image and plumb lines, by feel from a scaffolding, the mortar and rock lifted in hoppers by a pulley system. It had been built to last forever. He moved into the flat and the heat. He thought about stone and gazed across the site—sand, nothing but sand, turned, graded into a gentle incline, and packed down, and before he, Phil, and the other dozer operator had worked it nothing but sagebrush, volunteer alfalfa, weed, and sand. And where he walked, weed and sand. The stone had been hauled from across the river, maybe—quarried there, cut, floated over, and dragged.

He glanced back. Iris still stood between the horses, but Jones had gone to her and she was bent over, scratching the dog's ears. She looked up, catching Lafleur's glance, and Lafleur felt his limbs quicken. Jones's tail whipped back and forth. A haze still hung over the corral. Lafleur looked away, up to his right. The dust raised by the plane was slowly rising and diffusing into the sky, and beneath it was a tighter dust cloud, raised by the company pickup that had just pulled up at the runway. That was where Sabat was. Down below, Phil had started the LeTourneau's engine. A thick plume of black exhaust hung in the air above the machine. The surveyors were still at work and Lafleur rehearsed what he would tell them: lay the two trenches in two straight lines between the Housing Unit and Support Building. That was all.

As he walked, his thoughts reentered the array of items stuck to his brain, bits and pieces: pump types, water connectors, feeder lines and breakers, light fixtures, grates, hinges, flue inlets, overflow drains, fire dampers, lag piping, fan systems, trough drains, valves, bends, hydrants, preheating coils, fume hood connectors, and the numbers, and the clumpy, strangely abbreviated language. Little of that was meant to be remembered, but only to be found when needed, then forgotten forever. But the forgetting had a cost attached to it, he thought. The things he had to cast from his mind to make enough room to fill with what he needed still left faint trails to be confused with other trails.

His mind was suffused with Iris, too. She'd sneaked in there as if to keep his idiot company.

He had the silo on his mind, built by touch. It would be destroyed.

He had the blueprints, the drawings, which seemed afloat, dimensionless and abstract. The plans were an elaborate map, an intricate, extended foreplay to the act.

He moved into the envelope of noise made by the LeTourneau's engine, and down toward the machine itself, near the river. The LeTourneau dwarfed the backhoe, bulldozer, and the two surveyors. It coughed out another plume of exhaust, then the engine settled. The machine moved backward and turned slowly. Phil looked like a toy behind the glass. The machine looked as if it were rearing, as if it were being laboriously cocked, the high cab like the snout of a behemoth poising to strike.

The smell of diesel cut through the air. He looked back and saw the plane up on the runway, and the pickup, and Sabat standing next to another man. The plane's propellers slowed and became visible, stuttering in the sunlight. It was proper, Lafleur thought, to know certain things in detail and to allow other things to fall away. He had to be simultaneously in the plans for the project and above them. He had to be in his life and out of it at the same time. It was as if he were required to have an out-of-body experience, and he smiled to himself, thinking that. He'd seen an image of just such an idea in Sabat's study after dinner the first night.

It was a drawing of a ship. It hung on the wall along with other framed drawings of ships and, facing each other from opposite ends of the room, two large oil-painted seascapes. There were also models of ships on the shelves, even one in a bottle, and a quantity of books. There was heavy furniture in the room, and a desk with a computer, screen, modem, and printer, and on a table a plexiglass model of the project. Lafleur and Sabat had been looking at the model: the cubes for buildings implanted in a sheet of plexiglass that represented the slope of the site, the parking area and spherical recreation areas, the three guard towers, and the double ring of fencing made out of tiny metal posts and mesh to depict the chain link and razor wire. The river was a ribbon of smoked glass at the bottom, and at the top was the runway with a toy airplane parked on it. A group of five figures—prisoners—stood in one of the recreation areas. They had rosy cheeks and smiles. Lafleur looked up from the model and found himself staring at the pen-and-ink drawing just to the left of a window. It had two ships in it, one above the other.

"Colnett," Sabat had said. "That drawing's one of my prizes."

Lafleur leaned nearer and read the inscription at the bottom of the drawing:

The upper sketch may be of Hanna's Green island, from which Colnett took his departure. Neither the island nor the view can be identified on modern maps. The lower sketch is of Hachijo Jin, one of the Fatsiziu group, on Captain Cook's chart, lying about 100 miles south of Yokohama in longitude 140 degrees approximately.

The two ships were placed each in a different seascape with a scantily traced land formation in the background, the lower ship with its port side toward the viewer, the upper ship with its stern foremost—taking its departure. "Interesting," Lafleur said.

"They're maps," Sabat said.

In the upper drawing the island had a tiny compass reading written in above it: *N' 4.* "I've never seen anything quite like it," Lafleur said.

"They're fine," Sabat said. "It's a late-eighteenth-century charting by Captain Colnett. The drawing's original, pirated actually. Colnett was engaged in the China fur trade."

"But they don't know where the top one is," Lafleur said.

"No."

"Still?"

"No."

The two men were side by side, leaning over the model and looking at the picture. Lafleur grew fascinated by the very idea of such a drawing, with the rocks or islands in the background serving as a map, by the utility of such art, by its primitiveness and by the exquisiteness of the draftsmanship, and mostly by the ship, the act of displacement the artist had performed—himself presumably on the ship, at sea, and yet portraying each ship as a kind of demarcation, a compass. The artist was at once on the deck of the ship and floating above it. Despite his extraordinary fatigue, the trick of perspective fastened Lafleur's attention.

"You're interested in the sea," he said.

"I should have been a sailor," Sabat said. "I should have been alive two hundred years ago. The danger, the loneliness." He laughed, then added, "The adventure."

"The distance," Lafleur said under his breath, thinking that if the picture communicated anything, it communicated that.

Sabat seemed not to have heard. "The fortunes to be made. The honor!" His voice had taken on a curious tone of self-mockery. He paused, then said, "Do you like maps?"

"Naturally," Lafleur said. "I have to."

"They're dreams in a way, all of them," Sabat said.

Lafleur could smell Sabat—sweat and cologne, a not unpleasant oily odor with an aromatic tinge to it. They breathed almost in unison as they leaned toward the picture, looking. Their shoulders touched. Lafleur began to feel as though he were sinking into a dream. He thought of the bedroom they had passed as they walked down the hallway between the kitchen and here. The door had been ajar and he'd looked in, seeing a plush gray carpet, a dresser, the closet near the window, one bed made up with a deep-red bedspread, and the second bed leaning against the wall, a heap of bedclothes on the floor. That, too, was a map, a partial charting of the argument he'd overheard . . . *the neutral zone, beds* . . .

Sabat straightened up abruptly. "Speaking of which . . ." He moved to a corner of the room and came back with a large tube and a thick binder. He grunted as he hoisted the tube up onto the desk and set it on end. He laid down the binder next to the computer. "The complete plans and Project Manual," he said, then smiling, he added, "These are stamped." Lafleur touched the tube and tipped it a little, hefting its weight. When he released the tube it rocked slowly back and forth before settling. "I don't mean to be difficult, but I could have used these a couple weeks ago."

Sabat hiked himself up on the desk next to the tube, crossed his arms, and smiled. "Yes. I'm sorry."

"I'll have to go through them for changes."

"The changes are redlined," Sabat said. "And you can check anything with Iris."

"I don't want to start out on the wrong foot."

"No, of course not."

"But the changes may slow things down. The rock, too. The drillers said they hit rock at four-and-a-half feet. The plans I had didn't have test-hole specs in them, so I had to guess. I didn't guess solid rock at four-and-a-half feet, I'll tell you." He paused and gazed at Sabat. Sabat's face was still as clay. Lafleur wondered if he had made himself clear. "Say I find a change in the plans that affects the bearing of a wall. With something like that you'd want to be sure. You'd have to check through it again. The change might even be wrong. It might slow us down. I'm not responsible for changes or for oversights and I'm not going to get into a speed-up, either. This should be understood."

The face of clay moved. "What you're saying is that we have to pay."

"Yes," Lafleur said. "I'll do everything I can for you. I'll eat my mistakes, but I won't eat the architect's or the owner's. I should have had the plans. I should have had test-hole specs. That's all I'm saying."

"Fine," Sabat said. "The test holes, perc tests, and compaction specs, all those are in there." He tapped the Project Manual. "And here, too," he said, reaching back around the tube and touching the computer monitor. "The changes as well. We're piped into Reno and Alameda and changes come through the modem. Do you know how to use one of these?"

"Nope."

"Iris'll show you, but you should remember that this is one of two complete printouts on the site." Sabat touched the tube and made it rock lightly again. "I've got another set back in the corner, and then there's the computer. That's all. Access is restricted."

"What about the foremen?" Lafleur said.

"Besides your set, the plans have to go out piecemeal. Even the set the building-codes people have is restricted. It's for security."

Lafleur looked away and closed his eyes, then opened them again and stared stupidly for a moment at one of the seascapes, which depicted a becalmed sailing vessel. He was beside himself with fatigue, but he turned back to Sabat and said, "Because of the government?"

"We make guarantees to the government. Among them is the integrity of security. For example, you've been cleared."

"How?"

"How what?"

"How? What clearance?"

"By your record. Vietnam and Alaska. You were a captain with a grade six security clearance."

"I see," Lafleur said, startled. He moved to one side and perched himself on the arm of an easy chair. He didn't like this, any of it, not the sense of invasion he felt, not the nagging confusion he had over the government's part in the project, and not the suggestion that the job might be anything like the Army. He certainly didn't want it to be like Vietnam, or like his stint with Army Intelligence in Alaska, either—the white cubicle in the white, boundless tundra, where he'd been supplied with stacks of satellite photographs and asked to postulate the capacities of roads and runways, the design and storage capacities of buildings, to form images of interiors and to hypothesize subterranean structures from humps on the ground, and to match his postulations with the lists of specifications for what he'd supposed were nuclear plants, weapons systems, aircraft, missiles, munitions, research facilities.

"We're very careful about confidentiality," Sabat said.

"Secrets have their uses, I guess," Lafleur said, "but on general principle I don't like being kept in the dark, or . . ." He paused, searching for his words and experiencing a powerful, almost sexual sense of voyeurism again, but not his, now—Sabat's. "Or to have others rooting around in what is properly my personal darkness."

"Wonderfully put!" Sabat swayed, chuckling with pleasure. His heels knocked against the base of the desk. "But you've nothing to hide. Is it a point of honor with you?"

"Call it what you like," Lafleur said, and then he caught Sabat's eyes dancing about his face, checking the bandages on his cheek and head. He didn't like that, either. Because of his fatigue, and the drink at dinner, and now this conversation, which sapped his remaining resources, he was riding the last edge of his strength. He'd forgotten about his bandages, but now, quite suddenly, his head ached again, and then down in the thickness of the hurt something turned up like the corner of a single page being carefully lifted by a fingernail. It seemed that the way Sabat checked his wounds exceeded propriety. It seemed rude and excessively personal— voyeuristic. Lafleur was angry, and yet his anger seemed out of proportion to the provocation. He couldn't grasp what he was responding to. He steadied himself and spoke. His voice amazed him with its calm: "If you think my work with Army Intelligence means anything, you're wrong. I knew nothing. I was a functionary."

"It means we can trust you," Sabat said. "And that's all we need."

Lafleur paused, registering that . . . *Trust me!* He said, "To tell you the truth, any kind of hocus-pocus with the government bugs the hell out of me. I'm through with that."

"Look," Sabat said. "It pleases the bureaucrats to know that the job's being supervised by somebody with your background. That's all. Otherwise, it has no bearing on you."

Lafleur looked down at the rug, and then over at the model of the project. He turned back to Sabat, who put his hands on his knees and leaned forward expectantly. Lafleur said, "On the phone you called it a storage facility."

"That was an inside joke," Sabat said. "Until recently the company's main line of interest was data storage. We got into software and vocational programs a few years ago. Now we're going directly into prison management. Of course, it's a prison. I'm sorry if I disturbed you."

"But private," Lafleur said, more to himself than to Sabat.

"That bothers you, too."

The fatigue was coming back at Lafleur in a wave. He grunted incoherently, then forced himself to look up and say, "Yeah. It does."

"It's no different from public-health offices and research facilities all across the country, which are contracted out to private interests. Or from private timber management on federal land. The private interests are cost effective, or should be. That's what separates them from most government operations."

Lafleur had been watching Sabat's lips, which moved elastically. He felt dazed. "Reagan," he said.

"Reagan didn't invent the idea."

"But this is a prison," Lafleur said.

Sabat held his hands out, palms upward. "So?"

"I don't know," Lafleur said. "Maybe I always thought it was the people's responsibility to take away criminals' liberty."

"The courts take away their liberty." Sabat gazed at Lafleur with his small, bright eyes. "All we'll do is implement punishment and while we're at it run a better, more up-to-date facility and reduce the cost to the public."

Lafleur looked down at the model again—the tiny buildings, tiny rosy-cheeked prisoners held captive by tiny fencing. He looked up at the window above the model and stared fixedly at its blackness. The construction site would be visible through the window in daylight, allowing a view of progress just above the mockup: the survey flags, soon excavation, berming material, then concrete work, and eventually the elevated guard towers and the buildings to house a thousand souls. "But the prison," he said, turning back to Sabat. He heard his voice as if it were someone else's. "That's pain. It's the pain the public suffered, first, the pain given to them, and then it's the pain of punishment returned to the criminals. No matter how inefficient or messy, it's the people's pain."

Sabat's face clouded. "Some would call it rehabilitation."

"Would you?"

"Not always."

"Not often."

"Probably true."

"So why should a corporation be allowed to take advantage of this pain?"

"Why not? Why not decrease its cost? Besides, the public doesn't want to hear about prisons."

"That's not the point," Lafleur said, though he felt himself descending into uncertainty, bothered by the abstraction of his objections and uncertain of what he'd meant, uncertain of what had angered him in the first place.

"What is the point?"

"I'll be damned if I know," Lafleur said, and for an instant he rose out of his muddle-headedness and smiled at himself.

Sabat laughed softly. "I'd say it's a rather subtle moral point." He stood and stretched out his legs by rising to the balls of his feet, then sat in the desk chair. His face, wreathed with wrinkles, had become warm and engaging. "Certainly you're not thinking about backing out."

"I've signed a contract." It was a reflex response, and as he said it, he felt himself sinking farther into himself, thinking: I signed my name to form a partnership with Blaylock, to take up my father's part, I put in my own capital in the form of machinery which I would never have owned

anyway, deeded it over, though still it amounts to almost nothing, all that.
. . . "I'll do the work," he said. He heard something click deep within him
like a door snapping shut.

"Quite right," Sabat said.

. . . and there's the percentage, Lafleur thought, of what is not mine
to go to Gus and Jewel and another percentage to Penny and the children,
which is fine, that they should have it, but I'm out here building a prison
for this man, for a purpose I might find loathsome if I could think clearly
enough to understand it, which I might even have refused to build on
principle, if I had known what I know now, and yet there's the other
principle, my word, the first signature joining me with Blaylock and the
second one enjoining me to build here.

"Exactly what I would have expected from you," Sabat said.

The words sounded remote, as if they were spoken from the far end
of a tunnel, and Lafleur thought, *Expect! Me!* But he had to build here,
he knew, because of the principle. He had to hold fast to the principle
no matter what pain it carried with it. That was just what he'd been
arguing for the public: the pain would be his to absorb. He stared at the
window as if stunned, at the glossy mirrorlike blackness darker than the
night outside. The reflected images of the room swirled in it. He moved
from the arm down into the chair and leaned back. His head felt dead
on his shoulders. He thought that if he were to close his eyes he might
never open them again. "Why build a prison here?" he asked.

"Here?"

"Here."

"But it doesn't matter where," Sabat said. "We picked up the lease
from the family that used to run this farm. It's remote. Easy to secure.
Problems with building codes are minimized. Sometimes we'll hold illegal
aliens, the spillover. We want a low profile."

In response, Lafleur grunted. He knew little about the operating proce-
dures of prisons.

"There's a prison like this open in Texas, and one about to open in New
Mexico. A couple in Tennessee. This makes one over in this part of the
country. That's all. Otherwise, location is immaterial."

Lafleur rose out of himself again for a moment. He didn't believe that
location was ever immaterial. Location was always material. What was
location if not material? "Location is my material," he said.

Sabat laughed delightedly and said, "I guess that's why you're here."

Lafleur stared at the window and thought about excavation. He thought
about the holes he and Phil would dig, about the holes he had dug—how
they were ordinary through daily contact but capable of yielding the
unexpected, the quirks of mechanics and sediment leading to inexplicable

problems of siftage and slide and fault lines, and how sometimes the strangest things were found in holes, pieces of old things, bottles or pots, hunks of iron. He thought about the mass grave his unit had been assigned to dig in Vietnam, of how they'd used a loader to move the bodies, and of one of the few times he'd seen what was called "action," the Vietcong tunnel he and the Combat Engineers had been sent to blast out, a tunnel reported as abandoned and which was not. His fatigue gripped him. He was sinking. Holes grew strange as they went deeper, dark and dank, the inexplicable and explicable flickering back and forth in them. He had dug up an entire bed, once, made up with blankets and a pair of rotted pillows—that, too, in Vietnam, on the site of a bombed-out whorehouse. He thought about the beds down the hall, the one with the crimson covering, the other leaning against the wall. Beds filled his mind. He thought about how sleep was like a hole, ponderous at its bottom and fragile in its walls.

Suddenly he stood up. His pants stuck to his legs. He was sweating profusely. He picked up the rolled-up plans from the edge of the desk, then took a step and looked at the painting of the becalmed ship that hung to the right of the window. He heard Sabat's voice from behind him: "That's Cook's ship, the *Resolution*. A man up the road painted it. He paints seascapes. You never know what you'll find in a place like this."

"Smythe?" Lafleur said.

"I beg your pardon?"

"Nothing."

"A primitive."

Lafleur glanced back. Sabat was gazing at the picture. The face appeared to be made of clay, a grim Buddha-face. Lafleur looked at the picture. The ship was becalmed, but there was turbulence in the background of the otherwise glassy sea. Something frothy rose in the distance. Lafleur looked on the other side of the window at Colnett's picture. The entire marginless map seemed to float. That ship, the compass point, was afloat in blank space. The plans grew heavy as a pig in his arms.

"How long have you been working for this company?" he said.

"God. Years," Sabat said.

"Fuck, I'm tired," Lafleur said.

He was on the other side of that window, now, out there, low on the slope, within the thrall of the noise of the diesel. The odor of exhaust tasted like brass. He jerked his head at Phil, signaling to go ahead and cut.

The LeTourneau pulled out, turned, and passed. The machine held itself high off the ground like a huge mantis. It had the narrow swivel between the head and body, and the hydraulic hoses in there were filled with fluid like big veins. Out of its belly a big jawlike scoop flapped open and shut as Phil tested it. He circled and came back, turned into the alley marked by flags and lowered the scoop. The scoop sucked up earth for the length of the cut, just skimming it as Phil judged how deeply he could penetrate over the distance.

Phil turned and drove back along the riverbank toward Lafleur and the surveyors, passed beneath them, turned again, and dropped the earth in a line just south of the site. They would build an embankment there of earth to be used later as berm material. Phil drove uphill, threading his way through the flagged sectors. He went up nearly to the crest of the ridge, then turned back against the slope. The bed and cab of the Le-Tourneau tipped in opposite directions. Because of the spaciousness of the site, the distance of the low ridge, and what Lafleur took in from the periphery to the south—endless desert and remote ridges—the Le-Tourneau looked absurdly small for a moment. It seemed to have stopped moving. It was like a boat, like a small dredge merely tossing up and down in the lonely waste of the sea. It completed its turn and aimed its snout downward. It came at them, growing suddenly large. Dust churned around the wheels and blew up in a fan. The machine whipped around and roared by again, dipping its nose into the cut. It was nearly concealed by a wall of dust. Phil goosed the throttle and took the cut at speed. When he came to the end of the cut and turned out of the dust, earth could be seen boiling up to the rim of the bed.

"He drives that mother," a voice said.

Lafleur turned to the lead surveyor and grunted. The surveyor was blond and sunburned. His pale eyelashes and eyebrows were filmed with dust. His pink skin looked garish under his Day-Glo orange cap. The other surveyor stood several paces away with the transit. He revolved, watching as the LeTourneau went by between them and the river, unloaded, and headed back up the slope. It circled. The noise of the engine changed pitch and bounced off the cliffs in varying volumes and pitches according to its position. It came at them again, the noise like a single bass note played over and over, growing huge, overwhelming everything else. The LeTourneau turned and entered the cut. It skimmed the sand. Earth boiled up in the bed. The engine crackled as the machine cut downhill.

Lafleur knelt and unrolled his blueprints, opened them to Plan Y. The lead surveyor squatted next to him. Lafleur searched with his fingertip. Already, the paper was coated with dust. The LeTourneau roared beneath them. "There," Lafleur said, speaking into the surveyor's ear. He traced a line between a corner of the Housing Unit and the Support Building. "Flag it there. Two of them." He took a pen from his pocket and drew two light-blue lines.

The surveyor looked down at the plans, then up and into the maze of flags before them that marked out the Housing Unit. Beyond that would be the Support Building, which Phil was excavating. The LeTourneau was in the cut and dust obscured the flags. Even if he had been able to see clearly, Lafleur would have had to work to make his image of the completed building connect to the abstraction of the flags. The surveyor bent and spread out his much thinner roll of plans, his portion. He opened them to the page and marked out the trenches without even looking back at Lafleur's set. For him the flags were definitive, the end product. He was large, young, and soft. A fold of fat hung over his belt, his thighs were thick, and he had a cushion of skin under his chin. Lafleur had the impression that beneath the soft layering he was as strong as a bull. "That's all?" the surveyor said.

Lafleur shrugged. "The plans are screwed up."

"Fixing it that way seems awful easy."

"I know," Lafleur said. He looked up when he heard the LeTourneau strike something—a thump at the scoop. Rock.

"Even so, it's another thing to do. We're supposed to fly out of here tonight," the surveyor said, peering at his watch. He rubbed the dust off the crystal. He waited as the LeTourneau turned at the end of the cut and passed beneath them, then said, "We've still got a building to flag."

"Right," Lafleur said. "I know." The LeTourneau unloaded on the pile and headed up the slope. The surveyor and Lafleur both had ducked their heads against the billowing dust.

"Holy Christ," the surveyor said.

Lafleur rolled his plans into a tube and stood. The LeTourneau came toward them. Lafleur signaled Phil to go in more slowly. He pointed at the surveyor. Phil eased up. As the machine turned in and moved through the cut, the engine burbled. There was a string of knocks at the scoop. Lafleur walked into the dust to the cut and looked down at a slab of scraped rock about three feet down, a sheet of rock, the bottom, and not even as deep as the drillers had told him it might be. He looked up along the cut, a clean hundred-foot incision in the earth, and saw another exposed slab about halfway to the end. Phil drove along the riverbank, going slowly. Lafleur signaled that there was rock, then pointed at the surveyors and motioned for Phil to start cutting higher on the slope. Phil nodded and goosed the throttle. The noise slammed against the cliffs. Lafleur walked to his bulldozer, which was parked just past the berm pile next to the compacter and the tank truck they used for fueling.

The LeTourneau turned at the top of the ridge. Lafleur climbed onto the track of his dozer, reached over the engine housing, set the choke, and started the engine on gas. As soon as it kicked over he knocked the choke in. Black smoke poured from the exhaust pipe. When the carbon burned out of the cylinders and the exhaust whitened, and he hit the lever to switch the engine over to diesel. The engine caught and the exhaust became invisible. He smelled raw diesel and the cooking odor of oil on warming steel. It smelled good. It was like a drug to Lafleur. He let the dozer idle and turned around on the tracks and looked out.

Three figures stood in front of the glassed-in porch at the house—Sabat and two other men, U and the pilot, Lafleur surmised. He could tell that Sabat was talking by his gesturing arms. The sun glared against the windows of the porch and darkened the outlines of the figures. Lafleur looked up at the cliffs. Dust rose in the updrafts, swirling like smoke. He licked the grit off his teeth. The LeTourneau was up at the ridge again, making its turn. The masons were up there, working on the wellhouse, and just over the top of the ridge Lafleur could see the Cessna standing on the runway. He saw Iris on the black horse above the metal building. She leaned forward and the horse broke into a gallop. The LeTourneau turned down, raising a thick cloud of dust. The masons disappeared behind it. Iris appeared at the edge of the cloud, heading northward out into the flats. She bent low over the horse's neck. The horse's tail streamed. Iris and the horse grew smaller. The LeTourneau grew larger as it came. It spun, and dipped into the cut, and passed above the two surveyors.

The dozer engine had settled into a steady pulse. Lafleur reached under the seat for the dust mask, pulled it over his face, then slid behind the controls. He lifted the blade off the ground in front of the dozer and raised the ripper at the back. He pulled out and headed for the bottom of the cut. He revolved on the right track and lined up the machine with the flags. Dust blew toward him, then arched across the river. He could just see the cliffs, a columnar expanse of pale green. As he pulled into the low side of the cut where rock had been bared, Phil passed beneath him. Everything became the color of dust. The LeTourneau itself was hardly visible. There was just the earth trembling under its wheels, and the roar of the engine and glints of metal from within the billowing cloud.

Everything became invisible except the dust and the controls right in front of Lafleur. He lowered the ripper and edged the dozer forward. He felt the claw jolt over rock, then grab. He hoped for fissures and seams. The sensation of the tension on the claw and the slight bucking of the dozer was pleasing. He geared down and edged forward again. It felt like something up in the nose, a blockage touched and about to be pulled loose. This was what he desired, to be cast into a carnal relationship with earth and work. He leaned over the controls and peered into the obscurity and saw Iris and the black horse in his mind, galloping across the sand, tail, mane, and shirt whipping. She was in his blood. He eased the dozer forward. Through the levers he felt something crack at the claw, a cleavage giving in the rock and a slab of it tipping up.

Lafleur and Phil quit at five, showered, changed, and walked down to the house. Lafleur carried the plans, Project Manual, and Addenda. Diane was in the kitchen, washing pots. The others awaited them at the table— Iris and Sabat; the pilot, whom Sabat introduced to them as Byron Blylite; and Clinton U, who was Chinese, or part Chinese. He wore a three-piece pinstriped suit. Sabat said, "Clinton U."

Lafleur shook U's hand and said, "We missed each other in Portland."

"You were hard to find," U said. He had dimples close to the corners of his mouth, which deepened like two small sinkholes and drew a smile across his lips. His thick glasses made him appear owlish. He had a square torso, a headful of stiff black hair, and a small patch of freckles on each cheek. He passed over a plate of chicken as soon as Lafleur took his seat, and smiled more deeply and furrowed his brow at the same time so that he looked at once worried and happy. On his left hand was a ring with a large red stone.

"We're dropping off the survey team, then flying on to San Francisco tonight," Sabat said.

As they passed the chicken, mashed potatoes, and salad around, Iris held Lafleur's gaze for an instant. Her face was still. She had changed into a white dress that made her skin look darker. Sabat had quickness like a rodent in his face, and U the owlish look. Phil, who felt out of place here, Lafleur sensed, was solemn, attentive to the food. The pilot looked around, taking things in. The faces around the table seemed like masks on the spikes of a fence.

"I have the incentive package to show you," U said.

"Okay," Lafleur said.

"Afterward," U said.

They talked about excavation as they ate, and everyone looked out the windows at the site, at the lengthening shadows, at the chunks of bedrock that littered the long, dark cuts on the bright surface. The river looked like a metal ribbon. The surveyors were still at work. Their Day-Glo caps were like buttons of fire. One stood bent over a transit. The other held a marker flag. Everything out there was still. Soon the sky would become radiant. Already the light from the descending sun crept across the floor of the porch toward the table. They talked about Sabat's boat in Sausalito again, his favorite subject. He planned to check on it tomorrow, he said. They talked about the heat, the dust, the emptiness of the desert, and about the light plane, the Cessna, about the hazard of the drafts over the mountains.

There was a pause as they finished. On the floor, the line of light crept toward the table leg just to the right of Lafleur's foot. He glanced at Iris, who sat between Sabat and U, and felt himself filled with her, as if he had a compact with her. He glanced at Sabat, who was staring at the ceiling as if dazzled. Phil finished and abruptly left. Iris rose to leave. Her legs moved darkly under her white skirt as she passed before the glass. She touched the top of Lafleur's chair as she rounded the end of the table. Lafleur didn't move a muscle. He watched as U caught the pilot's eye, then jerked his head toward the door. The brutality of the gesture was startling—U's chin set and his eyes glaring behind the heavy lenses.

The pilot left. U went to the corner of the room and came back to the table with a thin, shiny briefcase against which the sun flashed. He took out a sheaf of papers, passed it to Lafleur, and began to speak in a gentle, clipped voice. It became increasingly clear to Lafleur that his first impression of U as slightly fuzzy had been incorrect. The contents of the papers, over which U had complete mastery, pertained to Lafleur's tenure as supervisor, to his function as a partner with Blaylock. They included the contract with International Data. Lafleur found nothing to surprise him, including the inclination of the figures to grow wild and to veer into the hinterlands of his debts and his company debts, his share in ownership, and his utter lack of personal solvency. Viewed from a certain perspective, he was dead broke.

He looked up. "I've signed this. I know all this."

"Of course. Forgive me," U said politely, although there was no doubt that the rehearsal of Lafleur's obligations had been intentional. "There's a rider," he said.

"The bottom sheet," Sabat said.

Lafleur flipped through the papers and found a shareholder's affidavit, signed over to him.

"It's your bonus clause," Sabat said.

U glanced at Sabat with annoyance, then turned back to Lafleur and explained that the shares had a retroactive clause to release them if he left the job early, that they would not be activated until the completion date, that the clause was contingent upon maintaining quality and the schedule.

"Shares?" Lafleur said.

"I trust you knew this was coming," U said.

"Yes, but not in shares."

"I see," U said. He sipped his coffee, then said, "Vic tells me you've had problems with the plans."

"You expect some of that."

"You need to keep good records, so that if you're over schedule we can determine the cause."

Lafleur nodded.

U said, "The shares are valuable."

"I'd rather have cash."

U said, "This is what we're offering."

"You mean I have to accept the shares?"

U looked at him, puzzled. Sabat leaned across and touched U's arm. "I told you he might be a hard case." He grinned and winked at Lafleur. U ignored Sabat. "It's tied into the contract."

"Why?" He'd hit metal, it seemed.

U repeated himself. "It's what we're offering."

Lafleur gazed through the window at the site. The sun was about to drop beneath the eave of the house and shine directly through the glass. The two surveyors were walking diagonally across the site. One carried a tripod on his shoulder and both held aluminum cases. The swinging cases flashed in the sun. The edges of the horizon had begun to turn red. It looked like a distant range fire. From the kitchen he heard Iris and Diane talking, their voices lapping softly like water. The line of light had reached the edge of the table.

"I'll have to send it to my lawyer," he said.

"I've sent him a copy," U said.

"Blaylock has one, too," Sabat said.

"I see." Lafleur looked at Sabat, then at U. "I'll have to check with them."

"Of course," U said. "But it's simply a bonus. It's usually considered exemplary to include employees among the stockholders."

"I understand," Lafleur said. "It gives them a stake in the operation."

"Exactly," U said, smiling.

"But I'd do the job, bonus or no bonus."

"Naturally. And we wish to reward you for that."

"Maybe I'd just as soon skip the bonus," Lafleur said.

"But the incentive clause," U said, "with the amount and manner of payment to be specified at a later date, was part of the original contract."

Lafleur stared at him, thinking: He considers me absurd. He might be right.

"You can always sell the shares," U said.

"Or give them away," Sabat said.

Lafleur looked down. The sunlight bathed the tabletop. The sheets of paper were blinding in their whiteness. He looked up again. The two men's heads were ringed with light. It shone against Sabat's bald pate and was punctured by U's stiff hair as if by thorns. Although he could hardly make out their features in the brightness, he knew that they were gazing at him. They looked like negative images. He also knew they considered him absurd, but still he felt he had to resist them. Even if it were true that his independence would be compromised by accepting shares in the company, still it wasn't even that, principally, that he was resisting. He wasn't sure what it was. Maybe it was the growing sense he had of the power that emanated from U and in which Sabat shared that made him recalcitrant, even afraid. He didn't know. An important moment was passing by, but he couldn't get a grip on it. Finally, he said, "All right. But it depends upon my lawyer's approval."

"Fine," U said. His head tipped toward Lafleur and came up again, then his hand, bleached by the light, reached for the papers. In a moment he had packed up and in another moment he had shaken Lafleur's hand and was moving into the kitchen. Sabat's silvery silhouette hustled past the windows after U. Lafleur heard Sabat asking Iris to drive them up to the runway. He heard them going out the door. He heard Sabat's voice calling to the surveyors. Lafleur stayed where he was, staring out at the iridescent site. The sun was setting. The light deepened. He heard the pickup spitting gravel. The wall at his back thumped in sympathy with the dishwasher. Pots clattered. He picked up his papers and went into the kitchen. Diane was bent over the sink, scrubbing. He walked down to the study. The bedroom door was ajar and he looked in as he passed, seeing the two beds, now, made up with crimson bedspreads. They stood six feet apart.

He moved into the study and set his paperwork on the desk. Rose-colored light streamed in through the window. It made the plexiglass model of the project glitter. It heightened the richness of the room—carpeting, shelves of books, paintings, drawings, and models, the heavy furniture. It made the room seem even more like a lair. Iris returned. Her skirt flicked as she turned into the study. She pulled the cover off the micro-processor and snapped on the power. The screen lit up. It said, "Command."

Iris switched on a lamp that cast a circle of light on the desk, then picked up a five-by-eight plastic card and showed it to Lafleur. It had the codes for the plans, the Addenda, the Project Manual. There was a command for change orders, too, and then the buildings were broken down into segments in accordance with the paper documents, and there were more commands, a score or more of them. She brushed his hands with hers as she showed him. "You punch the code, then just use your page and item numbers," she said. "Now, where's the problem?"

"Maybe Plan Y," Lafleur said. He bent and slid the heavy rubber band off the plans and spread them out on the carpet. Iris sat at the keyboard and typed in the code. Plan Y came up on the screen in amber light. Lafleur looked down at his plans, then back up at the screen. "Nice," he said. He moved to the desk and leaned toward the screen, searching for the trenches. "They're not there, either," he said. "My trenches."

"Your trenches?" she said, looking up at him. She had spidery smile lines at the corners of her mouth.

"I need those trenches," he said.

"What trenches?"

He frowned quizzically at her. "They're not there."

She laughed softly and said, "Wait. We need a search command. So we can check for consistency. The computer won't answer open-ended questions. Where in your materials are the trenches?"

"Ah," Lafleur said. "It's a question of angle."

"Oh?" she said, leaning back a little and looking at him again.

Or of sex, he thought. *Angle of approach.* He leaned forward to show her the Addenda. He showed her Sheet B-7, f, and Sheet E-9, Sheet M-14, d, Sheet M-23, and explained how he thought the trenches had been there, but were to be relocated, and then got dropped somehow in the process. As he spoke, he heard a distant roar as the Cessna rushed down the runway, then a whine as it ascended. Iris leaned near him, her bare arm touching his. He felt his blood jump. Iris pulled back and put the items up on the screen, proceeding painstakingly so that he would understand. She put up the items from the Addenda and he checked them against his document. They were identical. She told him that the plans had been revised on three occasions, that they could call up each stage, and laminate any changes from the Addenda. The sound of the Cessna had vanished. It was gone.

"Laminate?" he said, thinking of veneer, plywood, of laminated beams, of separate bodies pressed together.

"Overlay," she said, "like with transparencies. Look." She punched the code for stage two, Plan Y, then punched codes to laminate his items from the Addenda, and they came onto the screen, blinking slowly off and on.

"Oh boy," he said. He bent close to the screen and saw the added items quite clearly: feeder, breaker, recirculating line, hot-water line, 220 lines, and then he found the original trenching for his electrical and water lines, or where they had been once. They wound an absurd, circuitous route to get from the Support Building to the Housing Unit. "There," he said. "That's them."

"Okay," Iris said. "They really screwed them up. For starters, we'll scribe the item and send it back as a question." She punched the graphics key, and scribed a square around the trenches. "What else?"

You, he thought. He said, "The excavation detail. Plan OO."

He watched the screen as Iris punched the keys. The excavation plan came up: contour lines, cut lines, drain detail, riprap, and clay fill. The contour lines were curved to chart incline, abutment, ridge, outcropping, and were placed by degrees according to a scale. The tiny numbers made the lines mechanically coherent. Lafleur found himself burrowing into the image on the screen. The essence of a contour line was in the space around it where nothing was drawn, the diagrammatic ghost of the earth in its actual pitch and slope. It was like the powerful desire he felt, the sexual termination of the desire that he longed to realize, a mere marking of the pitch of emotions that encompassed it.

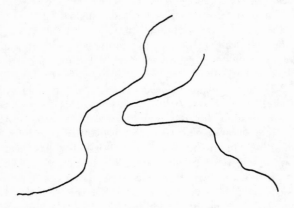

"The problem's the drain tile," Iris said. "And they didn't solve it. They just dropped it."

She was right. The trenches deviated in order to avoid the tile. He touched the screen and drew two imaginary lines between the Housing Unit and Support Building. "That's where I had the surveyors flag them. But I was winging it."

She scrutinized the screen, then said, "Not bad." She punched at the keyboard and a detailed grid came up. She scribed in the two lines. "Okay?"

"I guess."

She called back Plan OO. His two lines were where he'd wanted them. "There," she said.

"Now what? You send that on as a query to the designers?"

"You're getting the hang of it. But you're going to have to set the drain tile lower."

"Right."

"So we have to let them know about that." She typed in a note, then showed him the card again, pointing to a heading entitled "Architectural Query." She punched that code out. "That'll flag it for them. Then we send the whole works to Alameda."

"And that's it?"

"It's there now," she said. "We should get an answer tomorrow."

"It beats the hell out of riffling through the pages."

"Yes." She looked directly at him. Her eyes tunneled into him, as if she were reading his contours. He rocked ever so slightly back and forth on the balls of his feet. He smelled her laundered scent, tinged with perfume. "You come on fast," she said.

"What?"

"I don't think much of games," she said. "As you know."

"I do?"

"You know. The twin beds?"

He blinked and didn't speak, though in a flash he understood that she was referring to the bedroom conversation he'd overheard. He smiled and said, "Shit."

"I don't mean to embarrass you."

He was embarrassed, and looked away toward the window. The rose-colored light that streamed through it had deepened to magenta. It made the room luminous. Beneath the window was the model. Beside it was Colnett's drawing. He took a step sideways and looked out at the site. The work they'd done showed up as slightly more deeply colored rips in the ground. "I didn't mean to hear that conversation," he said.

"Of course not. Good heavens!" She switched the computer off and moved next to him.

"And what I heard I couldn't make heads or tails out of," he said, thinking, *Beds, pig, stirrups, killer.*

"Probably just as well."

"It looks like hell out there," he said. At the far edge of the site, the LeTourneau, bulldozer, compacter, backhoe, and tank truck were parked in a line. Iris touched the inside of his arm with her fingertips. He inhaled deeply. When he exhaled his breath shuddered in his chest. "I've got one question."

"Vic?" When he nodded, she said, "It doesn't matter."

He turned and took her wrist in one hand. He heard her breath, too, shuddering. He touched her hip lightly. His head swam. She leaned toward him, touching him. His body went light and he bent his knees as if he were about to lunge.

Chapter Ten

Before breakfast, the blaster arrived in an old International pickup that had a wooden sign with red lettering—EXPLOSIVES—wired to each side and hanging against the fenders. On the tailgate hung another sign that said POWDER MAN, ROME, OREGON. The condition of the truck and the glimpse Lafleur caught of the man, an old one with a gnarled straw hat pulled low over his eyes, had given him pause.

The first blast shook the dining-room windows as they were finishing breakfast. The silver rattled on the table and everyone looked up— Lafleur, Phil, Iris, and Sabat. The percussion from the second blast whammed against the house and Diane appeared in the doorway between the dining room and kitchen, wide-eyed.

"We're blasting," Phil told her.

"Oh," she said. She stared fiercely out the window. Lafleur turned in his chair and looked, too. A thick column of dust drifted at a tilt toward the river. There was a swollen place on the ground and a heap of rubble. Lafleur heard Diane retreating to the kitchen. In a moment she could be heard scrapping violently at something. A third blast rattled the windows and china. Lafleur felt it under his feet, the floor muttering as the shock waves were gathered up by the foundation from the earth.

As he and Phil rose to leave, Sabat said, "Kasanian's no friend of the project."

"The blaster?" Involuntarily, Lafleur glanced at Iris, as if for help, and in the instant, a flickering of the eye, he had a deep sense of misgiving because he feared that Sabat, who'd just returned from his three days in San Francisco, would see the exchange. Iris held her face still and gazed back steadily, granting nothing to anyone.

"He had us before the County Commission," Sabat said.

"So I heard," Lafleur said, turning to Sabat.

Sabat said, "A good trick is to smother your opposition with love."

"Even when their trade is dynamite?"

"Most of all then," Sabat said, and he glanced around at the others, chuckling, then lowered his head and laughed softly, as if there were levels to his joke that only he appreciated. Iris's eyes cut to Lafleur. Her stony expression gave just a little. Lafleur and Phil went out.

"That guy's a lunatic," Phil said.

"Sabat?"

Phil grunted. They passed out of the shade of the house and into the sun, then dipped down to walk along the riverbank. To their right and above them the earth was gouged and littered with rock. The blaster's old pickup was parked high in the far corner of the site next to the wellhouse. Lafleur saw the man up there. As they neared the machinery, Lafleur said, "I'll get the dozer. Check with him and make damn sure I can go in with it. Look him in the eye, for God's sake, when he answers."

He got the dozer, and when Phil signaled to him to go ahead he drove around to the topmost hole. Chunks of rock had been blown out of the bottom, split and scattered by the blasting. He went in and pushed rock while Phil started up the backhoe and went to work on the scoop-sized rocks that Lafleur left behind. Lafleur worked rock out the south end of his hole toward the embankment. Sometimes he lowered the claw of the ripper to dislodge a trapped chunk. He caught glimpses of the backhoe, the scoop rearing and dipping. The walls of his hole were damp. The work became hypnotic. The trembling of his machine was constant, its motion repetitive, the peculiarities of rock and sediment just varied enough with each load to hold his attention and also to allow him to think.

He thought about the masons, who'd left yesterday, but who would be back soon with an entire crew. The wellhouse was built and roofed with stainless steel that glittered in the sun and matched the metal building over by the corral. He thought about the surveyors, who would be back as soon as the blasting was done. He thought about Clinton U. He tried not to think about the snarl he was almost certainly headed for with Sabat over Iris. It gave him a queasy feeling. He thought about Penny and his kids, and he had a sense of guilt, of somehow having betrayed Andy and Tricia by being here. He thought about Blaylock. He thought about Iris. Her face hovered in his mind, green eyes, her straight, white teeth and the delicate smile lines at the corners of her mouth. He thought about Jewel and wondered what she would think if she knew all of what she'd got him into. He thought about Blaylock. He thought about his father, his dazzled face and blasted-out eyes. Both the welcome and the unwelcome people moved freely in and out of his mind as if they all knew each other and were having a party in there.

He pulled out when he'd cut down to the rock slab. Phil had already parked at the top of the hill. Lafleur drove up and parked, then joined Phil and the blaster. The blaster had a twisted, heavily weathered face to match his sweat-stained straw hat, and he sat on a camp stool he'd brought along. He was extraordinarily soft-spoken. One had to lean toward him to catch his drift. He introduced himself to Lafleur as Abe Kasanian, but said that a lot of folks called him the powder man, that Lafleur could call him Abe or anything else he damn pleased. "Call me Bare-assed Bonzo if you want," Kasanian said, laughing voicelessly. "I bet they told you that rock was eight feet down."

"Six," Lafleur said.

"Six, shit," Kasanian said. "Maybe one time out of twenty you'll get six foot of sand that low to the river. Usually four. Sometimes two. Sometimes nothing. Half the time you got that scab rock right where you want to plant yourself, speaking of bare asses."

"Can you break it up any smaller?" Lafleur asked. "In the top cut, anyway. We have to go deeper there."

"I can put in more charge and sink it deeper. The silo may come down."

Unsure whether or not the man was joking, Lafleur looked at the silo. "It has to come down anyway." He was thinking he would just as soon have Kasanian shake it down as have to doze it over.

"My uncle and me built that," Kasanian said.

Lafleur bent and picked up a weed stem and stuck it between his teeth. "This was your uncle's place?"

"He built it up," Kasanian said. "And before him his daddy did, then my cousin Ruth got it and it went downhill because of her husband. Nothing wrong with him, mind you. Dandy fellow, in fact, except he wasn't cut to make this place go, no sir. You got to like pain to ranch out here. It's in the boot."

Phil chuckled. "I haven't heard that one for a while."

Lafleur couldn't remember ever having heard it. Kasanian looked from him to Phil and laughed voicelessly. It was just air, his laugh. "You know about the boot, huh?"

"Either you got pig shit on your boots or you don't," Phil said.

"Ha! That's it," Kasanian said. "Pig shit, chicken shit, sheep shit, goat shit, all kinds of shit you can get on a pair of boots, human shit like a sewage man or bullshit like a salesman, or grease like a mechanic, or stirrup grooves like in the old days. Or you got carpet-walking boots, sponge-soled ones like a dentist, or nice shiny ones like a banker. Or you got blood on your boot like a butcher, or just the pure, fast, slippery air like a politician, or maybe no boot at all, no shoe, just a little bit of skin down there like Raquel Welch," Kasanian said. He stopped, sucked air, and raised his eyebrows. "Me, I got blasting powder on my boots. Ruth's husband tried to put on the wrong pair of boots and now I got mine on out here and the joy of blowing up their hayfield, for Christ's sake. I don't know how many times I hauled a disk across that field, or a baler, or set the irrigation lines for my uncle. It sure makes a fellow think."

His eyes took on a distant look. Lafleur thought about the County Commission and about Kasanian coming up against the likes of Sabat or Clinton U. He felt bad for the man. In a moment Kasanian said, "You boys going to let me work, or what?" Phil chuckled again. "Smaller?" Kasanian said.

"If we can get it small enough to use the LeTourneau on it, that'd be fine," Lafleur said. "Save us a day, maybe."

Kasanian got up and dragged a carton of dynamite along the bed of his pickup to the tailgate, then another carton. The boxes bounced along the metal as he dragged them. Lafleur blinked and looked at Phil. Phil tipped his head back and grinned. Kasanian had a gasoline-powered auger resting against the tailgate and he groaned as he hoisted it up to his shoulder. "You boys want to help?"

"The only thing I ever learned about dynamite," Lafleur said, "was to not touch it."

"That's right, by God. Don't touch it. Just touch one of them boxes."

Kasanian headed off, gimpy-legged under the weight of the auger and extension bit. Phil and Lafleur followed with the dynamite. Kasanian stopped and turned back. "That stuff's a little old. Don't jostle that box, neither." Lafleur and Phil, who were carrying the box between them, halted dead in their tracks. Kasanian bent double, laughing. The tip of the two-inch bit rose above his head. Then he straightened and went on, staggering to and fro.

There were three huge holes, arranged in a triangle: one for a Housing Unit; the second, nearest the river, for the second Housing Unit; and the third, the largest hole and nearest the ranchstead, for the Gymnasium, Support Building, and Industries Building. Each building was to have a subterranean level, and beneath the Industries Building there were two underground levels, the lower of which the plans called the "pit." Kasanian worked deliberately, drilling tubes into the rock at the bottom of the holes. The brace of the auger thumped violently against his leg. When he finished each tube he carefully inserted the dynamite. The work took an hour. Kasanian ran the wire, then they went back up to the pickup. Kasanian pulled three beers out of the cooler he kept in back with the dynamite.

"I think I can save that silo for now, but I don't know about the river," he whispered. "I may have to move that river."

He sat down on his camp stool and set off the charges in the first cut in sequence, with ten-second lapses between. Then he set off the remaining two banks of charges. Dust was still rising from the first blast when the last one went off, and for a long time the echoes whammed back and forth across the canyon. Lafleur had been watching the silo. He thought he'd seen it shift a little when the last bank was set off, or expand as if taking a breath. Startled ducks flew overhead in pairs, quacking through the dust that rose above the cliffs and hung there. The detonations made a deep, resonant, skull-rattling noise.

"I spared you the river," Kasanian said, looking upward.

Kasanian's methods were antiquated. He said he used powder because he'd never learned plastics. He said he'd been blasting part time for the last thirty years since he got out of the Army. He'd worked for his uncle on this farm and also blasted out the earthen tanks farmers in the area used to catch the spring runoff for summer stores. He'd been in the Combat Engineers during World War II, he said. Lafleur said he and Phil had been in the Construction Engineers, that he'd also seen a little duty with the Combat Engineers.

"No kidding?" Kasanian said.

"Some of us were officers," Phil said. He grinned at Lafleur. It was an old, half-serious joke and a half-grudging granting of authority that Phil liked to remind Lafleur of occasionally.

"Hell," Kasanian said. "In Combat Engineers everybody thought he was an officer. You guys drove those things?" He nodded at the machines parked above them.

"Part of the time," Lafleur said.

"Some of us more than others," Phil said, grinning at Lafleur again. "We had bridge duty. Making dikes and temporary bridges."

"In combat?" Kasanian said.

"We met in Vietnam."

"Yeah," Kasanian said, confirming something known only to himself. "I saw action. I blew a few bridges, too. We're a confused bunch of assholes, if you ask me. We build these things, then blow them to smithereens. The rest of the time we sit around with our heads up our asses." Kasanian's tone was bitter, and Lafleur and Phil exchanged a look. "Time," Kasanian said. It came out a kind of moan. "Goddamn it, that's something else to make you think. The future's slow, but the past is awful goddamn fast." They sat quietly for a moment, sipping beer, each of them entangled in his own thoughts. Phil stared at the ground. Their entanglement was mutual, too: war, about which they would not speak further just then. After a moment, Kasanian said, "So the silo comes down." Lafleur nodded and looked across the bright, torn sand toward the silo. "Want me to blow it?" Kasanian said.

118

Lafleur shrugged. "It's kind of close to the barn."

"Could be done, though," Kasanian said. "Your boss mentioned it, but the truth is it would kind of hurt to do it."

"Then don't," Lafleur said. "The barn is reason."

"I'd rather blow the barn. Would startle those horses, though. Nice-looking critters."

Lafleur smiled. "I guess the barn's kind of close to the house."

The old man laughed voicelessly. "Shit, yes. Scare the bejesus out of the boss." His face grew somber. "Sabat." He looked at Lafleur and smiled faintly. "Me and my uncle spent months building that damn silo. Hauling the rock and cleaving it, and setting it up. We had a gin pole and pulleys. He was quite a man. He could work, by God. He worked like the devil, but he died bitter."

Lafleur would have liked Kasanian to talk more about the silo and his uncle, but he was hesitant to ask. He and Phil went to work. The rock was broken up small enough for the LeTourneau to scoop it as long as Phil took it slowly. He worked in the large hole, hauled the rock out of it, and drove over to deposit it on the embankment. He moved in tight circles, cramped by the ranchstead and river. Lafleur worked the first Housing Unit. Each time he pushed up out of the south end he saw the earthmover at some stage of its circuit—the big pale-green machine taking earth up, dumping it, or swinging around in a storm of dust. When Lafleur had his hole down nearly to eight feet and had started hitting hardpan again, he moved into the hole for the second Housing Unit.

He thought about Iris again as he worked. He thought about her angular way of moving. He thought of her head on the pillow, of her hip rising under the crimson bedspread, and of her bare arm stretched out over it, of her shoulder, her throat. He became lost with her for a moment. The dozer rolled forward on its own, angled sideways, and he grabbed the lever just in time to escape gouging the wall of his hole. He liked the way work called one back to reality. He liked thinking about Iris, but when he thought about Sabat back from San Francisco and sleeping in that room last night, the queasiness returned and abruptly swelled into a powerful fit of jealousy. Then he thought that he didn't care. Something about Sabat, something about Sabat's self-containment, made Lafleur not care, and for the moment that was enough for him—to have the pleasure of his impetus toward Iris, even the bite of his jealousy, and to not care about Sabat. Just that. He attended to his excavation.

When he finished, he joined Phil and Kasanian and helped to set new charges. Kasanian opened up the second box, and they set light charges for the concrete pads at the bases of the four guard towers, then they returned to the pickup and sat and sipped beer while Kasanian prepared to detonate the charges. He set them off in rapid sequence. It sounded like mortar fire.

"I like variety," Kasanian said. They watched as the dust slowly filtered down and blew this way and that in the drafts. The sound died. In the silence a boulder dropped from the cliffs into the river and sent up a spout of water. "Sympathy," Kasanian said, smiling at them, then he said, "This is quite a deal you got here."

"Yeah," Lafleur said.

"Some of us fought it."

"So we heard," Phil said.

"And lost."

"Those battles can be hard to win," Lafleur said.

"You're telling me? Maybe we could've won if we'd had the numbers. Hell, there ain't that many of us to start with, and then you got to discount them that has to be squeezed half to death before they'll come out from under cover."

"What is it? That it's a prison?" Lafleur said.

"Partly. One of those city boys breaks out and you know damn well where he'll have to light. There's gonna be a loaded gun leaning up against every doorsill for miles around. We got our laws, some of them unwritten, but laws just the same. We respect the law. That ain't gonna be our boys inside those walls." Kasanian took a gulp of his beer, then leaned forward and spoke with force, though it still came out a whisper: "This is God's country, goddamn it!"

Lafleur and Phil were silent. Kasanian's statement had encompassed everything. The air was slowly clearing. Phil bent and slapped the dust off his pants legs. Lafleur put his elbows on his knees and stared at the ground. It felt good to sit in the sun.

"Some folks are hoping there'll be money in it," Kasanian said. "Times are hard. The ranchers are having a hell of a time. Me, I'm getting top dollar for this little job, but there ain't no connection between that and how I feel." He tugged on his hat brim and set his jaw. He was an old rooster. "Nossir," he said.

"If it's just laying there staring you in the face, you got to pick it up," Phil said.

"That's it," Kasanian said. "They had the Bureau of Land Management at the hearing. The Interior Department, a couple guys from Federal Corrections. Christ, there were more bureaucrats at that hearing than folks, and talk about boots . . . the shoes those guys wear don't tell you a thing except that they're damn expensive and you'd better not step on them. We didn't get snot out of the commission." Kasanian paused and finished off his beer, then twisted the can between his hands. "The BLM buys and sells the County Commission, anyway. Them BLM boys have been jerking us around for years, way back to the beginning: you can run so many sheep on the land, then you can't run sheep, you got to run cattle, then they lower the quota on you just when you're getting your nut built up. You got to take care of the weeds somebody else brought in, you can fence it, then you can't fence, you can build such-and-such on it, then you can't, you got water rights, then you don't. And the wild horses. We used to shoot the wild ones on sight. They eat up the range. Now they're protected, for God's sake. Where did those wild horses come from? They're the bad-bred bunch nobody wanted to chase down. That's D.C. law, not ours. We got our own law. We know about those horses, but you got to watch yourself. Some SOB back in D.C. farts in his sleep and everybody out here has to duck."

Phil chuckled and nodded at Kasanian. Lafleur stretched out his legs, digging his heels into the sand. Kasanian flipped his empty can over his shoulder into the pickup bed. It rattled against the metal. "Yeah," he said. "We were lucky to get a decent price for the lease and ranch buildings. So Ruth and her husband got something back."

"The government bought it?" Lafleur asked.

"No, this company, what is it?"

"International Data."

"That's it. I guess they transfer it over." He gave Lafleur a look.

"It's private. The whole deal is private," Lafleur said. Kasanian kept scrutinizing him, and Phil, too, had grown alert. "The company leases the ground from the BLM, then leases its buildings and services back to the government."

"I never did get that straight," Kasanian said. "What does it mean?"

"I don't know."

"Yeah," Kasanian said. "And probably a good thing, too, not knowing. It used to be what you could take off the ground. It was hard and broke a few folks, but there was plenty and it was honest. Now it's mostly what you put on it, or what you change it into, and how fast you can run once you get your bundle. Life is easier and longer, but somehow there ain't enough of it, if you know what I mean. It ain't the same."

"We're just digging holes and building that embankment," Lafleur said roughly. He was telling them less than he knew, and he had a queasy feeling again, as if with jealousy. He was telling them what he wanted to think. He added, "Then we'll pour concrete."

"By God, that's the truth," Kasanian said. "You hang on to that. A fellow's lucky if he's got that much, to know what the hell he's doing day by day." He paused and pushed his hat back on his head and looked up, then pulled his hat back down. He twisted a Red Man packet from his hip pocket. He held it out to them. They shook their heads. He extracted a hunk of tobacco and put it into his mouth.

"You boys are lucky to be friends, too. There ain't nothing like an old friend, believe me. I've lost a few and having them ain't like nothing else in the world." He spat to one side, tongued the wad into his cheek and grinned at them. "When you get to be my age you say what you damn please. You get tired of holding it all in." He looked away, down toward the silo, and his expression saddened. Touched by what Kasanian had said, Lafleur felt the weight of the words coming near him, even dangerously near, as if the old man had seen right through him. Kasanian rose. "Well, shit. Guess I'll be back in a few days."

"We'll need you," Lafleur said. "We have to go deeper in that hole."

Kasanian slid his auger into the bed of his pickup, groaning under the weight. Phil and Lafleur helped him load the rest of his gear, then Kasanian closed the tailgate and climbed into the cab. He stuck his elbow out and peered at them. "Tell you boys what. Nobody believes in nothing anymore except themselves and the almighty dollar, that's the problem. No wonder we got a trade deficit. It makes me sick." He spat through the window, drew the brim of his hat lower on his brow and drove off. His head rocked stiffly. The wooden signs banged against the sheet metal and the whole bed of the pickup tipped and swayed at cross-purposes with the cab. The pickup bounced along the top edge of the site, then circled down out of view behind the metal building and bunkhouse.

"It's a wonder that load doesn't blow up right behind him," Lafleur said.

"He likes it chancy," Phil said. "What is this about a private prison?"

"That's what it is. Otherwise, I don't know."

"Never heard of anything like it."

"I know."

"What kind of boots you got on?"

"Huh?" Lafleur darted his eyes to Phil. Phil grinned at him. Lafleur lifted his foot and looked at the boot—crepe sole and cheap leather. "K-Mart specials."

"How do they feel?"

"They burn."

"Right," Phil said.

Lafleur looked down at Phil's boots, black ones with eight-inch uppers, rawhide laces, and shiny brass eyelets. He'd seen Phil labor over them every three or four nights, cleaning and oiling them. "I thought you meant something else."

"Maybe," Phil said. He looked down at his boots. "But this, too. These are White's. A place up in Spokane that makes a hell of a boot. You ought to get some." He poked Lafleur lightly in the ribs. "Look. If you need help, I'm behind you."

"Do I need help?"

"Something's eating you."

Lafleur looked over toward the ranchstead. He was embarrassed, but also grateful that Phil felt free to speak his mind in this way. "Thanks."

"I'd watch out for that woman," Phil said. "The architect."

"Yeah," Lafleur said gruffly.

They went back to work. Lafleur climbed up onto the dozer and drove into the hole for the first Housing Unit. He pushed rock out the south end in a pile. Phil worked the big hole. After a while, Lafleur moved into the hole for the second Housing Unit and Phil worked the surface grades. Lafleur now thought about nothing but the work before him. By evening they had the site roughed out and the embankment built up to better than ten feet. They would continue tomorrow and bring back the other dozer operator, another backhoe operator, and run two dump trucks to finish the holes. In a couple of days the concrete crew would move in and construction would begin in earnest. Soon Lafleur would stop pulling double duty—working and supervising.

By the time he drove his dozer out of the hole, Phil had already parked his machine and left. Lafleur parked and switched the dozer off, then stepped down and looked at it for a moment. It was covered with dust. Tomorrow, he thought, they should change oil and filters. He was covered with dust. He needed a shower. He needed to take a leak. He moved behind the berm pile and stared at it as he relieved himself. Already it was ten feet high and a good eighty feet long. It was as profound as the walls of the holes had been—dark, damp, and compressing under its own weight. It was a junkyard of a sort, an organized pile of reusable waste— sand, thick with chunks of rock. Behind it, he was completely cut off from the ranch and site. Just below, the river hissed softly.

A shadow flitted by on the ground before him. He looked up. A hawk circled overhead. He heard something in the brush. He looked and saw movement several feet away. He leaned forward for a better look. Enough of an undulating body came out from cover for him to see that it was a snake. He froze. It was a thin, seemingly very long snake tangled up in a loose knot, a shiny snake in a new skin, a sidewinder. He threw all schooling to the winds and leapt backward. When he landed he caught himself and stood stock-still.

The snake's rattle had cut through the air as soon as he moved, and he stood in a sudden cold sweat as the snake moved toward him across a bare stretch of earth. Aghast, he watched the snake come near, not even seeing it exactly, not registering its curious motion, but seeing pure menace. He held his breath. His scalp prickled and his mind raced. The snake came near enough for him to step on it. He wondered if he should chance it, if he could move his foot fast enough. It seemed as if the snake were about to crawl over his boot toes, then in an instant in which the air around him seemed to condense, the snake veered away. Lafleur let his air out slowly. He stood absolutely still and breathed as gently as he could. His pulse pounded in his temples.

The snake's motion was like no motion of snake, sidewinder or otherwise, that he'd ever seen or heard of. It appeared thoroughly entangled upon itself, its contortions an almost acrobatic tying and untying like a complex and animated flower with the swollen head in the center—a stem there, erect, beaded and beady-eyed, and still. That the creature moved at all across the sand appeared an accident, or an act of defiance against the revolutionary undulations, and yet it did move slowly and steadily, still rattling, charting a wide arc. He breathed more deeply. A gust blew up from the water and cooled his neck. There was far too much snake there to be so narrow-bodied.

He searched it, looked at the stiff head, then found a second head several inches down from the first, grasping with its jaw the neck of the other. Then again, understanding now and growing more astonished, he traced the first body with his eye and located the point where the two bodies were pinned to each other. He took a step nearer and crouched— not too close. The snakes went on, oblivious of him. The head that grasped the other body he took to be male, though he was far from certain of that, and the other head, then, female, raised as if to spot the route like a pilot, but otherwise there was no distinguishing the two bodies caught up in themselves and made to appear as one. What came to amaze him most was the ambulation the snakes executed in synchrony with everything else—the quivering rattles, coiling, matching tails, and ecstatic bodies twisting around the coitus at the center.

The snakes slipped under sagebrush. The dry branches crackled softly. The tails whirred. He lowered his head to see. The color of the branches absorbed the color of snake. Then the snakes vanished. The sound vanished.

He stood up. Before him the desert was still and big, too big. Even the profundity of the berm pile had come to seem paltry. The desert absorbed everything, all motion, the teeming of insects, reptiles, rodents, and small birds in the bush. He moved alongside the berm pile toward the river, smelling earth and the coolness of water and the astringent odor of limestone. He crouched at the edge of the river, ruminating. The water touched the toes of his cheap boots and seeped into the seams. The shadow flitted by again.

Overhead, the hawk circled and searched the desert floor. It made a spiral that edged toward the cliffs. There was an affinity between the hawk's wide scribing and the snakes' entanglement. Lafleur felt as though he were floating between them, embraced by their encirclement at his head and feet. The cliffs, struck directly by the descending sun, glimmered. He looked to his left and saw Diane in the distance, standing at the far edge of the site, a solitary, forlorn figure, looking out at the damage.

He looked down at the water again. The river was slow and dark. Blue dragonflies hovered over it and spiders jumped on it. Upriver, the pumps ran day and night, drawing from it for the alfalfa fields. He looked back across the site. Diane was gone. He turned back to the river. All activity became fervent here. Even the grass on the bank was green. The scabrous back of a carp slipped through the surface of the water, rolled heavily, then sank, and then as if from the bottom of the river itself he heard a distant, soft wail . . . *Nicole!*

Chapter Eleven

Lafleur headed down to Sabat's study before breakfast to work over the schedule and inventory. The pale yellow morning light spread from the east. The pigs grunted softly in their shed as he passed. The sheep eyed him through the slats of their pen. Sabat had flown out late last night for Reno or California. Lafleur wasn't sure which. The porch creaked as he stepped up onto it and the screen door's coil spring sang as he moved inside.

The kitchen was filled with the odor of baking bread. Diane was slicing a slab of bacon. He eyed the coffeepot, which had just begun to perk. Diane smiled and said, "Five minutes." He moved down the hall. As he passed Iris's closed door his pace slowed. His weight hung for just an instant and his mind hovered. In the past week while Sabat had been here, Lafleur and Iris had kept their distance from each other, waiting, and—he thought—letting the dust settle. He was wary of Sabat, of the injury to him. He was also precariously tilted toward the woman.

He went to the study, sat at the desk, switched on the computer, worked his way through the opening commands, and promptly snarled himself in a loop somewhere between the inventory file, the architectural directory, and the exit key. He heard Iris's door click open, then her footsteps going toward the kitchen.

He expected that she would come to the study, and he tipped his chair back and gazed at a picture that hung on the end of a shelf next to the desk. It was another of Colnett's. It had the same primitive and exquisite draftsmanship as the one next to the window. *Colnett's sketch of his Pinnacle rock,* the caption said, *Barren isle, and Bell rock near Guja Shima or Kogeja Shima in Tokara Gunto (Loochoo islands), near the southern entrance of Colnett strait.* Lafleur looked at both drawings nearly every

time he came into the study. The possessive *his* intrigued him in this one, *his Pinnacle rock*, and the perspective struck him as it did with the other picture—the artist, Colnett himself, the *captain*, on the ship and floating above it, using the ship and the promontories at sea as demarcations by which he could navigate through *his* own strait. For a moment Lafleur grew lost thinking of all that, of himself and Iris, of Sabat, of Blaylock, of possession and perspective.

He heard Iris's footsteps coming his way. She appeared, tall and resplendent in a blue velveteen robe. She'd brought a cup of coffee for him, which she set on the desk. He gestured at the computer. "I'm stuck. I can't get the inventory schedule." She reached out and punched a series of keys. The inventory index came up on the screen. "Aha," he said. "The index." He peered at the screen. A fold of her robe brushed his elbow. He found the file number and punched it in. The inventory list he wanted appeared, the one arranged according to delivery dates. He scrolled down the list, then took a sip of coffee and looked back at her. "We're missing a rack of twenty-foot rebars."

She leaned toward the screen. Her leg pressed against his arm. Besides serving as a liaison between the site and designers, and keeping abreast of the project's progress, and exercising quality control, Iris was in charge of the inventory. "You mean I messed up?" she said.

"More likely the carrier. They're not on the site, that's all, and we're about three days away from needing them." He made his eyes move slowly down the column of items, the clumps of numbers and unpronounceable abbreviations that constituted a kind of code for that part of what had happened in the last week. The power lines had been spooled from Rome. A chain-link compound had been erected on the south side of the metal building. The concrete crew had arrived. An on-site concrete plant had been built and foundation forms mounted. Some concrete had been poured. If he had gone to the window, he could have seen portions of the foundation, pale gray in the soft early-morning light, and the concrete plant, the mixing bins poised high on steel stands, and up on the flat at the top of the rise between the runway and site, the growing encampment in which the workers lived, a circle of trailers and camping rigs, and then at the far corner of the site, just past the wellhouse, the last pole of the power line like the torso of a person with arms akimbo, strung puppetlike with cable, and impaled by the dark shaft. Next to it stood the smaller drop pole. From there the cable would descend in an armor and go underground.

He scrolled the screen down again and said, "I know they're listed here."

"Leave me a note."

He murmured, then—almost involuntarily—reached out and touched her leg. She bent over him. His chair rolled out from under the desk. He ran his hand inside her robe and felt the moistness of her mouth and body letting itself loose, then suddenly she pulled back. "Whoa!" she said.

Dazed, he straightened up, and in the corner of his eye he caught a glimpse of a large, dark shape moving by the window. In the same instant Iris's head jerked. He looked at the window and saw a man move out of sight. He looked back at Iris. Something dark and sharp had moved into her eyes.

"What?" he said.

"Nothing." She slid her hand down the lapel of her robe. "It's the security guard."

He'd heard that a security guard was flying in last night, that the metal building was to be his quarters. "What's wrong?"

"He gives me the creeps," she said. She smiled and cut her eyes back to him. "We could meet in the barn."

He squinted at her. "The barn?"

She smiled. "I'll meet you."

"Ah," he said. "An adventure."

She bent over the desk and riffled through a stack of papers in a metal organizer, took out an envelope, and handed it to him. "That came in last night." It was a Mailgram and through the cellophane window he saw Louis Brenneman's name. Iris touched his shoulder and cocked her head at him. "In a half hour? I'm going to shower first." He nodded and watched as she left. When she turned into the hall, her body swung lightly and the hem of the loose blue robe flicked in her wake.

He turned back to the screen and found the rebars. They'd been ordered and paid for. He left a note on Iris's pad—where the rebars should have been shipped from, when, by whom, and by what lot number. "Not your mistake," he wrote. He opened his envelope and read:

> No problem with I.D., so far as records show. No visible problem with shares in bonus if you want them. Maybe an opportunity for you to take over Blaylock & Lafleur. Call me.
>
> Louis

Lafleur set the slip of paper down on the desk and stared blankly across the room at Sabat's bookshelf, then he tore the envelope to bits, dropped it into the wastebasket, and read the note again, word by word. Agitated, he checked his watch. He knew Louis was an early riser, that he was usually in his office by seven. Lafleur dug in his wallet for Louis's home number and dialed it.

"It's six in the morning," Louis said.

"It says call you," Lafleur said. "What do you mean 'take over' the company?"

"Christ, Henry," Louis said. He sighed heavily. "I gather you don't like the shares they're giving you out there."

"I don't want them."

"Wait," Louis said. Lafleur thought he heard a refrigerator door opening and closing, then Louis came back on the line. "I think Blaylock might take them in trade. I think he'll let the company go."

"Completely?"

"Well . . ." Louis said.

"Yeah," Lafleur said. "You've talked to him?"

"Yes, but not about this, exactly. I've been talking to him about the payments to your father, which we've got worked out. Gus should be getting a check by the first of the week." Louis suddenly slipped into gear, then, and began to talk fast, as if he were in his office. He went on about the accountant and how she'd put the clamps on the books. "We just touched on your shares. It just floated by on the water, but I've got a feeling he might go for it. Get him to float, too, you know. Get you floating. Get everybody out there floating." Louis laughed. "He's a fox."

. . . *shark* . . . Lafleur thought. "Maybe he knew about the shares from the start."

"Maybe."

"I don't know," Lafleur said.

"He's already got some International Data shares," Louis said. Lafleur held his silence as he ruminated over that. Louis sounded as if he were chewing something, then he said, "There's nothing unusual about a contractor picking up a few shares from the principal."

"I suppose not," Lafleur said.

"So sign for them, then use them as ante."

"Ante," Lafleur said flatly. He closed his eyes and opened them and gazed at the sketch . . . *his rock.*

"Look," Louis said. "If you call me at this hour in the morning, you'd better take my advice."

. . . *his own strait.* "Okay, but don't commit me yet."

"I wouldn't do that," Louis said.

A rumbling noise from outside struck sympathetic vibrations in the structure of the house. Lafleur heard diesel engines, trucks, and he sat up straight, remembering that a Lima crane was being hauled in from Boise this morning. He heard the trucks looping above the ranchstead, heading to turn onto the site. He looked for them through the window. He saw the edge of the workers' encampment. The sun now cast its light in earnest, glinting on the chrome. "It's good about the payments to Gus and Jewel," he said.

"Right."

They hung up. The trucks went by—two flatbeds and a double-tandem lowboy loaded with the large parts of the crane. The dark figure, the security guard, went by the window again, going the other way. He hung in the window for a moment, then swung outward toward the site. The man wore a black uniform and he was big, his long arms hanging from massive shoulders. He had an odd, almost delicate way of walking, as if it hurt. The man disappeared. The trucks circled at the top of the slope.

Lafleur made a note to himself to call Jewel. He tore the Mailgram to bits and dropped it into the wastebasket. He punched the key to bring the Project Manual back up on the screen, and found his place in it: trenching for the main power line, pads for the guard towers, drain tile for the second Housing Unit, more forms for the first Housing Unit and the Industries Building, the deep one, and foundation work on the Support Building so that soon there would be the large outline of concrete roughly in the shape of a trapezoid superimposed upon a rectangle, silvery in the sun. Phil was to finish with the LeTourneau so that it could be loaded on the trucks that brought the Lima in, then carted back to Portland. In two days they would begin pouring wall slabs. The Lima would be used to lift them into place. Lafleur made more notes to himself, charting specifics as a double-check against one line of work's interfering with another. He stared at his notes, then added, "Raze the silo."

Perspective, he thought.

Distance.

Outside, he heard the truck engines shut down. He placed his notes in his shirt pocket, got up, and went into the hallway. The shower was running in the bathroom.

Iris.

In the kitchen, he filched two boiled eggs from a bowl on the counter and moved outside. It was six-fifteen. Morning light flooded the air. He heard men shouting, then the engine of the small crane, the Pettibone, starting up. They were preparing to unload the Lima.

He walked to the barn and stepped in through a side doorway. The door thudded softly behind him, reverberating in the space. A group of swallows darted frantically to and fro and disappeared. In the three weeks he'd been here, he'd come inside the barn but once—four days ago with Abe Kasanian. The barn was airy and luminous with the light that slanted in through the roof and the slits between the floorboards of the loft. The barn needed a roof. It was large. It had a row of stalls against each side wall and a double row in the middle. Its breadth was spanned by twelve-inch hewn beams that were supported by Y-bracing along the walls and by four rows of posts that ran lengthwise along the ends of each row of stalls. A pair of steel tracks, suspended from the beams above each alley, led to the sliding doors at the far end. At his end, a manure dolly hung from each set of tracks.

Lafleur peeled his egg as he moved. He made a trail with the shards of eggshell that he dropped onto the fine powder of dust and rotted matter on the floor. The barn was built solidly, all right—the beams, braces, and posts notched, bolted, and strapped with iron. There was a fervency and discipline in it, in the properness of things in line, and in the time that had obviously been given to handwork. There was the touch of something even wild and sensual in the heaviness and rightness of it all. It was immensely pleasing to Lafleur just to look at the barn in the sharp morning light, which fell in strips across the floor and over the rows of stalls and the two alleys. It aroused in him a remorse for his lack of a chance to build something like it—*by hand.*

The place had a pervasive, faintly sweet odor of decomposed organic matter, and through that a scent drawn almost like a line—the fresh horse manure in the two stalls at the end of the row that Iris was using. Her horses were out in the corral now. Through the opening in the sliding doors she'd given them the freedom of their stalls and the corral. There were swinging gates that could be used to divide the space and to close off the alleys at several positions for the sake of a system, which, Lafleur supposed, could be changed according to the kinds of animals kept, the numbers of them and their uses, the time of day. He found himself envying that, too, a system which though manipulated by hand was complicated enough, but never so complicated that it couldn't be apprehended in its entirety. The system of construction he had charge of was far too elaborate for him to contain in his mind.

All the gates were closed now except for the one through which Iris's horses could pass in and out. He bit off half an egg and chewed. It tasted sweet. At his back were two doors that led into rooms, and between them a ladder that led up through the hatch to the loft. Just next to the hatch hung a short length of frayed rope that Abe Kasanian had shown to Lafleur. The rope was knotted severely in a tack bend to an iron eyelet.

After Kasanian had detonated his last bank of charges four days ago, he, Phil, and Lafleur had walked down to inspect the holes. On the ground between the bottom hole and the river, a green stone had caught Lafleur's eye. He bent over and picked it up. It had been broken in half. It was wedge-shaped, and had a deep, smooth, truncated groove in its center, which was what had caught Lafleur's eye—the evidence of the stone's having been worked, or perhaps eroded with remarkable symmetry. "What's this?" he'd said.

Kasanian took it. "Where'd you get that?"

When Lafleur pointed, Kasanian moved to the spot and bent over, looking. He moved to the hole and looked into it, then came back with his gimpy-legged strut. He scrutinized the piece in his hand and when he reached them looked up from under the brim of his soiled straw hat. "Maybe a straightener."

"Indian?" Phil said.

"It could be a net weight," Kasanian said.

"Net weight?" Phil said, frowning.

The term had given Lafleur pause, too, until he thought it through: a weight for nets.

"But I think it's a dart or arrow straightener," Kasanian said. The three of them moved to the edge of the hole and looked in. Inside the hole lay a rubble of sand and broken-up rock. Above them, well past the topmost hole and next to the chain-link compound, workers were in the final stages of mounting the concrete plant. Storage mounds of gravel and sand had been trucked in, and one of the two semi-trailers, loaded with cement and covered by a bright-yellow tarp, had been pulled in next to the plant. Two men, a black man and a deeply tanned white man, each wearing a hard hat and otherwise naked to the waist, were up on the platform, turning down bolts.

The squeak of metal being cinched tight and the back ticking of the heavy ratchets pierced the air. The sun glowed on the men's torsos, and on the red bins, on the yellow tarp on the semi-trailer, on the white mechanical supply van from which small parts were doled out by a heavy-set lady named Pansy Stanton. There was the metallic glint from the Pettibone crane's cables, from the chrome on the waiting mixing trucks, the chain-link fence, and from the roof of the metal building over to the right. Surrounding these flashes of color and glitter was the gently undulating desert rising to the blue sky. Lafleur looked down into the hole with Phil and Kasanian. The three of them waited there for a moment, silent and solemn.

Then Kasanian spoke: "If there's anything else in there, it's wrecked for damn sure." He passed the stone back to Lafleur and said, "I always thought there should be stuff here. It's a hell of a campsite. Water and shelter from those cliffs, and plenty of game. That's why my granddad built here. The old bastard was no fool." Kasanian gazed meditatively into the hole, then turned around to face the river. Phil and Lafleur turned with him.

Lafleur looked up at the cliffs, then down at his stone. They were the same. "Limestone," he said.

"Sure," Kasanian said, then he pointed up at the cliffs. "See that tree?" A twisted, bushlike thing clung to a crevice halfway up the cliff. "Mountain mahogany," Kasanian said. "They used that for arrow shafts, and those, too." He pointed at a clump of tall bamboo-like reeds growing at the riverbank. "Phragmites. Arrow-shaft cane. They heated the shaft, then ran it through that groove."

"I guess they had it all here," Phil said.

"Christ, yes," Kasanian said. "But it was a hard sonofabitch."

Lafleur mused over that—the tool he had in his hand and the tools at his back, the trucked-in concrete plant, the Pettibone crane, conveyor rigs, backhoes, dozers, and the LeTourneau hauled in, and the supply van out there loaded with bins of parts.

"Used to be good fishing in that hollow before the bend," Kasanian said, pointing. The river widened there before an outcropping of the cliff narrowed it and then bent it out of sight. It was not far from where Lafleur had encountered the snakes. "Good-sized trout and rock bass. Catfish, believe it or not. Salmon, too, in the old days. It was a damn feedlot when the salmon came in. You boys fish?"

"Some," Phil said.

"Yeah," Kasanian said. "That ain't the same, neither."

Lafleur hadn't answered. The question had raised a terrific longing in him to fish again, for something that simple—line, fly, and tricky fish.

"I want to show you boys something," Kasanian said. They followed him along the river, then turned upward behind the animal pens. They moved toward the cement plant, but before reaching it Kasanian led them inside the barn by a side doorway. It was a door directly opposite the one Lafleur had come in this morning. They moved to where Lafleur stood now, waiting for Iris beneath the hatch into the loft. "Hung himself," Kasanian had said, looking up at the rope. Startled, Lafleur and Phil had looked up and were quiet. "My Uncle Spence," Kasanian said. "He had the two boys and lost one in Korea and another in an auto wreck, and he had the daughter, and me working here much of the time, and the daughter married a man that was no farmer. Why should she have done otherwise? She had the brothers to be here before they passed on, and then why should she stay behind for the suffering? Spence bore up under all that, but when his wife went it broke him."

Kasanian stopped and looked down the barn. It was late afternoon and a softened version of the light Lafleur saw now filtered in from the west side. Kasanian looked back up at the rope. Neither Lafleur nor Phil spoke.

"Not right away. At first he bucked up and brought his daughter back and the son-in-law to try him out. That's the one in the wrong pair of boots," Kasanian said, smiling faintly. "We had some funny times with him. Nice enough fellow, but he didn't know a five-bottom from a baler and couldn't keep it straight even if you parked the both of them next to each other and showed him. Poor old Jim." Kasanian laughed voicelessly, nodding his head, then he fixed his gaze on Lafleur. "Your boss bought some paintings. Ships. Seen 'em?"

Lafleur nodded. "I think he's got them up in the house."

"Good," Kasanian said. "That's him. Jim Basto."

"No kidding," Lafleur said.

"Talk about talent," Kasanian said. "But he didn't work out as a farmer, no way. Spence talked about leaving the place to me. For a long time I thought he should've, by God, left it to somebody who knew how to care for it, and it kind of bent me out of shape when he didn't. He might have left me an interest, or custodianship. Course it don't matter now. I'd've been cheated out of it anyway."

Kasanian stopped again and swallowed, then went on speaking softly, not whispering quite, but standing near to them and speaking low, carefully, and quietly. "We built that silo a year or so after the wife died, him and me. Strange, when he could've had a metal one trucked in and installed in a week, he had to build out of rock. The place needed a silo, all right. No argument there. We'd had an old wood granary that fell apart, so there wasn't nothing wrong with the idea of having a silo, you know, but the longer we worked on it the more I got the feeling the purpose of it was just a kind of excuse. It was like he was building something else, or just building. Wasn't until later that I understood his wife dying had broken him clean in two, and not for her, either, but him, for himself. He was more surely broken than she was dead. The silo was just a last fling, like a last dance, you know, but with him it had to be something he could finish and call useful. So he could die useful for Christ's sake. Too much will in the man. Enough will for a bear to choke on. More will than he could handle, or even live with, alone, anyway. So long as he had no woman around to take up his slack otherwise. He had no way to set back and take things in for a while when he needed to. I came in one morning a few weeks after we had the silo up and found him there, hanging from that rope underneath the loft. He'd just climbed up there and tied himself on and jumped through the hatch. I cut him down. Ruth, the daughter, wanted to take down the rest of the rope, but I told her no, leave it, that's his monument, too, by Jesus, and our reminder of how to live and how not to."

Kasanian looked down and nudged at the dust with a boot toe, then looked up and grinned at them, nodding his head. "Bet you boys are wondering why the devil I'm telling you all this."

"Nope," Phil said.

"Just listening," Lafleur said.

"Yeah," Kasanian said. "I like you boys. You ought to come out and visit me."

"That'd be all right," Phil said.

"Long as you're out here, you might as well see something besides this damn place. Besides McDermitt," he said, his eyes twinkling. "You boys been to McDermitt?"

"Yup," Phil said.

Lafleur had not, but Phil had told him about the tavern that straddled the Nevada and Oregon line, and about the red line painted on the floor and up over the barn, and how you could get one kind of drink on one side of the line and another on the other side, and how you could gamble and play the slots on one side but not on the other, and about the women, how on one side they propositioned you and stated their price.

"I bet you have," Kasanian said. He drew a map, then, that showed how to get to his place: out to the highway and across, south on the Rome road two miles and the left fork there onto Skull Creek Road, and past China Gulch and Scott's Ranch, and three more miles past the Owyhee Springs and the diversion dam for which there would be a sign, he said. Past that and another four miles or so southeast to an old wagon road on the left and across the cattle guard to his place, coming near the river again. He'd been leaning up against the wall, writing on a pinkish strip of paper that looked a great deal like a scrap torn off a dynamite casing. He pulled back and handed the paper to Lafleur.

"Or you could put a boat in the water, something light enough to port around the dam. It ain't much of a dam, hell. I could blow it with a couple sticks. That way you come eight miles or so upstream to my place. You can tell it by the copper rooster on the roof. I got a nice little place on the river," he said. He looked away from them, down the length of the barn toward the open sliding door, with a grim set to his jaw and the melancholy deep in his eyes. "Nice as this and not near as much ranch by God to break your back over."

Chapter Twelve

Lafleur waited for Iris underneath the hatch from which hung the length of rope. Methodically, he peeled his second egg. One of the two doors in the wall beneath the hatch was ajar. Through it he could see harnesses hanging from pegs in the wall, the leather cracked and rotted apart. In the center of the room were three saddles on sawhorses, two new ones and an old one. The old one had been recently oiled. There was a chair next to it, and soap on the floor, a can of leather grease, and a small heap of rags. The floor had been swept. He guessed that Iris had been working on the old saddle in her off hours. He pictured her there—her jaw set and eyes intent with concentration, her long fingers probing at the leather. The saddle had yielded to her and it glowed now with a sheen. He breathed deeply. Thinking of her filled him with expectation.

He bit off half the egg, pushed open the second door, and looked in. When he stepped inside a lizard scurried across the floor and up the wall, then stopped dead. He took another step and the lizard flicked out of sight through a tiny hole in the ceiling. There were footprints in the dust on the floor, the heel and sole of boots clearly distinguishable, small ones. Iris had come in to look. He followed her prints to the center of the room and stopped where they stopped. The room had plumbing and cupboards, a steel sink and a long counter. It was a milk room. It had a large electrified stainless-steel cooling canister, and holding canisters, compressor-run feed lines, and an elaborate array of copper tubing. Steel milk drums were lined against one wall, and over in the corner a small, heavy machine on a stand with a handle and spigots, and a large funnel mounted on top and a plumb bob hanging from a string. He recognized that, a hand-operated cream separator.

Everything in the room was coated with a thick layer of dust. But there was no debris, nothing, no scraps of paper, no hanks of string, no bits and pieces of things, no junk, just mouse droppings mixed in with the dust. Nothing in here appeared to have been touched for years. It was as if the place had been arranged one night for the next morning's work, then suddenly and utterly abandoned. The orderliness was eerie and cruel.

He thought of Tricia and Andy, just then, in his sense of barrenness. He thought of the snakes. He thought of his lost daughter. He seemed to hear a distant ululation—*Nicole!*

He made himself concentrate on the room. He imagined a person at work here, the wife, perhaps, the one without whom Spence had been unable to live, the woman who in the old way was the stitching that held together the strained cloth of the man. Lafleur's sense of her presence was mobilized by the equipment: the milk came through the doorway in buckets, he supposed, and was picked up, set on the counter and filtered, and run through the cooling canister. There would be noise and smell, the compressor whirring, water running in the sink, and milk steaming and the smell of it, and the smell of animals out in the barn, of hay and dung, and the cows lowing and their hooves shifting and stalls creaking from weight cast against them, and the sound of work out there, the children old enough to work, and maybe Spence milking, or back here spinning the valves, and calling down into the barn to keep everything running according to his exactitude, and voices calling up and down the length of the barn, the barn ringing with them, and here the milk sloshing as it was poured into the canisters and released through the spigots into drums. That much of it seemed almost like an idyll.

Lafleur stepped beyond the end of Iris's tracks and touched the crank of the separator. The bearings rolled easily and the separator revolved. He had turned one of these when he was a child—back in Quebec at an aunt's farm, where his mother had taken him after visiting his grandmother. He remembered marveling then at how stiff the crank had been and how the bowl turned so quickly once it was going, and though he understood gearing and leverage now, he marveled again at the speed of the thing— very fast, fast enough to set gravity and centrifugal force in opposition so as to distinguish cream from milk. The separator was mechanical in the way of old machines—like old well-drilling rigs, old tractors, old motorcycles, old sewing machines, old wringer washers. It was composed of a myriad of small, largely visible parts—nuts and bolts, valves, needles, and spigots. He liked that, but he knew that the separator had to be disassembled each night and cleaned piece by piece. The separator's position of prominence in the room suggested that it had been used along with the more efficient air-driven equipment right up to the end. He suspected that the woman cleaned the separator, that she'd accepted the brunt of the

138

inefficiency and toil that came with all of Spence's adventurous, half-realized schemes. The thought made him uneasy.

He turned the crank until the separator began to hum. The bowl whirred. The room grew tremulous. The air quivered. A door creaked out in the barn. He went through the doorway and found Jones, who had found Iris. Iris held up a green horse blanket and said, "It's clean." Lafleur chuckled and gave the manure dolly nearest him a light shove. To his surprise, it rolled freely on the tracks, and slowly kept rolling the length of the barn, flashing under the strips of light. It raised a rumbling sound that filled the barn, then it hit the stop at the end of the tracks with a boom. Out in the corral a horse snorted. Hooves beat and the two horses cantered by the open door with their tails raised. When the boom receded the cream separator could be heard still humming. Iris moved to the ladder that led to the hatch in the loft and said, "Up?"

"The loft?" he said, smiling.

"Where else?"

He gazed at her. Her lips were full for the angularity, otherwise, of her face—prominent cheekbones, the long, straight nose. Her hair was pulled back. He glanced up at the square opening above them. "It seems funny," he said.

"It is," Iris said. "These old jokes have their roots."

She turned and started up the ladder. He watched her long legs. Halfway up, she tossed the blanket through the hole. She followed it, her feet turning and vanishing, and he started up. Jones lay down at the foot of the ladder, sighing as her body struck the floor. The cream separator was still audible, humming faintly. As soon as he put his head through the hatch he met the strong, musty odor of decayed matter. Motes shimmered in the shafts of light. Dust was everywhere. Old hay bales slumped in stacks around the edges of the loft—what had been left unused, or left in storage for the use of the succeeding winter that had never come. The bales, turning to dust, were in the process of slipping loose from their twine. He eased through the opening, grasping the short length of rope for leverage. Iris was kneeling, spreading out the horse blanket. He bent down and unlaced his boots. He removed his socks and stood. The coarse wooden floor and bits of hay felt good under his feet. Iris stood and slipped out of her blouse. He ran his hands lightly down her bare arms. She stepped out of her sandals. She unbuttoned his shirt and came near so that the tips of her breasts touched his chest, and they stood that way for a moment gazing at each other with half-amused expressions—the adult in each of them, perhaps, amused by the children in them who had come out to play. The voices of concrete workers could be heard as the men gathered at the plant, then an engine started up and roared, sounding nearer than it was, and Iris jumped.

"It's just a truck," Lafleur said, smiling. "They're unloading the crane."

The truck moved, positioning itself. Behind it the rumble of the Pettibone could be heard. "Are they going to miss you?"

"How long am I going to be?"

"Not long enough to make them come looking, I hope."

"Oh?"

She smiled mischievously and came against him. Her breasts squashed against his chest. It was warm in the loft from the sun beating on the roof, but the air moved, too, from the open doors below and up through the holes in the roof. The warmth of the air felt good, her warmth felt good. He felt his warmth swelling between his legs. He felt her tugging on his belt. He struggled out of his trousers, then his underwear. When he moved his organ swung like a boom. She stripped. What had been almost chaste in their waiting gave way suddenly to heat and motion. Her face was flushed. Her nipples stiffened against his chest. He reached around and lifted her up against him, then let her down gently. He felt the suction, the tension under the wetness, the vestige, perhaps, of what he had seen as too much hardness in her at first and of what Phil disliked in her—too much brightness, a cosmetic sheen that made one's eye glance off her. But now it was a tensile hardness that matched his hunger for her. They went to their knees. She lay back. He went down on her, reached under and grasped her shoulders and pulled himself up.

They sat on the blanket naked. "If somebody comes in I guess it's not going to matter whether we're dressed or not," Iris said, touching his knee. "We'll just have to face them down."

She reached for her skirt and he thought she was going to dress after all, but she pulled a pack of cigarettes out of a pocket and lit one. She brushed away the dust and hay stems from a spot on the floor next to the blanket and set her match there, then leaned against him, her arm and leg touching his. What she granted him through the touch of her body made a powerful emotion rise in him. This was what he had missed—not so much the act of sex as the union afterward. He'd been without it for a long time, long enough to have confused sexual desire with it, to have forgotten what a woman meant. The touch of Iris's thigh and hip and arm to his was warm and firm, a complete relinquishing of distance between them. The emotion he felt made his eyes well and he looked down to keep his face from her, wanting to hold things just as they were, afraid of showing too much.

Outside, the LeTourneau's engine caught and snarled. Iris's body

140

twitched. It was Phil out there, also starting early so that the earthmover could be hauled out. If Lafleur had turned and risen to his knees he could have seen the earthmover through a hole in the roof, and the gathering workers at the concrete plant, and the trucks, the Pettibone, the Lima in pieces partly off and partly on the trucks. He didn't move. Iris reached around his leg and hugged it, then leaned away and carefully flicked the ash of her cigarette onto the bare patch of floor. She leaned back against him. "We don't want to start a fire," she said.

"It would solve the roof problem."

"Might draw attention to us, too," she said.

He chuckled and looked at her. He liked her long legs and pendulous breasts, her face shining through the makeup, and her hair disheveled. He liked seeing her this way with the creature showing through.

She looked down at the floor and held his leg and rubbed his ankle with her toes, then bent over and ground out her cigarette butt on the floor. She took care with it. "I have to tell you something about Vic," she said.

He stared across the loft at the bales slumping from the stack. He'd known that this would come.

"He builds a house of cards. If you shove, it might fall in on you. But it's his house of cards, that's what you have to remember. It has nothing to do with you."

He said, "He's hard to read."

"Yes."

"Seems like he enjoys being mysterious."

He felt her body stiffen and she whispered with a vehemence that startled him: "Yes. But not me. I'm not one of his mysteries. Not anymore."

He sat still. She reached for her cigarettes. They were French, Gauloises. She had them mailed in by the carton. She lit one. The tobacco had a pungent, slightly acrid scent. A swallow flew in through the large opening in the roof and glided around the loft, swooping gracefully up and down, circling the upright posts and grazing the pile of hay bales. They eat insects, Lafleur thought. It flies that way in order to match the chanciness of insect flight. Outside, the LeTourneau was going around. The engine roared as it ascended the grade, then burbled as it began to descend. Iris exhaled smoke. The pale, blue-gray smoke flattened, then rose on a draft toward the roof, spun, and vanished through the hole. Lafleur looked down between his legs. A drop of semen fell from the tip of his penis to the blanket and spread until it was the size of a dime, glistening and silvery, then it seeped in slowly, darkening the green cloth.

The swallow looped back from the far end of the loft, cutting through the shadows, and when it flew into the rectangle of light it banked, scattering the motes and flashing its russet belly and the white strips on its tail feathers. Not ten feet from them, it seemed to stop, or its image stopped in Lafleur's mind and stayed even after the bird suddenly disappeared through the hole in the roof. It was as if it had been jerked out by a string. "I was just an appendage to him," Iris said. "When the company wanted to promote me and send me out here, that was just fine, even though I knew Vic had influenced the assignment. But I'd let myself be his appendage, and when I think about it now it seems horrifying. Old female habits. Maybe I had to attach myself to somebody else's motion because I still didn't have enough of my own. That's the rebound, I guess. From the divorce. You're just up there spinning in the air. But it seems like I took an awfully long bounce. It's five years since I split the sheet."

Lafleur murmured. On their first night together, in the study, they'd talked about each other's histories in an almost formal way. It was a data check. Iris had told him that she was divorced from a fruit grower in California, that she'd used her settlement to go back to school and finish her architecture degree, and to take a master's. She'd moved to Reno, started working for International Data, and met Sabat. She had no children.

"But you must have liked him," Lafleur said now.

"Sure," she said. "I was his protégée. I was desperate to be taken away from where I'd been. I wanted to be taken somewhere, anywhere, and I guess I still needed someone else to do the legwork for me. But it's going to be all right, him getting me out here. Now I'm running on my own power." She reached up and touched Lafleur's cheek. "Besides, look what I found."

He smiled as if he were making a joke, but when he spoke it came out huskily: "You'd better be careful. I like you." Her eyes widened and she looked startled. Her face seemed to open with her eyes to let what he meant come in, almost as if she'd been hit but did not feel the pain yet, as if she were caught in the instant between surprise and the huddling around the injury, that instant when the world rushed in. She stared at him, drawing him in, too. Lafleur felt he was hardly breathing.

Iris bent and nuzzled his shoulder. They were quiet for a moment. They were stalking each other like large cats. Now, Lafleur thought, they would wait, alert to movement, and divert their conversation. "Listen," Iris said. "There's a lot of money tied up in this project. Millions. Enough money to make people unimportant. Do you understand?"

He picked up a stem and stuck it in his mouth. "It's a little over sixty million."

"Of course, you would know that. I'm not saying what I mean." She paused, then said, "It's not the money, exactly. It's what it is. The prison.

142

It's Vic's baby. It's the first time the company's really turned him loose on something."

"Yeah?"

"Yes," Iris said. "Construction is just the beginning so far as he's concerned. He's staying on here for a while."

"As the warden?"

She smiled. "I guess you could call it that. He's the manager. He's bucking for a vice-presidency. It's not just prisoners we're dealing with here."

"I know," Lafleur said. "I've figured that out."

"It'll be more like a colony than anything else, like one of those old penal colonies, and he's got to make it show a profit. He controls the money and he's taking a lot of the chances. And people when they fall into his orbit become like money to him."

"Okay," Lafleur said. "I got it. You're warning me."

"Yes," she said. "If you ever get down to it with him on a personal level, which you probably will, for God's sake, don't let him make you part of his process."

"Over you, you mean?" Lafleur said. This made him uneasy. "Get down to it with him over you?"

"No," she said. "That's not what I mean, but there's that, too. When it comes to women he covers himself awfully well. Money and power are much more important to him than women. For the women it's a different story, or it was for me. When you're inside a process like his it's hard to extricate yourself because you can't see anything. Everything's in a fog."

"That's what you meant about being part of his mystery," he said.

"Not being, now," she said, nudging him. She went on: "You have to make him be himself, his own raunchy, voracious self. He has one considerable strength, which is his systematic nature, his ability to keep a project like this under control. But, when something starts to suck him dry, it becomes a weakness. His intelligence switches over to the cold zone. Then he manipulates everything so he can hang on to his control. When he does that the animal in him, which is dangerous enough, but trustworthy in a way, dies. You don't want to have to deal with him on that level, not when he's empty. You have to watch out for that."

"Okay," Lafleur said, although he didn't understand what she was driving at. He wasn't even sure that she understood. There was a flicker of movement at the slumping stack of hay bales. Something was coming out. It moved again, darting several feet across the floor, then stopped in a strip of light—a lizard.

"There are others over Vic," Iris said. "There's a consortium."

"That guy U, for one."

143

"Yes, U . . . but he's a go-between, too. I met a couple of the others at a dinner, a man from L.A., another from Salt Lake City. And your partner, Blaylock."

Lafleur rocked back. "I just learned this morning that Blaylock has money in this project."

"Convergence."

"I guess."

"You're smiling."

The lizard darted forward another several feet, and stopped. "You've met Ned Blaylock?"

"Just that once."

"There's raunchy for you."

"And that's funny?"

"In a way." The picture he had of Blaylock at dinner with a consortium of investors was inescapably amusing.

"He's rich, you know," Iris said. "Vic told me he's got investments squirreled away all across the West. Vic says that when Blaylock sits down to trade you don't know what parcel of what podunk outfit he's going to put up on the table—timber shares, bits of mines, machinery, Alaskan real estate, offshore drilling leases."

"That sounds like him." Through the holes in the roof Lafleur heard an engine whining. The higher pitch cut through the noise of the Le-Tourneau, which was like a weight slung from a cord, going around and around. He straightened his back.

"What?"

"The Pettibone. Sounds like they're lifting the new crane." He stood up and looked through a hole in the roof. The three trucks had pulled side by side just this side of the workers' encampment. The carriage and engine housing were on one trailer, and the cab on another. The Pettibone crane was there and it had lifted the cab up about a foot from the one trailer bed. A bulldozer was there, too, and men were fastening a cable between it and the carriage. The dozer would pull the carriage off the trailer, then the Pettibone would set the cab in place. It would take the day to assemble the Lima crane. Down at the bottom of the site, near the river, the LeTourneau turned and moved laterally along the lower edge of the buildings.

The security guard stood just up from the barn. The light glinted off his belt and the brim of his black hat. The shadow of the top of the silo extended above the shadow of the barn like a big stack. The man stood there with his upper body in the light and his legs shaded by the silo. He lifted one arm to put something in his mouth. The arm went back down like a lever. The motion of the man seemed familiar, somehow, to Lafleur, but he couldn't place it. Lafleur looked over at the silo, at the webwork of mortar and heavy rock. From this perspective it seemed delicate and fragile. He sat down again, brushing against Iris.

"It's about time to move," she said.

"Pretty quick. Today's mainly mop up and get ready to roll, so far as I'm concerned. I'm going to take the silo down myself so we don't have to call back that other dozer operator. He's too slow."

"And I have to check through the excavation before the inspectors get here. The idiots." For a moment the sense of work to be done, of the exactness of obligation, welled between them, then she said, "Listen. When Vic finds out about us he will try something. He'll probably try to use me to hold you in line somehow."

A cold ball formed in Lafleur's belly. It was because she'd said *when*. And yet he knew it was the truth, that it would happen.

"But it'll just be an exercise for him because he doesn't care about women," she said. "That's what I'm trying to say, that you'd have to watch Vic anyway. No matter what. But this is between you and me. There." She pulled back and looked into his face. They were stalking each other again, moving up on each other, and she said, "It's just us here, you and me."

He reached behind her head and ran his fingers through her hair, then clutched her neck and drew her near until her forehead touched his nose. He released her. "I think I understand," he said. "But so far as Vic is concerned, I have to wait until it comes."

Her face grew still and she gazed at him. Her eyes glittered. Then she looked down. "But it has come," she said, looking up and fastening him with her eyes. "He is manipulating. You have to understand that and be ready right now. Don't let him draw you out there where he's sucked dry."

"Then I'll have to remember what you've said and make him be himself if I can," he said, not quite believing her. "Nobody has that much power."

"Power?" Her voice rose and she drew back. Her long neck arched. Her eyes burned into him. She grew beautiful and forbidding. "What I'm trying to tell you is that you'll be dealing with a dead man. Ultimately, that's his power."

"Ah," he said, startled.

She turned away and stared at the hay bales. Her smooth leg stayed against his, their ankles touched, their hips and sides grazed each other, and her one hand rested on his knee; as they breathed their rib cages filled and emptied in a rhythm, but he felt that she'd left him. He wondered if the flickering he'd observed previously in her eyes was a flickering of her being, an abnormal quickness of mind that led her to see too much, including the dead housed in the living. He sensed that if she looked too long at one thing the emptiness she would find there would engulf her, and that her habit of looking away was a question of survival with her. He wondered what she'd seen in him, what death, or what inclination of his own to veer away: his reluctance, for example, to take Sabat seriously, no matter what she said, or his willingness to supervise a project he probably objected to, or to engage in a partnership he questioned, or the conditional language he'd noticed himself using lately—the *mights*, *woulds*, *probablys*, and *ifs*.

He thought that Iris had been badly hurt, and he felt a wave of anger toward Sabat. He remembered the conversation he'd overheard his first day here, the rancor in it and the glide of Sabat's mocking voice. Now Iris had scared him. He felt something behind him like a cold, dark pocket up here in the sunlit loft. It was her being, demanding that he see what she saw. It was coming at him, blazing and chill as a ghost.

A horse fly landed on his left forearm. It lowered itself on its bristled legs, preparing to bite. Transfixed, he stared at it. The horse fly had green, translucent wings and yellow rings around its eyes. Suddenly, Iris was there, leaning across him to flick it off. "For heaven's sake!"

The fly flew around his head, buzzing noisily. "It's going to land on my ear," he said.

It landed on his forehead and she flicked it off. The fly buzzed away heavily, veering suddenly when it almost hit a post. "There," she said.

He ran his fingers down her back. She arched, moaning softly, then leaned toward him, placing one hand on his belly. He bent and took her nipple in his mouth. She straightened and gasped, then turned to him. They kissed. The coldness passed away from him. The longing rose, then ebbed. Their embrace became affectionate.

"Who's Smythe?" he said.

"Smythe? He runs the bar at the intersection. Why?"

"What did Vic do to him?"

She looked puzzled, then suddenly she smiled. "You did hear something when you were eavesdropping!"

"Not that much. Mainly I heard trouble, I guess."

"Vic bought the pigs and sheep from him. He wanted to rip the guy off, that's all."

"And the soldier of fortune you found in the file?"

"Him?" Her face took on a haunted look. "It's nothing. Just one of the henchmen the company keeps on its payroll. It upset me at the time because I was so upset with Vic."

"You called him a killer."

"I did? You remember it better than I do. I was out of control." She paused, then said, "Did you ever hear the one about the coyote and the knife?"

"A story?"

"They take a double-edged knife like a Bowie knife, that big, I mean, and stick it hilt down in the ground and bait it."

"Yeah?"

"You've heard it?"

"Maybe." He felt that he had. As soon as she'd begun, he felt he'd heard the story a hundred times, but he couldn't remember anything that happened in it. "Maybe I heard it with a wolf," he said.

"You bait the knife with red meat, with blood still in it. The coyote comes up to steal the meat, but you've tied it down with wire so the coyote really has to go to work on it. While he's doing that he cuts his tongue on the knife."

"Yeah," Lafleur said.

"You know it?"

"Maybe with Eskimos and bear blubber and a wolf."

"Maybe it's a better story with a wolf."

"Maybe. Maybe not. I can't remember how it ends."

"He gets the bait loose and swallows it, but comes back to the knife for the remnants and to lick off the blood. It's his own blood, too, along with the blood of the bait, and he can't tell the difference. So he licks and keeps cutting his tongue. The more he licks the more he bleeds. The more he bleeds the hungrier he gets. He's bleeding to death and he thinks he's starving, so he keeps on licking the knife blade."

She'd been looking toward him as she talked. Now she looked with him across the loft toward the ancient, sagging hay bales. Bits of dust floated in the air and elaborate cobwebs hung between the posts and rafters. Their bodies had bits of grit all over them. They were like two desperadoes, like a pair of bad ones who had managed to get away without their clothes, sitting there, the expressions on their faces resigned and faintly aghast, as if it were all nearly over and they were looking out at the rubble, just waiting for what would come next. Outside, the earthmover looped around and around. He saw the lizard again. It had changed course on the floor and climbed halfway up the low wall to the left. As he watched, the lizard flicked into motion and vanished behind a beam, then it reappeared and stopped, poised upside down, hanging onto the underside of the beam with its sticky little toes. Like magic. The horse fly buzzed haphazardly toward the lizard. A swallow flew in, looping elegantly and flashing its russet belly. The horse fly flew near the lizard. The sand-colored lizard stayed still. The swallow swooped and ate the horse fly. The swallow disappeared through a hole in the roof. The lizard stayed exactly where it was. Lafleur heard a clanking—the Lima's carriage, he thought, being pulled down the ramp. Once assembled, the Lima would be used to lift concrete walls into their positions on the foundations. Once that process began, the prison would suddenly take shape.

"Did you know the story?" Iris asked.

"Yeah, but I'd forgotten it."

"Everybody knows it, I guess," she said. "It has a lot of applications." Her impish look made him laugh. She laughed back at him and he laughed harder, feeling a little wild. It felt good to laugh. Down below, Jones began to bark and Iris grabbed for her clothes. "Shit. Somebody's come in," she said.

"No," Lafleur said. Jones's barking resonated through the barn. "She always barks when I laugh."

"Oh," Iris said.

Her expression and the sight of her, standing clutching her clothes, made him laugh again. Jones's barking increased in intensity.

"Maybe if you'd laugh a little more often she wouldn't get so excited," Iris said.

Lafleur grunted. He got into his underwear, stood, and pulled on his trousers and shirt. He stuck his head through the hole in the roof and looked out. A breeze rose from the lower floor of the barn to the hole and blew under his shirt. Convection. It felt fine. Jones had quieted. Down below, the LeTourneau had made long swathes around the excavated holes and foundations, taking earth off the humps and dropping it into the dips. Now Phil was working down near the river at the southeast corner. He was grading the recreation areas, the two circles, each of which would contain two softball diamonds. A cloud of dust hung above the site, drifting almost imperceptibly over the river toward the cliffs, drawn in that direction by a chimney effect. Convection and landforms. He could see the complete site, the hundred-fifty-foot-long berm pile just past the recreation areas and then nearer to the barn the outlines of the building units like huge geometrical figures on the ground—the partially constructed forms for the Industries Building, the deep one, the plywood forms for the Support Building, and poured foundations for the Housing Units, the Gymnasium, the excavated squares in which the pads for the guard towers would be poured, and almost directly across from him at eye level the bins of the concrete plant. Men were gathered around its base. A mixing truck had pulled under the bins. Everywhere there was the radiating array of trenches. In the distance was the pumphouse with its blinding metal roof and beyond it the power poles, and up on the slope, this way, the three semi-rigs, one of them still loaded with the crane's boom, and a two-ton closed truck that had just pulled in and which Lafleur figured carried the hooks, spools of cable, and small parts for the crane. The perspective gave him a sense of dominion. His mental map was making its excursion into reality.

148

The security guard hadn't moved. Lafleur could see the guard's chin, lower cheek, and a fringe of hair beneath the black hat. He was pale, red-haired, and freckled, Lafleur knew. Seen close, his face was boyish, almost puckish, which made an odd image in a man of his size—a good six feet five. Iris came up and stuck her head out the hole. "What's that character's name? The guard," he said.

"Bill Snediker."

He looked at her. Her face was still. Her lips were parted. She didn't look back. She had left her blouse unbuttoned. It fluttered open. "If those guys down there see you, they'll go crazy," he said.

"People don't usually look up."

"Yeah," he said. He looked up and out across the desert—the cliffs, the dark, twisting river. Dragonflies, he thought. Frogs. Fish. In the distance were the sandstone formations, the low bush and sand. Snakes. Coyotes. Lizards. Scorpions. Mice. There was nothing visible out there except desert. "This is some damn place."

"I have to give you a book to read," Iris said. "It's about this desert. A guy named Zeta wrote it."

"Zeta." He peered over to his right at the silo, thinking that he could squeeze in razing it this afternoon. He looked past the silo and watched as the Pettibone crane lifted the Lima cab a couple of feet off the running gear. The men were apparently having a little trouble getting the two parts to mate. Two men shoved on the cab to guide it as the Pettibone lowered it again. He heard a thunk when the cab hit the chocks.

Iris leaned against him. She pleased him. She scared him, too. He thought he'd acquired a slightly dangerous ally, but at the moment it seemed right.

That afternoon, Lafleur started up his bulldozer and drove to the silo. He climbed down and located a shoulder-high crevice in the mortarwork that he'd seen earlier—a place where the rock had been laid with less variation and the mortar had weakened and showed a fissure. It was not a serious enough weakening to endanger the silo itself, but it might be enough to give him some advantage. He didn't want to push the bottom out and have the rock come down on him. He wanted the silo to tip. The rock was hot to the touch and warm to be near. He stood back and marked the position of the fissure in his mind, then climbed back onto the dozer.

The metal in the dozer cab was hot. To his right a concrete truck had pulled under the bins of the concrete plant. The truck's mixer revolved slowly as it was filled. The driver had climbed the ladder at the back of the truck and was spraying out his gutter with a hose. As Lafleur watched, the driver lowered his head and ran the hose over it. Jones sat beside

Lafleur. She licked him in the face, which gave him pause, considering the carrion, the dead jackrabbits, ground squirrels, mice, deer legs, coyote heads, and bird bodies she'd been hauling around lately.

He pulled forward, raised the blade, and touched the rock with it. He geared down, jacked up the throttle, and eased the clutch in. The silo swayed ever so slightly under the pressure, then the dozer's tracks broke loose and turned freely in the sand. He backed off four feet or so, then came forward and bumped the silo. The dozer jarred and Jones's front paws slid off the seat and she knocked her snout on the dashboard. The silo had swayed ever so slightly. He pulled Jones up by the scruff of her neck and placed her sideways on the seat, then backed off and bumped the silo again, harder. A crack shot horizontally through the mortarwork. The impact knocked Jones completely off the seat. She was on the floor, tangled in the levers. He left her there. The silo would go. He disliked taking it down—out of respect for Kasanian—but he fixed his thoughts on the mechanics of what he was doing. He backed off and returned, bumping the silo delicately to ensure the cleavage, then throttled the machine until it roared, and he snapped the clutch into place. The cleats on the tracks dug into the sand and the silo toppled as gracefully as a big tree. It shook the earth and made a deep crashing sound. Scattering rocks bounced as high as the dozer cab. A cloud of dust ascended. The echo of the crash resounded back from the cliffs.

As he backed off, Lafleur saw Iris's horses to his left, galloping around the corral. To his right, the truck driver still stood on his ladder, but faced Lafleur now. A glistening arc of water rose from his hose and descended and splattered against the dry, packed earth. The two plant operators watched. One of them raised his eyebrows and hands and shrugged. Lafleur smiled. The security guard—Snediker—was out there, too, watching. Lafleur lowered the blade so as to scoop under the foundation. He took one side first, pushing rock over and lifting out half the concrete foundation. It came in chunks. He took the other side, knocking out the remaining rock and most of the foundation, then backed up and made another pass, pushing rock and concrete into the center. He'd driven around to begin pushing the scattered rock into a pile when Jones, still standing on the floor, snarled at him.

"Hey," Lafleur said. He tried to drag the dog up onto the seat. Jones faced him, her upper lip flicking back. "No!" Lafleur said. Spooked by being jerked around the cab, Lafleur guessed, but chastened now, the dog gazed at him mournfully. Lafleur worked. Slowly, he fell under the spell of the engine, the throttling run by the governor assist, and the forward and backward motion of the machine. He made a pile. It was satisfying like sweeping, like raking, like piling brush.

He thought of his twenty minutes razing the silo and of Kasanian's uncle's efforts in putting it up. He thought of lineaments, or of fibers, in this case the mineral fiber of mortar with which the rock had been bound together, and how such binding affected not the construction itself but the life of the builder, too. He thought about how working on the silo probably made an elaborate stitching of rock and of thought and of the attention of many days in succession until the work became subliminal, the stuff of dreams, and so—*expert.* In the case of Kasanian's Uncle Spence, Lafleur guessed, the work had been a requiem, an expert and yet desperate attempt to bind his doom to what would remain afterward, the living. Lafleur mused in this fashion as he worked, reconstructing what he had just destroyed. Violent as his work was much of the time, he had also a deep dislike for violence.

In time he had the ground nearly clean of rock, except for the pile. The absence of the silo had opened up a new alley of perspective down along the back sides of the barn, the sheds, and the house to the river. He drove in arcs, hunting down the stray chunks of rock. Jones snarled again. Her hackles went up in a rooster-like fringe. "Hey," Lafleur said. "Easy." He knocked the clutch lever free to stop the machine, and leaned toward the dog, meaning to extricate her from the levers and let her back up on the seat. She planted her feet and kept snarling. She came near enough to bite and Lafleur quickly shoved himself out of the cab and stood on the track, glaring at the dog. Jones lunged at him. Lafleur jumped to the ground. The dog came out onto the track, and as he stepped back Lafleur caught a glimpse of a figure in the corner of his eye. He turned and saw an old man, thick in the body, wearing bib overalls and laced-up boots. He had a shock of white hair through which the light shone. He stood sideways to the dozer and clutched a rock against his chest.

Jones growled, low in her throat now. "Easy," Lafleur said, holding up his hand and thinking—it's not me, but him. "Easy, girl." Jones stopped, then started in again. "Easy, fucker," Lafleur said. The dog growled. "Easy," he said.

He had no idea where the man had come from. Something about him—the light in the hair, maybe, or the way he held the rock, almost cradling it, or the utter stillness with which he stood, or his obliviousness of the running machine—gave Lafleur the chills. Then the man moved. He was truly old. When he moved, Jones leaped to the ground, grunting, and stood between the man and Lafleur. She kept growling. Lafleur stood stock-still, thinking, protecting me, maybe, or maybe not me but him, or what the hell? He was not afraid of the dog, but certainly spooked.

Over at the concrete plant, the mixing truck had pulled out and another was positioning itself beneath the bins. The plant operators had the conveyors running and a front-end loader was scooping rock and sand from the storage piles to the belts. Phil had just driven the LeTourneau up near the runway, where he would park it until the time came to load it up. The departure of the LeTourneau would mark with certainty the end of a phase in the project, that which Iris had spent her morning measuring—grades, excavation, the compaction in the big holes. . . . Since then, she'd disappeared into the house with her transit, tape, and clipboard full of notes.

The LeTourneau's dominance would be taken on by the Lima crane, whose body had been bolted down to the running gear, the boom affixed to the cab. The boom's strutwork stood high above the horizon. Two men were stringing cable. Another was in the cab, hooking up the controls. A fourth man was adjusting the tension in the track. He used a big-jawed, three-foot crescent wrench. Lafleur saw him shove his foot against the bracework and lean back to pull. The Pettibone crane was still there, steadying the Lima's boom. The security guard was there, watching the one crane piece the other together. It seemed strange to Lafleur that business went on as usual all around him. He flicked his eyes back to the old man, who bent stiffly and picked up another rock. His hands trembled, holding the rock.

The old man cradled the two rocks together, straightened up, and shuffled forward a few steps, and it dawned on Lafleur that, ancient as the man appeared, and though his hands trembled, he was holding a good hundred fifty pounds of rock. And, though the man shuffled, there was an eerie lightness to his movement. The man bent again—gently—and set the rocks up on another one. Lafleur reached out and touched the track of his dozer—for its stability, perhaps. Jones growled at him. Lafleur scrutinized the dog, then grabbed for her collar to catch her and make her stop, but he missed and caught his boot in the bottom of the track and nearly fell. He looked down to free his boot, then looked up and saw that the man was gone—vanished.

Only the dog remained, sniffing the air, calm now, herself again, his dog, and behind her the three rocks stacked one on top of another where previously the silo had stood. Then Iris appeared. The back of the barn, struck full by the afternoon sun, radiated heat waves, and Iris moved into that undulating air. Her figure appeared insubstantial, and gazing at her, Lafleur thought, It was nobody there, it was only her, I'm not seeing things, it was Kasanian, maybe, his tale, and then her talk of alive people being dead that made me see that phantom. She moved rapidly. She had a worried expression and Lafleur wondered, what now? She stepped out of the mirage. Jones danced around her, snuffling and wagging her tail. When Iris reached Lafleur, breathless, she said, "You have a phone call."

He took the paper Iris held out. It had a telephone number on it. He stared at it stupidly. It was his own, his own home phone. "Why?" he said. No—he thought—Penny's phone. He felt wooden and filled with a deadening fear and he looked away from Iris, afraid, and saw the security guard in his black uniform moving down toward the ranchhouse—the odd, delicate, loping gait, the equine bobbing of the head and the big, powerful body positioned at a slight cant, leading with one shoulder. Suddenly he knew where he'd seen the man before. He disbelieved what he knew even more than he disbelieved the phantom, and yet he knew, and it was unfathomable, and deep down he knew why, too, but couldn't say so, not to himself even, couldn't form that yet—it was the man in Zymanski's lot.

He heard Iris's voice coming at him as if out of a dream: "It's urgent."

"Yes."

"She wants you to call immediately."

"I know."

Chapter Thirteen

"Money is mass and class in action," reports the pseudonymous Dr. Loon in his essay on the economics of the Humboldt Bay region—*Tusk Shell, Gold Dollar, Pulp Note and Weed.* But what if there is no massing together and no class stratification? What about a society that is thoroughly democratic, and made so by hardship so insurmountable that all are equal under its yoke?

Yoke is the wrong metaphor. It has the European tinge. It suggests something heavy, carved or forged by some artisan at someone else's behest, a mechanical apparatus placed upon the shoulders of the ox-like unfortunate. With the Northern Paiutes the yoke was as inescapable and endless as pure air. There were no such artisans here, and fabricated articles, even the large burden baskets, were light, portable, fine, and degradable. Even the willow, rush, and brush houses were light, quickly made and quickly destroyed, a kind of skewed precursor to the mobile home culture of the west.

All were unfortunate in this dry place, presumably. No person stood apart. Ideas were spiritual, daily, and useful. And not much weirdness here, either, or not that weird, abstract way of seeing to make the dangerous weirdness, none of that European weird marauder's mind. Virtually no coinage of any kind here in the old days of the Great Basin. Nothing at all here but those two great worlds of things—those things that directly supported life and those that were spirits, the sun, say, landforms, large rocks, coyotes, and lizards.

Few coins here to trade for unconsumables, few coins to receive for the excess of consumables, virtually no excess, no wealth, and nobody standing apart. Not much coinage of personality, no kings, no presidents to appear on metal or pulp, no Babe Ruth, no Marilyn Monroe to be gilded in the imagination, no Jim Morrison to emboss the weirdness, no Tom Mix, no Al Capone, no Brigham Young, no Malcolm X, no Mary Baker Eddy, no Mary Kay, no Dr. Moon, no Rajneesh, no Rev. Falwell, no Michael Jackson. None of that.

"Wealth goes upstream or downstream," says Dr. Loon, "toward the stream or away from it. Up and down the coast, the currency also flows either downstream or upstream. Get a sense of that reckoning, forgetting about grids and projections—considering only places you might be in, and how the current flows through them."

But what if what little water there is does not flow out, but evaporates into the air? This is close to true. The Klamath River, the Humboldt, and the Owyhee Rivers do flow out of the western, northwestern, and northeastern fringes of the Great Basin, and Indian money, clam shells—*dentalia indianorum*—did change hands at the Klamath, for example, but there was in fact very little in the way of trade goods in the basin to have come out, or to draw trade in. The controlling reality was otherwise.

Lafleur stopped there, placing a finger on the page to mark his place, and let the book sink to his chest. He looked up at the mauve drapes drawn over Jewel's front window and thought about where the project was located—at the northeastern fringe. He lay on the couch in Jewel's living room here in Portland near the confluence of the Willamette and the Columbia, where matters were dense and had always been so. He had his head on the armrest and a quilt drawn over his body. He had moved a lamp over so he could read. He thought about the river out in the desert, the Owyhee, about how as one approached it the air cooled noticeably, how the smell changed, how on the banks of the river there was even a sudden, fecund rush of green.

He had never read anything quite like this book, which Iris had lent to him. He questioned it at every turn, and yet he kept reading. Wealth did not just go upstream and downstream, he thought, not even under the circumstances that Zeta chose to idealize. It was never that simple. Wealth was also osmotic and in a way it didn't matter how much of it there was for it to communicate its qualities. He himself felt filled with his father's ghost. His father's quirks and gestures, his very enzymes, and all the little trade secrets, the precise method of acquiring wealth—by the services of his machines—all this of his father seeped through and percolated in Lafleur's body. He felt like a Chinese box. If his skin were slit open, his father would be found in there, and inside his father was his mother, inside her was his grandmother, inside her was his grandfather, and Nicole was in there, and inside her the phantom of the silo, and on and on endlessly through unknown dead spirits to the ephemeral kernel of Lafleur's life. That, too, was commerce.

He turned his head and gazed through the doorway into the dining room. It was dark in there. Only the chandelier caught glimmers of light from Lafleur's lamp. Sandra, Jewel's daughter, was in the guest room and Jewel was in her bedroom. The last time he had looked he'd seen her light leaking out from underneath her door. Now the light was off. He hoped she slept easily. He could see the front of Gus's wheelchair—the small truck wheels, footrest, chrome hardware. The old man had died in the wheelchair. Jewel said she'd come out of the kitchen and found him there with his head on his knees. Before she touched him, she said, she knew he was gone.

Lafleur had been in Portland for two full days and he was on his third night. Though he had slept, fitfully—the first night at Penny's and the second night here—his stay seemed to have been one of very short, unbroken, sleepless, and tangled duration that began with the drive from Rome in the company pickup truck. He drove across the desert and over the mountains on the twisting route, down into the valley and then to Penny's place. He felt numbed, but he also felt that his shock, like the death, was inevitable, and so, as was his way, Lafleur felt something and looked at it at the same time.

Penny had prepared the couch for him. She told him that Jewel was bearing up well, that her daughter, Sandra, had flown in from San Diego, that her son was flying in the next day with his family from Minneapolis in time for evening rosary. "And your aunt," Penny had said.

"Aunt?"

"Jacqueline."

"No kidding. From Montreal?" He had two aunts that he knew of. He'd had three formerly, and an uncle, but the uncle and one of the aunts were dead. Another aunt, he'd heard, was infirm. He knew the name, Jacqueline, and he'd met her years ago along with the other three when his mother took him back home, but now he had absolutely no idea which of the women Jacqueline was.

"I'm going to put her up," Penny said. "Tomorrow night you'll stay with Jewel." She said it matter-of-factly. "Her son and his family are going to a motel."

"Fine."

"Sandra's been a big help," Penny had said. She raised a hand and brushed a wisp of hair away from her forehead. She looked exhausted. Her cheeks were gaunt and her eyes hollow. Seeing the share of the grief she'd taken on, Lafleur suddenly felt the knot in his belly loosening. He dug his fingers into the back of the couch, looked down, and fought off the urge to cry. Penny grasped his arm. "Hank, I'm sorry."

"He's gone," Lafleur said.

"Yes."

He stood for a moment, rocking. "Maybe it's for the best," he said. "For Jewel."

"Perhaps."

"You didn't need to do all this."

She didn't reply. Her face was still except for her eyes, which went down and came up again.

"I wish I'd been here to help," he said.

"You can't be everywhere."

He looked over at the dressmaker's dummy. A brilliant green fabric hung in festoons from its headless shoulders to the floor. He looked back at Penny. "I loved him," he said. "He could be a sonofabitch, a hard, demanding, unbending sonofabitch sometimes," he said, his voice breaking. "But he was a good man."

"I know," Penny said. She held him, and he felt her body straight as a pole against his, then softening . . . chaste and familiar and lending the support of the years it had taken to learn this touch. His body began to shake.

"The kids?" he said.

"They're fine. They're anxious to see you."

"I'll be glad to see them, too," he said.

At the funeral mass two days later—today—Lafleur had been astonished by the numbers in attendance. There were old acquaintances and associates of his father, familiar faces he couldn't place, and complete strangers. It gave him a sense of his separateness from his father. He sat in a front pew with Penny, their children between them. His Aunt Jacqueline, a well-built, vigorous old woman who'd begun to weep as soon as she stepped across the threshold of the church, sat to his right, and then Jewel and her children—Sandra and Mike. Deeply tanned and scrubbed to a shine, Mike had a roll of flesh above his collar and he responded to all intimations of difficulty with the same statement. Regarding his mother's grief, he said, "It'll come." When the hearse was a few minutes late for rosary last night, he'd said, "It'll come." He'd said, "It'll come," when the beans burned on the stove. Lafleur thought Mike meant that all things would come to him, without fail, forever. With Mike were his wife and two daughters.

Jacqueline smelled strongly of perfume, like a jungle in the cool sanctuary. The black casket, cloaked with a white pall and encircled by six lighted candles, stood before them at the head of the aisle. Reflections of the flickering flames danced on each end of the casket. Another candle burned to the right of the altar behind the priest, Father Bernard, who spread his arms and spoke in a rich voice: "On the day of his baptism, Gus put on Christ. In the day of Christ's coming, may he be clothed with glory." Lafleur heard a sigh at his back, long and hollow as if drawn collectively by the assembly. The candle flames bent. Jacqueline sobbed loudly and buried her heavily powdered face in a handkerchief that she kept tucked under the cuff of her dress. Lafleur glanced at Jacqueline, then past her at Jewel, who smiled faintly back at him. The wrinkles in her face sought the old forbearing, hopeful grooves. Her eyes were dry. Up to that moment, Lafleur had seen her face only flat and stunned, still as the desert.

Andy slid his hand lightly under Lafleur's arm and held his coat. Aunt Jacqueline's sobbing set the boy on edge. At rosary last night, both Andy and Tricia had been alarmed by the open casket in which Gus lay ensconced in white satin—his nose sharp and his brow like stone, his cheeks rouged—ghastly. After rosary, as Lafleur waited on the landing of the church with Andy and Tricia, the boy had said he thought that whenever somebody died God took the body away. There'd been no body at Nicole's services. Lafleur told him that his grandfather's spirit was with God, that the body didn't matter anymore. He hoped to offer solace to the boy, and to Tricia as well, who listened attentively from a short distance. He'd wanted to give them both something to grip.

Father Bernard delivered the homily from the pulpit. Next to Lafleur, Jacqueline dabbed busily at her face. Father Bernard talked about how Gus, an immigrant, had come to this country with little but his dreams and his willingness to work, how he became a success, and a family man, a rock in the community. As the Lord was consumed by the world, said Father Bernard, so too Gus had been consumed at last by the world he had made his own. Lafleur thought about the swallow and the horse fly up in the loft of the barn. He thought about Iris's tale of the coyote that drank its own blood. He thought about Iris on the horse blanket, and of the slants of brilliant light and dark, the motes in the air, coating his body. He thought of Iris's pendulous breasts, of the nipples he touched with his tongue. He thought about the security guard, Snediker, and his body jerked with rage, but he caught himself . . . *not now, not here, don't even think about it.*

Gus's soul, the priest said, had passed on to the mystery of the Lord's victory over death. Like a bird, Gus's soul was in flight after the long travail of his life. Those loved ones who remained were witnesses to his life and to his release just as they were witnesses of the Lord's resurrection.

Andy leaned his head against Lafleur's shoulder and placed his hand over Lafleur's hand. Lafleur saw that the boy was staring at the shiny coffin, poised on its rollers like a bomb. He looked at the boy's soft, pudgy hand against his own dark hand, and he remembered how his father's hand had seemed to him as a child—the veins and extruding cartilage bands, the calloused, weathered skin, the blunt, powerful fingers. He thought about how Gus's hands were now, crossed on his chest—thin, white, and fragile from lack of use.

Last night as Lafleur waited on the landing outside the church with Tricia and Andy, it had rained steadily, as it had all that day and the day before. He, Tricia, and Andy had been sheltered on the landing. He'd gone on to say that it was who you were inside that mattered. That was the spirit. Gus's spirit wasn't gone, he said, not any more than Nicole's spirit was. Nicole's spirit and Gus's spirit were still with them as well as with God, he said, though he had trouble with Nicole's part in that. He felt himself choking up.

Andy's eyes, dark as an animal's, had inspected his father. Tricia, too, had attended him closely, both of them alert to his emotion. "Like ghosts?" the boy said. "Maybe," Lafleur had said, "and maybe not, but it's like a ghost in a way. The ghost is a way of picturing it." The boy said, "I haven't seen Nicole." And Lafleur said, "No. You don't have to see them to know they're there. There are different ways to see. They probably wouldn't look the way you think they would." He felt his mind veering wildly toward the old man at the silo. His scalp prickled. "The ghost is what you see. It's not the ghost, exactly, that makes itself seen," he said, though he wondered about that. The boy said, "I don't think I want to see it." And Lafleur said, "Yes."

His eyes went to Tricia, who bore more than her share of the weight for Nicole's loss because she'd been told to watch the young ones, because she was the eldest. She was twelve now, almost a woman. She watched him with almost a woman's eyes. Her life had been crossed. Lafleur went on, answering the boy, who was six, but speaking as much or more to the girl. "Yes," he said. "It's you seeing it in your own way." And the boy said, "I don't think I want to see it." Lafleur said, "Yes. That's fine, too." "It hurts too much," Andy had said, though he spoke without showing hurt, but only that same dark, animal alertness, and Tricia watched with her steady, complicated eyes. He pulled them both to him and stood there, holding them, rocking gently.

"You don't need to be afraid," he said. Andy was still. Tricia, almost up to Lafleur's shoulder now, almost the size of a woman, hugged him fiercely like a child. He looked down at the street. Penny's white car hissed in the moisture as it pulled up to the curb. White exhaust curled from the tailpipe. He saw her face dip down to look up and find them. "But I am," the boy said, speaking softly. "I am afraid." Lafleur had felt the boy's chest filling with air, then, just as Tricia's hold on him softened, and he replied, "Yes."

At the mass this afternoon, Father Bernard had moved out from behind the pulpit to the center of the chancel and called for communion. Those in the front pew rose and moved toward the aisle. Lafleur found his eyes drawn to a large, plaster-colored orb of a face near the back of the congregation—Blaylock. Next to Blaylock sat a woman with a face white as snow and dyed, dull jet-black hair—his wife. She wore bright red lipstick. She looked like death. Lafleur turned into the aisle and stared at the back of Penny's head. Her blond hair was stark against her black hat and dress. Her head was erect, her shoulders squared. He looked above her at the stained-glass window. It was divided geometrically into four outer parts and a fifth, central part by the stem and arms of a cross. The whole was in the shape of an arch. The outer portions depicted a winged man, a winged lion, a winged ox, and an eagle. In the center was the lamb. The window was ringed by an endless string of fish that swallowed each other's tails.

He brushed the glossy surface of the coffin as he passed, then knelt to receive the sacrament. The priest placed the wafer on his tongue. Lafleur pressed it against the roof of his mouth. The wafer turned to paste, its taste intensely familiar. The church, located in south Portland, was his boyhood parish. The kneeler and altar rail separating the chancel from the nave were also familiar. So were the worn pads under his knees, and the stained-glass window overhead, the suspended cross, the plaster statuary, the Holy Mother carved from white marble and leaning toward the congregation, the musty smell of the place, the sharp smell of burning candles, the stiff, crinkling sound of the priest's vestment and even the smell of soap on his hand, and behind the priest the altars, and back in the corners of the chancel the obscurity, and at the sides of the nave the dark alcoves, the darkness of the confession booth. All this was a part of him. He was still inescapably a religious man. His life had become a large warehouse, which was dark in places and lit up in others, far from empty, but with things stacked up against walls and forgotten things in remote corners on long-forgotten shelves, and here and there heaps of debris, the junk parts of himself that he tended to avoid. Religion was one of those heaps, dense with relics and curious taboos. Sometimes he would drag a half-rotted item off the heap, sometimes toss a fresh scrap onto it, but no matter how dormant it might seem, the heap was permanently there. It had the power to make him stumble across it, to require his attention, to inflict him with guilt for things he had misperceived or done wrong, for omissions . . . *Nicole!* As he accepted the Blood of Christ from Father Bernard he felt himself descending deep into the tangle of that heap, and ruing his habit of keeping the guilt for his errors to himself, his habit of carting around a personal darkness in which he roved and turned like a mole in its tunnel, his habit of taking offense at anyone who intruded upon his darkness, and his requirement that he be in complete possession of his own guilt. Now it was he who reached out and touched Andy's arm for support.

After mass they followed the hearse to the cemetery. By the time they reached the gravesite, the casket was poised above the hole, suspended by straps and a cable from a small winch-operated crane. The hearse glided away. The people gathered, their umbrellas like slick turtle shells. There were only twenty-five or so here—Lafleur and his family, Jewel's family, Aunt Jacqueline, a few more that Lafleur knew, including Blaylock and his wife, Louis Brenneman, and some Lafleur had never seen before. He stood next to Penny. Tricia and Andy stood in front of them. The priest blessed the grave and prayed. The rain filtered softly over them.

Lafleur had not brought an umbrella. Penny moved near him, placed her hand inside the crook of his arm, and held the umbrella above both of them. She stood straight. Lafleur reached out and touched Tricia's head. The children edged back until their bodies touched their parents, safe under the umbrella. Up on the hill above them, a backhoe labored. It had a wheel stuck in the water-soaked ground. Lafleur saw the tire spin, spitting mud from its ribs. The operator was taking precisely the wrong approach—better to plant the pods and armature and allow the machine to free itself. The engine roared and ebbed as the operator dug deeper into the ground. The machine began to tilt. When Father Bernard finished his prayer, he glanced at the mortician. Lafleur watched the mortician move away.

Father Bernard sprinkled the grave and casket. Aunt Jacqueline sobbed. Jewel stood to Lafleur's right and he grasped her elbow. He felt her body tip toward him. He saw the mortician speaking to a groundskeeper, then he watched the groundskeeper weave his way among the white crosses and markers up the slope toward the backhoe. He heard a voice above the engine, swearing. The backhoe engine shut down. Lafleur caught Blaylock eying him, almost grinning. Lafleur smiled and looked down into the hole beneath the casket and thought about his father, how the last time Lafleur had seen him he'd been trying to get out of his body in the only way he knew how—by sending his son on to continue his battle. The mortician returned, slipped up to the small crane, and switched on the electric motor. The casket descended, swaying gently. Jacqueline sobbed loudly. Lafleur thought about how Gus might have enjoyed this toylike apparatus mounted on stands stabilized by sandbags, and how it took the casket right out from the back of the hearse and slid it along on a pair of tracks until it was perfectly centered above the hole, and then how the winch, soft as a computer motor, lowered him to the earth.

The casket struck bottom. The straps went slack. Jacqueline tottered at the edge of the grave, sobbing, and the others looked anxiously at her. Lafleur felt Jewel's arm tighten under his grasp. Jacqueline muffled her sobs with her handkerchief. They recited the Lord's Prayer. Lafleur merely mouthed the words and thought about how Gus would certainly have enjoyed the backhoe. He imagined Gus leaping out of the grave and scampering up the hill on his skinny white legs to give the operator hell. The two men, the backhoe operator and groundskeeper, stood up there in the distance now, looking at the buried wheel.

Lafleur thought about how startled they would be if they turned and saw the ancient apparition darting toward them. He thought about Gus being up there, directing the operator to lower the pods and then the armature, to swing the armature to the machine's low side and plant it, and use it to lift the machine, and then in tandem with the wheel that still had traction to swing the machine away from the hole it had dug for itself. He saw Gus up there, buck naked, his legs and back and old, flaccid buttocks pale in the rain, and he saw Gus gesticulating with his arms, bending and then coming up straight to give commands for the work. He saw the machine revolving away like a cockroach on its two hind legs. He saw the pods retract, the armature lofting upward, and then the machine backing off. Gus turned, looking for more work, for that which had pleased him most in his other life, then he strode away up over the hill and out of sight.

Lafleur was smiling. Jewel glanced at him, then smiled through her tears. "Amen," the people said. A shovel handle appeared in Lafleur's hand. He plunged the blade into the ground and sprinkled earth over the casket.

Now, on the sofa in Jewel's living room, Lafleur tipped his book up and gazed at it. The word *death* appeared near the top of one page and then again at the bottom of the next page. He read, picking up where he'd left off:

> There was flow, the flow of air, the flow of footpaths, and of the people passing, carrying nothing but light stores, their hunting and gathering implements. Walking, they traded the labor of one day for the breath of the next. The groups were called after what they ate—Fish-Eaters, Cattail-Eaters, Jackrabbit-Eaters, Rockchuck-Eaters, Cui-Ui-Eaters.

. . . Death was unimportant. Life was wired to the desert. Death was simply life switched over to another circuit.

Travel in family groups was the favored method of survival and for obvious reasons—the balance struck between the need for sufficient hands and the encumbrance of too much mass—but there were also seasonal gatherings—roots, fish, the pine-nuts—when larger groups of people came together. At such times there may well have been plenty, even excess, enough to trade. Early white explorers tell of finding the people at such times and of trading for food. And certainly such an occasion would be the time for celebration, and for gambling and games—hand game, to-kill-the-bone game, stoneball game, hoop-and-pin game—for the men to paint their bodies and to dress in their rabbit skin robes, for certain leaders, the healers and "captains," to step into the open, and for arrangements to be made for the marriages of the young—that form of trade. It was the time for the dreams to come out.

Social life is always contradictory. The archeologist, out of a scarcity of information, or out of *la rage de vouloir conclure,* may incline to set contradictions aside. It may be that the image I, too, have of paleolithic Northern Paiute as a naked nomad living in a vast, hostile world where spirit and concrete object are indistinguishable, where idea is as daily as the hand, where the line between life and death is as translucent as the sac that bounds the bulging innards of the jackrabbit, is the gilding of my own white man's desire to coin a new Eden.

Lafleur liked this passage better, though he still found the writing strange. He liked the conclusion, but the writing made him fear that he was missing a joke. Things seemed to be displaced in the writing, like knee joints operating as elbows and wrists revolving impossibly and stretching like the necks of large water birds.

He reread the passage, dwelling on the closing lines—*the hand, to coin, the rage to conclude.* He let the book sink to his chest and stared at the ceiling. After the graveside service and reception back at the church, he'd ridden to Jewel's place with Penny and the kids. Penny asked about his work. He said that it was fine. She asked how much longer he would be out there, and he said a month or two on the job, then he would come back to Portland, probably, and travel to the site for a few days every couple of weeks.

Their words were like pebbles dropped into a pool, surrounded by stillness. "And you?" he said. "The shop?"

She frowned as she turned the wheel for the corner. "We think we'll show a profit next month."

"Great."

"You seem changed."

He glanced back at the kids. Their silence was intense. "Better?"

Penny smiled. "Too soon to tell."

He stared through the windshield. The wipers slapped rhythmically to and fro. A wind had come up and the streetlamps jiggled on their poles. The light from the lamps flashed across the white hood of Penny's Honda and up the windshield. She asked if he'd ever heard from the police about the pair that had assaulted him. He paused, wondering if he should tell her. As soon as he'd got in the car he'd thought that she would ask about it, and even then he had resolved not to tell. But he told her, and by doing so his sense of the trouble he couldn't fathom and yet feared he was in hurtled at him. He saw the big one here in Portland, vanishing behind the line of machinery in Zymanski's yard, and out there in Rome—the black uniform, shiny boots, the snub-nosed revolver on his hip, the man standing, watching, moving about and watching with the bleached, dead-looking eyes set in the boyish face. "One of them's on the site."

"The site?" she said.

"He works for the company rep, the boss," Lafleur said.

They were at a stoplight. A white paper bag blew across the intersection. Penny had her hand on the shift lever and she turned toward him. Her black dress crinkled as she moved. "You've got to be kidding." The light changed to green and she pulled forward. "How can that be?"

He shook his head. Water from a puddle thudded against the undercarriage of the car. "I don't know," he said. "I don't have any idea. He just turned up."

She looked across at him again. "Does Ned know?"

"I don't think so." He'd talked with Blaylock at the reception and learned that there was another contract on line, that Blaylock was coming out to Rome in a couple of weeks. Blaylock was pinching the handle of a dainty cut-glass punch cup between his massive fingers and he swung it dangerously as he leaned toward Lafleur and said that he wanted to see the work for himself. He nudged Lafleur and said, "The old fart would have liked what we're doing. Remember that." He pulled back, tottered, and grinned at Lafleur. His wife, a small woman, stood next to him, furtively rubbing the palm of one hand against her dress. Her dark eyes burned like coals in her white face. Blaylock rocked back on his heels and chuckled loudly, and all around the eyes of the startled guests turned to him.

"Christ, I hope not," Lafleur said to Penny.

Penny murmured. They'd come to Jewel's street. They passed the old houses that had porches with false pillars and tiny front lawns. The working-class district had been kept up and now it was a racially mixed, faintly stylish neighborhood. The limbs of the stately maples swayed in the wind. The houses—their windows pale yellow under the deep eaves—looked snug. Lafleur longed to live in such a place, to find refuge in such a place.

"What are you going to do?" Penny said.

"First, make sure."

She pulled up in front of Jewel's house. The tires rubbed the curb. She jerked up the parking brake. "And report it?"

He leaned back against the headrest and smiled. "You bet. Don't tell Jewel."

"God, no."

"She doesn't need to hear about that."

Penny switched off the lights and windshield wipers. "No."

"Or anything like it."

"No."

"You probably don't need to hear it, either."

She turned the engine off and dropped the keys into her purse, then rested her hands on the bottom of the steering wheel. Outside, the wind wound around the car. Rain spattered the windshield. "It doesn't hurt," she said. "It's happening to you. You're the one who doesn't need it."

"Maybe so."

"But things happen."

"That's true."

"The frightening things just come at you."

"Lord, yes," he said.

"The older I get, the less I think people have any control."

"Yes."

"The best you can do, it seems, is just try to nudge things in the right direction, but even then some of them have a way of breaking loose."

"Yes," he said.

"Yes," she said, and they stayed there another moment. Lafleur stared through the windshield and down the glistening street. A car swished by. He felt strongly the presence of the woman next to him, her body poised and her mind sharply focused on the void out of which things came. In the back seat the children were silent. The air was electric with their listening.

They got out of the car and walked to the house. The children came behind, moving with great caution. Even on the plywood ramp their feet made scarcely a sound, and then they all paused, bunching up at the door. To their left the swinging divan swayed lightly in the wind. The big azalea's leaves trembled. They went in. They ate soup, bread, and chicken salad, which Sandra and Penny had prepared the night before. Afterward, the adults sat around the dining-room table, sipping coffee. Aunt Jacqueline held court and the others were pleased to defer to her because they were tired, and because Jacqueline was their senior and had traveled from Montreal to be here. The children had the television on in the living room. Periodically, canned laughter seeped through the doorway.

"He was the baby of the family," Jacqueline said. She sat in Gus's place at the head of the table. To her right was Jewel, then Sandra. They were opposite Penny and Lafleur. Mike and his wife, Cynthia, sat down at the far end. "He cut the King's picture out of two twenty-dollar bills, once," Jacqueline said. "Papa was furious. We were poor, then. God, we were poor. Papa had put his money into minerals. He was old. He lost everything in the crash."

Jacqueline's bracelets clinked against the arms of her chair as she gestured. Tricia and Andy appeared in the passageway and hovered there as if checking to make sure no one else had disappeared. Lafleur motioned to them to come. He wanted them to hear. "He came from a good family, Papa did," Jacqueline said. "They were in law and politics, and he scandalized them. Indenturing himself to a fur merchant and coming back with weeds in his beard, and wearing skins, and marrying Mama, too. He liked to do things his own way. Gus was his own son that way, more than the rest of us, and even though he hardly saw Papa. Papa was hardly there when Gus was little, and then the crash came, and then Papa took sick, and he died when Gus was ten. It was 1932. I was twenty. François was eighteen. Claude was nineteen. Sophie was twenty-one."

Jacqueline's eyes moved sharply from person to person as she spoke. Her face filled with warmth when she turned to the children who stood between Penny and Lafleur. Lafleur wondered which aunt it was whose farm he had visited when he traveled to Quebec with his mother. He had no idea. "Mama had the four of us in a row like kittens," Jacqueline said. "Then eight years after François she had Gus, and she kept him with her after Papa died. We had relations, Papa's people, who were in the professions, and they were glad to help us older ones along. They even sent Claude to the university. They would have taken Gus in, too, but Mama kept him. She sold the house and took him down to live with her people in the city, in a district. She raised him there."

Lafleur remembered the squalid place and the old woman. He had the image of her hawklike, fearsome face glimmering in the darkness, and of her large gnarled hands resting on her knees. He saw her in Jacqueline, he thought—a certain ashen tinge to the skin beneath her makeup, the dark, flashing eyes, and under her ample flesh something angular in her bone structure, a suggestion of power in her large, be-ringed and braceleted hands. He saw, then, the family resemblance between her and Gus, which had escaped him earlier—and to himself, and glancing at Tricia, who stood next to him, he saw it in her face, too—the arching nose, the darkness like an umber sublayer under the powder-white flesh. "We didn't treat Mama well, the rest of us, at least not until she took sick. Maybe we were so glad to be out of it, even to have suddenly found ourselves on a higher road in life. We were too pleased to think about it. But partly it was the way Papa had always treated her, as someone who didn't count. Now it seems cruel." Jacqueline had begun to weep. Jewel stirred, reaching out to touch Jacqueline's hand. "We thought little Gus was lost!" Jacqueline cried.

"But look. Look at this," she said, lowering her face and sweeping the air with her hand. She stopped at Lafleur and Penny and actually shook her finger at them, admonishing them. Penny looked down at her coffee cup and smiled. Jewel smiled. Sandra smiled. It was as if the three of them had made an impromptu pact, and then Jacqueline joined them, chuckling huskily as she shifted her weight and drew the handkerchief from her cuff. She patted her face with it. Outside, the wind soughed, rain thudded, and the branches of a shrub clawed the window. The joke had to do with his marriage, Lafleur supposed. It was a moment in which everything might have been all right if he could have been amused, too, but he could not be. He glanced down at Mike and Cynthia. Even they were smiling. Jacqueline settled back in her chair and continued: "When Gus came out west . . . that was long before Mama died . . . we thought, ah, just like Papa. But of course we didn't know him, except just a little bit. We knew Marie a little."

She turned and squeezed Jewel's hand. "You don't mind, do you?" Jewel shook her head and Jacqueline went straight on, talking of Marie, Lafleur's mother. "She came up to meet us all, and we weren't unkind to her, but we weren't especially kind, either. I'm sorry," she said, nodding at Lafleur. It was like his mother, he thought, to make a point of visiting each of his father's relations, to bridge that gap for her husband. Thinking of his mother conjured up nothing like the antic image he had of his father—scampering up the hill in the graveyard. She, who had left the world too soon and had left in pain, aroused in him an inexpressible sadness and an image of obscurity, a darkness descending on him as she had bent to kiss him goodnight when he was a child, her hair falling across his face and her breath filling his nostrils.

Lafleur hadn't known about the class difference between her and his grandfather's family, nor that Gus's brother and sisters were that much older than he, that they'd been taken in by relations—none of that. All he knew was that there'd been pain somehow, that Gus had seemed to want to forget his mother. "Marie waited for him two years while he was out here," Jacqueline said. "In those days a man felt he had to prepare things before marrying. Marie had no family. She stayed with Mama and cared for her," Jacqueline said, and that, too, was something Lafleur had never heard about.

"She waited," Jacqueline said. "A woman could wait. It was different then. Nowadays, if young people don't start breeding within hours of contact, they think they've failed." Sandra and Penny exchanged amused glances. Lafleur looked at Tricia, who was frowning, but beneath the frown her eyes were alert and inquisitive. "We had a different view of time back then," Jacqueline said. "It passed. Time passed. It was never empty. He came back to get her, but we didn't know this until later. We'd hardly known he was ever there, so how would we know when he left, or when he came back and left again? Years later, when Mama started to fail, the authorities called to ask if she was my mother. François and I went down to Montreal. Mama was slipping away, and we wanted to know from her where Gus was, so we could get him to come, but Mama said, 'No. Leave him be.'" Jacqueline paused. Slowly she turned one thick bracelet around and around her wrist.

Lafleur said, "What did she mean?"

"I don't know," Jacqueline said. "She loved him. Her life was hard. But he got out. I think she meant that."

"Hard, yes, but otherwise got out of what?" Lafleur said, meaning: What happened? When did he leave? Who was she? How had she survived up to that point? He felt he had to know that because those years had made his father who he was, and his mother then, too, whoever she was, poor orphanlike creature in Jacqueline's tale, who herself had never talked about that time in her past but only took her son to visit the place.

"I don't know," Jacqueline said. "But he came out here and did every bit as well or better than the rest of us back there who thought we were too good for him."

"Ah," Lafleur said, thinking of his father's ambition, and understanding that a little more, and even understanding, perhaps, why he still found himself at once rebelling against and fulfilling that. He thought about how even in death he saw his father running up the hill to fix something, to make something run right. He looked about the table at the women, at Jacqueline, who resembled his father and the old woman he remembered seeing, his grandmother, and at Jewel, who he'd thought more than once bore certain resemblances to his mother, not so much in looks as in manner, in her forbearance and buoyancy, and in her hands, perhaps, which were firm as his mother's had been, and as Jacqueline's, as his grandmother's. He looked at Sandra, who seemed just like Jewel in these ways. He glanced to his left at Penny, whom he had always thought to

168

be unlike his mother but now he wasn't so sure about that. He thought of how she had stood straight next to him at the graveside, and sat next to him at rosary and mass, and stayed near him at the reception, not putting on a façade of unanimity with him, but actually entering and exerting that unanimity, and who had talked to him as a friend because they were, after all. They had those years together, and were obliged to be friends, not to be fools in this trouble. And so she together with the others—even Cynthia, even Tricia, becoming a woman—were also showing that female stalwartness, for whatever reason, cultural or sexual, or whether or not at their expense, he didn't care at the moment. They all accepted, it seemed, the fact that trouble would come. They had a sense of doom, almost, which paradoxically seemed to grant them a keen ability to see things as they were and to find joy in that, while men like Gus and himself, as good as they might be, in their adventurousness, in their wild, ambitious, unreasonable hopefulness, were prone to climbing out on limbs until they became imperiled.

He felt himself surrounded by powerful female strength, and carried away by it, or down . . . carried straight down to his root. Something—shock, perhaps—must have shown on his face. Jewel leaned toward him and said softly, "Hank?" He looked at her, then around the table again, and found that almost by accident he had entered a collective gathering of emotion that swirled around like the wind outside. The women were weeping, and he realized that he had been given a gift, never mind the fact that the rip in his father's history remained largely just that, a rip. He realized that Jacqueline's speaking as she had of his father was a gift to him in his grief, given freely and out of her own desire to travel across the continent to tell it, and then given again by the others in their listening. They had entered his darkness and allowed him into theirs.

Lafleur bowed his head and the large, stonelike lump that had formed in his throat moved and he wept for the first time—for his father, for Nicole, for Penny, for Jewel, for Jacqueline's remorse. His body shook. He felt his daughter's hand slide around his neck to hold him, and he looked up at her first, as the tears streamed down his face. "I'm sorry," he said.

"No," Jacqueline said, reaching across to squeeze his arm. "You're French."

At the foot of the table, Mike moved. He shifted his legs and straightened in his chair and finally said it: "It'll come." There was a pause in which breath seemed not to be taken, a stunned silence, then the women began to laugh. A confused expression filled Mike's face, and then he laughed, too. Everyone laughed—at themselves and for Gus.

Then they left. First, Mike and Cynthia and their two girls went back to their motel. Penny prepared to leave with the children and with

Jacqueline, who would catch a return flight to Montreal in the morning. Jacqueline wept again at the doorway. She embraced Lafleur, engulfed him. It was dark. The wind had died. The rain came down lightly, steadily. The exhausted children walked to the car. Jacqueline followed, rocking as she moved. Penny and Lafleur exchanged a long look that carried a high-speed freight, as light and as potent as electricity. Then she went on, and he, Sandra, and Jewel moved to the kitchen to wash dishes. Soon Sandra went to her room to sleep. It was late. Jewel and Lafleur were left there and she said, "You were smiling at the cemetery."

"I know," he said. "It was the backhoe. It made me think of Dad."

"I thought so," Jewel said.

Lafleur leaned back against the refrigerator. The dishwasher gurgled as it drained. "I'll want to put the house on the market," he said.

Jewel paused, then said, "He left that for you, in your name."

"Yes. I knew he would, but I want to sell it and divide the proceeds between Penny and the kids and you." Earlier that day he'd paid a visit to the old family place to see what repairs needed to be made. He had the idea to hire help to refurbish the house, and then to put it on the market. The place had jolted him. The smell of the earth and of the rain on the leaves of the deep foliage, and the near-darkness, the thick outlines of the buildings and the obscure shadows were at once intimately known to him and strange. The chaos in the toolshed made him wonder how he'd lived in it. That tangled-up, idiotic man, trapped in that filth for months, seemed to him to have been a different creature, and when he looked at the sand spit, which was the same and always different, and at the river roiling around it, dark and oily-looking beneath the rain, he'd found himself on the verge of weeping—those tears the same as the old ones that had tried to come, and the tears he'd choked back last night, those he'd felt rising in him as he sat on the pew between Andy and Jacqueline, those that had come at the table, and these now, yet again, as he lay on the sofa in Jewel's living room, staring at the ceiling and listening to the rain, the same tears flooding from the same well of pain.

In the kitchen, Jewel had hung a wash rag over the water spigot in the sink. "But the house isn't mine and never was. It's yours."

He bent to put away the pots, closed the cupboard door and straightened up again. "There're his medical bills you've got," he said. "I want to make sure they're covered."

"Oh, Hank," she said.

"I'm not asking," Lafleur said. "Once the will clears, I want to talk it over with Penny and have Louis work on the papers, then put the place on the market."

"I don't know." She bent and opened the door to the dishwasher, which had shut off. A cloud of steam rose. She switched off the coffeepot. "What about the company, then?"

"Nothing. I think that's basically set. There'll be some changes, and we'll need to discuss it," he said, though the idea of any further changes gave him a quaking feeling. "But what would have been Dad's percentage will still be yours."

She sighed heavily. "I don't know. I'm tired."

"Yes," he said. He had never seen her look so tired.

"I'm going to go down and stay with Sandra for a while."

"That's good," he said.

"The rest of it, the company finances and what-not," she said, smiling weakly, "I'll leave to you. I'm only afraid you'll try to be too generous."

"No," he said, and he meant it. "There's the law, too." And there was, and beyond that it still wouldn't be a question of his generosity, but almost of survival—of himself and Jewel and her children, Penny and his children and his father, even the dead one, surviving in one another's company, of scouring themselves clean and of surviving even the tears and gashes in the fabric that bound them together. He thought of the snakes, of their glimmering, complicated weaving around and through each other as they moved across the sand.

"I'll trust those arrangements to you," she said.

Lafleur murmured, the thought behind the sound incoherent even to him—something to do with trust not being the issue, but grateful to be trusted, and also wary of it, of the weight that being trusted carried. Jewel's face had lighted up as she spoke, her smile locating its old paths in her skin. She would be all right.

She had gone to bed and he'd come here to the couch. He'd set up the lamp and waited for sleep to carry him to morning when he would get in the company pickup and drive back to Rome. He tipped up his book and read one last paragraph. His eyelids grew heavy even before he finished it, and when he awoke to the hard, rainless, early-morning light he found himself precisely there—on his back with the book on his chest, the lamp still burning:

> The Paiutes wore little clothing. They had bulrush sandals and the rabbit skin robes that they might wear around camp. In the cold men might wear buckskin jackets and leggings. The women wore an apron of sorts, either of buckskin or woven material, which, wrote Fray Escalante in 1776, "hardly covered what cannot be looked upon without peril." Much of the time the men wore not a stitch and the women just those aprons. Genitalia had not been coined for them, and the women's

apron, I would presume, was born of need—the great openness of the female genital region. Something that flapped kept the bugs off. When the white man came (or when I myself came to the history, thinking weirdly this way), the Paiutes took to clothing, partly, no doubt, at missionary urging, but largely, perhaps, out of a long unsatisfied yearning for adornment. These costumes were often remarkable, especially in the men: Army coats and flat-brimmed "agency" hats, trousers and breech-clouts both, boots, feathers, watchchains, buckles and buttons. By taking on the adornment they coined themselves at last. It was so that they came out of the desert into the imaginary life.

Chapter Fourteen

Detritus, that which is left after the rubbing away, is what we have of lost cultures, things of stone and shell and bone, and of what fiber chanced to be mineralized or preserved in dust, and words only when incised into something hard. Some concrete facts we have, but what of softer facts, the flesh that clung to the bone, what shape had that flesh, what sign of wear did it offer? And words, what of words, or even of inarticulate murmuring passed in the deepest night between a woman and a man, what of children waking in their trouble, what of the comforting of them, what of ghosts they saw, what of their eyes at dawn still struck by dreams? What of their faces taking in the light stitched between the reedwork of their hut? What of adult brows baked in the sun? What of the hands, the torn hands, and what of the weary legs? Of all this, the true decomposable substance of history, we have nothing but what the air and fundamental chemistry have carried to our imaginations.

Hector Zeta,
Manifesto for Spirits

Waxing, the moon grew more luminous each night. Because of the reflective powers of the desert, and the scarcity of electric light, the night air would seem shadowless and weirdly alight. Soon everything would have almost the same pale hue—the aligned concrete foundations and pads, the

173

ranks of machines, the concrete plant, the encirclement of trailers and campers, and the items that had appeared as if from nowhere inside the chain-link compound, the dismal little heaps of clothing and broken-down chairs, the flimsy, deftly constructed cardboard awnings, and the fence of the compound itself a luminous pewter color, and the metal building next to it in which slept the twelve or so men and one old woman. They were prisoners, illegal aliens, brought in while Lafleur was gone. They were Hondurans, he had been told.

They were released into the compound early each morning, and then, excepting the woman, taken out and put to work. They had already gathered up the rock from the razed silo, and now they quarried more out in the open desert northeast of the house, or sometimes in the distance to the east amongst the stone formations. Their pale-blue denim shirts and dark heads bent and swung as the rock was pried or chipped loose with picks and steel bars. They formed a brigade to pass the rock to the flatbed hay wagon that was attached to an old wheel tractor. In the afternoons they were marched back. They unloaded the rock and put it in place. A wall was being built around the ranchhouse. The security guard, Snediker, watched over them. On his belt he now carried the revolver and a billy club. A new shotgun was slung across his shoulder.

The night Lafleur returned from Portland, he told Sabat that Snediker was the one who'd beaten him. Sabat said that it was impossible. Lafleur insisted. Sabat's hand moved stiffly from his leg to his shirt front, then down again. They were in the study. Sabat sat at the desk. Like a captain he positioned himself at the helm while Lafleur sat in the easy chair.

Sabat said he would look into it. Lafleur said he had more than looking into it in mind. "It's called aggravated assault," he said. Sabat blinked at him. "And theft," Lafleur said. "He and his sidekick owe me two hundred dollars." He turned his head and stared at the window that reflected the room. On the other side of it was the project, which he could not see. "Why?" he said.

"Why?" Sabat said.

Lafleur turned back. "Why did he do it?"

"Why would be the question, exactly. There's no imaginable reason for it." Sabat smiled confidently, revealing his gold incisor, and he spoke with such conviction that Lafleur began to doubt himself.

But he said, "I want him off the site."

Sabat said, "Let me talk to him. I'll get back to you."

The next day Snediker was still there, and the next. . . .

Lafleur came near Snediker often enough, usually out at the high corner of the corral, where Snediker liked to station himself in the evenings after the prisoners were put away. His size and bearing communicated terrific physical power. His mechanical way of moving and his paraphernalia—boots, leather straps, gun, the black uniform—made him menacing. His face—the puckish nose, freckles, and drooping lower lip—was the face of a child, or of an idiot. His pale eyes were in fact blue, but they looked milk-colored. As Lafleur passed on his way to or from the bunkhouse, Snediker would bend stiffly, smile, address Lafleur politely with his breathy voice as "Sir," and gaze beseechingly with his dead eyes, as if there were nothing in the world he wanted so much as to draw Lafleur into that emptiness.

A week after his return, in the evening, Lafleur came across Snediker at the corral. Snediker was looking intently over the fence at the ground. Iris's horses were in there. The white mare lazily flicked its tail. The black was drifting toward Snediker with its head down. Snediker stood still. The black went nearer to him. Lafleur, who was coming from the site on Snediker's right, slowed. Beneath the bottom rail of the fence, he saw a small dust-colored thing lying low against the ground. It was penned in by the white horse, the approaching black, by Lafleur and Snediker. Snediker's body sank ever so slightly, poising itself, and suddenly the thing sprang and became big as it elongated in mid-air, then gathered itself up as it fell, bounced off the ground, and shot toward the corner of the corral. In the same instant, the black horse snorted and danced off, and Snediker pounced sideways with startling agility, and pinned the thing against the corner post with his leg. He crouched over the animal, reaching for it. The two horses spun in the center of the corral and trotted to the far side, their hooves clopping against the hard earth. Snediker's arm jerked. There was a soft, high scream. Snediker stood up, holding a dead jackrabbit by one back leg. The other back leg kicked spasmodically. Its neck was broken.

Lafleur kept going, warily. Snediker smiled, held out the rabbit body as Lafleur passed, and spoke in his sweet, breathy voice: "See? That's one less jack." Aghast, Lafleur went on to the bunkhouse without speaking.

Whenever he passed Snediker after that, Lafleur felt himself filled with loathing. The man nodded at him and smiled, and made half-audible remarks about the weather, the work, this truck, that machine, and kept addressing Lafleur as "Sir." Once, he pulled out the bright blue bag of sunflower seeds he kept in his pocket and held it toward Lafleur, offering him some.

Lafleur shook his head. Snediker shrugged and gazed sadly down at him. Lafleur walked on, feeling Snediker's eyes on his back. He told himself to be patient. If he went back to Sabat now, he knew, it would be like confronting mercury. The conversation would split up into a myriad of bright, skittering pieces, and he also had the doubt about Snediker, just a sliver of it raised by Sabat's conviction: *There's no imaginable reason for it.* " There was Iris, too, that unspoken, loaded intervention into the two men's relations, even though Lafleur's dealings with her since his return had been strictly—almost fiercely—professional.

He was still within the thrall of his grief. Iris deferred to that. Chastened by his father's death, he was waiting to steady himself. He had told her, "Look. I'm kind of a wreck," and saying it he'd realized it was more true than he'd known. He felt as though a flood of alien matter had passed between himself and Iris. He made a habitation out of his work, a comforting raiment, which he drew close about himself. He was engaged with Iris inside that shelter: her work, his work. He wished that Sabat would simply act on his own, fire Snediker, get him out of here. In his inwardness, he'd begun to feel as though he were dreaming Snediker.

One night two weeks after his return, he stepped outside the bunkhouse and noticed a wad of chewed-up sunflower shells on the ground just outside the door. He stopped, fixing on the shells. The little heap lay in the rectangle of light cast through the doorway. He turned it in the dust with his toe and thought first only that Snediker had been there, and wondered when, and why, and felt again the galling, perplexing anger. He thought about how those little wads of masticated shells were everywhere—on the route between the metal building and house, out in the yard in front of the house, and sometimes in places as odd as this, sometimes in the trenches on the site, inside the barn, down by the berm pile, next to the machinery. . . .

It came to him, a little leathery knot in his memory: the small pile of dried, chewed-up sunflower shells in his dump truck, down on the floor on the passenger's side. He struggled for a moment, standing there, wondering when he'd seen them. He thought it was the day he'd driven out to Rome, weeks ago, and then the realization came fast on him—the obvious. He remembered the salty, slightly rancid breath of the man in the cab of his truck. He remembered the man spitting. He remembered the man eating seeds back at Zymanski's lot, across the street under the awning in the rain, the hand moving stiffly like a lever end from his pocket to his mouth just as it did here.

Lafleur wheeled back into the room, and searched his top drawer for a flashlight. Phil, who was lying on his bed reading, looked up. "What's wrong?" Lafleur waved him off, went out, and walked back across the site to his dump truck. He climbed up on the passenger side, swung the door open, switched on the flashlight, and peered in. There were grimy bits of paper on the floor—the notes he'd written to himself before coming out here, which had been scattered from his wallet the night he'd been assaulted. He'd also forgotten about them. He gathered them up. On one the words *Storage Center* were scrawled, followed by a question mark, and he paused for a moment, looking at that, then bent deeper into the cab and saw what he was looking for, the dust-coated sunflower shells wedged in along the dark groove between the floormat and the hump of the gear box. He picked at the bits and pieces of dried shells with his fingernails. He lifted one shard, then dropped it. It floated through the beam of the flashlight to the darkness of the floormat.

He pulled back and stood on the step at the side of the truck. The waxing moon hung above the cliffs. Beneath him, under the pale light, was the site—the foundations, cement plant, trucks, and machinery, and beyond it the barn and house like silvery negative images of themselves. To his left, squares of dim yellow light shone from the workers' trailers and campers. For a moment he felt a powerful sense of the calm that came with finding affirmation of what he already knew and had doubted, and with the narrower, more certain articulation he was able to give the question that had been hounding him for weeks: Clearly not who, now, and not why generally, but why exactly, and for what purpose, to make him do what?

He walked back, skirted the encampment, passed between the corral and the compound, where the chain-link fence glittered eerily and the cardboard constructions looked like steel. He swung down to the ranch-house, found Sabat in the study, and started in immediately: "Now. I want that fucker out of here."

Sabat sat at the desk in a pool of light. He revolved the chair and said, "Snediker?"

"Right," Lafleur said.

"I've talked to him," Sabat said. "He was in Portland, after all."

Lafleur paused, pricked by despair. His discovery, the proof he hadn't even yet tendered, would gain him nothing. He took a breath, then said, "You bet he was."

"But not at my behest," Sabat said.

Lafleur paused again, and said, "It doesn't matter."

"He was sent to see Blaylock, not you," Sabat said, and he motioned to Lafleur to sit. Lafleur sat. Sabat said that Snediker had been sent to deliver papers to Blaylock.

"What does that mean?"

"That's all I know."

"It's not enough."

"You're right. It's not," Sabat said.

"You didn't know?"

"Of course not."

Lafleur took in more air. It was as if he were loading himself with air. He sat poised on the edge of the easy chair, alert and disappointed. "Blaylock?" he said. "Who sent him to Blaylock?"

Sabat shrugged and shook his head. His hands moved to his shirt, and back to his knees, then he clasped them awkwardly over his belt buckle. "I don't know. Somebody in Reno."

"Why?" Lafleur said. "For what possible reason?" Sabat raised one hand and shook his head slowly. The hand hung for a moment, then fluttered home to the other hand. "Have you asked?"

"I've let them know that we have a problem," Sabat said.

"And they say?"

Sabat said, "So far, they say nothing." His denials seemed to cock back degree by degree and then to be abandoned, left there with the spring of an invisible machine distended, just there, aimed at Ned Blaylock, or at some unnamed one in the Reno office, at anyone left out in the open.

"U?" Lafleur said.

Sabat hesitated, frowned, then chuckled. It was the confusion the name caused. He grinned. He opened his mouth like a fish. "I don't know."

Lafleur moved his eyes from Sabat's face to his soft hands, which were resting over the buckle. The hands moved, as if they knew they were being scrutinized. They parted and spread awkwardly, one on each leg, and Lafleur thought: His hands, he doesn't know what to do with his hands. "It makes no sense," Lafleur said, looking up.

"Power," Sabat said. "Power can be complicated."

"I'm sure," Lafleur said, "but so far as I'm concerned that explains nothing. It's a crock."

"Yes," Sabat said, smiling faintly. "But I live in that crock. There are some things I can do on my own, and others I can't. Personnel changes directly connected to the company have to be routed through the main office." His smile froze on his face. In his mind, Lafleur tried to reconcile this with what Iris had told him about Sabat's job here. He said nothing. They paused again. Finally, Sabat said, "We're waiting for clearance."

Lafleur took in air, then let it out, and said, "Get it. If you don't, I'll go to the police."

Something happened in Sabat's face. It went flat. His eyes turned steely and Lafleur paused again, and took in air, loaded himself. The coldness in Sabat's face was another denial, cocking back one more degree. Lafleur felt the coldness coming into himself. Coldness, and the sense of each other's barbarity, swelled between them—Snediker, Iris, the sense of mortal affront. Lafleur got up and left.

Snediker remained on the site. Lafleur waited. During the day he inhabited his work. He avoided Sabat. At night he burrowed deep into his personal darkness and dreamed wildly. Now he simply wished to awake and find that Snediker had vanished into thin air.

It was so, understanding him, that Penny had questioned him: "What are you going to do?" And then, as they sat out in front of Jewel's house in the car in the rain, the children rapt with listening in the back seat, the electric, alive silence back there, and the others awaiting them in the house, Penny had turned to him. The windshield wipers hummed and slapped softly. The leaves of the old maple tree next to the car twitched in the wind. Penny's face looked delicate and white. Her eyes widened. She jerked up the parking brake. Still capable of fearing for him as she might fear for herself, of taking on his care as her own, she had said, "And report it?"

In the evenings the prisoners were released into the compound. One of them, a man called El Gallo, wore a soiled turquoise shirt and a belt studded with silver. He had a heavy, leonine face, and at times when Lafleur passed the compound he would catch El Gallo fiercely scrutinizing him. At other times, when their eyes met, El Gallo would raise his hands and grin, and say, "How's it going, man?" Lafleur felt he was being mocked. Sometimes El Gallo could be seen striding back and forth in the pen, loosing a stream of words that arched into high-pitched shouts. From a distance it sounded just like what his name suggested—the cry of a rooster.

The others, excepting the old woman, played cards in the dust or gathered in knots under the makeshift awnings and stared through the chain link at the work on the site, with hard eyes set like stone in their faces. They seemed profoundly indifferent. They looked ready to kill at an instant's notice. But El Gallo, with his heavy face and eyes that flashed like knives, could look even more dangerous than the others.

The old woman usually sat in the one intact chair—all day long, getting up only to drag the chair back into the shifting or dwindling shadow of the building. Queenly, hawk-faced, and wearing the same dark-blue dress day after day, she looked almost like a nun. She had a softness in her dark eyes, an absorbent steadiness, as if she were prepared to see anything and to accept it for precisely what it was.

Two nights after his last conversation with Sabat, Lafleur was asleep and aware of the full moon. There was brightness everywhere. There was red in his eyelids from the light that passed through the blood and a light around his brain, as if his brain were resting on a white dish. Asleep, he was in a state of clarity.

The old woman was in the metal building now, along with the men. She had her own cell. All of them—the woman curled on her side and the men with their kicked-out legs and glistening faces in the rows of bunks—were there in the obscure, weirdly alight night air that slid through the miserable grates mounted under the eaves. Snediker was in his private room, his face the color of pewter. Outside—the weathered ranch buildings, already patinaed with age, and the surface of the river like polished aluminum, and the earth itself and even the cliffs— everything took on the whitened silver of the moon. Lafleur lay dreaming. He was sprawled on his back with one arm flung out and his mouth open, drinking in the whiteness and snoring softly. He was bathed in the moonlight that flooded through the window beside the door and the one above Phil's bed.

Then he became aware of the door in his sleep. Something was at the door, jostling it. Something bumped the door repeatedly and made the latch rattle, then he felt the door swing open, felt a greater whiteness in the room, and heard hinges creak and then footfalls coming slowly across the wood floor. There was a clicking sound with each footfall. He thought of El Gallo with rooster feet, the brittle nails striking the floor. The steps seemed uneven, as if lame. The clicking came near, then turned away, circled and came back again. It did this repeatedly. When it came near, Lafleur thought, Good, now it will go away again, and he stirred in his sleep, thinking of El Gallo. Oddly, the thought that El Gallo might have broken out and come in here looking for something, for food, or for a weapon perhaps, did not frighten Lafleur. Even the thought that the others, the ones with the dangerous eyes, might have followed El Gallo on their soft, silent feet did not frighten Lafleur. For the moment he felt safe in his cloud of sleep. Then the thing stayed near him and breathed into his face. The breath had a rank odor and he thought—this, in his sleep, still: It's the dog, Jones.

The breath stayed there, reeking, coming into his face, the creature not moving. Lafleur thought, It's Jones who has learned how to unlatch the door from the outside. Last night, Lafleur had awakened to see Phil's figure hovering over the dog just outside the door, shaking his fist and whispering hoarsely, "Stay, motherfucker!" Now Lafleur thought, It's only Jones here. She's eaten something bad again. She might jump on my bed as she likes to do. This made him anxious, the anticipation of Jones jumping onto the bed. The dog didn't jump. He waited. He thought he had better get up and put her out before Phil awoke, so he did. He got up and walked to the door, put the dog out, shut the door, and came back to bed, but as soon as he closed his eyes he found the dog still there, waiting, breathing into his face. He thought, I didn't do it. I only dreamed that I put the dog out. I'd better do it. He got up and did it again and came back and found the dog still there. He thought, I'm dreaming. I have to wake up and do it. So he did, but when he came back and closed his eyes the dog was still there.

180

Lafleur lay paralyzed in his sleep. By its refusal to leave him, the creature became grotesque. It would not move. It breathed into his face and he could hear a rasping in its throat. The smell was like carrion. Lafleur thought, It's a dead thing. A dead thing is waiting to jump on me. The creature walked in circles again, the sound of its walking uneven because of the lame foot, its nails clicking against the floor, but then he realized that while the creature was walking it was also standing at his side, breathing into his face, and he thought, It's El Gallo, after all, limping around and looking into everything with his dangerous eyes, and all the others are crouched in all the corners and perched on the window sills and hanging like spiders from the ceiling, staring at me, and the old woman, the nun, is near me, breathing death into my face. The circling sound came closer and closer until it was going round and round his head. He felt a tremendous pressure at his temples from the circling, from being watched by the dangerous ones. The carrion reek filled his nostrils. Now— he thought—I'm going to die if I don't open my eyes. He opened them, but everything was the same. He thought, I didn't open them. He opened them again and saw Jones's eyes looking right back at him from six inches away, and teeth, and a glossiness the color of silver in her mouth. Lafleur jumped violently, then calmed himself, thinking, It's just Jones here.

Jones edged nearer and Lafleur felt her damp throat against his arm, then she dropped something onto his pillow. Lafleur raised himself on one elbow and looked. It was a hand. This did not, somehow, seem remarkable to him. He thought, This is one of those hands Zeta talks about, or this hand goes with the man I saw carrying limestone blocks, or it's the substantial hand of my father brought to me as a gift by the dog, or—his thinking winding toward delirium within his strangely calm body—it's the hand of a prisoner, or it's a distillation of all those hands lifting stone, or maybe it's just my other hand that I've cut off the circulation to by sleeping on it. He touched the hand lightly with his fingertips and felt nothing in it, and he thought, Yes, of course, it's my hand and I need to move it around and get the blood back in it. He moved his arms, both of them, to be sure, and he felt his hands on the ends of them, dangling by the wrists just as they should have. He thought, I still haven't opened my eyes. When do I stop dreaming and open my eyes?

He put his head back down, sighing heavily, or dreamed he did. He had his head beside the hand he was dreaming or not dreaming. Jones stood there. The room was white. I give up, Lafleur thought. I give up, he repeated to himself, carefully forming the words with his lips and listening for the whisper of them. What I need to do, he thought, is get up and throw the hand in the trash, whether or not it's real, and put out the dog one more time, then maybe I can get some rest. So he did that. He sat up, slid his feet out from under the covers, and touched them to the cool white floor. He stood, picked up the hand, and walked over to the trash bucket next to Phil's dresser. He dropped the hand into it, listening as it slapped against the bottom. He attended carefully to all of that—the sound of the hand, the feel of the floor under his feet, the whiteness of the air he inhaled. He grasped Jones's collar and led her outside, closed the door behind her, and walked back to his bed. He looked over at Phil, who lay on his stomach with his thick, hairy hand clutching the pillow over his head. Lafleur lay down, drew the blanket up over him, and fell asleep. He thought, I've just dreamed all this, but it's fine now because I've taken care of it and I'm not afraid.

Just before dawn he was awakened by a shout. He opened his eyes and saw Phil fully dressed, bent over the trash bucket. "Holy Christ!" Phil said. He looked over at Lafleur. "What the fuck is that?"

Lafleur slid out of bed and stood beside Phil. He felt dazed by his sleep. "A hand," he said. It was there, truly, a hand gnawed off at the wrist, the socket bone split and ragged. The flesh was more decayed than not and had an opalescent color. It was a barely substantial slime clinging to bone down in the bottom of the bucket. Lafleur bent toward it.

"Don't," Phil said.

Around one finger was a thin silver ring, the flesh puckered under it. It was a left hand, small but perhaps adult, perhaps that of a woman, and he had a horrible dreamlike sensation that it was the old woman's hand, cut off by Snediker. He caught himself, telling himself, No. The hand stank. "Jones carried it in."

"And you put it there?"

"I thought I was dreaming."

"Uh huh," Phil said. "Look, Hank. That's a fucking hand. Where's the body?"

"Body?"

"The hand came off a fucking body."

"Ah," Lafleur said, thinking of the woman again, but quickly he told himself, No. This hand's been around awhile.

Phil closed and opened his eyes. "What about tonight?"

Lafleur stared at the hand. It appeared delicate down there, the moist flesh creased along the palm toward the fingers and the whorls of skin still partially preserved. He reached out and opened one of his dresser drawers, took out fresh underwear and laid it on his bed. He pulled off his pajama top and pulled on an undershirt. "Tonight?"

"What about tonight when fucking Jones comes in with the poor motherfucker's other hand, or Christ knows what?" He scowled at Lafleur. "Shit, Hank, wake up."

"Maybe it's a woman," Lafleur said.

"What happens when I get up in the morning and find a toe in my boot?" Phil said. He began to smile. "Let's do something."

Lafleur grinned back foolishly as he put the shirt on. "What?"

"Take it to the house. Get the boss to report it. Go look for the body."

Lafleur liked Phil's sense of consequence, of how one thing led to the next. He put on his trousers, socks, and boots, and walked down the hall to the bathroom. He shaved and wiped off the lather and peered at the lean, old-looking spook in the mirror. When he returned to the room, Phil was bent over his tiny refrigerator. He fished out a can of wheat germ. Lafleur walked out the front door.

"Hey," Phil said.

Jones was outside. She pranced around Lafleur's legs. He crouched to scratch her ears. She moaned with pleasure. He rubbed her neck and shoulders and scratched under her jaw, and he marveled at how hard she had grown. It was the nighttime running, the frantic digging. Her throat was a-quiver with wildness. He found a small sheet of cardboard he'd remembered blown against the wall of the bunkhouse, and walked back in. He went to the trash bucket, bent, and rolled the hand out onto the cardboard. Phil watched, chewing his wheat germ.

"Okay?" Lafleur said.

They walked out into the pale air of dawn and moved toward the house. Jones followed with her nose lifted, sniffing eagerly. Lafleur glanced back at the top of the site. He could see the roofs of trailers over the rise and a thin wisp of smoke snaking into the sky from someone's cooking fire. Lower down was the metal building and chain-link compound—empty. He and Phil walked the length of the barn, and then as they passed the pens he looked over at the site. The walls of the lower Housing Unit had been placed, and beside the building stood stacks of spandeck that would be laid on top of the walls. The site looked ominous in the gray light. The walls had begun to be set for the Support Building and beyond it for the Industries Building and the second Housing Unit. More panels would be set today. Panels lay in forms on the ground, the concrete setting up in some and others ready to be lifted. The Lima crane stood there with its pods down. Its boom had been lowered to the chucks. The cross-braced member pointed at an angle of thirty degrees toward the cliffs.

The three pigs hurtled out of the shadows and rushed the wall of their pen as Lafleur and Phil passed. They thrust their snouts between the boards and grunted, hoping to be fed. Jones charged the pen and barked back at the pigs. The noise made Lafleur's ears rattle. The pigs jerked back and stopped suddenly on their stiff legs. The dog straightened up and stared at them, then curled away and fell in step behind Lafleur and Phil.

Lafleur held the hand some distance in front of him like an offering. "We're pretty early," he said.

"Maybe we should look first," Phil said.

"I'm not going to cart this hand around while we do it," Lafleur said. He stepped up onto the porch. The boards creaked under his feet. He peered into the kitchen. It was dark. There was a shelf against the wall and he found a box on it. The hand rolled as he eased it into the box. In the bottom of the box it looked more alive than it had out in the open, palm up and fingers slightly bent as if to close on something round, an apple, a stone.

He rejoined Phil and said, "No telling how long that hand's been dead."

Jones trotted ahead of them toward the river. Her coat glistened and Lafleur remembered how she'd felt wet last night, or thought he remembered that. "I bet it's been someplace wet," he said, nodding at Jones. They followed the dog around the twenty feet or so of low wall the prisoners had built. Lafleur picked up a shovel. They dropped down and passed beneath the first Housing Unit, the recreation fields, then the berm pile. They moved out into the open. There was a breeze. They were silent. Though it was cool yet, they both were watching for snakes. They approached the bend Kasanian had said was good for fishing, and Jones splashed across there, clambered up the bank, and began digging furiously at a shallow indentation. Lafleur shouted, ordering her off, and for once she obeyed. He and Phil pulled off their boots and socks and waded across from a spit, seeking the shallows, and came out, climbed the bank to the indentation, where they pulled up abruptly, appalled.

A shoulder joint lay to one side. What was left intact in the depression was the top of a ravaged human trunk, the bones and gelatinous matter clinging to bones, a dried slime clotting the sand, and the top of a pair of trousers, mostly rotted, and a belt with a metal buckle encircling the pelvis. The head was there, barely strung to the torso, the jaw agape, the meat rotted.

"Shit," Phil said. "The dog's been at it."

Lafleur poked with the blade, then dug it in where he figured the legs would be. He went deep enough to get under them. Quickly Phil moved upwind. Lafleur dug around, then under, and pried and felt weight against shovel. A piece of something came out. It had a shoe on it.

"Wait," Phil said. "When you dig it out, then what?"

"You're right," Lafleur said, but he moved around and pried, and more came out, then he worked upward and gradually levered out the two legs. Sand stuck to the legs. Maggots, startled by the light, crawled over each other in confusion. The body had leather shoes and jeans, into which the flesh had rotted. It was a boy, Lafleur saw, or a small man. Just to the side of the left hip he spotted the glimmer of a triangular piece of metal. He bent to pick it up.

"Hank," Phil said. "Stop."

Lafleur grabbed up the triangle and recoiled, gagging, then moved beside Phil. He crouched and cleaned off the triangle in the sand, and turned the metal triangle in his fingers. It had what appeared to be Chinese characters on each side. He put it in his pocket and stood up, gazing at the remains.

"Easy, Hank," Phil said. "Somebody else will dig it out. All we have to do is tell them where it is."

"Right," Lafleur said.

"Are you okay?"

"Yeah," Lafleur said, but the body had an effect upon him that was disproportionate even to what it was—a body. He was affected by something greater than his natural inclination to be revolted by human remains—even after seeing the caveful of Vietcong lacing the exploded earth, the dead ones moved by front-end loaders, the body bags, and his father enveloped in white satin, even that.

"Look," Phil said. He pointed to their left.

"What?"

"Up there."

Lafleur looked and saw nothing.

"Look at the weeds," Phil said.

Lafleur bent and sighted along the flat above the bank, and he saw it, then, in the sharp early-morning light: the weed in two faint parallel furrows the distance apart of vehicle wheels. There was a steady breeze here in the riverbed and it gave the weed a distinct motion. In the furrows the weed was shorter than the weed around it, more grasslike, and it caught less wind. It was greener from collecting moisture, and thicker, and so affected differently by what breeze it did catch. There was a music in the motion, a subtle, swaying counterposition. It was a memory in rhythm of those who had passed there—murderers, perhaps. Exquisite, it brought tears to Lafleur's eyes.

"Hey," Phil said, touching Lafleur's shoulder. "Are you sure you're all right?"

"Yes," he said, wondering, What's wrong with me? "You've got some kind of an eye."

Phil released his shoulder. "Somebody's been here, all right."

"Yes."

"Shall we head back?"

"Let's check up there."

They walked onto the wash, and there the ground was more obviously compressed into two overgrown furrows. They looked back in the direction of the ranch and saw the furrows veer and stop before the outthrusting cliffs. They looked the other way—south, upstream. Jones had trotted that way and they followed her. Within fifty yards the furrows broke into a more recently, more heavily used roadway that seemed headed in the direction of Rome. They stopped and looked back toward the ranch again. From this position the furrows weren't visible at all. They walked a little farther and Lafleur picked up a shotgun shell he saw lying just off the roadway. He turned it in his fingers, judging by its faded pink casing that it had been out in the weather for a year at least.

He held out the shell and looked at Phil. Phil grimaced. They talked about the road. They guessed it might come out on the highway, maybe up in the direction of Arock, or even just this side of the bridge at Rome. They didn't know. The breeze had risen. It had a pull to it, and in the distance to the southwest a thin black line stretched across the sky.

Chapter Fifteen

Early that afternoon Lafleur stood at the "pulpit" with the concrete foreman. They were surrounded by noise—the engines of backhoes and loaders, cement trucks, cranes, power compacters, saws, drills, and the racket of hammers and of sheets of plywood being thrown into stacks. The noise swirled around in a wind and reverberated off the walls. They had the plans open and were thrashing out how the Lima crane could negotiate the open trenching, when Sabat appeared at the bottom of the site, stopped, and looked around. The concrete foreman, Red Jackson, was going on about the crane and trench. "You can't drive it there. It'll cave in the fucking trench," Jackson said, punching the plans with a thick finger. He jerked back and stared furiously at the actual trench, the water trench that ran from the pumphouse to the center of the project.

A cement truck rumbled around the storage shed at their backs. The plans fluttered in a gust of wind and Lafleur slapped his hand down to hold them. The black line he and Phil had seen had turned into a storm cloud. It darkened the sky to the southwest and was headed their way. The wind had been steadily rising all day. It blew in gusts and wound around the site in all directions.

Lafleur glanced down at Sabat, who had put on a white hard hat. He was coming. He moved near the Support Building, then disappeared behind a wall plate. The "pulpit" Lafleur and Jackson stood behind was a plywood slant board mounted on a rough cabinet. It was located high in the site, and blueprints—those parts of the whole that were doled out piecemeal—were kept in it. From the pulpit the foreman, Lafleur, or Iris could examine the plans and view the work going on around them. There was an error in the Project Manual. The water trench had created an island inaccessible to the Lima crane, and they had just brought in a rigger from Portland to execute a series of difficult crane "picks." The Project

187

Manual was right on those, putting the picks in a sequence so as to reduce the time they would have to keep the rigger on the site, but now half the picks were even more difficult and one of them couldn't be made at all until the trench was filled in and packed.

"We'll just have to keep the rigger over another day," Lafleur said.

"It'll cost you," Jackson said.

Jackson didn't care about the cost, not this cost, anyway. What bothered him was that he would have to reschedule all the pours and picks over the next few days.

"Who screwed up?" he said.

Lafleur shrugged. It was tied into the error in the plans he'd discovered when he'd first arrived, and which he'd hoped he'd fixed back then. The missing trench between the Support Building and the first Housing Unit had to be added, and drain tile had to be adjusted again, and another trench had to be moved, and yet another delayed, and then the water line that fanned out at its terminus to the various buildings had also been delayed. It was all in there, buried deep in the prohibitive, cross-referenced, unreadable language of the Project Manual and Addenda. "It's in the plans," he said.

Jackson snorted. Lafleur smiled. He liked Red Jackson, whose belly swelled under his shirt and hung over his belt. His body showed who he was, one who in his thirty years of working had battled his way up to foreman. He abused himself. He was a bull. One day he would drop dead of heart seizure on a job site.

"Maybe we could divert some of the men and finish pouring the walls in the Industries Building," Lafleur said.

Jackson snorted again. "The pit?" The two of them gazed out at the Industries Building, a large hole rimmed by plywood forms, then Jackson bent over the plans. Lafleur glanced at Sabat, who had come out on their side of the Support Building and stopped just beyond the cement plant to talk to a concrete worker. His white hard hat swung to and fro and paused, then bobbed up and down. Garrulous, Sabat liked to talk to the men, to fix them with his eyes and to carry them off on wildly wending conversations. A bag, one of Snediker's bright-blue sunflower-seed packages, blew by Sabat, turning end over end. Jackson pushed back from the pulpit and said, "The trucks'll have to drive around the fucking crane all day long."

Lafleur shrugged. "Drivers are cheaper than crane riggers."

"We'll lose more than a day on this screw-up," Jackson said.

"We'll try to make it up."

"Horseshit."

Lafleur smiled at Jackson again. Jackson stared back with his small eyes set right in the center of the pale, fleshy sockets. His jowls hung. Lafleur put the plans under cover inside the pulpit and said, "Let's go check the pit."

When they set out, Sabat turned and looked up at them. Lafleur pointed down below the center of the site at the open space between the buildings. Sabat moved that way, picking his way around the stacks of plywood and rebars. He went alongside the lower Housing Unit, which with its wall plates partially installed looked like the huge gap-toothed grin of a monster. All the buildings were that way to varying degrees, the big twenty-foot concrete plates standing on end, sometimes affixed to adjacent plates, sometimes standing alone, like a bigger, more complicated, more askew Stonehenge.

A concrete truck pulled up to the second Housing Unit. The driver swung down from the cab, walked to the back, and pushed out the trough. He switched the release spout open, then shut. A line of concrete hissed down the trough. A concrete inspector held a plastic test cone under the trough, filling it. He crouched and slapped the cone down on a square of plywood, then lifted the cone. Lafleur eyed the dark gray cone of concrete as he passed. It stood there, visibly paling in the dry air, which was precisely the problem here—the amount of water that had to be added to the mixture to keep it from drying too fast. If too much water was added, the mix would come out structurally unsound. The wind only made matters worse. The inspector, who was employed as a safeguard against government inspectors and who reported to Iris, moved his calibration stick next to the cone, looked at his watch, and knelt there as if in prayer, deeply attentive to the infinitesimal movement of the tip of his cone down the stick. If the concrete sagged too quickly or not quickly enough, he would reject it.

Lafleur and Jackson walked single file across a plank that spanned a deep trench for the tunnel that would run between the Industries Building and second Housing Unit. From one end of the tunnel came a steady throb of hammers—the carpenters building forms down in the pit. To the left, Sabat came into view from behind a wall plate in the first Housing Unit. Beyond him, down near the ranchhouse, were the prisoners, swaying and bending as they passed the rock hand to hand from the hay wagon to the wall at the house. Snediker stood there, a large, dark figure, the shotgun slung from his shoulder and the barrel rising above his head. Lafleur understood that the wall would be continued so that the house would be completely cut off from the prison, protected. The wall would be six feet high and topped with razor wire.

He and Jackson stopped at the water trench, the one in question. The blue sunflower-seed bag blew into the trench and danced along it. Lafleur watched it, then raised his eyes. The trench curved around the second Housing Unit. Phil was up there in the backhoe on the side of the trench, filling the trench with earth, working this way. Behind him came two men with power compacters. They compressed the fill. They were down in the ditch and all Lafleur could see of them was their yellow hard hats bobbing with the vibration of their machines. The fill was to be entered and compressed in layers. Phil would go back all the way to the pumphouse and make another pass with the fill, and another, the compacters following him down each time. The object was to recreate the indigenous density of undisturbed earth, as if there had been earth there instead of rock.

The compaction rates were checked by a second inspector, who also reported to Iris, while Iris herself kept track of the structures. She'd been out on the site with her clipboard not long ago. She had a daily checklist to run through. Lafleur had seen her conferring with the inspectors, then striding rapidly through the Industries Building. If he had spotted her now, he would have asked her to come along.

He'd seen her earlier, too. After he and Phil returned from the river, he'd called Iris out of the house to the porch. She appeared, wearing her work clothes—boots, jeans, white shirt, and white hard hat. He took the box down from the shelf and showed her the hand. Looking, she leaned against him. He felt his arms loosen at her touch. He found himself wanting to talk to her about something other than bearing tolerances and supply shipments. At the same time he felt a click in his blood, as of two inert things meeting—a knife blade tapped against a stone. He stood absolutely still, receiving the touch of her leg and elbow. She reached into the box and poked the finger that was banded by a ring. The hand fascinated her.

"There's a body," Lafleur said. "We found it."

They stood there, the two of them, gazing at the half-putrefied hand, and he told her about Jones bringing it in, and about where the body was, and that somebody should call the sheriff. "I guess Vic should know about it," he said.

"He's still in the shower." She looked at him, her face still—lips, long nose, angular jaw, and green eyes underneath the white hat. She was calling to him to come out from cover.

He said, "I guess things are complicated."

"No kidding." She prodded him in the ribs and smiled. "But not that way. I'll phone the sheriff and tell Vic when he gets out."

A dust devil danced around the bottom of the second Housing Unit, jumped the water trench, and vanished into the deep trench for the tunnel. It bounced out of the trench, carrying debris, and whirled past the concrete inspector. The inspector dodged it, then gave the concrete-truck

190

operator the sign. The operator swung the trough over the water trench so that the end of the spout hung above the foundation forms of the Housing Unit. He throttled the engine. The truck's revolving canister accelerated. Concrete poured down the extension and slopped down a full story to the floor. Men could be heard down there, shouting at each other, readying their tools. The dry, limy scent of fresh concrete wafted through the air. The dust devil had disappeared over the crest of the slope, but Lafleur saw that it had left the blue sunflower packet behind on the ground near the pulpit.

He and Jackson moved to the Industries Building and stood at the head of an earthen ramp that descended to a second, makeshift landing and ramp, which in turn led down to the second subterranean level—the "pit." Carpenters were down there, deep in the obscurity, building forms for the walls. The carpenters worked in the pools of light cast by drop lamps. Sabat came up and stopped behind Lafleur and Jackson.

"Look," Lafleur said. "If we get a couple more men down there to help with the forms, we can probably start pouring here today. That'll keep the trucks running while we wait for the trench. We can put another backhoe on the trench and have it ready by tomorrow."

"You don't want to hurry that trench," Jackson said.

"No."

"If you drive the crane over it before it's ready, you'll crush the fucking pipe."

"Right."

"If you get one of my trucks or the crane sunk in that trench, I'll make hell for you."

"Right," Lafleur said, smiling. He liked Jackson's sense of proprietorship, and his theatrical sense, too—talking this way with Sabat standing right behind them.

"You get this concrete work too far ahead, you'll make hell for the mechanical workers," Jackson said. "Then I'll have Lopez on my ass."

"Put him on mine," Lafleur said. "It's all stubbed in, but you're right. We don't want to reschedule the mechanical work."

"You don't," Jackson said, glowering at Lafleur. His pink, sunburnt skin drew tight across his brow, then he grinned. He turned away and stared into the pit. Lafleur stared. Over on the other side of Jackson, Sabat stared. The racket slowed and the pit boomed as new sheets of plywood were slapped into place. "Even with the trench backfilled, I'd want to bridge it for the crane," Jackson said.

"Right."

"Compact the holy shit out of it, squeeze that ground, then maybe use some of that spandeck for the crane to cross on."

"Right," Lafleur said.

"Okay," Jackson said. He started down the earthen ramp. Lafleur followed. Sabat followed Lafleur. They were like swimmers stepping daintily down into the pool of darkness, out of the wind. Twenty feet deep, the bottom was profoundly dim and damp. The makeshift landing jutted out over the pit. Jackson moved to the edge and called over a senior carpenter. Lafleur hung back. Sabat stood near him. Jackson crouched to talk to the carpenter, who had climbed the first couple of steps of the wooden ramp. In a moment the carpenter looked directly up at Lafleur, registering something Jackson had said, something, Lafleur was sure, to do with the "screw-up," and then Jackson rose and went by Lafleur, barely nodding. He bent and swung his arms stiffly as he labored back up the earthen ramp. He entered the light at the top, his figure a cartoonlike silhouette for an instant, squat and thick, then he vanished.

The carpenter returned to work with the others, the ten or so of them in the pit. Some positioned sheets of plywood for forms. Some attached the tie wires, pulling them through the forms and twisting their ends with pliers. Others hammered at the two-by-four supports. They worked in clusters. Their yellow hard hats dipped in and out of the light. They looked like mud daubers hovering over their nests. The floor of the pit was strewn with cable, and under it was a plastic laminate, there and on the outsides of the wall forms, to guard against seepage. The place, Lafleur knew, was crawling with salamanders. They came out of the damp earth and crept through the tears in the plastic. More laminate would be laid. The concrete would be treated. A heavy steel mesh had been entered into the wall forms for security, and more mesh would be spread over the floor before the concrete was poured.

The pit was studded with plumbing and electrical stubs fitted through the forms and poking up through the floor. Lafleur had seen the blueprint file for the pit on the computer screen. It was marked *Code One: Supervisory Review Only.* It formed an image in Lafleur's head of a macabre dungeon of heavily reinforced cages and isolation tanks, high-pressure hosing and high-voltage wiring. Everything was wired—entryways, floor and wall grates, ceilings. Entire cells were interfaced into circuits, and there were padded cells, and cells with what Lafleur could only make out to be manacles affixed to the walls. It had made him wonder, and he wondered now, looking down. Every time he looked at it he had a sense of foreboding.

Sabat's soft, insistent voice spoke into his ear: "Problems?"

"We have to re-sequence the work," Lafleur said.

A voice called out at them from the top of the earthen ramp, "Crane!" A figure was up there, black against the air, which had turned gray. The figure's arms went up and down. Down in the pit, the workers scattered.

The tip of the boom of the Pettibone crane appeared above the top of the forms. A load of plywood hung from a noose, coming down. The load hugged the wall forms opposite Lafleur and Sabat. The two of them turned and started back up the ramp.

"About that body," Sabat said. "The sheriff's office called back. A deputy's going to be out in an hour."

They stepped out into the open. The leading edge of the black cloud had reached the site, blocking out the sun. The site fell under a strange, temporary twilight. It had begun to rain softly. The cloud was like a big sheet of black floating up there, moving fast. Beyond it to the southwest the sky was blue again. Lafleur and Sabat swung right, crossed over the trench, then turned again and moved toward the Pettibone crane. Cable fed out from the spool at the tip of its boom. The cable glistened with moisture and it twanged as the descending load shifted. Lafleur checked his watch. "You want me to take him out there?"

"You or Phil. Frankly, I would prefer you."

Lafleur nodded. They turned away from the Pettibone crane and picked their way through the stacks of materials.

"Iris said you told her there was an access road."

"There was a road."

"The sheriff's office seemed to know it. They're sending in a man by it. I said somebody would go out and meet him."

"Fine." Lafleur touched his breast pocket, feeling for the metal triangle and the shotgun shell. He and Sabat walked on. To their right, over on the other side of the Industries Building, the yellow bucket of a loader heaved up, then tipped, dumping a load of sand and gravel onto the cement plant's conveyor. The conveyor carried the load up toward the bins. A man stood on the platform at the top, monitoring the flow. His orange shirt flapped in the wind. It looked as if he and the blue bins were floating above the barn, up there in the gray air beneath the black cloud. A wall had been poured on the ground just below the cement plant. Over the wall, workers were running a power screed, a long, winch-operated blade on tracks that moved the length of the slab, smoothing it. Down from that slab, another was setting up, and then between the Support Building and the animal pens, union carpenters were assembling forms for two more slabs. Lower yet on the slope, not far from the ranchhouse, were four wall slabs ready to be lifted, but only the two for the Support Building could be installed until after the water trench was filled.

Here, in the center of the site, inside, outside, and alongside the trenches and foundations, mechanical workers were crouched, assembling water lines and feeding power lines from large spools, running them in the trenches and through the ports in the concrete. Red Jackson stood bent over a transit, double-checking the sight lines for the walls at the Support Building. The Lima crane had moved around the top of the site, and now passed to the right and began edging between the concrete plant and the Industries Building. Its cab was red, the boom black. Because of the problem with the water trench, the crane would work from the periphery of the site rather than from the center. The loader darted out of its way. The top of the Lima's steel crawler track was visible, glinting above the foundation of the Industries Building.

The cloud was directly above them now, and it had begun to rain hard. The drops raised puffs of dust. The wind had stopped completely. The men looked around at each other and grinned with pleasure. The cloud was roughly in the shape of a parallelogram, and beyond each of its sides the sky was clear. Sunlight poured from around its edges as rain poured from its center. Lafleur turned to his right, and passed through a door opening into the Gymnasium. Sabat followed. "Take the pickup," Sabat said.

Lafleur nodded and glanced at his watch again. It was almost three. They came out on the other side of the Gymnasium, then moved down to a position from which the Lima crane could be seen. To their left, the horses were next to their water tank, standing in the rain. Rain dripped from the edge of Lafleur's hard hat in front of his face.

"Jackson's not giving you trouble, is he?" Sabat said.

"Christ, no. It's the Manual. There's a mistake and we have to keep the rigger overnight. The crane's supposed to be picking from the middle, not down there by the house."

Sabat murmured. Lafleur stopped. He looked past the concrete plant at the Lima as it moved by the wall plates and the pile of limestone pushed up next to the barn—all that was left of the silo. The crane passed the animal pens and headed in the direction of the house. The prisoners were down there, working on their wall. Snediker stood watching them. For an instant, Lafleur's head swam—with the sweet smell of the earth dampened by the rain, with the work that swirled around him, with the prisoners, with Snediker and the excessively wired pit, with his dreams, with the roadway faintly etched into the weeds, with the appalling corpse of the boy out there, and with the dismembered hand. He kept seeing that, the whorled palm and the flesh puckered around the ring, the fingers curled as if to gently hold something, and he heard his father's voice as if he were no more than ten yards away, calling him, *"Hank. Hank."*

He looked around. The rain was letting up. He looked out at the low hills to the southwest. A line of sunlight came across them, approaching the site. He turned his head back and looked at the Lima crane. The tip of the boom etched a small, dark circle in the air. The body of the crane turned ponderously next to the Support Building. It pulled forward a few yards, then stopped and lowered its pods. The boom swung around. The picking bar, suspended from the cables, swayed and descended, and then the crane raised and leveled itself on the pods. Each pod sank several inches into the soft earth.

The bar, a half-ton, wedge-shaped chunk of three-inch steel, had a line of twelve two-inch eyelets along its lip for receiving hooks and pulleys. The crane lowered the bar to its side and two men moved to it, dragging their loops of cable, pulleys, and hooks. One of them was the rigger who'd been brought in from Portland for the series of difficult picks. The pick he was preparing now was one of those, an unusual six-point hook-up on an off-balance slab. The rigger was expert, one who mixed in logarithmic calculations with experience and touch. He was in an elite cadre of the construction business, fiercely independent specialists such as structural welders, high-rise riveters, nuclear-plant steam fitters, crane operators, sometimes ripper operators, demolition blasters, and heavy-equipment operators such as Phil. This cadre often made more than foremen, sometimes more than supervisors. The rigger had pulled in last night in a black four-wheel-drive pickup with oversized mud tires, three sets of shocks, anti-sway bars, an array of fog lights, and a carburetion system that could be switched back and forth between two thirty-gallon gasoline tanks and a fifty-gallon butane tank. Half the camp had gathered to look at the truck. The rigger had claimed he could drive from Portland to Fairbanks without stopping for fuel.

The rigger and his helper crouched beside the bar and began snapping in their hook-up. Lafleur glanced down at the prisoners. Their heads and bare arms glistened. El Gallo was among them, distinguishable by the bright blue of his shirt. Lafleur couldn't help but think it a strange form of torture, the prisoners kept working there while the construction of their permanent quarters went on right before their eyes. Sabat was still here. He wondered what Sabat wanted now.

"Nice rain," Lafleur said.

"Nice for those prisoners," Sabat said, "working on that rock. We're not really ready for them, yet."

Lafleur glanced coldly at Sabat, then turned to the crane, which had raised the bar and revolved its boom so that the bar dangled above the slab that was to be picked. From the bar hung strands of cable. The rigger and his helper stood to one side. Slowly, the crane operator dropped the bar toward the slab. The cables touched and drooped. Lafleur and Sabat took a few steps to their left for a better view. All across the site the men had turned toward the crane. They had paused in the hard rain, set down their power tools, and allowed the engines to fall to idle, and now they

195

stayed where they were for the moment. The line of sunlight bisected the site, and it kept going, visibly moving northeast. A faint vapor rose from where the light struck the damp earth and concrete.

"You've lost time because of the rerouting?" Sabat said.

"Maybe two days. Maybe less if we can fill all the cracks in the schedule. It's in the Manual. It's not us." Lafleur glanced at Sabat again and saw a darkness flit across his face. Sabat didn't speak.

Lafleur looked down at the crane's picking bar, which was still being hooked up to the slab. He took a few steps forward, as if to free himself. Sabat followed. They stopped near the concrete plant. The shadows of the plant's struts climbed up the side of the barn, bent crazily at the eaves, then disappeared into the edge of the rain cloud's shadow that fell across the roof. The sun heated the right side of Lafleur's body. He had a clear view of the crane and the slab about to be picked. The picking bar kissed the slab. The slab was L-shaped and the mica in it sparkled in the light. It was to be picked as an upside-down L and set in place that way, hence the complexity with balancing its weight. The rigger, a handsome man in his thirties with black hair and a trim, black beard, watched as the helper forced the six plugs one at a time into the slots in the slab. Lafleur watched the rigger. He had a stand-offish, insolent air. In one hand he held a sheaf of papers, the engineer's Pick Manual.

"If you've got your records in order, you should be fine," Sabat said.

Lafleur said nothing, but kept looking—at the rigger and then at the helper, who drove the plastic-coated, steel expansion plugs into the hollow plastic cylinders that had been placed in the forms before the concrete was poured. He looked at the maze of cables that ran from pulleys at the picking bar to the expansion plugs. He thought about friction. Feeling himself growing angry with Sabat's manner, he forced himself to think about that—the friction between the plastic slots and plastic-coated plugs, which was all that would secure the slab as it was lifted. That was all. Friction. No threaded fasteners. It was as simple as gravity, the holding power of friction counteracting the force of gravity and poised delicately between the crane and the fifteen-ton slab. In a way, he thought, friction held everything together—the friction of bolts and screws, the friction of nails, the friction imbedded in the weight and the inertia of one thing resting on something else, the molecular friction of welds and poured concrete, and the psychic friction of his obligations—to Jewel, to Blaylock, to Penny, to his children above all. The friction of all his connections kept him silent.

The rigger's helper had the plugs secured and he went around the slab once more, double-checking pulleys, plugs, and whipcords. The rigger went with the helper, now, bending over each connection. They checked the cables, running gloved hands along them, making sure the lines wouldn't snarl. The rigger signaled to the crane operator. The operator's whitened hands could be seen moving over the controls. The bar began to rise. The crane's engine accelerated to a low roar. The rigger and his helper watched intently. All around the workers watched. The carpenters had left their hammers alone, the concrete workers stood still, and the man up on top of the mixer hung by one hand and leaned out from the catwalk to watch. Over in the site, to the right, the mechanical workers looked up. Lopez, the mechanical foreman, and Red Jackson watched from the pulpit. Down by the house, the prisoners paused to look. Lafleur saw El Gallo rise and lift his leonine face to watch. Snediker watched. At the window of the house's dining area, a figure obscured by the sun glancing off the glass—Diane, most likely—stood watching, and another figure watched from the window in the study—Iris. Even Iris's horses had hung their heads over the top rail of the corral. It was as if the air of watching were magnetic, drawing everything to attend it.

Slowly the slack left the crane's cables, then the cables went taut, and the bar, pulleys, and cables quivered in the air. The cables were like guitar strings attached to the bar as bridge, and then to the huge concrete slab. The slab tipped up, the top of it rising slowly until the entire piece came vertical, and it rocked for a moment, twanging the cables, and then the boom of the crane rocked, and the red crane body tipped ever so slightly on its pods. The slab settled with its end just off the ground. The crane operator paused there and the rigger moved around for one last look at his hook-up. He looked at the connections and carefully up at the bar, then at the boom. He signaled to the operator to go ahead.

The slab left the ground. The boom of the crane quivered. Lafleur found himself taking a step back. Everyone watched. The watching gathered densely like air inhaled into a huge lung. The operator turned the boom and the slab swung gracefully toward the lower corner of the Support Building, its path just trailing the trajectory of the tip of the boom. The shadow raced along the ground. Up in the air against the now clear blue sky, the slab glimmered and looked at once delicate and ponderous. The cab turned as the boom turned and light flooded through a side window, illuminating the operator. He took the slab just past the targeted wall, then swung the boom back a little so that the slab stopped dead, steady. The crane body rocked lightly on its pods. The slab hung for a moment, then began to descend. As it neared the ground the operator slowed its descent to a crawl and adjusted its position while workers with probing poles guided it from the ground. The slab passed between two adjacent, already installed slabs and settled onto the footing with hardly a sound, safe. That was all. The operator's hands pulled back from the controls.

Red Jackson had come down and set up his transit to check the slab's position. Lopez disappeared behind the second Housing Unit. The workers with the poles moved back, set their poles down, and carried ladders to the slab. Two welders already had their torches lit to fasten the weld plates between the slab and foundation and the adjacent slabs. Once the plates were welded, the rigger's helper would detach the plugs, then the crane would swing the boom back for the next pick. All around, the men turned back to their work.

Sabat turned to Lafleur, his eyes flashing with pleasure. "That is really something." Then his face abruptly grew solemn. "I'm having more problems with the owners."

"Over what?" Lafleur said.

"There's infighting and I'm getting the flak."

Lafleur didn't respond. He didn't want to hear this.

"Now there's a body out there," Sabat said. "It has nothing to do with us, of course, but these things can get twisted out of proportion. You never know. We have to protect ourselves."

"Sure," Lafleur said, though he didn't understand what Sabat was driving at.

"I have enemies," Sabat said. "They'll use the slightest excuse to scuttle me."

Lafleur looked away. Just down from the concrete plant, the men had started up the power screed again. As the screed smoothed the freshly poured slab, two men rode at the ends, watching, and a third shoveled fresh concrete mix into the low spots. The loader came back and plunged its scoop into the gravel pile. Below that, the crane waited, its engine idling. In the distance, Lafleur heard the compacters hammering at the trench. The rising noise seemed like quiet to him, like a calm. He wished to fall deeply under it. Through the struts of the concrete plant, down past the crane, he could see the prisoners working again. One group transferred the stone by wheelbarrow from the wagon to the wall, and a second group mortared the stone in place. They made their progress by almost infinitesimal stages. The rock wall had begun back at the low corner of the house and now had been built half the distance up one side so that it was just visible from where Lafleur and Sabat stood. Snediker was down there, a large figure in black. One arm lifted mechanically. His hand put something in his mouth—the sunflower seeds upon which he seemed incessantly to feed as if he were a large bird. The arm lowered.

"And I don't want the deputy on the site," Sabat said. "I don't want to see him."

The Lima crane's boom stayed poised, the cables cut the sky, and beneath the boom the helmeted and masked welders crouched over their fires. The pale incandescence flickered against the concrete wall. Lafleur looked at Snediker again, past the crane. Snediker hadn't moved.

"Why not?" Lafleur said.

"Why?" Sabat said.

"What's the problem with the deputy?"

"He's local. We don't want to mess with local authorities until we're ready."

"Because of the Hondurans?"

Darkness moved over Sabat's face again and at the same time he smiled strangely. He had a band of tension between the right side of his nose and the corner of his mouth. It pulled his upper lip out and made the smile lopsided. "They were delivered to our personnel by the Border Patrol, so we're legitimate, if that's what you're suggesting," Sabat said. "But, if we get into it with the locals, then we'll probably get into it with the Portland press. The last thing we want is bad press, or any kind of press at all. I'm not ready to deal with that yet."

"All right," Lafleur said, though he knew that Sabat was up to his trick of throwing him off by impressing him—troubles, infighting, and bad press. "But as far as I'm concerned that deputy is the law. I won't bring him over here unless he wants to come. If he wants to, then I'm out of it. I don't want to mess with him, either, or with you, or with company politics, or with any of that."

Sabat looked down at his toes, then up again. "You're wise."

"Maybe," Lafleur said. "What I'm saying is I'll do what I have to for my own reasons. Not yours. The only thing that'd make me bring a sheriff's deputy onto the site is to arrest that motherfucker down there."

"Look, I'm sorry about that," Sabat said. "We've been cleared to hire replacements. We're waiting on them, but we have to have security until they arrive. Snediker's been given notice."

Lafleur said nothing. It was obvious by now that Sabat said whatever he pleased. He left it to others to try to figure out which of his statements were lies. Lafleur looked up at the barn to his left. The shadows on it were lengthening. The swallows swooped in circles around the eaves. The black cloud hung in the sky in the distance. It looked like a floating tray, black and oddly geometrical. As he looked the hand came into his mind again— soft and dark and delicate, seeking to hold something.

Lafleur looked at Sabat, whose face seemed dense as clay. Sabat didn't turn to look back, but Lafleur sensed a weird ferocity building in the man's silence. He didn't care.

He hitched up his trousers and said, "I've got to find another backhoe operator and put him on that trench." He turned and started back up the slope. A breeze skittered the blue sunflower-seed bag under his feet. The black horse nickered at him as he passed. He eyed the old woman in the compound, her dark figure still as stone on the chair she had pulled into the narrow ribbon of shade at the front edge of the metal building. She watched. She seemed to watch everything. He cut through the Gymnasium to the center of the site. There were puddles of water on the floor. He was surrounded by the working men, by the clatter of their tools and machines, and for the moment he felt calm again.

He used the tack room in the barn to pen up Jones so she wouldn't follow him. Iris appeared and said that she wanted to come along. The pickup was just outside, she said. She'd already put the hand in it. He located a shovel and they got in the pickup and headed down below the house and along the riverbank at the bottom of the site, going south, upriver. Iris drove. She turned up behind the embankment and found the same trail Lafleur and Phil had walked earlier. Lafleur glanced over at her long, brown bare legs. She'd changed into walking shorts and sneakers.

"You look like you bit into something rotten," she said.

He gazed through the windshield at the expanse of sagebrush, arroyo, and sand. The limestone cliffs loomed above the river to the left. "Wait until you see."

Their bodies swayed with the motion of the truck through the ruts and hollows. Iris said, "I'm moving into the bunkhouse." He looked over at her. A wisp of hair hung across her cheek. "In one of those empty rooms. I'm not obligating you to anything, or trying to. I'm sick and tired of sleeping on the floor of the study, that's all."

"I didn't know you were doing that."

"I didn't think you did. I'm tidy." She smiled weakly. "I've got to get out of the house. I could just up and leave, I guess. But I've got to see this job through. I can't quit the job. It's pretty damned awkward."

He looked back out the windshield and raised one hand to shade his eyes from the glare. Across the river, he saw the slightly darkened, freshly turned earth with which he and Phil had covered the body. There was no sign of a sheriff's car. He pointed and said, "There." Iris cranked the steering wheel hard to the left, and stopped on a low, rocky place just above the bank. He stepped out and took the shovel from the bed. She came out the other side of the truck with the cardboard box. They moved onto a sand spit that reached halfway out into the water. "Wade or jump," he said. He backed up and leaped, coming short of the far bank and splashing himself up his trouser legs.

Iris pulled off her sneakers and waded. "You can be nowhere anywhere," she said, looking down at her legs going into the water. "Anywhere you want. But this place makes you think like that, I guess. This place is really nowhere, so I might as well keep my job and be nowhere here for a while longer." She stopped and looked down over the top of her box. She'd stepped into a hollow and the water rose to her waist.

"These dragonflies are screwing. They're all flying around screwing."

Amused, Lafleur stroked the side of his nose. All up and down the river the brilliant emerald dragonflies flew in twos, one on top of the other, hooked up like refueling jets to tankers. Some hovered together over blades of grass to lay their eggs. As Iris neared the bank, darting dragonflies parted in the air for her. Water spiders ran away from her legs, dimpling the surface. There were butterflies as well, black ones, and small clouds of gnats. There was great activity at the river. The grass was lush on the banks. On his side he could see minnows darting in the shallows. Iris came out, dropped her shoes, and slid her wet feet into them.

"No cops yet?" she said.

They walked up the bank toward the mound. Lafleur started digging. Without thinking about it, he was digging again. A hunk of the torso appeared and he shoveled gingerly, not wishing to lacerate the gelatinous flesh.

"My lord," Iris said. She moved upwind exactly as Phil had.

"Stinks," he said.

"But that's the positive influence of this place."

"The smell?"

Iris narrowed her eyes. "It's not really nowhere. It's not nowhere on a map, not any more than anywhere else. It's there on the map, but there's nothing in it, that's all. It's blank. Nothing in that place on the map."

He looked up and said, "That's why we're here."

"Yes," she said. "And that's what a map is for, to find out what you can use something for, usually. But look at it. Look at you. Talk about detail."

He kept shoveling.

"The way we stick out here. Talk about exposed. What a place."

He leaned against the shovel handle and pried gently at the legs. The pair of them emerged, parting the sand. They were like puppet legs, loosely connected to an unseen body. Darkened by moisture, they sent up a reeking cloud. He turned away, then held his breath and pried suddenly at the top of the body from the very tip of the handle. The slime-encrusted head came out and lolled, one side of the neck pulling apart from the shoulder like boiled meat from bone. The head came to rest. The mouth was wide open. Something moved in the mouth. Still holding his breath, and realizing now what he'd done—brought the shovel, and dug out the corpse as if he were in the grip of a ghastly curiosity—he leaned forward to look. The thing was glossy. It distended like a tongue, as if the corpse were struggling to speak. Suddenly, the thing flew out of the mouth. Lafleur jerked backward. It was a frog. The frog hopped across the torso and over the shoes and then along the sand to the bank.

"Did you see that?" he said.

"What?"

"That frog?" His voice sounded frantic to him. Iris frowned quizzically. He stuck the shovel in the ground and moved up beside her. "A frog jumped out of his mouth," he said. He heard a splash from the river. "There," he said. "It just jumped into the water."

"A frog?" she said.

He exhaled slowly, feeling a shuddering in his throat. "He had a frog in his mouth," he said.

"A frog?"

"Yeah," Lafleur said. He stood for a moment, then said, "I guess this place was someplace to him, all right. The boy."

"I guess."

"Lonesome," he said, feeling a melancholy rise strongly in him.

"Is that bad?"

He didn't answer. He had no answer. He heard a voice from his memory—*So lonesome . . . it's no way for a young one to die!* Hearing the voice, he began to understand why he'd been willing to come back here. It had nothing to do with Sabat. He said, "For a child? A boy?"

Iris murmured. It was a contained noise, a moan of recognition, a soft, womanly, mysterious sound. He gazed at her. Her cheeks were flushed. He admired her lack of squeamishness, the reach of her emotions, and her directness with him when she said, "What about death? Is it so bad?"

"I don't know."

"Sometimes it doesn't seem important at all." They walked farther up the bank.

"Maybe you're wiser than I am."

"Maybe more detached, just now. But it's everywhere. In a certain way, there's nothing special about death." She grasped his arm, then released it. "I'm sorry. I don't want to upset you."

"No, don't worry." He'd told her about Nicole some time ago, and about his mother, and he knew that she understood he had them on his mind, too, not just his father. "I've even thought something like that. That it's the beginning point, not the end. That we start with death," and saying that he saw his father scampering up the hill in the cemetery to help out with the backhoe. "But when someone you love dies," he said, "there's a part of you that snaps, no matter how well you think you're taking it, no matter how prepared you were. You've lost a presence in your life. I keep hearing voices."

"I know," Iris said. She had lost her father, too, when she was young. They walked along the roadway, or along the two almost invisible furrows. They stopped where the roadway became distinct. A light gust rattled the weeds.

"This is it?"

He shrugged. "I guess."

They were in the dead of early evening. It was dry and hot, and the only trace of the rain cloud that had passed over was the shallow dimples in the sand. There was not a bird in sight. To their left the cliffs towered above them. Only down at the river in the shade and wet did the fervent, crazed activity continue. Iris held his arm and he felt himself a vessel like the river, moist and glandular, his skin like water, shifting under her touch.

"I've come to like this place," she said.

He nudged the sand with his boot toe. "The desert's getting to you."

"These last two weeks have been hell," Iris said.

"Vic?"

"He's in trouble with the owners, I think."

"So he keeps telling me," Lafleur said, still disbelieving it, or certainly disbelieving the reasons Sabat offered for spreading the news around. "Maybe he's just overextended."

"He lives and breathes overextension."

"Right, and that's unhealthy."

"For him and for others."

"It's a ghost," he said. "You make ghosts that way."

"Ghosts?"

"Bad ones. They'll haunt you," he said. He thought about the figure he'd seen after knocking the silo down, what he'd come to suppose was an apparition born of some receptivity in himself. He thought about Hector Zeta's remarks on hands, about the hand in the box, about his father's hands, about Andy's hand holding him, and Tricia's hand resting on his shoulder as Aunt Jacqueline talked, and about his own hands coming, it seemed, into an increasingly abstract relationship with work, and about the prisoners building that wall, using as a base the very rock of the silo Lafleur had wrecked, and then about Sabat, whom he thought to be overextended deep into an unmanageable illusion even as the project he oversaw became increasingly, heavily, dangerously concrete. Lafleur said, "You've got to stay grounded, somehow, and stay in touch with the good ghosts."

"You're sounding pretty metaphysical."

He smiled faintly and stared over the river and across the desert toward the distant sandstone formations. He was unnerved by what he'd begun to see in Iris, through her words and the way she looked at him, the way she addressed him in general, bodily—that she was deeply attached to him, that what he had construed for the last two weeks as distance granted in consideration of his grief was not just that, but also the fear that if she pushed him the distance might never be bridged again. He was galled by his own foolishness, the excessive inwardness that prevented him from seeing what lay before him.

But as was his way . . .

. . . or as had become his way, perhaps, through the influence of his work and Victor Sabat . . .

. . . he, too, *quick to learn the language of a new reality,* all those little quirks of speech and expression and inflection, the weird little circuitous and deflecting avenues of thought and language with which he now fed his idiot . . .

As was his way, he persisted in seeking the core of the matter by a divergent route. He said, "Vic doesn't want to unload Snediker."

"Of course not."

Her matter-of-factness surprised him. "You knew that?"

"Of course."

Lafleur looked down the road. He thought he saw dust in the distance, coming toward them. "Sunflower seeds," he said. "I remembered there were sunflower seeds in my truck the other day, from the man spitting them. I checked. They were there."

"It was your proof."

"Yes. Not that I doubted it in the first place, exactly, but it's different when you're certain."

"And you think Vic sent him."

"Who else?"

Her face grew somber, then she touched his waist with her hand. Gently, she slid her hand around him and leaned against him. "I don't know who else," she said softly. Down the road the dust had come nearer.

"But why?" he said.

"I don't know why," she said.

He believed her, but also thought she was holding something back, or that there was something within her she couldn't dislodge. "It was a felony assault, for Christ's sake. That keeps hitting me."

She didn't move.

The fan of dust rose and spread. He saw the flash of chrome, then the shape of the car itself coming fast up the road, bouncing deeply in the ruts. Iris pulled away. The car came alongside them and stopped, shifting forward on its springs. Dust blew over the roof and hood. The officer opened his door and got out—a young man dressed in a green-and-gray uniform. He nodded at them, then went around to his trunk, opened it, and pulled out a folded body bag.

The man came over and held out his hand. "Bob Brown."

Lafleur shook his hand, then led him to the remains. "We dug it out," he said.

The three of them stood upwind and looked. "Not much to go on," the officer said.

"There's a hand," Iris said.

The officer didn't seem to hear. He didn't seem to have observed that Iris was with them. He shook open the bag, moved to straddle the feet, bent, and slid the mouth of the bag up along the legs. He came up with a revolted expression on his face. "God!"

"Smells," Lafleur said.

"Good God!" the officer said, bending again and struggling to work the bag up to the hips. Lafleur stuck the shovel in the ground next to the hips to hold them. The officer worked the bag up. Lafleur eased the head in with the shovel blade, then shoveled in the loose pieces—shoulder joint, forearm . . . The officer tipped up the bag and parts slid into the bottom with a sucking sound. "Jeeze," he said. He held his head back as he tied off the top. He dragged the bag up the slope to his car. Lafleur followed. Iris followed him. They made a short parade. The officer lifted the bag into his trunk and closed the lid. "Thank you, folks," he said.

"There's this hand," Iris said, passing over the box. The officer opened it and looked in. "Fingerprints, maybe," she said.

The officer blinked slowly at her.

"A dog dragged it in," Lafleur said. "That's how we found the body."

"You never know," the officer said. He opened his trunk, put the box in, then closed the trunk again. He had a clipped mustache, clear eyes, and a tanned face. He was a young one, a little cocky, one from whom, Lafleur thought, such trouble still slid easily.

"What will you do with the body?" Lafleur asked.

The officer took a matchstick from his pocket and placed it in his mouth. "Not much. Report it. Let the county examiner take a look. Pauper's grave." They stood. The air was still. The engine of the car ticked softly. Lafleur caught the officer looking in the direction of the construction site. "It's different when you have someone reported missing, then find a body. That's a whole different proposition," the officer said. "These, sometimes they just turn up."

"Lost integers," Iris said.

The deputy blinked at her again. "Maybe an itinerant," he said, "living out here with no relations. Maybe a killing. We'll report it, put it in the pipe, and we'll get calls from hell and back, Chicago, St. Louis, L.A. Folks with lost ones. There's a lot of that, but not here. Out here, somebody's missing and you know. In Chicago, I hear, they've got twenty unsolved missing persons a week. And those are the ones reported. Sometimes you'll find a body and identify it, maybe an ex-con with records, fingerprints, dental charts, and nobody even knew he was missing." The officer blinked slowly at them again. "Most folks are lawful, but you got to watch out," he said, giving his words a little edge. He leaned toward them and smiled broadly, showing them his white teeth with the mashed matchstick wedged between two front ones. He had a way of speaking that made one expect an accompanying slide show. He looked toward the site again. "Quite an operation you got there."

"You ought to come by and take a look at it," Iris said.

Startled, Lafleur straightened up.

"Maybe next time," the deputy said. He squinted at the distant site, which appeared as a snarl of clutter and glitter, dense in the center and sending its fingers out into the sands. "Now, there's something out of control," he said. "The aliens we got sneaking into our country." His voice grew heavy with meaning, and Lafleur imagined a slide with figures on it, statistics and a graph, crime rates and illegal aliens and missing persons compared to grains of sand passing through an hourglass. "Best be on my way," the officer said. He took their names on his pad, got into his car, started it, turned, and gestured woodenly at them as he drove off. The car tipped and swayed and a fan of dust built behind it. Lafleur thought of the body in the dark trunk, the chewed, dismembered remains, the parts converging upon one another in the plastic bag, rocking with the car, going away. . . .

. . . somebody's boy.

"That took a lot of nerve," he said to Iris.

"Inviting him out?"

"You bet."

She laughed and they started toward the river. Lafleur picked up his shovel. "Think I'll wade this time," he said. He knelt on the bank and unlaced his boots, took them off, then his socks, and rolled up his trousers. He stuffed the socks into his boots. Iris went ahead. He glanced back at the hollow in the sand. There were stains. That was all. He looked down the road. The car had become a dot of metal under the dust fan, going away. He felt something ring in him and heard his daughter's name . . . Nicole.

For once it was not a wailing cry, not Penny's voice hanging and falling to a sob, but his own voice softly saying the name. He remembered the sand spit and the heron, the line of fog, the yellow bathing suit bobbing farther and farther away from him, and Penny's wrenched face, Tricia's and Andy's stunned, bewildered faces, and Mrs. Good's Abyssinian jack and her daughter, the shirt blowing up above the hollow of her back, and Mrs. Good coming into the kitchen, and the cow bodies and dead chickens, the timbers and roofs in the river, the whole terrible telemetry of the Willamette that absorbed the body of his daughter into its vocabulary.

Now he had this, the telemetry of the soft, desert river, but consisting of the insistent mental image of a curled hand and of one resonant click, not thought but felt, grounded deep in his body. The boy was somebody else's lost one, just one from the host of missing souls, a long-lost traveler delivered up to him. It was as if Nicole had crept up on him, as if she'd come there to give him the body of the boy, and to say, *Here, accept it.*

That was why he'd wanted to come back here. He stood for a moment, rocking, and then thought of Andy and Tricia. He wanted them. He wanted to see them. His eyes filled with tears for the second time today. Iris called out to him. Where she stood the river came up to her waist. Lafleur went down and waded toward her. Minnows darted around his legs. The bottom was rocky at first and he walked gingerly, then it turned to mud. Hooked-up dragonflies hovered in front of his face. His head felt light and clear. The water was warm. He came near Iris. He had his boots and socks in one hand and the shovel in the other, balancing it on his shoulder. She reached out and touched his stomach, then grasped his belt buckle and tugged lightly. The clarity within his head become a sudden clarity of blood. He bent toward her, lost his footing, and swayed. Iris grabbed him. They flailed and fell in. They came up blowing. "I'm wet," he said. He tossed his boots, socks, and the shovel over to the bank.

Iris laughed, and then they stood still, facing each other. He put his arms around her and held her. The desert seemed an entirely different place here in the water—wet, bright green at the edges, filled with motion. Her body was wet and lithe, too much for him to resist. He felt giddy.

"I'm going to look funny going back there in wet clothes," he said.

"Dry them out."

Holding her, he looked over her shoulder up the river. Just above them the water eddied around the spit, and it had visible welts on its surface. He felt the light current dragging at his legs. Beyond the eddy the water looked like smoked glass. If he had looked at the spit and eddy long enough, he knew, he could have made the old blue heron materialize there, standing with its feet in the water, watching for fish. He looked over to his left and could see the faint trail of wheels above the hollow in the sand, and the music in the counterposed motion of the grass, and he thought, It's just the music there now, the music left in the softness of earth and growth by the life, the music in the path. That was all.

"So you're going to move into the bunkhouse."

Iris drew back her head to gaze at him. "I have no choice."

"I'm giving Vic one more shot at unloading Snediker, then I'm calling the police."

"Yes."

"I have no choice."

"Yes, but you have to remember that Vic gathers people around him to express parts of his personality."

"What do you mean?"

"Snediker."

"Vic?"

"Yes."

He hadn't thought of it that way. They paused. He became aware again of Iris's body touching his. "And you?"

She drew back. "Probably. Before. Not now."

"It doesn't seem to matter."

"Careful."

"Nothing seems to matter."

Iris leaned toward him and touched him through the wet cloth of his trousers. His blood thudded. "Nothing?"

"Maybe one thing."

She laughed. "Me or it?"

"Where it goes."

"Spoken like a contractor," she said, laughing again. She raised her hand to his waist. Her other hand, holding her shoes, was at his back. His footing was uncertain. They had just enough purchase on each other to keep from falling in again.

"Balance," he said, thinking of the concrete slab lifted by the rigging, the plugs, pulleys, cables, and picking bar, by friction. The current pulled at his legs. The coupled dragonflies, grown accustomed to their presence, hovered around them and went away, came back and went away, regarding them as a part of things—grass, weed, descending sun, water, and animal. "It's a question of balance," he said.

"It always is."

They moved to the spit. Sand mites danced around their feet. He found himself scanning the landscape. He saw no one—only the site and ranchstead in the distance. Heat waves undulated above the sand. The rain cloud was now a narrow, black line in the distant northeast. They moved to the truck, which was right there, its nose poised above the spit. He felt his feet and lower legs drying already, even his shirt stiffening against his skin. He put his hands under Iris's shirt and turned her to him, holding her ribs, then touched the lower moons of her breasts and reached for her nipples with his thumbs. She gasped and stepped back.

She pulled off her shirt and spread it out on the hood of the truck. He took off his shirt and spread it out beside hers. He got his boots and set them up on the rail of the bed, and hung his socks there in the sun. He placed the shovel in the bed. The metal there was too hot to hold his hand on. The sun was sinking, striking the earth almost laterally, but holding its power. The shadows lengthened. The sand was hot under his feet. When he came back to the front of the truck, Iris was removing her shorts. He inhaled deeply. The air was hot and dry in his nostrils. A lizard flashed out of sight beneath the truck. He could hear the whisper of the river and sparrows rustling in the brush. He grasped Iris. She came against him and lightly rubbed her nipples against his chest, then reached down to stroke him through his trousers.

"Off with them," she said.

He stripped. His swollen penis swung heavily like a gin pole as he moved. "I hope to Christ nobody's watching," he said.

"I want that," she said, pointing.

He heard crows cawing in the distance and looked up for them. They were nowhere to be seen. He opened the door of the pickup cab and looked in. "The seat's been in the shade."

Iris grasped him. His head swam from the excruciating detail of his pleasure. He clutched at her desperately, slid his hands down her back to her buttocks and lifted her. She hooked her heels around his legs and held on to his neck with her hands. He felt her heat against his belly and he slid her down, entering her. He went deeply into her and she moaned, "Easy. Slow." She pressed one breast at his mouth and he took the nipple gently in his teeth and searched its surface with his tongue. She shuddered and arched her back. He swayed, holding her, then walked her to the cab, feeling powerful and savage.

He lifted her onto the seat, disengaging himself. He felt the wild juxtaposition of the dry air and the moisture of body. The crows cawed hoarsely overhead. Their shadows flitted trickily across the windshield and through the cab. A fly buzzed raucously on the dashboard. He felt like a panther. Iris's face was flushed. He bowed to her, burying his face between her legs, and sought the detail of her pleasure with his tongue. He stretched out one hand to reach her breast and rolled the nipple between his thumb and fingers. He spread his other hand across her abdomen as if to hold her, and to feel there, too, for her darkness. His penis rested on the runningboard. Iris clasped his neck with her legs and moaned, lifting her hips from the seat for him. Questions ran through the back of his mind like a thin, frothy white line, *What am I doing? After this, what? What next?* The questions flickered and vanished, washed over by dark, barbarous enchantment.

Chapter Sixteen

The color of salmon, Blaylock's car came sailing along the road and turned down the drive. Its dust cloud swallowed it, then it nosed out of the dust and bounced along the crest of the slope to the site. When Lafleur walked up from the pulpit he found Blaylock decked out in checked polyester trousers, a bright red shirt, white belt, and two-tone white-and-brown shoes. His flabby arms popped out of the short sleeves. His face was touched with red. Lafleur greeted him, but Blaylock kept looking past him at the site, taking it in.

"Not bad," he said.

Lafleur grunted and turned to look with him. He'd thought Blaylock was coming just to see the project, and maybe for a dose of the open, bright desert air—this salamander-like one who was accustomed to the dark of his house, the darkness of engines, and to fumes, to solvents, oils, and exhaust—but he was dressed as if he'd come to party.

Lafleur showed him around. He introduced him to the foremen, Lopez and Red Jackson. He took him from one building to the next. Blaylock questioned nothing, but his pleasure came out sounding confrontational. "That's a load," he said, gazing down at the electrical conduits in the bottom of a trench. "That's a hell of a weld plate," he said, gazing up at the joint between two wall slabs in the Gymnasium.

They went to the Industries Building and stood on the landing above the pit, which Lafleur scrutinized uneasily every time he came near it— the walls poured by then and the forms stripped away, and the plethora of wiring and plumbing entered through the stubs, and the place crawling with mechanical workers. Not even Iris was sure what the pit was for. "Isolation cells, maybe," she'd said. Blaylock looked into the hole, then raised his head and swung it toward Lafleur. "Busy fucking place," he said.

When Blaylock saw the prisoners working on the wall, which they had built five feet tall between the river and the house, and begun up between the house and the project, he stopped in his tracks and chuckled. "You're kidding," he said. "Already?" Then he said, "Got some figures from our accountant to show you." He'd emphasized the word *our*, and he gaped at Lafleur, displaying his limy tongue. He leaned toward Lafleur, sending an odor of alcohol and something sweet like mint. "Do you want to deal?" he said.

Lafleur said, "Maybe."

Blaylock chuckled, stirring up the mucus in his chest. "Yeah," he said. "Cagy."

They left it at that. Lafleur turned him over to Sabat. Later, as Lafleur was closing down the site for the day, Iris told him that Sabat wanted to take them out to eat at Burns Junction.

"Me, too?" Lafleur said. "All of us?"

"I know," Iris said. "Are you feeling testy or do you want to humor him?"

"It probably depends on how close to him I have to get."

"The café's kind of interesting," she said.

He showered and dressed, then stepped outside and moved to a position near the corral where he would see when Sabat and Blaylock came out of the house, or when Iris, who was showering, emerged from the bunkhouse. It was the heart of the summer, now. The river was shrinking, the heat and irrigation lines at the farms drawing against its store. The water levels in engines had to be checked repeatedly. The earth, however faintly stirred, threw its powder skyward, and above the site itself hung a constant haze. It hadn't rained again. He looked through the haze, which softened the pastel green of the cliffs to the east, and southward over the top of the project, the blue of the hills. At the far, high corner of the site a mirage shimmered.

If he hadn't agreed to go out, he would have been walking now, which he'd taken to doing in the evenings after work. It was his time alone. He carried a staff to guard against snakes. Usually he ended up at the sand spit near where they'd found the corpse. He would sit and watch the shallow, slowly riffling water, the shadows of fish, the insects, or Jones as she splashed in the water and dug furiously at the banks in her endless quest for refuse. Once when Jones had worked her way upstream, a coyote appeared on the bank opposite Lafleur, scarcely twenty feet away. It was sand-colored and russet turning to black at the snout and the tip of the tail. Its bright black eyes took him in. By looking it seemed to articulate his presence, to substantiate the fact that he was there. It turned and trotted off, vanishing behind a swell in the earth.

The place filled Lafleur with melancholy, but it was a melancholy with which he was easy enough. He felt as though he became himself, the man from Portland who was nevertheless here. He felt momentarily freed from the trickiness of life on the project—even from Iris, surely from Sabat, from the deepening pall Sabat cast that seeped into Lafleur's daily work. When he received mail, he would bring it along and go through it on the river bank. Sometimes bills were forwarded to him from Portland, or sometimes he got a note from the realtor who was overseeing the painting and renovation of the house on the Willamette. Lafleur had gone ahead with that, and as soon as the will came out of probate, he planned to put the house on the market. Sometimes he got short letters from Jewel, and more rarely something from Penny—more bills, those that were his to pay but which had gone to her, and usually a note about the children. They were fine, she would say. Sometimes there was something from the children themselves, a drawing, a one-page letter, a photograph of Andy playing baseball or of Tricia on a Girl Scout outing. He missed them. He wanted to be with them.

Instead, he was waiting to drive to Burns Junction. Jones lay in the center of the corral with her head raised, looking expectantly at him. By her clock, it was time for their walk. The horses had grown used to the dog. A dead rattlesnake hung over the top rail of the corral down by the water tank. The horses didn't mind that, either. The snakes had come out into the open because of the steady heat. A prisoner had killed that one with a shovel. That was weather . . . the heat, the lack of water, rare clouds, frequent snakes. Although the largeness of the place, its lunatic spaciousness, seemed to grow more insistent in the heat, Lafleur had felt a narrowing of his eye for it, a kind of tunneling like a camera aperture wound inward to draw out darkness.

Up on the flat between the landing strip and the slope the array of trailers and campers arranged in an L had reached its maximum proportions. The full complement of mechanical workers had been called in—electricians, ventilation workers, plumbers. More concrete workers had arrived. There were nearly forty workers in all, but since it was Friday a good number had pulled out for the weekend. He could see some of those who remained passing among the campers and trailers, a couple of heads framed in lit windows, and a small group standing near a fire. They built a fire after work every day out of scrap lumber, and as night fell and the air cooled the size of the group swelled. It was a place for beer and talk.

There was equipment everywhere on the site—backhoes, ditch witches, loaders, transits, gradient sticks and flags, a file of power tools set up under a plywood roof. There were vans and panel trucks, cans of things, stacks of rebars, conduits, pipe, rolls of wire, bundles of fasteners, heaps of gravel and sand, and the spandeck, stacks of it, and trash, cardboard, plastic and steel straps, tangles of discarded wire, empty spools, and things the men had dropped—milk cartons, cans, cigarette and candy wrappers, beer bottles, and Snediker's blue sunflower bags, still there. Snediker was still there, three weeks after Lafleur's ultimatum.

Sabat had said they had the replacements, a team of two, that they were waiting for them to be released from another assignment. He said again that he was in a bind with the head office, that somebody there was making life hard for him, that he understood Lafleur's anger, that he'd been wrong in the first place to doubt Lafleur. He apologized and asked for a few more days. He said that Snediker had been put in a harness, that he'd been given a strict schedule and told to stay clear of the building site. It was true enough, Lafleur had thought, that Snediker had been much less in evidence lately. Sabat had two hundred dollars in cash that he said Snediker had asked him to return to Lafleur. Wishing to have as little to do with Sabat as possible, or—put more exactly—in a state of flight from his own loathing for the man, Lafleur relented once more. Offended by the short stack of twenty-dollar bills Sabat held out, but knowing—by the look in the man's eyes, the mark of greed—that he had no way to make his offense understood, Lafleur took the money.

The buildings were unroofed yet, although virtually all the wall panels were in place. Huge, gray, and tomblike, they cast deep shadows. Monumental, they seemed poised to complete themselves, to acquire their roofs, doors, and barred windows, their guard towers, to encircle themselves with razor wire. The littered site breathed an air of danger, as if an invisible thing were in there slithering through the doorways and windows and down along the trenches from one building to the next, a spirit filled with potency, probing to bind all the parts together, to make it into a prison.

In the corral, Jones sat up abruptly and looked toward Lafleur. The black horse turned toward him. The white shifted sideways. Lafleur straightened his back. He thought he heard whispering. The back of his neck prickled, and he looked down the alley between the barn and bunkhouse. Neither Sabat, Blaylock, nor Iris had appeared. Both horses faced him now. They switched their tails. Behind them the doorway was open to the darkness of the barn. He heard the whispering again, but distinctly. "Hey, man," a voice said.

Lafleur turned and saw El Gallo crouching behind the chain-link fence. The man beckoned. Lafleur approached. "The old lady, she's sick," El Gallo whispered.

Wary, Lafleur stopped a couple of feet away from the fence. El Gallo lifted his dark, deeply furrowed face. "Sick?" Lafleur said.

"Sick." El Gallo glanced back over his shoulder. "She'll die."

"Die? The woman?"

"The woman will die."

"How the hell did you get out here?"

"Saw you. Picked the lock." El Gallo shrugged and smiled as if at an absurdity. He looked back over his shoulder again, then rose. His clothes, the turquoise shirt and black trousers that appeared dashing from a distance, were in fact threadbare. They hung limp as rags on his thick body. His boots were torn open at the toes. Only his metal bore up—the silver belt buckle, the heavy silver bracelet he wore on his left wrist, and the spots of gold that showed inside his mouth when he spoke. "But don't worry, man," he said. "We get out of here, then what? Escape in a cement truck? Where do we go? Drive it down the river?" He motioned at the landscape. It was the gesture of an actor, encompassing the huge space of sand and rock. "Besides, the fence is electric." He spat at the fence and made it sizzle. "These last few days, have you seen her?"

It was true, Lafleur couldn't remember seeing her.

"Somebody has to do something," El Gallo said.

Lafleur looked distrustfully into El Gallo's face, and said, "Where's the guard?"

"The big one?" El Gallo smiled again. "He keeps watch."

"Inside?"

"Sure. Inside. Go in and look."

"What do you do if I go in?"

"When the big one lets you in the front door, I go in the back door."

"Maybe it's a trick."

"Of course it's a trick, my friend. But not on you." El Gallo spread his hands out. "She'll die."

Lafleur paused. "I don't know."

"Hey," the man said. "Take a look. That's all."

"Where are the others?"

"Locked up."

"You picked one lock."

"Sure. But he's got guns. He's crazy. To get out of here we either have to go through this fence or by him. Nobody's going to leave."

"Why me?"

El Gallo smiled. "He fears you."

Lafleur paused for an instant, registering that—what seemed absurd. "No, he doesn't."

"He walks us a half mile around to avoid you."

Lafleur dug at the sand with his boot toe. "Why didn't you tell somebody before?"

"Tell who, man? When? I've been waiting to catch you alone."

Lafleur looked over at the bonfire where the men were gathered, then back at El Gallo. "All right," he said. "In a minute." He moved along the fence, went past the metal building, and turned into the alley. There was still no one in sight down there, only the sides of buildings and the pens, in one pen the gently arched backs of two pigs, and the ranchhouse and the flat that sloped down to the river. To his right, the horses stood in the corral, switching their tails. Jones had disappeared. He slowed, doubting what he was about to do, then swung around to the front of the bunkhouse and went in the center door to the hall and through the doorway to Iris's room, or to what had become to some unclear extent his room. She had her back to him and was leaning toward a small round mirror on the dresser—his mirror.

"I'm coming," she said.

He said, "Will you go down and get Vic? And bring him up to the compound?"

She turned, holding a mascara brush between two fingers and looking past it as if she were sighting with it.

"There's something wrong," he said.

She lowered her hand.

"I may need Vic up there."

"Do you know what you're doing?"

"Hell, no." He smiled.

"Do you have a gun?"

"What?"

Her eyes flashed. "Take a gun."

He hung there, looking back at her, not questioning her, but taking it in. "Okay," he said. "Hurry." He turned back out into the hall and went into Phil's room, into what to some also unclear extent was no longer his own. Phil sat reading, his feet propped on his bed. His eyes lifted and followed Lafleur, who went straight to his dresser, pulled open the top drawer, and took out the hardwood case. He took out his father's old pistol, and screwed in the .410 barrel. He glanced at Phil, who hadn't moved in the least, except his eyes, which now narrowed like a cat's. Lafleur hefted the gun. He thought of a coat he had with side pockets capacious enough to hold the gun and went to the closet, found the coat, and put it on. He slid the Thompson into the side pocket.

"Warm for that coat," Phil said. He hadn't moved.

"We might have trouble," Lafleur said.

"I guess."

"I'm going into the compound," Lafleur said, and he paused, listening. He heard Iris's sneakers squeaking down the hall, then the door thudding as she went out. "Sabat's coming up. Will you keep an eye out?"

215

Phil glanced toward the dresser and Lafleur looked, too. Between the corner of the dresser and the wall leaned the case with the 30.06. They looked back at each other. "Okay," Phil said. Lafleur moved to the door, went out, and walked up to the metal building. The Thompson made his coat sag to one side. He touched the gun through the fabric, checking its position. He saw El Gallo crouched back in the corner next to the building, a hump of darkness. Over at the encampment to Lafleur's left, the group still stood around the fire.

He stopped at the door, inhaled deeply, and knocked. He waited, then knocked again. Footsteps approached the other side of the door and stopped. Lafleur straightened his coat. He heard a voice: "Yeah?"

"Open," Lafleur said. He heard keys, then the lock clicking. The handle turned and the latch snapped. The door swung inward. Snediker's body filled the doorway and his head inclined downward.

"What?"

"I want to see the woman."

"You can't come in here."

"Yes," Lafleur said.

Snediker didn't move.

"Now," Lafleur said.

Snediker's body seemed to swell. He gazed past Lafleur with his milky eyes. Lafleur looked back. There was no one in sight.

"He's coming," Lafleur said. "Sabat's coming."

"He says to let you in?" Snediker's voice came out breathy, as querulous as a child's.

"Yes."

Snediker moved like a large gate, swinging ponderously on its hinges, and Lafleur moved by him, feeling he was passing under something dark and heavy. He entered Snediker's quarters—three chairs, a bed, a dresser, a steel case, cooking equipment stacked on a counter, a table, and in the center of the floor a small, round braided rug. Its neatness struck Lafleur as deranged. There was another door to the left. Snediker had gone to it and stopped, and looked back out the open front door. Lafleur looked. He saw three figures down near the ranchhouse—Iris, Blaylock, and Sabat. "We'll wait for Vic," Snediker said.

"No, we won't," Lafleur said. Snediker gazed at him with his expressionless eyes. "Now," Lafleur said. To his surprise, Snediker fished through his keys and bent obediently to the lock. The door opened. Lafleur went in and found himself in a rank-smelling corridor, the left-hand wall of which quickly gave way to a collapsible floor-to-ceiling grate. It was pulled fast over a large room in which double bunks had been mounted against two facing walls. The men lay on the bunks, some on

216

their backs and others in various postures with elbows and knees akimbo. Faces were turned toward Lafleur and Snediker. The dark faces were highlighted by the small amber wall lights. The men were utterly silent and still. From them emanated the sharp smell of sweat, of clothing worn day after day. Lafleur scanned the room quickly as he passed, his eyes darting from one bunk to the next, and he found El Gallo, a dark hump hunkering in the shadows against the far wall. He was in the same position Lafleur had seen moments before in the corner of the compound. His belt buckle and glossy eyes caught the light. It was as if he hadn't moved at all, as if he'd been transported inside and reconstituted there. Lafleur passed by the end of the grate to a solid wall.

Snediker stopped and turned to hold the keys up to the light. Lafleur found himself flattened against the wall. The man was huge. Instinctively, Lafleur's hand moved to the gun in his pocket. The close quarters reminded him of the man pressing close to him in the cab of the truck. He remembered the smell of the man's breath, of wet wool, and the fist coming at him and his head rattling against the window. Suddenly, he was quivering with rage. Snediker turned and leaned down to the lock. Lafleur moved into the corner, cradling the gun in his fingers. Snediker unlocked the door and pushed it open. Lafleur followed him into a small, dimly lit room. It stank of vomit and excrement. A solitary bed had been pushed against a wall and, looking at it, Lafleur stopped, appalled. An obscure figure lay under a sheet, as still as a plank.

"Air," he said to Snediker, who hovered at the head of the bed. Snediker didn't move. Lafleur pointed at a doorway that he figured opened out to the chain-link compound. "Open it up." Snediker moved, fumbling with the keys again. When he opened the door a cloud of cool air entered the room. Lafleur edged nearer to the bed. He made out the woman's face, the white skin drawn like vellum over the bones, the eyes half-closed like slits. As he neared her, he smelled a distinct acrid odor, a line of foulness drawn through the air. "Light," he said. The light from the amber wall fixtures, even combined with the twilight filtering through the open door, was insufficient for him to see the woman clearly.

Snediker switched on the overhead lights, not one but a bank of them all at once. The woman rolled away and curled her body slowly, pained by the brilliance. Lafleur leaned over her and touched her arm. He felt the bone, the frailty under her sleeve. No one had changed her dress. Her bedclothes were grimy. The pillow case was gray. She rolled her head back and looked at him, her face and hawk nose gaunt, and from between the slitted lids her eyes were dark and luminous like a snake's eyes. Her granulated lips were drawn into a line like a snake's mouth. He touched her forehead, which was dry and hot—feverish. He looked up at Snediker.

Snediker stared back, his eyes hollow, then he revolved his head toward the doorway that led into the corridor, toward the sound of the others, now, coming into the building. Their footfalls clattered in the corridor, and then they entered the room one after another—Sabat, Iris, and Blaylock—and they slowed, forming a file, staring at the woman. To Sabat, Lafleur said, "What is this?" Sabat didn't respond, didn't move, although he had a shocked expression, and next to him Iris's face was wrenched with disgust. Blaylock's large, normally impassive face had expanded with surprise. Lafleur glanced back at the woman, who gazed up at him with her slitted, shiny eyes from under the heavy lids. Lafleur said, "There's no air in this room. No water. Her linen's filthy. What the hell?"

"I didn't know," Sabat said. The foolishness of the statement was manifest.

"She's sick."

"I didn't know," Sabat said. "She was supposed to be cared for."

"By him?" Lafleur gestured with his head at Snediker. "He's as dumb as a box of rocks."

Snediker audibly sucked air through his teeth. His chest swelled and his upper lip curled vaguely—even that, his anger at a direct insult, obscure, generalized. Lafleur fought the urge to put his hand in his pocket, to touch his fingers to the gun. He looked back at Sabat, whose small, hard eyes were moving now, darting from Lafleur to Snediker to the woman, and back again, his lips flickering at the corners. Lafleur thought, He wants a way out. He glanced at Iris, as if asking her help, and he saw her face quickening. Her face spoke to him—*Easy. Be careful.* Next to her was Blaylock in his checkered polyester trousers and red party shirt, stolid, his entire large, overweight body planted on his big feet, and Lafleur felt reassured by his presence, because he was the alien party here, a witness, and had the effect of adding a critical intelligence, even, and thus of balancing the situation, which otherwise might have swallowed up everyone.

To Sabat, Lafleur said, "We have to get this woman to a hospital," and saying that, he wondered, What hospital? Then to Iris he said, "Get Phil," thinking, More ballast, more balance. "Get him to bring his rig around," he said, and to Sabat, as Iris moved to the doorway, he said, "He's got that sleeper." And he wondered, To Burns, or over to Boise? To Snediker he said, "Water. Get some water. And a sponge so we can clean her." He reached out and touched the woman's arm again as he said that, and when Snediker didn't move, he snarled at him, "Get it!"

Snediker went out, and the others waited. An uncomfortable silence swelled in the room. For a moment only the woman's breath could be heard, shallow and dry. Snediker returned with a basin of water and a rag.

The rag would do. Lafleur dipped the rag in the basin, which Snediker held, and leaned over the woman, thinking, Now what? He started with her brow, carefully cleaning it, then cleaning her face down to the neck, stroking her skin gently and wringing out the rag. She looked at him with her luminous eyes from behind the slitted lids, and he thought, She's taking it in, everything. It's the completeness of death she's waiting for, and he straightened up, wondering, Now what? He ran his eyes down along her narrow body under the sheet, then looked over at Sabat and said, "Help me."

Sabat came. Lafleur gingerly picked up the hem of the sheet, holding it between his thumb and middle finger, then drew it down to the woman's waist and passed it to Sabat, who drew it to the foot of the bed. A waft of foul odor rose. The woman's dress was bunched up above her knees, stiff and encrusted with filth. "Jesus," Lafleur whispered, taking a step back. Sabat stepped with him. Lafleur rolled the bed out from the wall, moved around Sabat, behind the bed, and began washing one leg, below the knee, pausing when he saw the welt on the calf, and he froze for an instant, wondering what to do. Then he went on, washed the welt and moved down to the large, calloused foot. He reached across and dipped the rag in the basin, which Snediker still held—the big one there, close, looming, loathsome, and silent. Lafleur wrung the rag and held it out to Sabat, not saying it now, beside himself, speechless, but thinking, *Help me.* Sabat took the rag and looked down at the woman's legs, and Lafleur wondered, When we're done with the legs, then what? His answer walked into the room—Iris, followed by Diane.

Iris had a bundle of clothing and towels. Diane took one look at the woman and at the men standing there, and her face grew fierce. She moved to the bed and took the basin out of Snediker's hands. "Go," she said. "Out." Sabat, Snediker, and Blaylock left. Lafleur hung back and Diane said, "You, too. Out." Lafleur moved to the corridor. El Gallo had come near the barricade. Lafleur slowed and skittered his eyes from bunk to bunk, across the jungle of arms and legs and illuminated faces, then let his gaze rest on El Gallo, who stood near the barricade with his arms crossed. Lafleur stopped and took a deep breath.

"You were right," he said. "It's bad."

El Gallo nodded.

In the distance, Lafleur heard Phil's tractor coming this way along the crest of the slope. "We're taking her out."

"Good," El Gallo said.

"I think she's been beaten."

"Yes," El Gallo said. "Hopefully, that is all."

Lafleur's eyes jerked to El Gallo's heavy face. "Meaning?"

El Gallo shrugged.

219

"Who is she?" Lafleur asked.

"A teacher. A nun. She's a professor."

Lafleur paused. Something from his childhood rose in him, something from the heap of artifacts and taboos, a strong prohibition that bore upon the inviolability, the sanctity, the fearsomeness of nuns. "Why is she here?"

"Political." He tipped his head toward the men. "They're all political. But she most of all. Honduras."

"Ah," Lafleur said. He paused. He could hear Iris and Diane talking softly in the room as they worked. "And you?"

"Not political," El Gallo said. He smiled and his heavy face changed utterly. His white teeth showed, his cheeks lifted, and his eyes twinkled. "I'm a trader. I'm the guide. I was to be paid."

Lafleur smiled back. "I thought you were a lunatic, the way you carry on."

El Gallo chuckled. "I have a reputation, which has been damaged by this. I do that to keep their spirits up."

Lafleur looked down the corridor into Snediker's room. All he saw was a bare white wall. "The woman's old," he said to El Gallo. "Surely she didn't walk across the border."

"Surely not," El Gallo said. "These did." He gestured with his head toward the men again. "She was taken out."

"Taken?"

"Taken out. Taken out of circulation. Do you understand?"

"Extradited?"

"Extradition is a legal proceeding," El Gallo said.

"You mean just taken?"

"Taken. They flew her here, she says. Somebody must think she's dangerous," El Gallo said, chuckling again.

Lafleur heard Phil's tractor pull up in front of the building, then he heard Iris calling his name. He saw Sabat move by the doorway in Snediker's room, passing in and out of sight. "Why?" he said. "Why taken?"

El Gallo held his hands out, palms up. "Who knows?"

"Taken by whom?"

El Gallo repeated his gesture with his hands, and said, "I don't ask."

"Taken by the government?"

El Gallo shrugged. "So it would seem, but who knows?"

Lafleur gazed at El Gallo for an instant, then turned and moved back to the woman's room. Iris and Diane had stripped the bed. The filthy bedclothes lay in a heap on the floor. The woman lay on the bare mattress, wearing a long white flannel nightgown, which Lafleur recognized as Iris's. The woman's large, gnarled feet stuck out the bottom and her hands lay still on her abdomen. Her eyes were still slitted, her mouth drawn in a straight line. She looked desperately frail. She was shivering. "She needs a blanket," Iris said.

Lafleur bent and scooped the woman up. "Phil'll have one." The woman felt light as straw, light as a bird. He cradled her head in the crook of his arm. Her lightness had the quality of a fiberless, barely strung-together musculature that Lafleur remembered his father having toward the end. He carried her out, going carefully through the doorway. He carried her past El Gallo and into Snediker's room, where the others waited. They watched as he went by. Diane and Iris followed him. He carried the woman outside. Phil's Kenworth semi-tractor was there, vibrating in the twilight. He took one step up the side, balancing himself, and Phil reached down from the seat. Gently, they maneuvered the woman up and into the sleeper. Lafleur clambered up onto the seat. Phil bent into the sleeper and straightened the woman. The tractor hummed. Iris and Diane stood together on the ground. Phil pulled back. He and Lafleur were side by side on their knees, looking in at the woman. She was shivering.

"Blanket?" Lafleur said.

Phil bent deeply into the sleeper, found a blanket, and spread it over the woman, then settled back again beside Lafleur. "Where?" he said.

Lafleur twisted sideways and looked down at Diane. "Where?"

"Burns is fastest. There's a clinic," she said.

"Burns," he said to Phil. "Do you want me to come?"

"I'll go," Diane said from beneath them.

"Yeah," Phil said to Lafleur. "Diane knows Burns. You call ahead. And get Sabat to give them an insurance number or whatever the fuck they use for something like this."

Lafleur nodded, not moving. Neither of them moved for a moment. They looked in at the woman. "Jesus," Phil whispered.

"Right," Lafleur said.

"I'll call back as soon as I get her there," Phil said.

"Right."

"It's a two-hour drive."

"Right." Now Lafleur felt like a child, kneeling beside Phil as if at an altar. They gazed into the snug sleeping compartment. The woman's torso rose and fell ever so lightly with her breath. Her eyes were still hooded. The dark, glossy slits glistened underneath the white skin.

The four of them—Sabat, Blaylock, Iris, and Lafleur—went to Burns Junction, anyway. They rode crammed into the silver Mercedes-Benz. Sabat had insisted that they go.

Lafleur had said they must be back within two hours to receive Phil's call. Sabat had said it was only a half-hour drive. He called the clinic on his own. Snediker sat in his chair and stared disconsolately between his knees at the floor. His massive hands hung limp over his knees. Lafleur went in and washed his hands in Snediker's sink, then waited with Blaylock and Iris at the outside doorway. They listened as Sabat left an insurance number with the receptionist, and identified the woman on her way as his ward. He turned, looked straight at Lafleur, and told the receptionist he would take responsibility for the woman's care. Lafleur looked at Iris. Her face spoke to him—*Careful.*

Sabat gave the hospital his name. He gave the names of the people bringing the woman. When he hung up he moved to Snediker and said, "I want the keys." Snediker cringed and unclasped his keys from his belt. Sabat took them and went over and locked the door to the corridor, then moved stiffly to the outside door. The four of them went out. Snediker looked after them forlornly. Sabat locked that door and pocketed the keys. "He's not going anywhere," Sabat said coldly to no one in particular. His lip twitched. They walked to the car, got in, and pulled away from the house. They drove up the hill, passing above the landing strip and settlement of campers and trailers. The bonfire there silhouetted the group of figures around it and sent a spray of sparks straight up into the darkening air.

Sabat drove along the road to Rome, weaving among the sandstone formations. Dark lumps, the bodies of jackrabbits, littered the roadside. They passed the alfalfa farms. No one was talking. Blaylock sat in front with Sabat, his head tipping and nodding ponderously with the motion of the car. They passed a sprinkler system in a field—rainbirds attached to an axle made out of linked four-inch pipe, the whole long enough to span the field and mounted on large spoked wheels. The motion of the wheels, doubtless, was regulated to shed the amount of water the field needed, and the apertures of the rainbirds adjusted for that, and according to how much water the farmer was licensed to draw from the river. That was science, or science and government, Lafleur thought, sensing a kind of madness in himself, a compulsive need to name things, to reestablish the ordinary world. The field was deep green against the beige backdrop of hills and sandstone. The sprinklers made countless rainbows. The river itself flashed in and out of sight as they progressed. The sun kissed the horizon. They reached Rome and turned onto the highway. Sabat worked the car up through the gears to fifth and drove along at seventy-five. Lafleur had tipped his head to see the speedometer. He wondered if they would come up behind Phil's tractor, but he guessed not. Phil might be doing eighty-five.

They didn't talk. Burns Junction would be just that, as Lafleur recalled: a junction in highways 95 and 78, thirteen miles up the road from Rome.

Highway 95 led south to McDermitt; 78 led northwest to Burns and the hospital. One might choose to go south into Nevada from there, or northwesterly toward Portland and the sea. When he had passed through Burns Junction—just three times, once coming, and twice coming and going from the funeral—he had hardly noticed the place, but now it assumed grandiose dimensions in his imagination. If one were navigating oneself, it might be a turning point at which one could throw one's life one way or another. One might choose to go toward the coast, rain, green, and the volcano, or to escape south toward the casinos and deserts . . . Mojave, Arizona, Mexico. Everything could be different.

He smelled Iris's shampoo. Sabat had lit a cigar and rolled down his window several inches. The wind blew through Lafleur's hair. The odor of the cigar circled the car. It had a strong, thick, acrid smell while Iris's shampoo penetrated like a razor. The top of Blaylock's head lolled backward, and just to the side of the headrest the bottom of a Scotch bottle glimmered in the slanted light. The bottle vanished. Blaylock bent out of sight. He was setting the bottle between his feet on the floor. They were about halfway to Burns Junction. Blaylock's head came up again. The road dipped and they crossed Crooked Creek. Lafleur figured that Phil was past the junction by now, heading for Burns. He thought of Phil and Diane sitting up high in the tractor. He thought of the woman in the sleeper, her chest rising and falling with her feeble breath, her ears filled with the soft grumble of the engine, and her body in the darkness rocking gently with the road. The sun was setting. The desert shone. Lafleur ran a fingertip down a pleat in the red leather upholstery on the back of Blaylock's seat. Blaylock belched and for a moment the scent of whiskey mixed in with the cigar smoke and shampoo. Lafleur glanced at Iris and smiled. Sabat spoke: "Snediker's out of here."

No one replied. The car rolled on. Iris touched Lafleur's knee. In front of Lafleur, Blaylock's head was utterly still. Lafleur imagined him staring fixedly out the windshield. Sabat's eyes were reflected in the rearview mirror, looking back. Lafleur wondered what the original purpose of this venture to Burns Junction had been. He thought about Snediker, locked up in his room. Sabat spoke again in a tight voice: "He's nothing. He's just a loose piece gone awry, but the hell with the front office. He's gone."

Iris's hand tightened, then relaxed. Lafleur looked at the side of Sabat's face—the jaw and cheek rigid with tension. Burns Junction came into view ahead of them—a pair of fuel pumps, a long shed, and a building that had been a house, once, but which now had a blinking red neon sign in its window that said CAFÉ. Behind the café was a cluster of low stucco buildings that passed as a motel. Sabat slowed, geared down, and pulled into the far side of the lot. Turning, he passed a sign for the McDermitt traffic that said LAST GAS IN OREGON. He parked the car with the nose pointing toward the road, shut off the engine, pushed his door open, and got out. No one else moved. "It's interesting work, the construction business," Sabat said over the roof of the car. "You never know what'll happen next."

No one responded. Blaylock's head listed to one side, then righted itself. Lafleur got lost in his head, thinking about how this had nothing to do with construction, and then about how he liked the monotony of construction—the monotony of labor for its detail and for the detachment it gave, the monotony of digging holes, of hammering nails, the monotony of working with the same people every day, the monotony of a cup of coffee every morning. He felt dazed. Still, no one inside the car had moved to get out. Sabat was leaning against the roof. His narrow belt crimped his soft belly.

Lafleur looked at the work shed that stood just east of the café. It was dusk now and there was a pool of light inside the shed and another diffuse pool of light outside the open double doors. A man stood inside under the light at a work bench, half turned toward them. He moved outward into the darkness under the cave, between the two pools of light, and he hesitated there, then came out into the second pool, and stopped just beyond it in the near darkness, a slender, stooped figure. Sabat had parked in an indeterminate position between the café and the pumps. The man was checking to see whether or not they wanted gas. Sabat stepped back from the car. Iris pushed his seat forward and got out, and Lafleur followed, wedging himself loose from the back seat and coming out standing beside Sabat. He felt the weight of the gun in his coat pocket. He removed the coat, folded it around the gun, and set it on the back seat, then followed the others toward the café. He eyed the man, whose stooped posture gave him a furtive appearance.

"That's Jim," Sabat said softly when Lafleur caught up with the others. Sabat opened the café door and held it open. They went inside a long room—what perhaps had once been the living room, kitchen, and bedroom of the old house. Lafleur's eyes went immediately to the metal expansion struts at either end of the counter, which supported the roof where a wall had once been. The counter divided the space and both sides were crowded with things. On this, the public side, the four of them picked their way carefully toward the counter, sidestepping snack racks and little tables laden with small articles. Display cases and shelves of canned and packaged foods lined the side walls, and above them hung banks of oil-painted seascapes. The place had the air of dense, confused familiarity, as if a huge tool drawer had been left open.

Over on the business side of the counter a woman with a florid face awaited them. She waggled her finger at Sabat, and said, "We were about to turn off the burners."

"We like to surprise you," Sabat said. The lilting tone of his voice made Lafleur's head turn. Sabat seemed suddenly to have become himself again. He had the same old mischievous grin, just slightly skewed by the line of tension on the side of his mouth.

The woman leaned against the counter, flattening the flesh on her forearms. "Ever since you and your bunch arrived we've been in a permanent state of surprise." She raised her eyebrows, creating a labyrinth of contrarily arranged wrinkles on her broad forehead. "Chili?"

"We'd hurt your feelings if we didn't," Sabat said. He eased onto a stool and grinned at her.

The woman pulled back and beamed, tucking her chin against her chest, then suddenly she wheeled and called back into the recesses of the room, "Four chilis!"

There was a grunt from behind a pair of large upright coolers. Blaylock sat next to Sabat, gaining purchase on the stool with one buttock, then dragging himself to the center. He swayed and gripped the edge of the counter for support. He was drunk. Iris sat next to him. When Lafleur sat next to her, he saw a second woman seated behind the far end of the counter beneath a large oil-painted seascape. She'd been doing needlework. Like the other woman, this one appeared to be in her sixties, but she was trim-looking and had strong features and smooth skin and pleasant gray eyes, with which she looked up at them. Her shining dark hair was rolled into a bun.

The fat woman said, "Two new ones, huh?" She glanced congenially down the row from Sabat to Lafleur.

"Hank," Lafleur said.

"Sally." She held out her hand, which Lafleur took. It was large and soft.

Sabat introduced Sally to Blaylock, and Blaylock acknowledged her by swaying precipitously toward the counter. He caught himself and pushed back. His eyes were glazed and his face was pallid. "And Ruth," Sabat said, gesturing at the seated woman, who smiled at them, reserved, self-contained. "Frank's back in the kitchen," Sabat said.

Sally had reached under the counter and come up with glasses, cups, and silverware. She puffed each time she straightened. The other woman, Ruth, put down her needlework and came over to pour coffee into the cups. Sally filled the glasses with water, then moved back and leaned against a cooler. Her forehead was beaded with perspiration. Ruth vanished behind the coolers. Lafleur sipped his coffee and looked around. At his end of the counter were racks of potato-chip bags, peanut bags, candy bars, key chains, curios, and small toys—items for the traveler. Behind the racks and on the inside of the counter, a second doorway led outside in the direction of the work shed. The wooden door was chocked open, and night air wafted through the screen door into the room. Lafleur saw the corner of a stainless-steel counter behind one of the coolers, and he heard someone back there scraping at the griddle—Frank. He glanced back over his left shoulder at a small table with stacks of used Harlequin Romances and Louis L'Amour Westerns, and a sign that said 50 CENTS EACH. Next to the table was a glass case of cut and polished rocks. He looked up over Blaylock's head at the oil paintings—seascapes with price tags stuck to the corners. There was also a line of framed needlework above the far end of the counter—floral patterns with odd slogans, such as TAKE NOTHING FOR GRANTED and LADIES LOVE OUTLAWS.

Ruth did the needlework, it appeared. Somebody painted. It struck him that these paintings had been done by the same hand as the ones back at the ranch, by the son-in-law of the man that had owned the place— Spencer McHugh. If so, one of these women was the daughter. The paintings featured rock, surf, horizon, setting sun, the dark outlines of ships, and usually something violent—a hoary swirl of water, menacing rock, or a skeletal boat, sundered masts, and split prows. One had an arm and hand extended to the air from within the curl of a wave. Somebody collected rocks, too, and perhaps cut and polished them, and somebody read the books, a pair of them did, maybe, man and wife lying side by side at night, one reading the romances and the other countering with Louis L'Amour—suppressed eroticism on one side of the bed and pistol fantasies on the other. Things were ornate in the café. The lives of the proprietors, their ages, shown by what had been accumulated and by workmanship veering toward art, slipped through the jobbers' allotments of goods brought out in trucks from Boise and Burns.

He was naming things again, trying to discern where he was. He felt an almost manic need to do that. He was more shaken by the woman, the nun, than he'd realized. Sally had been watching him as he looked around, and he nodded and smiled faintly at her. To Iris he said, "Who paints?"

"Jim."

Lafleur glanced through the screen door out into the darkness. "They're for sale," Sally said. "He buys," she said, beaming at Sabat. Everything was for sale, Lafleur thought—food, rooms, gas, curios, sundries, and artifacts found and homemade. That was trade. He picked up his spoon and looked at the inscription. It said U.S. NAVY. "Abe spoke of you," Sally said.

Lafleur looked up. "Abe Kasanian?"

Sally nodded, then moved to open the cooler when Ruth came out with four plates of bread. Sally took out a butter plate, shutting the cooler with her hip. She skidded the butter plate down the counter. It stopped in front of Blaylock. She was a banger and a clatterer. Ruth, who handled things gently, went back behind the coolers, then returned with four bowls of chili, which she set on the counter. Sally set little packets of crackers next to the bowls. They had a routine. The griddle scraping resumed in the kitchen. Ruth returned to her chair and picked up her needlework.

Sally leaned against the cooler and said, "Abe doesn't let on much, but he didn't enjoy blowing up the old place."

"I guess not," Lafleur said.

"Did you know he was a nephew of the former owner?" she said. "And the great-grandson of the McHugh that homesteaded the place. His folks lived down in Steer Canyon. But he put enough time in up there. It was him more than Art or Stan that the old man put to work all along."

Ruth looked up from her needlework. "He was willing."

"True enough," Sally said. She was still looking at Lafleur, but not talking to him, exactly. It was a peculiar mode of address. "If anybody was willing, Spencer McHugh would find a way to use him."

"But willing on his own, just the same," Ruth said.

The women paused. Some old contention was rearing between them, whose release Lafleur had precipitated, because Kasanian had spoken of him. Lafleur felt a growing glimmering of understanding. Ruth was Spencer McHugh's daughter. The scraping from behind the coolers had stopped. Lafleur sensed listening back there. He spooned chili into his mouth and closed his teeth on it. The chili was fine.

"Now," Sally said, "as sure as God is good we'll have an escapee on our hands. You hear the like. That's what the old ranch came to. You put such people in there and they'll get out, you bet." She put her hands on her hips and addressed Lafleur directly once again. "Abe didn't like it."

"He cared about the place," Ruth said. "I didn't. Not that way. Not to work it."

They fell silent. This contention—Lafleur thought—was a ritual creature, one that heaved and rolled according to rules made by the ladies over the years. He wanted to ask Ruth if she was the daughter, to be sure of that, and to ask if she was the one who wanted the rope cut down, the one with the willing but inept husband, Jim Basto. Polite, he held his silence. Blaylock wiped his mouth with a blue handkerchief. Sabat leaned forward, listening, a smile fixed on his face. His teeth showed. Lafleur thought of the old woman in Phil's sleeper—one who was lucky to get out. He thought of her rocking, rocking gently with the motion of the tractor and staring straight at death with her serpent's eyes. From behind the coolers a dishwasher came on. The building vibrated. Lafleur felt the counter vibrating and there was a soft booming somewhere, something structural set sympathetically in motion. A man appeared from behind the coolers—Frank. Tall and rawboned, he had a slight paunch that had gathered stains and made a ring of dirty color on his apron. He moved next to Sally and collected her under his arm. She became a soft, smiling, worried ball there against his ribs.

"Hello, Frank," Sabat said.

The man nodded, then said, "Iris." He nodded at Lafleur, then back at Blaylock. With his appearance the atmosphere in the café had shifted. He opened his mouth and ran his tongue along his upper teeth, then said, "Got that prison in yet?"

"It's coming," Sabat said, glancing down at Lafleur. "The buildings are coming up."

Frank licked his teeth again and blinked slowly. Ruth passed her needle in and out of her cloth and glanced up and down from her work to the people with her pleasant gray eyes. She was stitching a large, red rose freehand, which Lafleur knew was far from a mean feat. Sally moved away from Frank, then out from behind the counter and to the front door, where she turned the OPEN sign around. She snapped shut the Venetian blinds over the windows on either side. The blinking neon light kept blinking, flashing against the blinds and radiating dimly across the room.

"It must be time to go," Sabat said.

Frank smiled, blinked, and licked his teeth. His mannerisms gave him an air of great deliberation, like a judge. "Are you expecting more workers?"

"We're at full strength. They'll be in and out. You haven't seen them?"

"A couple trucks stopped today," Frank said.

"You may have to stay open later than nine."

Frank blinked. "Probably should have got a beer license."

"It's not too late."

"Probably should remodel the motel," Frank said. "I guess there'll be traffic from here on out. Visitors and such."

It was a probe of a sort, a vague request for information to which Sabat did not respond directly. Ruth was attending the conversation closely. Her hands had stopped. Her needle was poised, poking upward through the cloth. Sally had come back to nestle next to Frank. In their expressions Lafleur saw twins poised to do battle, a pair in each face: the desire for profit, to get those trucks to stop more often, to cash in somehow, and at the same time resentment against the intruders and what they had brought—a prison. That was trade. Sabat spoke: "Hank here is the construction supervisor and Ned's his partner from up in Portland."

Frank's eyes moved to Blaylock, then to Lafleur, and he nodded again.

Ruth looked at Lafleur and said, "Abe spoke well of you." That was all. There was an odd moment in which the eyes were upon him, exerting a pressure to get him to speak, to say something, but he said nothing. He was thinking of the woman again—rocking, rocking gently, her eyes glittering as the Kenworth rolled toward Burns. The eyes in the room moved away from him. He turned and saw what they saw, a figure at the screen door just on the other side of the counter. It was Jim, right there, close. He stood touching the screen with the front of his body, like an insect drawn to light. The figure was immobile, the face dark, the hollows of eyes, cheeks, and mouth darker yet—a watcher, a listener. Everybody watched. Lafleur watched. The figure watched back. Lafleur glanced at Ruth and saw that her expression had grown anxious.

There was an encirclement here drawn around an unnamed chaos. At first glance an ordinary enough place, if ornate, and tangled in a way Lafleur would have found pleasing, the café had become quite strange. Frank sighed heavily. "We probably should expand the dining area."

"Sure," Sabat said.

"Guns," Sally said. "They'll have guns. You get liquor and they'll come after it. Their friends who come to visit will have guns."

"We got guns," Frank said.

"Guns," Sally said.

Lafleur thought of his gun, tucked in the pocket of his coat on the back seat of Sabat's Mercedes-Benz.

"Guns," Sally said. "We don't have guns for that reason. Do you see?" she said to Sabat. "This was God's country."

Frank murmured and gave her a squeeze. There was a silence, then Sabat spoke to Ruth. "I'm still interested in that painting."

"He has it in the shed," she said, her tone almost protective, motherly. "I'm sure he'd be pleased to let you see it."

The figure in the side doorway was utterly still, poised there like a very large moth with its wings folded down. Iris touched Lafleur's shoulder and he jerked. They were leaving. Sabat paid the bill. They said their goodbyes and went out the front door into the night, Lafleur and Iris first, then Blaylock. Sabat walked around the side to find Jim. To Iris, Lafleur said, "Did that get weird or is it just me?"

"It can't possibly be as weird as we are," she said.

They moved to the car. Blaylock came behind them, aspirating heavily with each step. Lafleur looked back at the shed and saw Sabat and the slender figure standing next to each other inside, looking up at a wall. "They don't like Vic," Iris said, "or anything about the project. They're upset, obviously. But Vic pays his way."

"Ruth and Jim are married?"

Iris nodded. "They owned the ranch. She inherited it and sold it."

"She's Abe's cousin."

Iris nodded again. "Jim's shy. Incredibly shy."

"His paintings aren't bad."

"God, no. Vic took a couple down to Reno and a gallery snapped them up. Vic's robbing him blind."

Lafleur grunted.

"It's sad."

"That he's stuck here?"

"That he's being ripped off."

"Maybe he doesn't see it that way."

"He will."

He put his fingertips into the rain channel above the door of the Mercedes and gazed over the roof at the desert. It looked like a line of phosphorescent white in the moonlight. Its slitlike appearance accentuated its endlessness. It could be mistaken for the sea. He narrowed his eyes and looked, catching what Zeta might have called Jim's fundamental chemistry—the sea, the eerie transliteration of it into seascapes here in the desert. It wouldn't have taken much to conjure up a ship out there.

"Maybe being lonely out here puts him in touch," Iris said. "He paints, God he paints. There's ten paintings in the café that weren't up a month ago. Can you imagine?"

Again Lafleur grunted, then he said, "Why the hell are we here?"

"Good question."

"So Vic could buy that painting?"

"Maybe. Things took a turn back at the project, so it's hard to say. Maybe he wanted us to see him in action with something he could control."

Behind them, Blaylock farted. Lafleur grinned and looked down. Blaylock's fundamental chemistry drifted by them.

"Failing all else, I guess he'll go ahead and screw Jim," Iris said.

"I get the feeling you know something I don't."

"Yes," she said. "Him." She looked back over her shoulder at Sabat, who was approaching them now, coming quickly from the shed. He'd bought the painting, he said. But it was big. He would have to come back and pick it up later. He grinned at them, and his eyes glittered feverishly.

The four of them got into the car and drove home, down the highway to Rome and off onto the gravel road. Blaylock took a pull from his Scotch bottle. Lafleur held his coat on his lap, feeling the weight of the gun. The car wound through the sandstone formations, then came out into the open. A herd of mule deer appeared in front of the car and ran alongside it, weaving back and forth, down into the ditches and along the edges of the fields and back onto the road, weaving, jumping the fences and negotiating the banks of the ditches with magical control, but locked into the thrall of the car's headlamps. They were like moths, but graceful and complex in their movement. They were like schooling fish, like birds landing in a tree, that complex, that organized. Sabat switched off the headlamps and for a moment the car moved in darkness, a silver glove probing the night, filled with amazed bodies. In the distance the lights of the encampment twinkled. The bonfire threw a narrow stream of sparks into the air. The tops of the pale, roofless buildings floated above the crest of the slope. When Sabat switched the lights back on the deer had vanished.

"Poof," Sabat said.

"Vic didn't show you this thing?" Lafleur asked, touching the top of the computer screen. He and Blaylock had been left in the study. He thought Blaylock had asked about the computer.

Blaylock's words had come out slurred, but Lafleur thought he'd said, "Do you use it?" Blaylock sat in the easy chair, staring fixedly at the computer screen. Lafleur switched the computer on, punched out the code for the index, then called out the file for mechanical plans. The file came up, the words made out of light. Blaylock sat with one hand on the arm of his chair, holding a glass of Scotch. His other hand hung toward the floor like a slab of meat. His eyes were hooded. Whether he had asked about the computer or not, Lafleur hoped that showing it to him would rouse him. Lafleur bent over the keyboard and scrolled through, not thinking about what he was looking for until he came to it, the mechanical layout for the subterranean level of the Industries Building, the pit. He straightened up and allowed his eyes to roam around the screen, following the circuitry.

A few moments ago Phil had phoned. Sabat had been there then, and he took the call. Sabat's perfunctory responses—yes, no, good—told nothing, but when he hung up he said that Phil and Diane were at the clinic, that the woman would be all right, they thought, that she was dehydrated, that they were feeding her intravenously, that she should stay there a few days. Then he left, saying he was going to make another call on the kitchen phone. Now Lafleur could hear him talking in the kitchen. Iris had gone up to the bunkhouse after they'd returned. He heard Sabat's voice going on at length, stopping, then going on again, but he couldn't make out the words.

He swiveled the screen so that Blaylock could see it. "That's the bird's-eye view of the basement in the Industries Building," he said. He touched the advance button. "North Walls." He ran it through the cross-sections to the closeups. "Individual walls, parts of walls, cutouts," he said, leaning toward the screen. In the time he'd spent at the computer over the last week, he had kept returning to this file, as if to a scab. He continued to be amazed by the amount of wiring the mechanical plan showed. He was looking at a door detail now. The door was wired, keyed to an electronic lock, and had double sets of conduits, one running to the exterior power source and one to a backup system. There appeared to be a coded manual override. The door opened to one of twelve cages in the basement and the cages were wired, too. The entire cell block, it seemed, was electrified. He glanced at Blaylock, who hadn't moved, then touched the button. "You can pop it back to the grid." He touched the button again. "Call up overlays. You can overlay plumbing, conduit work, the switches, the interior furring, or strip it all the way back to the empty hole. It'll trace feed lines." He paused, thinking, But it still won't tell you what the fuck it's for. He looked at Blaylock, who was almost stuporous. Lafleur stepped back and said, "They can draft with these things, and program them to set up the mechanical work, change a system, check structures, gauge compaction. You can run system checks against the codes. It's fast. It's going to change everything."

"I don't give a shit," Blaylock said.

Lafleur thought, He speaks. He switched off the computer and poured himself a glass of Scotch. He sat down between Sabat's desk and the model of the project, across from Blaylock. "I couldn't make this setup work until a couple weeks ago. Mostly, I'm still out there at the pulpit shuffling blueprints," he said, and he thought, Why am I telling him this?

"If they trusted you, they'd of trained you," Blaylock said.

Lafleur gazed into the man's stained eyes. "Maybe so."

"I said you choose it," Blaylock said.

"Ah," Lafleur said. He paused, then said, "I thought you asked if I used it. I thought you wanted to see the computer work."

"I don't give a shit about computers." Blaylock's words were barely intelligible. He didn't move. Only his mouth moved and his belly, rising and falling slowly. "We had machines when I was young. Things to change the world. Right now, I don't give a shit. The world doesn't change. It's always been a hellhole. I said you choose it. I mean your life. A lot of what happens you got no choice about. A little bit you do. If you're lucky enough to get a good start, then you got just enough left to choose yourself and fuck your ownself up. That's what I mean," Blaylock said, and then he laughed gutturally. His knees drew inward, then went out again.

"I see," Lafleur said, humoring him.

"For example, I choose to drink this crap," Blaylock said. He raised his arm and took a gulp out of the glass, then lowered his arm. His hand lurched, but he didn't spill the Scotch, not a drop. His hand lay there again, mottled, massive, and scarred, gently cradling the glass. "I could quit. But I choose to drink the crap."

Lafleur took a sip of his drink and looked away. Above the model of the project hung one of Jim's paintings. It showed a ship wrecked on the shore, pummeled down to its whitened timbers, which protruded like ribs. The surf crashed over the skeleton. In the background a monkey clung to the trunk of a palm tree and gazed back at the viewer with wide, astonished eyes. The painting was violent and ecstatic. Lafleur heard Sabat's voice coming in shorter bursts now from the kitchen. It was still just sounds he heard, not words, the voice punctuating the silence. Sabat was arguing, defending himself. To Blaylock, Lafleur said, "Why should they trust me now?"

"Who the fuck says they do?"

"You've got me there." He looked at the computer, then back at Blaylock. Bad as Blaylock looked, there was force eddying in the man, and once again Lafleur felt as though he were gazing at two different people in one body: the one, Blaylock with his arms out and knees apart, obscene, aggressive, and the other one, Blaylock crouched over some teeming center, huddled around himself as if around a hurt, drugged and possessed by himself. "I talked to Louis," Blaylock said. "Should we go ahead with it?"

"With what? Christ, Ned."

"Deal. Trade the shares."

Lafleur smiled. "I'd about decided you came out for a vacation."

"Not on your life," Blaylock said. He chuckled, then closed his eyes and left them so for a moment. When he opened them they appeared clearer. He straightened himself in the chair. It was as if he had consulted with himself and found himself able to proceed. "You've got International Data shares coming. I heard you didn't want them."

"That's right."

"You and Jewel have also got some shares in my concrete company, by the way."

"I've been busy," Lafleur said. "I don't know about that. I don't even know what my share of the excavation company's worth."

"Right," Blaylock said.

"Do you know what the company's worth?"

"It depends. We can trade straight across."

Lafleur looked away, then back at Blaylock. In a world where everything was as precisely quantified as possible—trucks, tractors, spare parts, wages, taxes, shelf space—Blaylock was talking as if they were swapping jack-knives on the courthouse steps. "Straight across what, Ned?"

"I don't want the responsibility. Maybe you do. Across that. Across my not wanting something and your wanting it, for Christ's sake."

Lafleur smiled and took a sip of his drink.

"Across your father's fucking dead body," Blaylock said.

Lafleur's eyes cut to Blaylock. "You're drunk, Ned."

"Right."

"You're in no condition to talk about this."

"Bullshit," Blaylock said. "I'm always drunk. Even when I'm not drunk, I'm drunk. Talk to me."

"We have to get a valuation."

Blaylock shifted his rump in the chair, then leaned toward one side and nearly fell across the arm. He caught himself with his right hand and hung there for a moment. Lafleur thought the man was about to vomit on the carpet, but then he lurched back and settled into the cushions. His chin sank to his chest and he closed his eyes again. Remarkably, he had again managed not to spill a drop of his Scotch. He lifted his head and belched. His body jerked. He held the air in his cheeks, then let the air out and opened his eyes. "Bullshit," Blaylock said. "The only thing that matters is what it's worth to you to have it and what it's worth to me to get rid of it. There's your damn valuation. Everything else is window dressing."

Lafleur took another sip of his whiskey.

"Christ," Blaylock said, shifting in his chair again and chortling. "Those shares of yours aren't worth anywhere near what they might be worth later, anyway."

"Are you telling me you're going to give me a break on them?"

"Hell, no. I'll give you what they're worth to me. That's the measure."

"You want them for speculation?"

"Speculation! No, for the cash income. I'm getting old, son. I'm damn near as old as Gus was and look at him. I'm sick and tired of sticking my head inside engine compartments. Besides," he said, "I already own a piece of International Data. I want your shares to add to my ante."

"I'd heard that," Lafleur said. "I'm working for you twice over."

"We're working for me."

"You've got the excavation company working for you."

"Who the hell's it supposed to work for?"

"Twice. You've got it working for you twice. Or three times for all I know. You've got the clone, too."

Blaylock widened his eyes and let his jowls sag. "What the hell? Talk English."

"The copy of the excavation company."

Blaylock laughed. "A paper company. I torched it. All it took was a match and a wastebasket."

"But it had assets."

"Sure. I siphoned them off."

"Into what?"

"This and that."

Lafleur snorted.

Blaylock smiled. Crooked and out of control, it was nevertheless a smile of genuine pleasure.

"How much of International Data do you own?"

Blaylock blew air like a horse. Lafleur smelled the whiskey. "One or two percent of a company like International Data is a hell of a lot of money, son."

"All right," Lafleur said. "But does it occur to you that it might look funny, whatever you've got?"

"Who the shit cares about funny?"

"The woman in Burns cares. The men up there crammed into that room like sardines care. The police are probably going to care. This is a strange damn operation, Ned."

"That's different. That's mistreatment. That's management."

"You've invested in it."

"Money. That's all. And part of it's yours."

"What?"

"It's a company investment and you've got your share, whatever the fuck your share of the partnership is. Plus the shares I told them to write in for you as part of your commission. That's what we're talking about. Get it?"

"I don't want those. I don't want any of that. I don't like this damn project."

"You don't like the management, but that's all right. The last thing you want to do is start liking management. You just got to keep on disliking management. That way you can keep your nose clean like mine," he said and he laughed at the ludicrousness of his own statement. His face turned a deeper shade of purple as his laughter rumbled in the room. His body shook, then he began coughing. He bent double and stayed there for a moment, gathering himself, then straightened up. He lifted his drink. His hand shook. He lurched the glass to his mouth. He gulped at it and held the whiskey in his mouth, swishing it around. When he swallowed his body jerked. His head turned and sank as his hand descended to the arm of the chair. He was watching to make sure his whiskey got there safely. He rolled his eyes up and looked at Lafleur from under his brow. "I had no idea these people would fuck up like this."

"Like with the woman?"

"Like the woman," Blaylock said. "Or all of them, the company bringing prisoners out here before the place is secure, or licensed for Christ's sake, and leaving them in the hands of that clown. Like sending him after you in Portland."

"Like what?" Lafleur said. He shifted to face Blaylock directly.

"Right," Blaylock said. "But Vic did that, sent Snediker to Portland. They got to keep a tighter rein on him. He's trying to weasel out from under it. But you got to figure, who else would do something like that except him?"

Lafleur uncrossed his legs, then crossed them again. He gazed past Blaylock at the doorway to the hall, amazed by what Blaylock had said and wondering how what Blaylock accepted as obvious could have been so hard for him—Lafleur—to see. He felt like an idiot. "Why?" he said.

Blaylock sucked on his lips and raised his eyebrows, then shrugged. "To scare you?"

Lafleur thought, Yes, I was afraid. No matter how circumspect I tried to be, I was afraid. He thought of his reaction in the hall of the metal building, of his dreams, of the beating itself. He remembered the metallic taste of his fear, and considered himself an idiot for not having understood the power fear could have over him. He felt the idiot within him, scampering around and laughing, and he found himself left with the same question, ringing with a different sound, but coming out, finally, exactly as it had for weeks. "Why?" he said.

"Hell, I don't know," Blaylock said. "Maybe he just likes his people scared."

Now Lafleur thought it, not saying it: Why?

"You've got balls, son," Blaylock said. "The owners were scared to death that you'd have the police in here. If it makes you feel any better, they're grateful to you for keeping your hat on so far."

"It doesn't."

"Right," Blaylock said, chuckling.

"Why didn't they just fire him? Or turn him in themselves?"

"They have fired him, but Vic drags ass on it. They're not exactly lily-white themselves and he's got his leverage on them. Either that or they're just not paying attention."

Lafleur inhaled deeply, then exhaled, and paused, looking at the doorway, thinking, Of course. He hadn't heard Sabat talking on the telephone for several minutes. There was a dead silence from the rest of the house, as if no one were there. He turned back to Blaylock.

"Look," Blaylock said. "So far as I was concerned, this was just a big fucking contract to go after. We got it. We've damn near got the sucker built. Whatever goes sour with their operation is no skin off your butt."

"That's easy for you to say," Lafleur said. "I've been dealing with this all summer. You've been sitting back and waiting, figuring you'd make a killing on the shares you dealt to me, which I don't want and never did."

"Try," Blaylock said. "Try to make a killing. There's a difference. But, if we're going to do it, I want to do it soon so I can get my bundle together. I can't unload what I don't have yet."

"You're worried?"

"Fuck, yes. Wake up, son. I want to be ready if the bottom falls out." He raised his hand and held up one finger. "But my nose is clean," he said. He laughed again, hacking out the phlegm until his laugh ended up low and velvety. Lafleur smelled the whiskey, and something else, a stench. Blaylock's eyes rolled upward and his head rocked crazily. He steadied it and said, "I'm about to pass out, though. I'll trade ten percent of the partnership for your I.D. shares. That gives you control."

"We have to establish value."

"Lord. Establish it and you'll see that it's a hell of a deal. You've still got your buy-back. You can end up with seventy, seventy-five percent."

Lafleur listened to the silence again. He wondered where Sabat was. Outside, he heard an owl hooting in the distance. He said, "You mean Jewel and I've got the fifty percent plus another ten percent for me if I trade, plus wherever the buy-back gets me, and whenever I want it, even after you're dead."

"Dead!" Blaylock said. He shook his head and whispered hoarsely, "Fuck!"

"You had this in mind from the start. Beginning with moving in on my father's interest."

Blaylock inhaled deeply and leaned forward, placing his weight on the arms of the chair. "I had to do something to shake you out of your tree. I was damn tired of running that outfit myself. Too much work. I thought the obvious would never dawn on anybody—you, Gus, or Jewel. And I set you up for supervisor out here, too, in case you've been wondering. But you've done a hell of a job, right? I wasn't wrong. You've even learned how to shake that sonofabitch Victor around. You're a harder fucking case than your old man was."

Blaylock sank back and Lafleur smiled, pleased despite himself.

"You betcha," Blaylock said, grinning apishly and nodding his head. "You've even been fucking Vic's girlfriend, I hear," he said. He began to giggle. His belly quivered. He looked like an obscene, ugly Santa Claus. His body swung sideways. He stopped giggling and listed to his left. The stench Lafleur had smelled before became stronger and he glanced down. He saw a stain on the insides of Blaylock's trousers, a darkness creeping out onto the upholstery of the chair. The man had defecated in his pants.

"Listen," Blaylock said. Aghast, Lafleur looked up. "You've got the buy-back. You'll have control of the company. You run the fucker. You can draw me down to ten percent if you want, so long as you pay. It's a hell of a deal. The missus and me have a lot in Palm Springs. Out in the sun. You get that sonofabitch Louis to set it up. I want to keep ten percent, that's all, so . . ." He stopped talking and lolled sideways. His head sank against the chair. He snored raggedly, wheezing and blowing.

Lafleur set his glass on the desk and rubbed his temples. Blaylock twitched and opened his eyes. With his movement a waft of the stink floated through the air. "So I can keep on pestering you," he said. He slid sideways again and snored.

Outside, the owl hooted. Lafleur turned and looked into the blackness of the window, then he got up and walked to the hallway. He stood for a moment, looking toward the kitchen. He didn't think Sabat was in the house. He looked into the study. From behind the back of the chair he could see the top of Blaylock's head hanging sideways and one arm draped toward the floor. From this distance he almost felt a tenderness toward the man. He thought that Blaylock liked him, after all. He wondered what to do. The telephone rang. Lafleur stared at it. He let it ring four times, then moved to answer it. "Hank?" the voice said. It was Phil. He said they were going to start back in about an hour, that they'd been talking to the police. He said the clinic had called the police. He paused.

"And?" Lafleur said.

"She's been raped," Phil said. "And tortured with a cattle prod or some damn thing."

Lafleur didn't speak.

"They need to talk to somebody," Phil said. "I don't know anything about this woman. She talks. She speaks better English than I do, for God's sake, but who the hell is she? They have to talk to somebody out there."

"Sabat," Lafleur said.

"I guess," Phil said. "She says she was raped, too."

Appalled, Lafleur said nothing.

"I know," Phil said.

Lafleur said, "Who's Sabat supposed to call?"

"The Burns police."

They hung up. Blaylock snored gently. Lafleur looked down at the model of the prison—the buildings about which he knew a great deal now, the double encirclement of fencing, the guard towers, the tiny smiling men. His mind was whirling. He told himself, One thing at a time. He moved to Blaylock and tried to raise him, but the limp weight was too much to manage. He thought, Get Sabat. Then he thought, Get the gun first. He picked up his coat, which he'd set on a corner of the desk, unfolded it, and put it on. It pulled heavily to one side from the weight of the pistol. He walked down the hall and into the kitchen. There was no one there. He moved out onto the porch and saw Sabat coming down from the direction of the metal building. Light caught the orb of Sabat's face when he lifted it to look at Lafleur. Lafleur felt himself fill with coldness. As Sabat came near, he jangled a set of keys and said, "I double-checked the locks."

Up past the barn the metal building was a glossy patch in the darkness. In the bunkhouse, Phil's room was dark. Iris's room was alight. Lafleur said, "Ned's passed out and crapped in his pants." Sabat moved up onto the porch. The porch creaked. The light from the kitchen glinted off his eyes and the bulge on the side of his face. They went inside and moved through the kitchen to the hall. "He dirtied your chair," Lafleur said.

Sabat went into the room first, and stopped before Blaylock. His head rocked back. "He's going to drink himself to death."

Lafleur reached out and extracted the glass of Scotch from Blaylock's fingers and set it on the desk. He and Sabat each took an arm and dragged Blaylock up, turning him toward the doorway. They tottered under the weight. The smell was strong. "Walk, Ned," Sabat said. He reached up and patted Blaylock vigorously on the cheek. "Walk." Blaylock moaned and moved a leg, then the other. Half-asleep, he took up just enough of his own weight for them to steer him out, down the hall, and into the bathroom. They leaned him up against the counter and Lafleur steadied him there. "I'll locate some pajamas. You get his clothes off," Sabat said.

Lafleur gave Sabat a look, curling his lip.

"He has to bathe," Sabat said.

"Yeah," Lafleur said. "I'll do this and you can call the police when we're done." Sabat glared at him. "Phil called," Lafleur said. "The police in Burns want you to call them."

Sabat spun around and went out. Lafleur grasped Blaylock's arm, guided him to the toilet seat, and sat him down. Blaylock's head swung back and banged against the wall. Lafleur undid his shoelaces, averting his face from the stink. He pulled off the shoes, then the socks. Blaylock's huge, knuckly feet looked like alien creatures on the dark tile. "Your shirt," Lafleur said. Blaylock moaned. "Get your shirt off, Ned," Lafleur said. Blaylock moved and fumbled with the pullover shirt with his thick, blunt fingers. He got his elbow stuck in the sleeve and Lafleur tugged on the cloth, freeing the arm, then stepped back. "The rest of it," he said. Blaylock worked his other arm out of the sleeve and sat there staring groggily at Lafleur with the shirt around his neck and his white, fuzzy paunch hanging over his belt. "Take it off," Lafleur said. Blaylock pulled off the shirt, then carefully spread it over his belly. He looked up sheepishly at Lafleur. "Your pants."

"The hell," Blaylock said.

"Stand up and take them off."

"The hell. I crapped in them."

"Right. Take them off."

"Screw you," Blaylock said.

"Stand up."

Blaylock stood and Lafleur reached for his belt buckle.

"The hell, that's mine," Blaylock said, clumsily swatting at Lafleur's hands. Lafleur leaned into the shower stall and turned the water on, hoping Blaylock would get the idea. Sabat returned with a pair of pajamas and set them on the counter.

"Smells like shit, huh?" Blaylock said, leering at Sabat, and then to Lafleur he said, "I'm not like him."

"Shut up and drop your pants," Lafleur said.

Blaylock put his hands to his belt buckle and undid it, then unzipped his trousers. Sabat turned the bathroom blower on. "That's it, blow it away," Blaylock said. "I'm not like that fucker," he said. "With him you never know."

"Drop them," Lafleur said.

Blaylock dropped his pants around his ankles and stood there, swaying. "You make a deal with me and you know. If it's crooked, you know. If you get screwed, you know how you got screwed. If you screw me, I'll let you know, by God, then you'll know I know, goddamn it. With Vic there you never know a fucking thing. He might be your goddamn uncle and you wouldn't know. He might screw your sister and she wouldn't know." Blaylock threw his head back and laughed wildly.

"Step out of those pants," Lafleur said.

Blaylock lifted one leg. "I'll fall."

Lafleur bent over and held the trousers, getting some of Blaylock's crap on his fingers. "Step up," he said. "Shit, Ned."

"Shit is right. The best there is," Blaylock said. He stepped up with one foot, then the other.

Lafleur stood, nearly gagging, and kicked the trousers past Sabat toward the door, then turned to the sink and washed his hands. "Get the underwear off. Do it yourself." He washed his hands for a long time, then bent over and splashed water on his face.

"I'm not like that fucker," Blaylock said.

Lafleur glanced at Sabat. Sabat's face was drawn tight with anger. Lafleur said, "He's drunk."

"You betcha," Blaylock said. "Truth serum. You know. You're my partner's son. We've got something between us. If I fuck you over I'll let you know, and you'll know exactly how I fucked you. That's education." Blaylock turned to Sabat. He tottered and said, "If he says I'm drunk, then by God that's the truth. I'm drunk as a skunk." Blaylock laughed giddily at his joke. "Skunk. Get it?"

"Shut up," Lafleur said.

Blaylock stood there, stinking, his legs stained, his head weaving. "With that fucker, Vic Sabat, he'll screw you from behind your back. After he's screwed you once, he'll screw you again while you're looking around trying to figure out who screwed you. He doesn't quit. Don't let him get his jack in you. He's all secrets like a goddamn Russian."

"Get your underwear off," Lafleur said. He pointed at the shower stall. "You need a shower." Blaylock bent and began to lower his underwear. "There," Lafleur said. He looked back at Sabat, whose mouth was twisted. Lafleur opened the shower door and a cloud of steam filled the room. "In," Lafleur said.

Blaylock stepped in, clutching the jamb to steady himself. "Balance," he said. He moved under the rushing water and stood for a moment, then stuck his head out and said, "Balance is the key." He laughed wildly again. Lafleur shut the door on him and kicked the rest of the clothing toward the pants. Sabat found a beach towel and nudged the clothing onto it with his toe. He made a bundle and set it out in the hall.

"I'll get Diane to wash those for him," Sabat said.

"Diane's in Burns," Lafleur said. "Then she's got her weekend off." He looked at Sabat and Sabat looked back with his off-kilter face. The exchange between them was of two men coming to know each other dangerously in the blood. Sabat's expression was rigid, ugly, and angry. His anger lent credence to Blaylock's words, and there was the woman in Burns, raped repeatedly, which Sabat probably knew that he—Lafleur—would find out about, and the prisoners, probably kept here illegally, and Snediker, kept on, and there were all the lies and manipulations, and then there was Iris. The look they exchanged carried a heavy, tottering cargo. It was a silent, mutual curse. Blaylock began to hum. Through the translucent shower door the white figure looked massive and diffuse, ghostly.

"She's been raped," Lafleur said. "The woman."

Sabat stared at him coldly.

"But then you already know that."

A smile squeezed its way onto Sabat's twisted face. "I was afraid of it."

"But not afraid enough," Lafleur said.

"He's gone. He's out of here. In the morning."

"You bet he is," Lafleur said.

"He's locked up for the night and in the morning he's out of here," Sabat said.

"That's not all," Lafleur said. "You sent Snediker after me in Portland."

"You're wrong about that," Sabat said.

"No, I'm not," Lafleur said. "The question is why."

Sabat didn't respond. His face moved. It was his mask, his smooth, unreadable mask of self-possession, that he was trying and failing to will back onto his face. "It wasn't me," he said.

"Bull," Lafleur said.

Blaylock began to sing in the shower, a happy, garbled version of "Tipperary."

"I didn't send him," Sabat said.

Lafleur leaned back against the wall next to the toilet. They were silent for a moment as Blaylock sang on. Lafleur looked in at Blaylock's shadowy, swaying form in the shower. He felt filled with a curious affection for the old bear, the naked, filthy one, the infighter, bully, the greedy one who showed his helplessness as easily as his rapacity, who wore his mortality right on his skin and who was deeply imbedded in nothing but who he was, who could be trusted to be himself. Lafleur thought he understood how his father had liked Blaylock, once, and he remembered the monkey wrench, but now he saw it descending to the man's leg, hanging there, and then the man stalking off. He remembered that part of it, first the anger boiling up out of the man and then the blow that was finally not delivered.

"Look," he said to Sabat. He'd been about to say that he had his work to do, that he'd be happy to stick to that so long as Sabat cleaned up the rest of it, but he didn't say it, knowing that it was foolish. Much as he wanted to flee back into his labor, to the plans, digits, unpronounceable words, and to the men, to escape that way, he knew that it was impossible. Almost desperately, he desired the calm, the distance that attended the work. He desired to cover himself with his work as if with a tent and not to come out from it until it was time to leave this place, but as he stood there looking into Sabat's face, which was filled with resistance and lies, he knew that it wasn't going to be that way. "Screw it," he said.

Blaylock sang away in a prodigiously deep, ecstatic, watery voice: "It's a long, long way to Tipperary. It's a long way to go."

"You never know about people," Sabat said, his voice curling with insult.

"I sure didn't," Lafleur said. He took the pistol out of his pocket and held it up by the barrel. It was heavy in his hand. Its bluing gleamed. "This is what I was brought to," he said. Sabat grinned his weird, twisted little grin, and Lafleur's eyes narrowed, seeking out the darkness in Sabat. He slipped the gun back into the pocket.

He went out, through the hall, the kitchen, outside. The porch sang under his foot. He went down and moved toward the bunkhouse. He could hear Blaylock. The singing voice came out the bathroom window and echoed softly off the Support Building. The pigs grunted as he passed. The owl hooted in the distance. The cool night air felt electric on his skin. He felt large in the night, like an oversized moth with great big eyes.

Chapter Seventeen

It was late August, another two weeks since they'd found the old woman nearly dead. Snediker was gone. The Cessna had come in the next morning and whisked him away. Sabat was here. Diane had moved into an empty room in the bunkhouse because she refused to stay in the ranchhouse alone with Sabat at night. Phil was still here. The prisoners were here, but they'd been moved into better quarters in one of the partially finished Housing Units. The old woman had been moved from the clinic in Burns to a Portland hospital. Four days later she vanished. The entire sequence of events with the woman was treated matter-of-factly by Sabat. One day, he said to Lafleur, "You know, in a way you're partly responsible for her escape."

"Bull," Lafleur said.

Sabat was amused. His words dropped from the side of his mouth. "As you wish."

"Personally," Lafleur said, "I don't know whether she walked out of there on her own power or if she was removed. Do you?"

"Is that an accusation?" Sabat said, still smiling. He positioned himself on his heels, then came forward as if he were about to jump. They were in the study, standing over the model and looking out the window at the rock wall that now cut the ranchhouse completely off from the project.

"No," Lafleur said. He was no longer cowed by Sabat. He was merely amazed by the casual handling of the old woman's mistreatment and disappearance. "I don't know, that's all."

"Then I guess I don't, either."

. . . *then!* . . . Lafleur thought. *What did the man mean?*

He had learned that Sabat's cryptic, inscrutable remarks always emerged from some inner logic, and so assumed that the *then* spoke to some sense of consequence understood only by Sabat. That was the way with the man: while talking with him one would not know what he meant, but later the words would swirl back up loaded with meaning. Lafleur had come to prefer not to know what Sabat meant much of the time. He continued to avoid him. At times he managed to go several days in succession without speaking to him.

After work this afternoon Lafleur had walked to the bend in the river. He'd had no mail today, so he was simply there, sitting on the sand. That was fine. Jones wandered upstream and disappeared. Clouds of gnats floated above the water and the bees were out—yellow jackets. They hovered at the edges of the shallows, dipping to drink. Water spiders scurried over the surface of the water. There were minnows just under the surface and Lafleur made them scatter by poking at them with his snake cane. Occasionally he'd see something dark move along the bottom—a catfish, perhaps, or if it was quick, a bass. The thought of bass made him wish he had a fishing rig. He often wished this when he came here. It was a rue that came repeatedly to him and passed. The water riffled around the bend and he thought about how the banks might be moved next year, after the winter floods, and yet of how, like the spit back at his old home on the Willamette, it might always be the same here but for the subtly altered shapes.

When he saw something large move at the bottom, he bent forward to see. It was like a pale shadow, long and big. It ferried the bottom toward the opposite bank, and came back, and disappeared, and then appeared again just upstream. It rose slowly in a shallow and rolled, breaking surface with its big, scabrous, ghost-colored body, and then sank and moved along the bottom against the current: a carp, feeding. Its paleness disappeared.

He settled back and thought about Andy and Tricia. He'd considered bringing them out here, but decided it was no place for them—maybe later. He was thinking seriously about taking a weekend off and going back to Portland. Across the river he could see the indentation where they'd dug out the body. He wondered if the body had been identified. He'd heard nothing more about it. In the weeks that had passed, the sand had shifted in the hole so that the indentation was smooth, contoured softly into an almost imperceptible echo of what had been there.

Something moved just downstream. He turned his head. A deer stood there, a doe. Its head came up. Lafleur sat stock-still. The deer didn't move. Unafraid, it watched with its big brown eyes, taking him in. It was a mule deer, brown and buff and darkening toward the tops of the legs and erect ears, and he was a man it was watching, the two of them incised into each other. The exchange seemed to be at once extraordinary and quite unremarkable, a daily thing. He'd seen several deer here just this way. They were emboldened by the lack of water in the hills, he guessed. He'd seen the one coyote. He looked down at his boots. He heard a rustling. He looked up. The deer was gone. He heard Jones, barking wildly. He sat still, listening to the sound of the dog as she cut across the sand, chasing the deer. The barking grew faint.

He felt a chill at his back, and turned to look. He saw nothing, looked back at the water, but still felt the chill. He rose uneasily, stepped toward the bank, and looked back in the direction of the site. He saw nothing at first—just the desert, the project in the distance, the glitter of metal, the ranch, and the river curling by it. There was a low rise not more than fifty yards from him. He saw movement there, a rounded protuberance coming up. It stayed still. If he hadn't been looking right at it, he wouldn't have seen it at all, and even as he looked the faint shape began to dissolve into the landscape. He began to think that his imagination had become precariously activated by the insects, the fish, the doe, that he was seeing things that weren't there. But he saw movement again, something long and narrow rising.

It glinted in the light. It tipped and came down beside the round thing, which might have been a head. He saw more movement—hands, perhaps, an adjustment of body to the narrow thing—and what it was, or might be, began to register: a gun barrel, a gun. He stood still, filled with disbelief, just looking, until finally his instinct responded to some firmness of intent in the figure, some gripping action, and he moved, catapulting himself toward the river, and as he landed he heard a bullet ringing against rock and then the report slamming against the cliffs.

He ended up on his belly, his head toward the river, his feet in the brush. Jones appeared, paddling gaily across the water toward him. He disentangled his feet and came up to his knees. Jones jumped up beside him and shook herself off. Lafleur grabbed her, jerked her down, then edged upward, and looked over the top of the bank. Again he saw no one at first, just the rise, the desert, and in the distance to his left the contorted sandstone formations. To his right specks of light played against the project. Jones slunk up beside him and licked his neck. Then the figure appeared from behind the rise. Dressed in black, it came up slowly to its full height. It mounted the rise with a characteristic, almost dainty, curiously mechanical, equine gait: Snediker. The rifle swung from one hand. He descended the rise and kept coming.

A string of thoughts rushed through Lafleur's mind: Snediker had been fired, Snediker was gone, he'd been shipped out a month ago and replaced by a pair of handsome, efficient young men. Lafleur tried to trick himself that way, but as he watched he saw that Snediker was truly there. The face had become discernible—the pouting lower lip and puckish, crazed expression floating above the huge, dark, mechanical body behind which the desert shimmered.

Lafleur slid down to the water and crossed it, soaking his boots and pants. He jogged upstream, staying low on the bank, then swung up behind an escarpment. Jones thought it was a game. She danced beside him. He hauled her down beside him and stuck his head out and watched again until Snediker came into view. He was walking, moving fast. His head nodded as he dipped down the bank to the water, and as he crossed the water fanned out from behind his legs. He strode up to the bank and stopped and his head revolved until it found Lafleur. The rifle came up. The sun glinted against the scope. Lafleur rolled back behind the escarpment, thinking that what was happening was absurd, ludicrous. A shot rang out and bits of rock sprayed against his boots. Amazed, filled with disbelief, he nevertheless spun around and fled for the cliffs.

He glanced back once and saw Snediker running toward the escarpment. He remembered a crevasse he'd seen before, an eroded runoff he thought he might climb. He was thinking he probably couldn't outrun Snediker, that somehow he had to get the advantage of height. He glanced back once again and saw Snediker on the road behind him, running as if in slow motion, like a machine, closing the gap. Lafleur hugged the cliffs, weaving in and out according to recesses and protrusions of rock. Ahead, he saw an outcropping, a kind of corner in the cliff. Behind it, he thought, was the crevasse. He ran and didn't look back now, but kept his eye on the ragged outline of rock, and reached it. He grasped the corner and pulled himself around, finding the crevasse. He didn't stop, but looked upward as he moved and glimpsed a shelf fifteen feet above him that he thought he could get onto, and beyond that the long, narrow V-shaped cut rising well over a hundred feet to the sky.

He got a handhold and hiked himself up. Beneath him he heard Jones whining and scrabbling on the smooth rock, struggling to climb. "Beat it!" he said. He hung on, twisted his body around, and looked down. The dog wagged her tail and barked. "Beat it!" he said. "Go!" The dog's ears dropped. He turned and climbed, clutching a fissure with his fingertips. Hauling himself up, he thought of snakes. Suddenly his body went cold with fear, and aghast, he said it to himself, hissing, "Snakes. Shit." Best of all, he knew, snakes liked the cracks and crevices in sun-warmed rock just like this, and worst of all for a person was to blindly stick a hand onto rock. He began flicking his hand at the rock before grabbing on, and taking an instant to listen before pulling himself up. He swung one leg first onto the ledge. His arms quivered. He got his second leg up and rolled . . . safe. He was on his side. He looked upward and saw another ledge ten feet or so above him. He got up and moved for it, trying to strike a balance between caution and speed. He heard Jones snarling. He knew by the sound that the dog had turned on Snediker. The snarling intensified, turning wild, and Lafleur felt hopeful for an instant, and to himself he murmured, *Jones, Jones, Jones,* repeating it like a prayer, and then he heard a shot just below him, whamming in his ears. He dragged himself up onto the second ledge and waited, listening. He heard nothing, just the soft soughing of the breeze blowing by the cliffs. He looked out on the river, the wide, brilliant desert, listening.

Snediker came into view, walking out from the cliffs. Lafleur crouched. Snediker turned and looked up, searching the crevasse. He spotted Lafleur and raised his gun. Lafleur flattened himself on the ledge and pushed back deep into the crack, and lay there. He heard nothing. He edged his head sideways and peeped over the edge. Snediker was gone. Lafleur waited, straining to hear, and then Snediker appeared again, dragging Jones by the collar. He turned, looked up at Lafleur, and called out in a clear voice, "Lafleur! Hey, motherfucker!" He lifted Jones's body, extending his arm straight out. It was as if the dog were nothing, weightless, a rag, a mere scrap. Snediker tipped his face back. The sun shone against his face. Jones's hind legs kicked weakly. "Want your dog?" Snediker called. He looked at the dog, and up again, then dropped the dog. Jones kicked and rolled in a death throe, shoveling her nose at the earth. Lafleur didn't move. His legs were shaking. He tasted acid in his mouth. Whatever doubt, what disbelief or amazement he'd clung to, vanished completely.

Snediker walked back to the cliff. Lafleur edged forward, clinging to the rock, and looked straight down. Snediker passed into the shadows at the base of the crevasse. The buttons on the epaulettes of his black shirt glinted. The lens of the gun he'd slung over his shoulder flashed. He started up, moving with surprising nimbleness. It seemed a deranged, preternatural motion, and for an instant Lafleur shrank before it, then turned and looked up. He saw thirty feet of very difficult climbing, then easier climbing, perhaps, as the crevasse sloped inward to the top. What was at the top he had no idea. He looked down. Robotlike, Snediker was coming.

Lafleur climbed. If he could traverse the cliff to where it began to slope in without losing too much ground to Snediker, he might gain the advantage of the top. It was hard climbing. He braced himself by pushing his hands and feet outward against the walls of the crevasse, moving one member at a time—a hand, a foot, a hand, a foot—and each time he moved a hand he flicked it first as a feeble precaution against snakes, and then sought whatever crack or protrusion he could find for support.

The late-afternoon sun beat directly upon the cliffs and the heat was intense. He was sweating profusely. He tasted salt on his lips, the astringency of lime dust back in his nose, and he began to feel lightheaded. His arms and legs trembled. He heard Snediker toiling behind him—a murmuring and faint clinking of gun and strap. At another ledge, on which he secured a brief holdfast, Lafleur looked down between his legs and saw Snediker about twenty feet away, hauling himself over a hump. The head came first, then the whole body like a large reptilian thing with the innocent face sliding out of its hole. The face fixed on Lafleur and the voice called out again, "Hey, motherfucker!" Lafleur was poised, hanging on with one hand, and he had the horrible thought that when Snediker got here he, too, might be able to balance himself and use the gun.

Lafleur hoisted himself up onto another narrow ledge, and went on, and reaching the inward slope found he could move at a half-erect crouch. He moved faster. There was loose rock here, and even a few wind-scoured scrub bushes to grab on to. He kicked at the rock and scooped it with one hand, sending streams of it down. He heard Snediker grunting. He looked down and saw precisely what he had feared—Snediker on the ledge that allowed him to hang on with one hand and handle the gun with the other, but he held the hand and gun up, just then, shielding his face. Lafleur took a fast deep breath, and scrambled upward, scooping at the rock as he went, hanging on to the starved bushes when he could, and filled with fear, expecting to hear the crash at any moment, to feel the bullet ripping into his back. He kept going, clutching and desperately knocking at the loose rock, and reached the top, put a hand over, kicked at a mass of small rock, vaulted over, and came up on one knee.

Cautiously, he peered down. Snediker stood with his head averted and his arm and rifle up. The rocks glanced off his body and pinged all the way to the bottom, striking in deeper tones the deeper they fell. Lafleur pulled back and looked for a larger stone, something big enough to knock Snediker down. There was no such rock. He listened. The last of the loose rock bounced against the cliff to the bottom, then there was silence. He waited. The silence grew eerie, and he thought, He's waiting, too, he's waiting for me to stick my head back over the edge. He thought, Don't do that. He turned and looked before him, thinking, Now, now what?

What he saw shimmered in his eyes: to his left open desert, a huge table set at a tilt toward distant ridges. To his right and circling around as far as he could see was a low, secondary cliff of volcanic material, irregular and craggy, and behind it the same ring of ridges. He saw dust in the air, the obscure outline of a mushroom floating above the long, low cliff, and he wondered if there was something going on over there, a field being worked, maybe, and he thought, My God. People. He thought he heard a barely audible, thin, distant rumbling, and he cocked his head toward the crevasse and listened for Snediker again. He heard nothing, and he thought, He's still waiting, or he's coming gently. The urge to look down was almost overpowering, but he did not. He stood and sprinted for the low cliff and ran alongside it, following its gradual curve, hoping to put as much distance as possible between himself and Snediker before heading into the rock. He wanted to be well into the rock before Snediker came out on top of the cliff.

He slowed when he felt winded and looked back. There was no sign of Snediker, but he could hear him moving, now, the loose stones pinging down the crevasse and thudding at the bottom. He moved into the rock abutment and went up it. It was fifteen or twenty feet of easy climbing. Near the top he looked back again—still no sign. He went over and slid down a gentle slope, coming to a stop on his back. He propped himself up and looked down, startled by what lay beneath him: a giant natural bowl, an amphitheater-like continuation of the table he'd seen previously, flat and tilted here, too, and rimmed most of the way around by the volcanic formation—basalt—and in the bowl a herd of horses being driven by three horsemen in bright shirts. On the far side of the bowl stood a green truck and horse trailer. Two horsemen rode front and rear point and the third cut his horse back and forth between them. The red, blue, and yellow shirts slipped in and out of sight in the churning dust. The horsemen were running the herd along the rim of volcanic rock. They brought the herd out of the shadows near the rock and made it circle into the light, then spiraled it in again, bunching up the horses and slowing them down. The beating hooves sounded like muted thunder. Sporadically, Lafleur heard the cowboys shouting, their thin voices slicing through the roar: Yip! Yip! Yip!

It was shaded where Lafleur sat, but the rock held the day's heat. His shirt was wet with sweat. His arms ached. The rock was black and the coarse sand at his hands was black. Down in the bowl itself the sand was white, bright in the full light, and the undulating horses multicolored under the veil of dust. The herd was perhaps a quarter of a mile away. All he had to do now, Lafleur thought, finding himself bedazzled, was to go down there and hug the black rim, strike a balance between the abutment and the proximity of the horsemen for protection, and follow the herd to the truck.

He stood and walked a few steps. The rock crunched under his boots. He stopped and listened. He heard nothing but the horses. He moved on, and when he came to a short, steep incline of sand and loose rock he sat down again. Just as he began to slide down he glimpsed something below him on the slope, a slithering play of dark in the shade, on the black sand. Sliding, he saw the thick thing twist suddenly, and then cursed himself for forgetting that again . . . a snake. He clutched at the rocks at his sides and slid sideways in a desperate attempt to keep himself from rolling right over it. He skidded to a stop just six feet above the snake. A rock tumbled over it. The snake leaped and snapped at the air, then coiled. Its rattling split the air and its body flickered against the black sand as it twisted upon itself. Lafleur stared and exhaled slowly. He was shaking. In the distance was the muted thundering of hooves.

He stayed where he was, motionless, sideways just above the rattler, propped on one elbow, his head up. The snake had its head up, too, erect and swollen above its coiled body. It was a dark creature. Its dark-gray blotches and bands were set against a buff color. The underside of its head was buff and the top jet black. The head tilted in Lafleur's direction. The tongue darted in and out. The tail vibrated violently. The snake was smelling him, checking him out. The rattling stopped, then started in again. Lafleur moved his eyes. He was quite conscious of that—moving his eyes and nothing else, moving them in their parched sockets to look down into the bowl where the horsemen had knotted up the herd. The herd milled around, raising white dust. The cowboys patrolled the herd, and a fourth man had appeared, standing beside the open door of the pickup. The backs and rumps of the horses looked shiny and the cowboys' shirts were like flags, the various colors making a mobile quilt in the dust and light—exquisite, inaccessible.

The snake moved, lowered its head, and its body began to twist, the length of it weaving over itself, the alternating deep gray and buff sliding and making the snake look like smoke. It was uncoiling. Half-uncoiled, it stopped. Gingerly, Lafleur tried to edge away . . . too soon. The snake recoiled, rattled, and hissed. Lafleur froze. From the other side of the abutment, at his back, he heard footfalls, crunching heavily in the coarse sand . . . Snediker. The snake rattled. It didn't move. Lafleur knew that he had to move now. The only way to know the snake's reach was to test it, but he didn't move. He heard a voice, a strange half-grunting, half-humming noise from the other side of the abutment. The snake, like smoke, began to uncoil.

Lafleur watched it. He heard the humming, a tuneless, percussive noise. The snake uncoiled completely and stopped, and Lafleur thought, Now, go away, go down, sideways, go somewhere. The snake lay in an S with its head lifted. Lafleur listened to the humming. It sounded as if it were right behind him at the bottom of the abutment. The snake moved. It came toward him. It was big and thick. Its beady body made a sibilant sound on the coarse sand. It came alongside him, its length paralleling his legs about two feet away, and Lafleur thought, or he prayed—like a child he beseeched God, and even named his wish to the old concrete God of his childhood in this strange, abstract place: All right, come this way,

251

come near me, keep coming, come close. He heard Snediker climbing the abutment. Level with Lafleur's hip now, the snake curled toward him, its head erect and its tongue flicking, near enough for Lafleur to see its sage-colored eyes. It came very near, the desert-colored thing, dark, buff, black, and sage. Lafleur awaited it.

It came, nearly touching his thigh. Its body swung around behind the head, and Lafleur felt his body pause breathlessly as if he were rising to poise himself in midair, and then he lunged and seized the snake right behind the head and rolled up onto his knees and held the head down. The snake hissed and twisted violently. Its tail whipped. Lafleur grabbed its midsection with his other hand and held it, and kept holding the head, and got his feet under him and stood, lifting the snake.

The strength of the creature was astonishing. Every movement of the rippling musculature sought to whip the hissing, agape head at him. It twisted its tail around one arm. He pulled the body against his chest and kept the head away. He squeezed the throat. The snake stopped hissing. Its body was filled with a terrible, still tension. Lafleur moved carefully up the ridge, slowing as he neared the top, peered down, and saw Snediker—gun, black uniform, epaulettes. He had his head down to watch his footing. Lafleur crouched and cautiously disentangled his left arm. The snake resisted him with its tension. He held it near the head still, and now near the tail. The ponderous midsection pulsed and twisted. Carefully, Lafleur turned sideways. Snediker heard him. His face jerked up and he swung his rifle around. Lafleur pitched the snake at him. The snake twisted in the air and landed on Snediker's chest and shoulder; it latched onto him just below the elbow, biting through the cloth. Snediker made a deep, guttural sound of horror and he pulled desperately at the snake, dropping his gun. Lafleur slid down the ridge, rolling head over heels, landed at the bottom, crawled toward the gun, and grabbed it up. Snediker had stumbled backward. He tugged at the snake, holding it by the neck. He ripped the head loose from his arm, and again made the low, grunting cry. Quickly, Lafleur eased the rifle bolt part way back and checked for the cartridge, then snapped the bolt to and released the safety. Snediker stood on the snake head with one bootheel, bent, then came up, sliding his hands along the body, squeezed its midsection, and pulled the snake in two. He straightened and looked at Lafleur, still holding the wriggling tail section. His breath rasped in his chest and his childish, freckled face was contorted and pallid. He stepped toward Lafleur.

"Not another inch," Lafleur said, pointing the gun at Snediker's chest. Snediker stopped. Just behind him the snake head flipped around in the black sand. "Sit down," Lafleur said. Snediker didn't move. Suddenly enraged, Lafleur raised the gun to his shoulder and peered through the scope, bringing the crosshairs to the button on Snediker's left breast pocket, and touched his finger to the trigger, deeply tempted, but he caught himself, thinking, no, not this one, not by me, not unless I have to. Snediker's eyes looked old and dead. "Sit down," Lafleur said. He spoke as he would to a child.

Snediker looked at him questioningly, then dropped the snake body and moved sideways to the abutment. He kept his eyes on Lafleur. The snake body writhed, knotting and unknotting. The head lay still. Snediker eased his body down, settling slowly, and rolled up his sleeve and looked at the bite. His upper arm was puffy and red. "It hurts," Snediker said.

Lafleur lowered the rifle. "Cut your sleeve off."

"Help me," Snediker said. His brow furrowed. "You cut it."

"I'm not getting anywhere near you," Lafleur said.

"Why?" Snediker said.

Lafleur rocked back onto his heels, thinking, The man is mad. "Do you have a knife?" he said. Snediker dug in his trouser pocket with his good hand and produced a knife. "Sharp?" Lafleur guessed it would be. Anything Snediker had that remotely resembled equipment would be kept in top condition—rifle, scope, oiled belt and boots, uniform, sharp knife, pistol. Lafleur inhaled suddenly, startled by his heedlessness.

"Toss me your pistol," he said. "Toss it out." He raised the rifle again. Snediker reached back to his holster and threw the pistol out. Lafleur picked it up and cradled the weight of the snubnosed .38 in his palm for a moment, then wheeled and heaved it over the cliff. He heard it pinging against the rocks down toward the bottom.

"Hey!" Snediker said.

"Shut up," Lafleur said. "Cut your sleeve off." Snediker obediently ripped the sleeve along the seam with the knife, then carefully pulled it down his arm. "That's a tourniquet."

"Sure," Snediker said, looking at his arm. A streak of red ran up to his shoulder.

"Twist it around your upper arm."

"I know." Snediker pulled the sleeve around his arm and cinched it, tightening it violently.

Christ! Lafleur thought. He's that way even with himself. "Lacking anything better," he said, "you're going to have to use the old method. Cut an X and suck it out."

"I know."

"Don't swallow the venom."

"Please, help me."

"After you do that, take off the tourniquet. You're damn lucky it didn't bite your neck," Lafleur said. "I'm going for help."

"You're going to leave me?" Snediker's face puckered.

Lafleur moved to the cliff. Over to his right he could see the crevasse he'd climbed, a slit in the rock. He followed it downward with his eyes. The thought of climbing back down made his belly turn. He could see Jones, a dark dot in the shadows at the bottom. He stopped a minute and thought of her, running, and of her holes, of the things she'd brought him, skunk tail, coyote skull, horse femur, jackrabbit and bird bodies, the human hand. He thought of her rituals, of how she'd tried to be friends with Phil. Just a dog, he thought, but his head shuddered as he raised it.

In the distance to his right he could see the construction site, the round playing fields, the pale concrete walls of the new buildings in the nearing dusk, the ranch buildings. The sun glinted against the roof of the metal building and the machinery, and against the trailers and campers at the top of the rise. The workers had the bonfire going. It looked like a pale candle flame and sent a thin line of smoke into the sky. Just above the encampment was the runway, a scrape in the earth at the foot of the sandstone hills. What seemed so big being in it, so complex, so nearly overwhelming, looked like nothing down in the canyon—tiny and harmless, a scratching at the earth.

He turned back to Snediker, who was bent over his arm, sucking. Blood trickled down to his wrist. The knife lay in the sand. "I'll come back with help," Lafleur said. "You'll want to stay still."

Snediker spat to one side and looked up. "I can hardly feel my arm. I might die." In his fright, the skin pulled back from around his dead eyes. "You're big."

"You had me fired. That's why."

"The hell," Lafleur said.

"I feel sick. What if I die?" His brow furrowed and his lips quivered. The breeze lifted his wispy red hair.

Lafleur moved off, walking along the low volcanic formation. He heard Snediker behind him, calling, "Motherfucker!" The profanity turned and sailed on the breeze. At the end of the formation Lafleur looked back. Snediker was hunched over his arm. Lafleur slung the rifle over his shoulder and set out across the big, tipped bowl. It gave him a strange feeling, walking at a tilt. It made the geometry of the world seem skewed. The sand was turning pink. The sun sank. The volcanic ridge and distant hills were utterly black.

The sky was red, blue, and yellow, the same colors as the three cowboys' shirts had been. Ahead of him, the horse herd, a dark clot in the distance, squeezed through the keyhole in the rock. The green truck and trailer rolled behind the herd. Dust rose, nearly invisible near the ground, but higher up it feathered and caught garish light. Lafleur quickened his pace.

Chapter Eighteen

It took him a half hour to reach the keyhole, the two high promontories nearly joined at the top. He went through and found himself on another table, or a continuation of the table behind him, tilted like that table. The white sand became luminous in the dusk. In the distance he saw a flickering orange light. He felt large in the vast open space. He saw the outline of a small shack. Gradually its details became apparent—the shed roof, the posts supporting a deep eave, a metal chimney—but the shack still seemed tiny even when he came upon it. The lantern glowed behind it. There was a corral back there, teeming with horses, and a cowboy, pitching hay into a crib. He looked up and touched the brim of his hat when Lafleur approached. He eyed the gun. He was young, twenty-five perhaps. Pale hair tufted out from under his straw hat. "Hunting?"

"No," Lafleur said. "There's a man out there. Snakebit."

"Bad?"

Lafleur shrugged. "Not too bad. But I should get him help. Is there a phone?" As he asked, he looked around, past the shack and across the vast flatland to distant ridges in the dusk . . . no poles, no power poles, nothing.

"Nope." The cowboy plunged the prongs of his pitchfork into the ground. "I got a truck. We could go out and get him."

The offer alarmed Lafleur. He turned and looked into the corral. The horses milled around slowly. Their flanks glistened. Lafleur licked his teeth, which had grit on them. "If I can get to a phone," he said, "I'll call for help and save you the trouble."

"You from the project?"

Lafleur nodded.

"Closest would be Abe Kasanian's place across the highway."

"Kasanian?"

"But town ain't much further. I can take you to town, or back out to pick up your man and then into town. I don't mind. These critters won't go nowhere."

"I know Kasanian," Lafleur said.

The cowboy disengaged the handle of his lantern from the hook on the post and started off. Lafleur followed. They went around to the far side of the shack, where the cowboy set the lantern up on the roof of an old Chevy pickup.

"I think this sucker'll run," he said. He lifted the hood and propped it open with a stick, then got a five-gallon gas can out of the bed. He opened up the air cleaner, washed it liberally with gas, and replaced the cover. "Got to prime her." He returned the gas can to the bed, climbed into the cab, and turned the key. The starter whirred. The cowboy stuck his head out the window. "Needs a Bendix." He tried again and the starter engaged. Fire flashed in the darkness under the air-cleaner cover. The engine caught and roared, sucking the fire into itself. A thick cloud of oily exhaust drifted forward over the bed, the cab. The cowboy hopped out and closed the hood, fastening it to the bumper with a bungee strap. Lafleur got in and held the rifle, barrel upward, between his knees. The truck creaked and dipped deeply on its springs as they started out. The cab smelled of mouse droppings. They drove easterly and then westerly in what Lafleur took to be a wide arc that carried them around the ridges to the highway.

"You must've walked all the way around by the Lassers' place," the cowboy said.

"Right." Lafleur had no idea what the cowboy was talking about.

The cowboy told him that his buddies had gone back to Jordan Valley. They worked for the Department of Interior, he said. The horses were wild—mustangs. There were too many of them. "They say they eat up the rangeland," the cowboy said, "though personally I think some landowner from San Francisco or Portland has scammed the government again. They're pounding another bucket of sand into a rathole. Them horses can't eat that much. They don't eat the same as cows. They sure don't eat a place down like sheep. But it's work, I guess."

They stopped at the highway, then crossed it. A sign said Skull Creek Road and Lafleur recalled Kasanian's directions from what seemed ages ago—something about China Gulch, Scott's Ranch, Owyhee Springs, a diversion dam, Skull Creek Road, and a copper rooster on the roof. "This Kasanian's a character," the cowboy said.

The road was deeply rutted. The pickup veered wildly back and forth. Ball joints, Lafleur thought. His body rocked with the motion and he grew aware of the aching in his legs, all the way up to his hips. His hands and shoulders ached.

"He could've been one of the biggest ranchers around, but he walked away from it," the cowboy said. "Smart, maybe."

Lafleur wondered how that tale jibed with Kasanian's tale of Uncle Spence.

"The horses were here first," the cowboy said.

"Sort of," Lafleur said.

"Yeah?"

"The Spanish."

"Yeah, I guess."

Lafleur smiled grimly to himself, thinking that what he'd seen in his desperation as an exquisite historical throwback—three cowboys skillfully maneuvering a herd of horses—was in fact another government-control program. The horses were like weeds, like rodents, like coyotes, like Bill Snediker. Once, the wild horses had been a liquid asset.

"Here we are," the cowboy said. They pulled into a drive and the pickup's headlamps swept along a low-slung stucco ranchhouse. An exterior floodlamp snapped on, revealing a yard enclosed by a rail fence and a plethora of large articles—wagon wheels and one entire wagon, an old hayrick artfully converted into a trellis, and flowers growing out of ten-gallon milk cans. The silhouette of a short, bowlegged figure appeared in the doorway. "There he is."

Lafleur offered to pay for the ride.

"Hell, no," the cowboy said.

Lafleur got out and moved through the gate. He called to the figure in the doorway of the house. The figure came outdoors. Three snarling basset hounds boiled out from under his feet and flew toward Lafleur. Lafleur stopped in his tracks. At a cry from Kasanian the dogs silenced and fell to snuffling at Lafleur's shoes and legs. It was Jones they smelled, the last of Jones. Kasanian came down the walkway with his gimpy stride, and waved his arms at the dogs. "Git."

The dogs sprayed across the yard and ranged along the fenceline, sniffing the ground. They snaked in and out of the shadows. The pickup pulled away. Gravel popped under the tires. The taillights bounced and quickly dwindled. "I'd about given up on you coming to visit," Kasanian said. "That the Llewellen boy?"

"Didn't get his name."

Kasanian looked up at him. "You broken down?"

"No." Lafleur heard the emotion in his voice, and felt his throat swelling. It was Kasanian, the presence of one he trusted. "I need to use the phone."

Kasanian scrutinized him narrowly, then touched his arm. "Come in."

The dogs boiled back through the doorway, sniffing Lafleur's ankles as they passed. Inside, the house was a denser, more exotic version of the yard. The walls were decorated with several of Jim's paintings—seascapes, wrecked ships, a large painting of a ragged man straddling a narrow plank in the high sea. Harnesses and cowbells hung on the walls, old tools, old rifles, old photographs. Kasanian led him across to the kitchen. They passed a silver-studded saddle mounted on a sawhorse. A cage hung from the ceiling above the kitchen counter, and in it a green parrot roosted on a stick. Kasanian saluted the bird as he passed and said, "Howdy, neighbor." The parrot spoke the words back in a cracked, acid voice, and Kasanian grinned at Lafleur. "The wise one greets you."

"I could sure use a drink of water, too," Lafleur said.

Kasanian filled a glass at the sink, passed it to Lafleur, and nodded at a black wall phone on the other side of the table. "Feel free." Lafleur gulped down the water and picked up the receiver. "Guess you don't need that hunk of iron to make a phone call, though," Kasanian said.

Lafleur touched the strap of the rifle.

"You kind of startled me at first out there, toting that thing." Kasanian laughed his same pleasant, voiceless laugh. He looked older without his straw hat. His thick gray hair was slicked down close to his head. "Beer or coffee?"

"Both?"

"That's my man. Contrary."

Lafleur propped the gun against the wall and dialed the number of the project, then turned and leaned back next to the phone. Kasanian passed him a beer. Sabat answered the phone. Lafleur told him that Snediker was snakebit, that he was out in the desert, that they had to go get him—just that, nothing more—and Kasanian looked sharply across at him. Sabat said, "Snediker's supposed to be in Nevada." His voice was cold. He, too, said nothing more. The question of where Snediker had come from, of why he was out here at all, hung heavily in the line. Lafleur said that Sabat should drive out so they could pick Snediker up. "Where?" Sabat said.

"Where?" Lafleur said to Kasanian.

"I can take you out," Kasanian said.

Lafleur shook his head.

"Probably be easiest if I drove you out to the highway, then. Tell him it's seven and a half miles east of Rome. Right there. Skull Creek Road."

The parrot flapped its wings and cackled: "Skull Creek Road!" Kasanian laughed voicelessly and bowed to the bird. Lafleur gave directions to Sabat, hung up, and then stood for a moment, looking down into the depths of the living room. The three basset hounds lay enthroned on three large cushions on the couch. The entire house was at once rustic and dense, not unlike the café at Burns Junction, but much neater—an old bachelor's quarters. Kasanian was at the table pouring coffee. He gestured at a chair and said, "Sit. It'll take him a good forty-five minutes."

Lafleur sat. On the wall across from him hung a pair of photographs—a woman and a man. Kasanian set the coffeepot on the stove and returned to the table. He saw Lafleur looking at the photographs and said, "Those are the ancestors."

"The ancestors!" the parrot said.

The man had a square jaw and wore a black flat-brimmed hat. The woman's hair was drawn back tightly, revealing a high, rounded brow. She had on an old-fashioned, button-down bodice, and her lips were drawn tight. They both had humorless gray eyes. They looked as though they carried the years of labor, and care, and the dust of the desert, as if they'd handled it by hardening themselves against it. "But they weren't near so nasty as they look," Kasanian said, laughing softly.

The parrot laughed, hissing rhythmically.

"They keep me company. Them and the dogs and that damn parrot."

"That damn parrot!" the parrot said.

Kasanian looked fondly over his shoulder at the parrot, and then up at the photographs. He turned back to Lafleur. "She was Spence's sister."

Lafleur remembered the frayed length of rope in the barn, and the old man picking up limestone blocks from the razed silo. He remembered how the old man cradled the blocks, and set them down, how Jones had barked, how the old man had disappeared. He remembered the small stack of blocks left behind. He had never understood it, but just now, because of his state, his scalp prickled, and though it sounded foolish to him even as he said it, he asked, "Does he have a ghost? Spence?"

Kasanian looked closely at Lafleur. "The kind of man he was, the old iron-willed sonofabitch, the chances are he's still haunting a couple dozen people around here. But that ain't what you mean. You seen him?"

Lafleur finished his beer and took a sip of coffee. "I saw something the day I took the silo down."

"It don't surprise me."

"Could be just what you were telling me about him. That probably spooked me."

"Maybe. I've heard a lot stranger, though." Kasanian fixed his gaze on Lafleur and his face grew solemn. "You look like somebody ran you through a rock crusher."

Lafleur looked down at his arms, which were scratched and chafed, and at his torn hands. "He tried to kill me." Kasanian's brow knitted and he kept gazing at Lafleur. Lafleur told him, at first just the facts of it— Snediker coming out of nowhere, the gunshot, killing Jones, climbing the cliff, the rocks, the horses, the snake in the rocks, how he'd used the snake, how Snediker ripped the snake clean in half. Then he told Kasanian about his disbelief, about how at first he didn't believe that Snediker could be trying to kill him, and as he spoke, Lafleur realized that he hadn't really believed it until just now, as if it took this, the telling, to make what had happened real. The longer he spoke the more his voice was filled with emotion. When he stopped he was shaking.

Kasanian listened attentively with his hands folded under his chin. "Personally, I'd have a few questions about anybody who'd keep one like that on."

"Sabat?"

Kasanian nodded.

"Snediker was fired almost a month ago. He was out of there." Lafleur's voice cracked with emotion, and he pushed back from the table and said, "Damn it, I'm sorry."

"It's all right." Kasanian smiled. "But it makes you wonder. Is it the operation that messes up a man's judgment like that—Sabat's, I mean? To let a guy like that run around loose. Or do you have to be that way to start with if you're going to run that kind of operation?"

"I don't know. I don't like to think about that."

"Talking to a man like that, Sabat, it's like he's looking over your shoulder all the time, hoping something better'll come along. It makes you edgy."

Lafleur smiled and looked out at the three basset hounds on their cushions. They were asleep. One twitched in its dreams. "That's true," he said. He ran his fingertip around the rim of his coffee cup. He'd begun to feel a little better.

"What kind of rattler was it?"

Lafleur shrugged. "Black and cream. Black, or maybe dark green diamonds. A kind of a diamond shape alternating with the cream color and turning into rings at the tail." He remembered the snake very clearly.

"A big one, you said?"

Lafleur paused, thinking of Snediker standing on the head and jerking the snake body apart. He nodded. "Maybe four feet." He smiled faintly. "A strong sucker."

"It sounds like a western black. The bite won't kill him. Make him sick, though, the sonofabitch."

"Sonofabitch!" the parrot said.

Kasanian grinned and saluted the bird.

The parrot cocked its head, looked down at them with one beady eye, and opened its yellow beak as if it were about to speak again. Its gray tongue stuck out.

"I don't know," Kasanian said. He picked up his cup and finished off his coffee. "South of here you got the bomb range. East, you got Boise. West, you got the Willamette. You go far enough north, you get Hanford. But I thought we was safe enough here, safe as a body can get, anyway. This place is like magic, and magic it'll be until the end of my days, I guess, but I hate to see the corruption moving in." He paused and looked down at the table, then up again at Lafleur. "We'd better go meet that asshole."

"Asshole!" the parrot said.

At the sound of the chairs scraping back from the table, the three basset hounds stood bolt upright. Lafleur picked up the rifle and followed Kasanian. As they moved to the door, the dogs ran silently around their ankles. The parrot cried after them, "Goodbye! Goodbye! Goodbye!" Lafleur heard it crying from behind the closed door as he and Kasanian walked to the gate. "Goodbye! Goodbye!" The voice sounded plaintive in the distance, like a child. Kasanian had an old Buick, and as Lafleur got in it he heard the voice again. "Goodbye!" The dogs stood at the fence and watched as they pulled away. The car rolled slowly along Skull Creek Road to the highway.

Kasanian told Lafleur to be sure to come back and visit him. Lafleur said he would. Kasanian asked how much longer Lafleur would be around. Lafleur told him two or three weeks. He said that after that he'd be in and out for a few months. Kasanian asked about the prisoners. They reached the crossroad and sat with the engine idling. The headlamps illuminated a wedge of desert across the highway. Lafleur told him about the woman.

"Jesus Christ," Kasanian said.

Lafleur told him about the woman disappearing from the hospital.

"Jesus," Kasanian said. "You sure you don't want me to come along?"

Unconsciously, Lafleur ran his fingers down the barrel of the rifle that he held between his knees. "No, I'll be fine."

A pair of tiny headlights appeared in the distance to the west. Lafleur felt his body tightening. He told Kasanian that the prisoners had been moved into one of the new buildings, that they had better quarters now. "But I'm not sure they're there legally."

"Christ," Kasanian said. "Listen. You're going to have to report this. You can't just let it ride. Sometimes you got to have help."

"I know," Lafleur said. The headlights approached, then slowed. Sabat's truck stopped in front of the Buick. Lafleur opened his door and tipped the gun barrel out.

"You be careful, now," Kasanian said.

"Thanks." Lafleur got out, moved to the truck, and pulled the door open. Sabat's eyes moved immediately to the rifle, then he turned his head and looked out the windshield. Lafleur felt a wave of anger. He slid onto the seat and positioned the rifle between his knees again. "Forward. About a mile." They drove in silence until they reached the turnoff. "Left." He guided Sabat past the now-darkened line shack. The old pickup was parked out front. He caught just a glimpse of the horses out back, their bodies glossy in the faint light. He directed Sabat through the keyhole and across the tilted bowl.

Sabat spoke: "I'm sorry you had this trouble."

Lafleur looked at him coldly, the round, smooth face tipped slightly back as he gazed through the windshield. Lafleur tasted his anger, like metal in his throat, but because of his distrust—of Sabat, of himself even, and of his sense of his own vulnerability—he said nothing more until they neared the volcanic ridge, then he told Sabat to go slowly, to watch for the cliff. As they turned around the ridge he found his hands creeping down toward the action of the rifle. He glanced at the door latch, marking it in case he wanted to get out in a hurry. The headlights probed the open sky above the cliffs, then swept in toward the low ridge. Lafleur leaned forward, straining to see.

They came near where he'd left Snediker. "Easy," he said. There was no sign of Snediker. "Easy. He's not there." Sabat didn't speak. He stopped the truck and Lafleur got out, carefully now, touching first one foot to the ground and then the other. He took the rifle with him. He turned a complete circle, looking into the night, then moved to the spot where Snediker had been sitting. He found the twisted shirt sleeve. He found the snake head, but not the snake's body. He went back to the truck and put the sleeve and snake head on the seat. "Here's his sleeve. The snake head. He pulled the damn thing in two." Then he said, "What the hell do you mean, trouble?"

Sabat gazed at him without speaking.

"The fucker tried to shoot me."

Still, Sabat didn't speak, and Lafleur thought, He's looking for his route. Either he's looking for a route out of this or for one to get to me. Then Sabat spoke, his voice low: "I'm sorry. The last I heard he was back in Reno."

Lafleur stepped back, nodding slowly, not speaking. He turned, moved to the front of the truck again, and looked around. He climbed the ridge to look, slowing as he neared the top, listening. The truck door slammed and he jumped. Sabat had got out and was standing near the left headlight, looking up at Lafleur, his shape dark next to the brightness. Lafleur took another step. He moved with great deliberation, fearing snakes again, fearing that Snediker would be up there awaiting him. He took a couple of more steps and stopped again, spooked. He listened, but heard nothing

262

except for the hum of the truck. He thought of finding Snediker on the other side—dead maybe, or maybe he'd discover Snediker's face peering right back at him. Lafleur's body froze. He couldn't make himself move for a moment. He slipped the safety off and held the rifle at ready, then he moved, crawled up and looked. He saw no one. He stood up straight, looking left and right. Loose rock rolled down from beneath his feet, making a dry sound. Behind him, the truck hummed. Lafleur's eyes began to ache from searching the darkness. There was no sign of anyone. He slung the rifle over his shoulder.

Below him lay the bowl, a large place in the moonlight hollowed like a lake, and beyond it were the even darker hills, then the somewhat lighter sky. A breeze ruffled his hair. He looked back at the truck. Sabat stood there with his hands in his jacket pockets, a rounded figure in the darkness beside the headlight. It occurred to Lafleur that if Snediker had been here Sabat would have been no help at all. He looked back toward the bowl. He saw movement, some flutter of motion near the base of the ridge. He gripped the rifle sling. Suddenly the thing rose. Fascinated, Lafleur simply watched it. It kept rising and then, construing the upward motion to be size, he thought, There! Snediker!—and quickly he swung the rifle off his shoulder, but the thing kept rising, kept coming as fast as the wind, and Lafleur stood transfixed, straining to make out the shape of the thing played upon faintly by light from the sky. It breached the sky and at the same time hurtled directly toward him, and rushed by, coming near enough for him to hear the air whistling in its wings and to see that it carried something long and thin in its talons—a snake or the snake body. He revolved and watched it—an owl. It became a pale, mobile sliver sailing out over the cliffs into the night, then vanished.

Lafleur clambered back down the ridge and moved to the opposite side of the truck from Sabat. He laid the gun on the hood and leaned against the fender. He touched the gun with his fingertips.

"Maybe he took off," Sabat said.

"Seems so."

"But not by the cliff, most likely." Sabat's voice was low and measured.

"No."

"We could drive back the other way and look."

"Did you see that owl?" Lafleur said.

"What owl?"

Lafleur didn't answer. They drove between the ridge and cliffs until the shelf became too narrow to proceed. To their right there was a gulf of darkness over the edge of the precipice. Sabat backed up and turned the truck around. Lafleur could see the project, the pinpricks of light gathered together, surrounded by night. They drove back around the end of the ridge and into the bowl. Slowly, they circled the perimeter. Lafleur leaned forward and searched the sand and the rough black volcanic formations as the headlights played across them.

"He's going to be hard to find," Sabat said.

"Especially if he's hiding."

"How far can he go?"

"Kasanian said the bite would make him sick."

"But not kill him?"

"Probably not."

"He's big."

They were speaking guardedly. They had driven halfway around the bowl. The sand was dotted with knucklelike horse droppings. Lafleur turned his head to the right and looked out the window. The volcanic ridge ascended and grew more complex. Large, fleeting shadows jumped across it as the truck passed. It was true that, if Snediker was up there staying still, he would be hard to see even if the lights fell directly upon him.

"Maybe we should head back to the ranch and check," Sabat said.

"Check what?"

"Go back and wait, then."

"Go back and call the police," Lafleur said.

Sabat turned the truck back toward the keyhole and accelerated lightly. The pickup jiggled as it sailed over the uneven ground. The gun barrel quivered in Lafleur's hands. He thought of the darkened line shack up ahead. "We should stop and warn the cowboy."

"Probably not necessary," Sabat said.

Lafleur looked across at Sabat, who stared straight ahead. "It would be a good idea to warn him."

"It looked like he was in bed."

"You don't get it, do you?" When Sabat didn't respond, Lafleur picked up the snake head and looked at it in the light from the dash—agape jaws, sharp fangs, entrails still hanging from where Snediker had jerked it off its body. He set it back on the seat and laid his head back, and allowed the gun barrel to rest against his right thigh. He felt cold. He saw the owl in his mind, the big bird rushing at him, then sailing out into the darkness.

"That he tried to kill you?" Sabat said.

In the corner of his eye, Lafleur saw Sabat's face turned toward him. "Right."

"I understand. But it's you, not anybody else. The cowboy's not in any danger."

"Just me and the old woman?"

Sabat lined the truck up with the keyhole. The slightly lighter sky was visible through the dark opening in the rock. "Look." He turned his head again. "Snediker gets fixed ideas."

"Maybe so. But the word for that kind of character is psychopath. All his ideas are fixed, and it's damn hard to tell where the hell he gets them from."

"Are you blaming me again?"

"I didn't say that," Lafleur said, and he thought—not even thinking it, really, He's setting me up. He remembered Sabat standing down by the truck when he was up on the ridge. He thought, then, too, allowing me to be a target. *Careful!* . . . he told himself. They entered the keyhole, passed as if through a ring of darkness, and then entered another darkness. "We're stopping to warn the cowboy."

The lump on the side of Sabat's mouth rose as he smiled. "You've got the gun."

Lafleur glanced down at the rifle that he held poised between his knees, the butt resting on the floorboard. The rifle swayed lightly with the motion of his hands and body. He hadn't dreamed of using it. In his guilelessness he found the suggestion that he might astonishing. He closed his eyes for a moment and saw the owl rush by him again. There was something in that owl, some meaning, and in his nearly inchoate state— afraid, exhausted, angry, still shocked, and sensing that he was caught on some very large, turning thing—he tried to hang on to the owl. It was phantasmagoric, a spirit that kept bursting into light and then flitted out again into the night. He had happened to be out there, that was all. The owl had happened to be there, like the carp, the doe, the coyote, like the heron back on the Willamette that always happened to be there. The owl had been feeding on the snake body, perhaps, which also had happened to be there. In the convergence of happenstance, then, he—Lafleur— came to be there, certainly, marked by the owl. The owl simply came to validate him, because he was there, because it was there, because the snake body was there. So it was. His mind leaped and a version of perception became certain, though truly, whether or not the owl had had *that* snake, or any snake, or if it were an owl at all—and not, say, an absolute hallucination—was immaterial. The version was what was material, even if it were a version granted him by ghosts. It was material for the essence it ghosted, for what like a surveyor's marker it triangulated between himself and Sabat and so . . .

. . . and so, he whispered softly to himself as he struggled to control his thoughts . . .

. . . and so, no matter what the willful or deranged reasons for Snediker's attack, or the attacks, both of them, tonight and months ago outside Zymanski's warehouse, they'd become inevitable through the conspiracy between Snediker's nature and—at the least—Sabat's neglect. At the very least, Sabat, who knew Snediker best, had allowed matters to run their course, had waited and watched just as he'd stood down by the truck watching, just as he watched Iris, just as he would wait and watch now if he were allowed to, taking a chance on Snediker and the cowboy. Snediker was the marker, that was all, the third point by which Lafleur would come to know Sabat. Lafleur had sensed something akin to this from the start, but he hadn't trusted himself, hadn't trusted the disbelief he'd been digging at . . . excavating . . . for months, and that was why he'd allowed the question of Snediker's presence on the site to float for so long. He believed it now. In his eyes the rounded figure next to him, manipulative in his quiescence, became suddenly and certainly evil.

They glided across the open desert. "Stop at the shack," Lafleur said. "We'll stop."

"Who the hell do you think you are?"

Sabat stopped the truck at the shack. "Look," he said. "I miscalculated Bill Snediker. I'm sorry." Then he began to chuckle. "Who do I think I am? Are you all right?"

Lafleur pushed open his door, got out and walked toward the shack. He glimpsed the wild horses in the back, churning slowly in the moonlight. He stepped up onto the porch. He heard footsteps inside. The door opened and the young cowboy appeared. Lafleur told him that they'd not found the man they had been looking for, that the man might be dangerous. Lafleur put his hand on the jamb, leaned forward, and said, "He's a little cracked." The cowboy slowly licked his upper lip. He was in long underwear. Button-to-button, the stretched fabric left diamond-shaped openings up his chest. He glanced at Lafleur's rifle. "I'm sorry," Lafleur said. He suggested that the cowboy bolt his door. The cowboy said, "I will," but he gave Lafleur a look that said, Who's a little cracked?

Lafleur and Sabat drove past Arock and out onto the highway, through Rome and up the gravel road. They didn't speak. It was midnight when they reached the ranch. Lafleur called the sheriff. He thought of Penny, insisting that he report the mugging back in Portland, and again, after the funeral, insisting that he report Snediker's presence on the site, and of Kasanian telling him to get help from the law. As he talked to the sheriff's dispatcher he stared at the window. But for the reflected light of the room, which made the window black, he might have seen the outline of the six-foot stone wall and of the tops of the buildings. Sabat stood behind him, listening. Lafleur thought that Penny had understood all along that the true function of law was to define trouble, to corroborate it when it occurred, to bring it out into the light, to name it, to make it real. The sheriff's office took Lafleur's description and said they would send a car.

When he hung up, Lafleur turned to Sabat. "You, too. They want to talk to you."

Sabat's face had become sleek. "Do you know what you've done?"

"To you?"

"Do you know what kind of company I.D. is?"

"More than I want to know."

"No. Not nearly enough. Do you know how big General Electric is? Or Bechtel?"

"Bechtel, sure."

"Multinational. Like governments. I.D.'s in that class."

"So?"

The sheen on Sabat's face was like another skin, translucent like plastic film. "So now it's you against them. Do you know how dangerous it is to fool around with such a company?"

Lafleur said, "You're threatening me?"

"I'm acquainting you with a fact. You're in trouble."

"For what? Turning in a lunatic?"

"For breaking cover."

"Cover! Whose damn cover?" Furious, Lafleur leaned toward Sabat. "Your cover, for starters."

"I've got no cover!"

Sabat didn't answer, but stood his ground. He smiled faintly as if he were being confronted by a complete novice, by one of little understanding. Lafleur turned away and left the house. He found Iris waiting for him in bed. He was still carrying the gun and her eyes widened as he took it off his shoulder and set it in the corner.

"What happened?"

"Snediker."

She hiked herself up against the pillow. "What?"

"It's all right."

He told her about it as he undressed. She sat up straight and listened with increasing attention as he went on. "He's still out there?" she said when he told her about not being able to find Snediker again.

He shrugged, and told her what Sabat had said about the company. "Is he serious?"

She lit a cigarette and tipped her head back as she inhaled, then watched the smoke as it drifted to the ceiling. She was thinking. "He's serious, all right, but my guess is he's the one in trouble. That's what he's worried about."

"It's not that big, is it? Not like General Electric?"

"No, but it's big enough. What executives do if they're ambitious is jump from I.D. to G.E."

"What does he mean 'cover'?"

"What does Vic ever mean?" She was sitting cross-legged now. Her bare knees poked out and her blue nightgown was bunched up between her thighs. "The company's obsessive about keeping a low profile. This place'll be crawling with police."

"Maybe the feds."

"Right. That'll blow his cover. He screwed up with Snediker." She took a final drag from her cigarette, then snuffed it out in an ashtray and took a long time poking at the coals with the butt. Lafleur had the feeling that she was off in another realm.

"What are you thinking?"

"Trying to figure out what it means."

"What's next?"

"Exactly."

"Should I worry?"

"I'd be careful with Vic."

"I'm going to be straight with the police."

"Of course."

He slipped into bed, pulled up the covers to his chin, and lay there straight as a pole. "I've got no choice."

"I was worried about you," she said. "I heard the pickup leave. I didn't know what was going on."

"A lot," he said.

He slept fitfully. Each time he awoke he found himself filled with an obscure sense of dread. Finally, he got up and showered and roved the building site until light. When the sheriff's car arrived, it was driven by the same deputy who'd come for the remains of the boy at the river. As they rode up to the line shack, the deputy told Lafleur that the boy had never been claimed, that there'd been nothing to identify him by, not even dental work, that he'd been buried at county expense.

At the shack, the cowboy was awaiting the semi-rigs that would haul out the horses. He hadn't seen Snediker. Lafleur and the deputy drove to the cliffs. Lafleur discovered that now he rather liked the young man, whom he had previously considered foolish. There was no trace of Snediker. Another deputy found a red car with Nevada plates pulled off the road between the project and Rome. It was rented. There was no evidence that Snediker had returned to it.

Lafleur and Phil drove down to the river later on and found that Jones's body was gone, too. They searched for signs of Snediker. They looked for the pistol Lafleur had thrown over the cliff, but couldn't find it. They found the cane Lafleur had abandoned at the river. Perhaps Jones had been dragged off by the coyotes. Lafleur thought it would be all right for

Jones to be devoured, to be refuse, to be scattered, to become a part of the desert that way. The deputy came again the next day to search. He interviewed Lafleur again, and Sabat, Kasanian, the cowboy, and as Iris had expected, he brought an FBI agent with him, who did the same round of interviews, including one with El Gallo. There were questions about the prisoners. Sabat became furtive and inaccessible. Warrants had been issued for Snediker's arrest—two counts of assault, one of rape, and one of attempted murder, but he was gone, it seemed, vanished.

During the day, Lafleur kept looking over his shoulder. With each passing night his dreams became increasingly vivid. He awoke in the dark and found himself sitting bolt upright with the sheet twisted around his legs. Next to him, Iris slumbered deeply. His head swirled with images— the distant floor of the cliff, Snediker coming up behind him, the rifle scope flashing, the snake coiling on the rock, Snediker ripping the snake in two, the horse herd passing through the keyhole in the rock, the owl flying at him, Sabat's smooth face poised above the steering wheel, and then again in the study, Sabat with the shine almost like a halo, and through it all the distant, terrifying cry of Kasanian's parrot, *Goodbye! Goodbye!*

Chapter Nineteen

Often there is no telling what the meaning is. An aboriginal tale is always "thrown" in unknown ways to some unknown but perhaps terrific extent.

Hector Zeta,
Manifesto for Spirits

Lafleur and Iris lay in bed facing each other. It was just before dawn. Her breath came into his face and he inhaled it with the air of the room. He inhaled her. He gazed at her face—jaw, cheekbone, nose, and closed eyes. This face and warmth of body were familiar to him by now, and a comfort, yet she was still a carrier of the unknown, the reasons in her for choosing him unknown, and his reasons for accepting her unknown.

Her fingers drifted across his belly. He rolled nearer to her. They lay quietly, gently aroused. She raised her head for a moment, glancing at the window behind her, then settled back onto the pillow and asked, "How are we this morning?" Despite himself, Lafleur chuckled. The amusement between them turned anxious. They lay still, allowing the unease to exhaust itself. Turned loose, their minds drifted and hovered, and darted and drifted again, bright as dragonflies.

After a while, he said, "I'd really like to stop worrying about Snediker." Ten days had passed since Snediker's disappearance and for half those days the police had conducted searches, but still whenever Lafleur ventured away from the site he carried the Thompson pistol with him, and otherwise he kept it loaded and in easy reach in the room. He'd set an old wooden milk crate on end next to his side of the bed. On it, underneath the Hector Zeta, the pistol lay ensconced in its hardwood case. The case was unlatched. The pistol had the .45 barrel screwed in. The two rifles, his and Snediker's, leaned side by side in the corner just beyond the milk crate. They were also loaded. "Maybe the asshole's dead."

She turned her head toward him and reached up and ran her fingertips along his cheek. "He's got to know he's in deep trouble if he comes back here."

"But he's crazy."

"Crazy enough not to know that?"

"Maybe the coyotes got him."

"Maybe."

From outside he heard a hawk cry. He imagined it circling in the dawn. "If he's managed to get back to Reno he'll just get pushed back into something like it again." He had concluded that Snediker had exercised very little control over his actions.

"Yes."

"He's got to know that the police are after him."

"He'll get caught."

They lay still. Outside, the cowbirds called to each other. Their call was exquisite. It sounded like water trickling over glass. Dungeaters, they were here because of the horses, pigs, and sheep. They followed the trail of dung wherever it led, all across the countryside.

Lafleur turned his thoughts to his work, as he did every morning in preparation for the day. The structural components of the buildings were complete now, foundations, walls, floors, and roofs, and the exterior detail well underway, the trenches and grades backfilled, the concrete plant dismantled and hauled out, the concrete crew gone and new crews at work on the interiors, ceilings, doors, lighting, heating and cooling, circuitry, plumbing, cabinetry, cages. The computer had been moved into the Industries Building and he supervised from there, inside the elevated central guard tower—an octagonal cubicle that eventually would be enclosed with bullet-proof glass, a high-tech "pulpit." Located near the juncture of the Industries and Support buildings, it offered a clear view across the main floors of both of those, and up into the Gymnasium as well. That was the intent. Later, the guard would be surrounded by banks of monitors and electronic control boards, and he could maintain visual contact with the prisoners lifting weights or playing basketball in the gym, or sitting in the library, or working in the "plant" which was to be devoted to computer fabrication. Much of the plant was already erected—the long counter rows and stools, conveyor belts, parts bins, magnification devices for micro-fabrication, soldering irons and power tools attached to collapsible overhead arms, the racks, and ramps that led out to the loading docks.

"He might get shot, too," Lafleur said, "if he's still wandering around out there." He was lying on his back with his hands under his head and his elbows sticking out like wings.

Iris murmured.

"He might've been shot already."

"True," Iris said.

"Some of these people around here are old-fashioned. They like their law close at hand, right there at their fingertips."

Again Iris murmured, and without looking he could tell that she was smiling. "God, yes. They're anarchists almost, they keep it so close."

The word *anarchists* raised in him not entirely displeasing images of fires, bombs, chaos. He thought about anarchy and the extremely lawful. He thought about lynch mobs. The idea of a lynch mob wasn't all that displeasing to him, either, not when he considered Snediker. Bad as a lynch mob was, he thought, at least some of the victim's presumed guilt was transferred to it. With the blood on its hands, at least the mob maintained traffic with its own bestiality, unlike this place he'd built, which promised to absolve the "innocent" completely from their share of the guilt.

In the three buildings that adjoined each other—the Gymnasium, Support Building, Industries Building—there were lesser guard cubicles in addition to the central tower. Eventually, they too would have closed-circuit monitors and their own control boards, and all visual matter would be piped from them to the main control tower. For now, he and Iris shared a table of raw wood in the central tower. They had the blueprints and manuals spread out. They worked together part of the time—he plotting what was next, she deliberating over what had just passed, or charting her inspectors' reports and tracking the requisitions and deliveries. He saw that her authority had increased. Sabat had become almost invisible, and in response Iris seemed to be covering more ground.

The two of them went back and forth in the printed plans, and from the plans to the computer. He would leave the tower to check the work itself, or to confer with a foreman, or she would leave, and then they'd come back and sometimes meet. While they were there they'd go away from each other in the plans and then sometimes they'd be surprised to discover themselves meeting as if by chance on a certain page, or bent over a certain farflung detail on the screen. The paths of construction they had to follow became increasingly circuitous. The work became digital, subject to their digits, their fingers, and to each separate brain activated similarly to inspect the density as if with a long, thin probe.

Working from the tower gave Lafleur a discomforting sense of power. At times, it seemed as though the workers were his prisoners. He could even move to the edge of the cubicle, look straight down into the lower level of the Industries Building, and catch glimpses of the actual prisoners, the "detainees," who were kept down there in the completed cells of the "pit." The image haunted him—the bodies catching light in the dim cells as they lolled on their cots or stood next to the bars, staring out at the workers putting finishing touches on the prison that housed them more and more completely with each passing day. Lafleur had thought that it must be like being buried alive.

When he was down in the pit he sometimes stopped to talk with El Gallo, which made him feel as though he'd become Captain Colnett— half of him down there with the man he liked and the other half floating in the air, up in the tower. A few days ago, El Gallo had leaned forward, brought his dark, heavy face near the bars, and said, "I'm guilty. But not this guilty."

As a result of questioning by the FBI, and then by immigration officers, El Gallo had been put in touch with a lawyer, who was seeking his release. He said, "I'm guilty of bringing in refugees. I admit that. I admit almost anything they want. I did it for money. I got bad breath. I bleed. My shit comes out brown." He laughed, stepped back, and spread his arms. His turquoise shirt was threadbare and had a rip down one side. His belt buckle gleamed. "I smell like a dog, but I'm a citizen of this country. Sooner or later, they'll have to admit that."

His face became somber. "What about them?" He gestured toward the cell next to him in which two men sat at either end of a cot. The two were watching with their narrow, angry, dangerous eyes. "And them?" El Gallo said, gesturing toward the row of cells on the other side of the hall. Some cells were enclosed with concrete walls. Others were simply barred. There were prisoners in each kind, placed there, Lafleur thought, at random. "That's why the authorities don't want to let me out. Even if I don't say a word, when I get out a little bit of them gets out. Like with the old woman. It's a leak. And if I do talk, just a few words, the leak grows bigger. If I talk to the people who hired me, then the spirit of these men starts to escape. That's what is feared, a flood of spirits. The bosses can't stand it, the idea of the spirit of these men breaking loose."

"I'm sorry," Lafleur said.

"No." El Gallo leaned against the bars and reached out and touched Lafleur's arm. "It's not you, man. You've done plenty."

But, filled with guilt for what he found himself unable to do, Lafleur had thought, *Not enough.*

He lay in the bed now, rapt with his thoughts of El Gallo, of his own inabilities, and of how his unconsidered, inescapable response—getting the old woman to the hospital, getting away from Snediker, and then calling the police—might seem considered and deliberate to someone else. He didn't deserve the credit El Gallo gave him.

Iris slid her knee up onto his thigh and whispered, "Let's screw." Her manner of approach set off an uneasy twang in him, but he rolled sideways and touched her hip. Her green eyes probed him. Outside, the cowbirds called. A flicker tapped at the barn wall. He heard pigs grunting, two of them probably contesting a scrap of food dug out of the earth. He slid his right hand under her and pulled her toward him, then moved his left hand up her side and placed one fingertip on the center of her taut nipple. He rolled her nipple against his thumb. His head was like an aerial seed pod afloat in the room, reeling and filled with chaos. She put her hands on his chest, then she tipped her head back and spoke, fastening his thoughts as if with a spike: "He's gone, Hank."

"I guess."

"Forget about him."

"I can't. Besides, if I stop worrying about him, then I'll have to worry about Vic and International Data. Maybe it's easier to worry about Snediker."

It was true. Sabat's threat had so far failed to materialize. Far from forgotten, it had nevertheless become generalized in Lafleur's mind, a scrim against which the palpable recollections of Snediker were incised. Lafleur had wondered if he was tricking himself again. That, too, worried him. At times everything worried him.

"The company's not going to do anything to you."

She seemed to be saying that with more certainty than he'd heard from her before.

"And if Snediker's gone," she said, "Vic's heart is gone."

"What?"

She slid her hands around to his buttocks, pulled him deeper into her, and slowly rotated her hips. "Don't you see?"

"Say that again," he said. His head listened. His body was poised and quivering. His body was like the snake head entering the liquidity of his mind.

"If Snediker's gone . . ." she said, but he groaned and rolled her over on her back. He dug his toes into the mattress, grasped her shoulders, and pushed deeply into her.

They lay naked under the sheet and blanket. Their legs were entwined. She had her head on his shoulder and they fell into a deep drowse, then slept. The lovemaking did acrobatics in Lafleur's dreams. Only when he awoke did he realize that he'd fallen asleep. Neither of them had moved. It was after dawn. The room was golden.

He turned his head to the left and ran his eyes over the two loaded rifles in the corner and back to the milk crate, to the case that held the Thompson pistol. He reached out and took up the book, the Zeta, and set it on his chest. "What about this?" he said, leafing through the pages with one hand. He knew that she also was awake.

"What?"

He found the place. "Here." He turned the book toward her.

She shifted, brushing his shoulder with her breast. "The Burns Paiute chapter," she said. He freed his arm and moved up beside her. They resettled themselves. "It's cribbed, of course," she said.

"Cribbed?"

"Stolen."

"He says that. He has a footnote."

Iris thumbed through the footnotes. "Right," she said. "Beatrice Blyth Whiting." It was from a book published in 1950. "Even so, he stretches it. You don't know where Whiting leaves off and Zeta starts in." She turned back to the chapter heading and gazed at the page and at the same time idly stroked Lafleur's ankle with her toes. "Zeta twists the material."

Lafleur rested his hand on her abdomen. "Sometimes you have to torque a beam to get things straight. Zeta says he does that."

Zeta had a disclaimer in which he admitted that he had collapsed the elements of two of Whiting's tales into one, but at the same time insisted that it was completely true to the original, as best one could construe that—*the original.* Lafleur liked that—the collapse of elements, torquing to get at the truth.

Iris ran one foot up his leg, then down again. "Maybe I don't remember it as well as I should," she said. She propped the book up on his chest, leaned over him, and read. Lafleur closed his eyes again. The bunkhouse began to reverberate with a rhythmic thumping noise. It was Phil, on his back on his pad, beginning his morning regimen with bench presses. Iris turned the page. Lafleur opened his eyes and gazed across the room at a short timber with a chunk of crossbeam that he'd found in the barn and carried in here to keep for Abe Kasanian. It had hay tallies on it, dating from 1902, written in pencil in a coarse, strong hand: 1902—25 tons, 1903—32 tons. . . . In the twenties, the tonnage was converted to bales: 1922—610 bales . . . It went on with the numbers and otherwise, he was sure, contained the record of what he was not prepared to decipher: underneath the indications of harvest, the subtle shifts in equipment and help, drought years, good years, sickness and health, questions of charac-ter—the irrational integer.

Iris turned another page. Lafleur looked at the book and read along with her. The passage was set in the 1930s in a camp just outside the town of Burns and had to do with the death of Mr. M., a northern Paiute.

According to Zeta (if not Beatrice Blyth Whiting), Mr. M. was a mild man who minded his own business and was not unpopular with the other members of the community. He was lame. He'd broken his hip in a fall from a horse and the injury had been poorly treated. While he did not move rapidly, he could walk at his own speed for great distances.

Mr. M.'s wife, Mrs. M., drank heavily and had affairs with other men. It was said that one of her daughters had been fathered by a man from Burns. Many felt sorry for the burden Mr. M. carried. Sometimes he took vacations from his wife by making long treks—sixty miles to Fort Bidwell, a hundred miles to McDermitt, and thirty miles northeast of Burns to Drewsey. When he was home, he and Mrs. M. fought constantly, or she fought him. It was she that the neighbors heard, her shouts and accusations. At times the fights reached such a fever pitch that the entire community witnessed them. One winter night Mrs. M. chased her husband with a club, knocked him unconscious, and left him where he fell in the cold. Another time, the neighbors were awakened in the middle of the night by screaming and moaning. Mrs. M. and her eldest son were mercilessly beating Mr. M. out in the road. Mr. M. seemed incapable of defending himself. The onlookers, fearful that he would be killed, finally pulled the two men apart and tied them to separate telegraph poles.

Mr. M. died quite suddenly when he was in his early fifties. Mrs. M. claimed that he had been sorcerized by Mrs. P., his own cousin, who'd come to Burns after having been driven out of Fort Bidwell. Mrs. P. was known as a sorceress. Back in Fort Bidwell, she'd put the blood curse on the family whom she blamed for the death of her son. She'd cut her arms and gone through their house, smearing blood on their chairs and sink and beds, and on the seat in their outhouse.

According to Mrs. M., her husband decided to take his family camping up at Drewsey and Mrs. P. said she wanted to come along, but Mr. M. told her he didn't want her. Mrs. P. said he would be sorry for not taking her. Mrs. M. took this to mean that Mrs. P. was threatening them with a blood curse. Mr. M. set out with his family and while he was traveling he saw a snake. That night he dreamed the snake was crawling around his throat and he awoke just as it was about to strangle him. The next morning he had a fever and they returned to Burns and summoned Dr. X.

Mrs. M. told Dr. X. that Mrs. P. was responsible. The doctor asked Mrs. P. to take a bath and call off her power. Mrs. P. said that she would, but admitted to nothing. She did so only for Mr. M., her cousin, and to satisfy Dr. X.'s request, she said. It meant nothing to her. She would lose nothing by it. On the contrary, since it was a favor, it would be her gain, and under no circumstances could she give up her power, certainly not the blood curse back in Fort Bidwell. That power was real and stayed on. It would be improper for her to try to call off power that was no longer even her own, she said.

Mr. M. recovered, but a month later he was sick again. This time, although Dr. X. administered to him for five nights, Mr. M. couldn't be saved. Dr. X. diagnosed the illness as caused by sorcery but refused to name the sorcerer. Mrs. M. and all the members of her family said it was obviously Mrs. P.'s power and they made it very uncomfortable for the P. family. Mrs. M. said she'd found blood in Mr. M.'s bed. The oldest M. girl accused Mrs. P. in public and attacked her with a club.

Some people didn't believe that Mrs. P. had done the sorcerizing and claimed that Mrs. M. had killed her husband herself. They recalled all the family fights the community had witnessed and said that Mrs. M. wanted to get rid of her husband so she could run around and do what she wanted. They said she was jealous of Mrs. P. because she and Mr. M. were so close to each other. They remembered when Mrs. M. was ill and Dr. X. had been called to work on her. They said that Dr. X. had told Mrs. M. that she was sick from her own power, bad power given to her by a black lizard. Dr. X. offered to take the power away, but like Mrs. P., Mrs. M. wanted to keep her power. This was fine, some said. Who, having power, would want to freely cast it away? But what you keep you must accept as yours, they said.

Mrs. M. said that Mr. M. had the power to travel long distances even though he was lame. He could survive on nothing for days in the desert. She needed all the power she had to keep a man like that who in his travels stretched her hold on him to the breaking point. But the people said that this story Mrs. M. told about Mrs. P. was indeed her own story. The blood was her own. The snake Mr. M. had dreamed was her lizard power.

The accusations were fueled by the community's dislike of Mrs. M. People thought that she and her daughters felt superior because they could always get work in town. The daughters were better educated than the other girls in the camp, too. And the way Mrs. M. and her daughters ran around with white men put all the women in the camp in danger. They said it was Mrs. M. who told Mrs. P. to stay behind when they went to Drewsey. Mrs. P.'s family, everyone knew, had the power of snakes and it was Mrs. M. who interpreted her husband's dream and expressed her opinion to Dr. X. Maybe there wasn't a snake in the dream after all. Maybe it was a lizard in the dream, ghosting Mr. M.'s breath as a lizard sucks an egg. It could be, they said, that Mrs. M. had made it all up so that she wouldn't be accused of murder.

That was the story. When Iris finished it she laid down the book and said, "Now I remember."

Lafleur said, "Whose story is it?"

"What do you mean?"

"Mr. M.'s or Mrs. M.'s? Or Mrs. P.'s, or even Dr. X.'s?"

"Wait," Iris said, tipping up the book and flicking her eyes from it to Lafleur. "Doesn't he talk about that?"

Lafleur murmured assent and waited as Iris read on. A moment ago, he'd heard Phil padding down the hallway to the bathroom. Now he heard the shower running . . . Phil at his ablutions. He heard Diane moving around in her room next door. He heard distant sounds from the encampment, a voice calling, a camper door shutting. He heard the cowbirds. He heard a vehicle pull into the lot in front of the ranchhouse, and wondered what it was. He couldn't bring himself to get up to look. The light had intensified. Soon, the sun would pour through the window. He stared over his feet again at the old timber, enumerated with harvests like a tablet from ancient Babylonia.

As Lafleur remembered, Zeta said this about the story: It is a cultural fringe tale. One of its strongest elements is mobility—the mobility of Mr. M. in particular, despite his lameness, and of Mrs. P., and as a background the incursions of Mrs. M. and her daughters into the town, or of the town into them. In the case of Mr. M., his lameness lifts his travels to a mythic level. There is the question of why he traveled so far—to Fort Bidwell to see Mrs. P., perhaps, or to Drewsey because it was a traditional gathering place for the fabrication of nets prior to the salmon run on the Malheur River, or to all places as a reenactment, whether purposeful or purposeless, of the man's traditional wandering in Paiute society.

The tale does not give us reasons or anything of Mr. M.'s psychological makeup except that he was mild and commanded the community's sympathy, Zeta said. Psychology has no place in the tale. Only sympathies, the response to what we know as psychologies, belong here. Looked at a certain way and remembering Mrs. M.'s claim that she wished to retain her lizard power in order to "keep" Mr. M., it is possible to see her in a light entirely different from that immediately shed by the tale. And what of Mrs. P.'s journey from Fort Bidwell to Burns? Why did she come to Burns?

As to white influence, what direct evidence there is of it in the tale is attached mainly to Mrs. M. and her educated daughters, and to scenic furniture, the telegraph poles Mr. M. and his son are tied to, and the chairs, beds, sink, and outhouse seat that Mrs. P. smears her blood over down in Fort Bidwell. In fact, Zeta said, the relative absence of scenic and historical context is interesting in itself. If one reflects upon this for a moment and knows something of the conditions under which the displaced Paiutes lived—impoverished, reduced to raiding the garbage bins behind grocery stores for food, degraded, racked with disease, moved by force from one place to another, and having seen their traditional gathering grounds despoiled and taken from them—then one would see that the white influence must be everywhere, seeping into the tale from all sides.

The role of Dr. X., for example, comes into question. What was his position in relation to white doctors in town, under what constraints or with what freedom did he administer to sickness, and with what despair at the abundance of disease? We do not know. And as to Mrs. M., who engaged in sexual trade with the white community, who succeeded in educating her daughters, why did she do this, out of what desperation, what will to survive? We do not know. We know only that the white influence was there, and that by its being there the tale is "thrown" in unknown ways to some unknown but perhaps terrific extent.

According to Zeta, the tale is skeletal, almost a cipher. Several interpretations of its central issue—that of who is to blame for Mr. M.'s death—are possible, but the notion that blame cannot be placed is unacceptable. The cause is in there (or *out* there) somewhere, however inscrutable it may be. Its inscrutability is its essence. The notion that Mr. M. might have died of natural causes or of disease begs the question and is equally unacceptable. What is most remarkable about the tale is the dynamism of its spirituality. The spiritual world remained a permeable gland—up to that time, in any case—a habitation like story itself, like language, like the Chinook dialect, capable of absorbing alien matter and of keeping its effect of placing human consciousness out in the natural world. The spirits—snake, lizard, and ghost—are out in that world. All things carry spirits. The tale asserts that human consciousness is a collaboration with spirits.

In the white world, in the grinding poverty of our humanism, Zeta said, we keep what we call our illusions to ourselves. If our illusions become too much for us to bear, we may expiate them to a psychoanalyst, who will help us to kill them, but always, nearly always, the killing is in terms of ourselves, our personal histories, and so it is a part of ourselves we kill. Through such an act we only enter more and more deeply into a solipsistic trade. Our lives are filled with illusions, the desperate little dramas we make up about ourselves and others and through which we attach blame, or by which we assert our superiority, or inferiority, as the case may be, and we have larger secrets, too, pacts of a sort—loyalties, religious pacts in which we ultimately disbelieve because of the lack of connections, the lack of traffic with the world, and nationalist and political pacts that sometimes spring into hate campaigns. We have dreams, a plenitude of dreams we don't have the faintest idea what to do with except to stir them in secret. Not even our religion helps us. All this dreaming and secrecy festers in us, spins without recourse, without the resistance of the natural world, creating an unbearable vertigo. . . .

Whenever Lafleur reached this point in his reading of the passage, or of remembering it as he did now, he paused and thought of his father, his father's company, and his—Lafleur's—coming into the company, and then of this, the project, of its purpose—the detention of people who would be put to work developing information storage systems for a corporation. He thought of the sheer, unmanageable, deathly, Byzantine weight of it all, and of how strange it was that a people would go to such an extreme to have its evils kept from itself and at the same time be so bent upon putting those evils to use. And then he would think of his father scampering up the hill in the graveyard to help with the tractor that was stuck in the mud, and of the ghost of Uncle Spence, picking up the limestone blocks, beginning again on the destroyed silo, and of the body of the boy that seemed delivered to him by Nicole as if to tell him to let her go and pay attention to her sister and brother, Tricia and Andy, and it made him wonder about his illusions, or ghosts, who conducted themselves in death exactly as they would have in life.

Iris looked at him. Lafleur knew that she'd read to the end of the chapter, where Zeta said that the names in the tale were nominal, the guilt shared, the death unimportant, the force of a public opinion ritual, and yet that the blame must be placed. But it is impossible to tell upon whom to place it. The blame can only be placed with the aid of spirits, Zeta said, but the spirits are beyond us. They hold us in their power, too. They are our resistance and our code, a way of talking and of living. They may even be tricking us. The only way to place the blame is to be in the story, Zeta said.

Iris said, "I forgot about what he says at the end of the section."

"How could you forget that?"

Iris shook her head. "I don't know."

"You gave me the book."

"I know. I knew that was in there. I forgot how it went."

"What do you think?"

"Think?" She closed the book and looked across the room. "He sure takes liberty with his sources."

"That's not what I mean," Lafleur said, annoyed. "What about the blame?"

"We can't see the cracks in his people. He's reconstructing a spiritual world, among other things, and the tendency, out of a desire, maybe, which in Zeta's case seems almost desperate . . ." She paused. She spoke with caution and at the same time almost nonsensically, as if she sensed that she was being brought near a dangerous center, and Lafleur thought, *Yes, desperate.* She went on: "The tendency is to make everything intact. According to scheme. To make everything of a piece. But what about the cracks, the daily tears in the fabric, the trouble and the doubt?"

"Exactly," Lafleur said, and he thought—she knows that, she's figured that out even though she couldn't remember the book. He said, "*La rage de vouloir conclure.*"

"The what?"

"The rage to conclude."

Her eyes widened a little. "What do you mean?"

"I mean Zeta, what he as much as says about himself, and what by admitting I guess he's trying to fight in himself. I mean Vic, and me, and you." As he spoke he felt that what he wanted to talk to Iris about, what he wanted her to tell him, was slipping away. He struggled to bring it back: "You get hooked into something and you don't give a goddamn about anything else."

"I see," she said.

"Men," he said. "Mainly men." Saying that, he felt himself about to smile and at the same time he was annoyed. "And sometimes women acting like men."

"Me?"

"Maybe sex has nothing to do with it."

Iris settled back beside him, nestling her head on his shoulder. "Sex always has something to do with it. And I don't mind your rage to conclude." She entwined her legs with his and reached under the blanket and stroked his belly, and slid her hand down to his scrotum. He closed his eyes. His head rocked dangerously like a small boat. "The more raging the conclusion the better," Iris said. They lay still.

"Who do you blame?" he said.

"Mrs. M.," Iris said.

Disappointed, Lafleur murmured. He had hoped she would say Mr. M., or Dr. X., something off to the side, something less obvious that might lead them somewhere.

"I wonder what Diane would say."

"No," he said.

"No, what? What do you want?"

"I want you to tell me something."

"Tell you what?"

"I don't know." He felt himself poised on the edge of what he wanted—some truth she could triangulate for him—but then it began to pass away again. "I don't know," he repeated.

"I think I will ask her," Iris said, and abruptly she had slipped out of bed, taking the book with her. He opened his eyes. She stood, searching for the place in the book. She was washed by a rectangle of light, and he passed his eyes coldly down her body—long neck, narrow shoulders, pendulous breasts, belly, russet thatch of hair, and legs. She had a pouting expression as she looked down at the book, then she moved, stirring the motes in the air, slipped on a housecoat, and went out to the hall. Lafleur heard her tapping on Diane's door. He heard the door open. He heard the two women talking. The door shut. He heard Phil in the bathroom, running water into the sink.

He closed his eyes. The luminousness in the room passed blood-colored through his eyelids. He heard sounds in the distance—voices, things clattering and slamming at the encampment, and the cowbirds. He heard a dove. He heard Diane and Iris laughing, their voices muted by the closed door. He lay with the bedclothes draped across his chest and reentered the tingling domain of near-sleep. He jerked when he heard footsteps and voices in the hall. Iris and Diane entered the room and he snapped up the covers.

"Tell him," Iris said. She sat down on the edge of the bed.

"There was a Porter, a lady I heard about," Diane said. "She might be Mrs. P. in the story, or her mother, but I don't know." Diane spoke with a slight lisp, her tongue touching her teeth. Her long black hair hung past her shoulders, down over her red shirt. She wore jeans. Her eyes gleamed. "It's a revenge story," she said. She paused and no one spoke, but Iris turned her head and gave Lafleur a long look, raising her thin eyebrows. Lafleur lay still. "I don't know if it's the same one or not, but Helen Porter used to go around telling the stories," Diane said. "People said she'd change the stories whenever she wanted."

There were footsteps in the hall and then Phil went by the open doorway. He stopped, stepped back, and came in. He was in white shorts and a T-shirt. His face and burly arms were rose-colored. He smelled of cologne. A damp towel was draped over one shoulder and in his hands he held cans of shaving cream and lotion, his mustache wax, razor, toothbrush, and soap dish.

"Not that the stories couldn't be changed, as a white person would understand it," Diane said. "There's a difference. If we change a detail it may not change the story because the history is still there. Helen Porter told the old stories, too. The anthropologist would come to somebody else and say Helen Porter told me this story. It went this way, the anthropologist would say, and the people would listen and not say anything. They would let it stand, just so. What could they say? Helen was telling the old stories and changing them as she wished and people would wonder, Why does she tell those? They don't make sense the way this person says Helen told them. Those are not Helen's stories to tell that way, either. So what does it matter, they would think, and not say anything. Helen Porter and some others were being paid to tell the stories. That was it. The ones like Helen would change things whenever they wanted according to their personal choice if they thought they would get paid more for it. Others would change things to make a joke." Diane shrugged. "The stories weren't meant to be written down, you see, not even this one, which is not one of our stories."

They were all quiet. Iris sat still and Phil stood there solemnly, balancing his articles against his chest. The fact that they'd never heard Diane speak at such length gave her words weight. Lafleur saw that the story was even more skewed than Zeta had suggested, that it had been skewed before Beatrice Blyth Whiting got her hands on it. The sunlight through the window struck the timber from the barn, and cast a strong shadow on the wall in the shape of a cross. The timber had a silvery hue, and the penciled notations stood out against the wood: the data, the record of labor: 1922—610 bales, 1923—544 bales, 1924—608 bales . . .

"It's a pretty good story, though," Diane said. "It could be a story somebody else told to get back at Helen Porter. Who knows? It's good gossip."

Iris laughed and shifted to look back at Lafleur.

He freed his feet from the pressure of the taut bedclothes and said, "Gossip?"

"Very strong gossip, but it's not history," Diane said. She smiled and Iris laughed again softly, and Diane laughed, too.

"What do you mean?" he said.

"History is the truth," Diane said. "It doesn't change."

"Ah," he said.

"This guy . . . what's his name?" Diane said, leaning toward Iris. Iris held up the book. "Zeta," Diane said. "He's right when he calls it . . . what? A house?"

"Habitation," Iris said.

"Like a house," Diane said. "I don't understand half his words. But he's right about that, even though it's just gossip he has there. You keep the windows open to let things in and out, but it's still the house you live in. That's history. It never changes."

"I see," Lafleur said, but he was filled with questions. He wanted to ask about those windows. He wanted to know about the lizards, snakes, and Mr. M.'s power of walking. He wanted to ask about snakes. He had snakes on his mind, the snake that ghosted Mr. M.'s breath, the snake he'd held, twisting violently in his hands, the two snakes copulating. He wanted to know about the owl. And what about the old woman? What about ghosting, and the curses left and taken away? He wanted to know all of that, everything, but he had a shyness that at least matched Diane's, and a sense of his privacy—as he lay there, naked under the bedcovers—and of hers, and an overpowering sense of his ignorance. He didn't ask. Instead, his mouth opened and a wild remark fluttered out on its own power: "It's awfully strange how things just appear and disappear around here."

The room fell under a startled silence, but then Phil said, "Easy, Hank. It's all right."

Lafleur had startled himself. "I'm sorry," he said. "I'm not looking for sympathy."

"Everybody knows it's a crock the way that sonofabitch was handled," Phil said. "It's a crock of shit."

Lafleur looked down at the shape of his feet under the sheet, understanding that he had allowed the incident to become too fierce in him. Phil's words entered like a beam of light, for which Lafleur was grateful. It also made him more embarrassed than he already was. He looked up at Diane. "Did you hear about that snake?"

"Maybe a friend," she said, smiling faintly and speaking in a tone of voice that made no particular commitment and gave up nothing of herself, that might even have mocked the idea of a snake being a friend.

"Yeah," Lafleur said.

"We gossiped about you," Diane said. Iris chuckled. Phil smiled. They moved around, the three of them, relaxing. Lafleur had to stay where he was. He felt like a hospital patient. A ring of power formed in the room.

"So who do you blame?" he said.

"Mrs. M.," Iris said.

"Helen Porter," Diane said.

"What the hell are you talking about?" Phil said.

Laughter filled the room. The laughter became nervous and ebbed, but as the four of them looked at one another it rose again. Like a live thing, the laughter jumped back and forth. When it ceased, the room was filled with calm. Phil left, and then Diane. Iris returned to the bed and leaned back against the pillows beside Lafleur. Dressed, she lay on top of the covers. "Things were set up for Snediker to do something like that. Don't you see?"

"Okay. I already got that."

"But not just set up in the sense of being arranged, though I guess there was that, too. That's grotesque enough. What's worse is that things were set up psychologically."

"Okay," he said.

"It's like Bill Snediker was Vic's tongue."

"Tongue?"

"Everything that pulsed and spoke . . . heart, kidney, lung and tongue. He was Vic's tongue in Vic's head and Vic is probably somebody else's tongue in their head."

"Tongue?" Lafleur said. "What the hell do you mean, 'tongue'?" Iris chuckled.

"Listen," Lafleur said. Suddenly he was annoyed again. "It's not funny. Tell me."

"What do you want to hear?"

"Say it," he said.

"Say what?"

"Whose fault is it?"

"What? That Snediker tried to kill you? That's what I'm trying to tell you."

Lafleur reached around and grasped her shoulder under her housecoat. Her eyes widened. He saw his anger reflected in her face. That, too, was a thing coming out of him on its own power and for an instant it made her look ugly to him—repulsive with her bright eyes like stones, plucked eyebrows, her long, narrow neck. He had a sudden urge to slug her. Appalled, he softened his grip and let his hand drift downward. The large buttons of the housecoat pulled loose. He moved his hand down to her abdomen and let it rest there, cupping her smoothness, her warmth. He stared with amazement at his hand, then let his head sink back to the pillow.

"What's wrong with you?"

He murmured incoherently and drew nearer, thinking, I don't know. She slipped her legs under the sheet and touched his ankles with her toes. Her voice sounded distant. "I'm sorry. I know it isn't funny, but Vic had to have somebody to do what he couldn't get caught doing himself. Do you see? So he arranged it that way, or didn't even arrange it. The psychological ground was prepared, or not even prepared, exactly—it's just there. It develops in a way that makes certain things inescapable. So far as Snediker was concerned, the person of Vic was an illusion that he entered."

Disturbed, Lafleur inhaled slowly and exhaled, then said, "So?"

"What?" she said softly. "Hank?"

"So you blame him? Vic?"

"He was a romance for Snediker, twisted as it was."

"Fine," he said, "but Snediker's not the point. Sabat is. The point is that Sabat used Snediker to try to kill me, for God's sake. And what about you?"

"Me?"

"He was a romance for you?"

"Yes. After a fashion, of course. Once. What do you mean?"

"You knew him," he said.

"Vic?"

"Yes. And you didn't warn me."

"I told you to watch out for him."

"Yes, but not to watch out for my goddamned life."

"I didn't know, Hank. I had no idea it would go so far."

He didn't respond for a moment. Outside, a flicker tapped at the barn. A sheep complained. A solitary horn blast measured the distance to the workers' encampment. The door to Phil's room opened and shut and then Phil's boots crunched on the gravel outside and steadily went away. The cowbirds' voices ran like water. It was now a melancholy sound. The room was yellow. Lafleur's anger had been rising in him again. He knew it by the responding alarm he'd heard in Iris's voice.

"Something's screwed up here," he said.

"It's all right, Hank," she said. "You're going to be all right."

"Good," he said, "but something's really screwed up and I wish you'd tell me what it is. Name it."

"I don't understand what you're asking."

"We're finished, aren't we?" he said. He'd startled himself, saying that, and yet he knew it was the truth.

Her voice came out thinly: "No."

But he could tell that she also knew.

"Why?" she said.

"I don't know."

He looked at her. She lay there, staring at the ceiling. Her face—the domed brow, angular cheeks, and straight nose—was utterly still. His body lightly touched hers, but the contact, so recently electric, had been neutralized. A part of him felt easier for this. Another part was afraid of what was happening, of what would happen next in their disentanglement. He felt his mind like a dark, slippery thing roving warily over her in the yellow world.

Chapter Twenty

It was mid-September, almost autumn. The light was lengthening. He saw Iris's figure outlined in the doorway to the Industries Building. She hung there for an instant and then entered briskly. She crossed the polished concrete floor to the ramp and started up toward the observation tower. Her brown arms stood out against her pale yellow blouse. Her face was dark brown. Her hair clung to her head like a helmet.

Lafleur stood at the computer in the tower. He was encircled by banks of security monitors and control decks, some of which were hooked up and operable, some of which were not. Mazes of wire harnesses hung from the backs of the machines and spilled over the counters to the floor. He looked away from Iris and gazed out at the main floor of the Industries Building, which stretched out before him in the shape of a large isosceles triangle. The tower was near what would be the hypotenuse, built up from the pit through a round hole in the floors. There was an observation deck for each of the three floors, and for the sake of visibility each deck was elevated from the floor it overlooked and connected to it by two ramps. Lafleur watched a man on aluminum stilts who roved the far end of his floor, near the apex of the triangle. The man was hanging gridwork from which the "finish" ceiling would be hung. He worked slowly outward from the apex toward Lafleur's right side. His stilts clicked as he moved.

Another man on a motorized lift worked ahead of the man on stilts, nearer to Lafleur. He edged along the outside wall. Soon he would cross to a round, two-foot partial wall that was suspended from the rough ceiling. The partial wall, which encircled the top of the space the tower occupied, would provide support for the gridwork. The man on stilts was tacking up a metal stringer. He had a power nailer that sounded like a gun when he fired it. Mounted on the wall was a laser level. The level spun a bead of red light around and around the space, ten feet high, marking the line at which the gridwork was to be hung. The bead moved along the outside wall, jumped to the partial wall and followed it, and then jumped back to the outside wall. It diminished like the tail of a comet at its end before it came around again and penetrated itself. If one were to look closely anywhere along the line, one would see the tiny comet-shaped bead. It was as if the bead were everywhere. No matter where one looked, it was there, but from the slightest distance the light appeared merely to be a perfectly accurate, uninterrupted trail of red.

Iris had come halfway up the ramp. The laser left a trail across her forehead as of blood seeping through a knife slit. With each step she took, the trail jumped several inches down her body. It cut across her forehead, her lips, her neck, her chest, and finally across her abdomen before its path was interrupted by the partial wall. She pushed open the gate and came in beside Lafleur.

"I bet you don't want to go out for chili with Vic," she said.

"Lord, no."

"I didn't think you would."

The gridwork the man on stilts was installing was made out of light-weight slotted steel bars, which he placed two feet on center with cross-pieces bolted on every four feet. The entire grid was attached at its edges to the metal stringers the other worker was tacking up, and then attached by the metal tie wires to the joists in the rough ceiling. The bars, stringers, and crosspieces were prefabricated, cut to dimension and calculated to bear just so much weight. The tie wires and bolts were prefabricated. On the grid would be mounted the light fixtures and electrical conduit, and then the ceiling tiles. The tie wires would stretch out equally under the weight of the tiles, making the ceiling absolutely level and tight like a drumhead—perfect.

Lafleur had been going through the Project Manual file in the computer, plotting out the next several days' work: interior walls, ceilings, Sheetrock, doors, fixtures, switches, locks, a host of finish installations, low- and high-pressure ductwork for the air-circulation systems, grills, flashings, distributors, acoustic systems, volume extraction units and sound attenuators, fixture systems, fixture carriers, hangers, supports, anchors, shock absorbers, dimmer modules, panels, Barry mounts, and within and emanating from the Support Building, the heat-extraction systems, generators, motors, back-up battery banks, the master clock, temperature-control system, laundry plant, water-treatment plant, and everywhere the fire-alarm and sprinkler systems. Attached to it all came the same prohibitive language—interior piping hydrostatically tested at 200 psi, transformers above and below 10 KVA with taps 2 and 2½%

full capacity, and 75 KVA transformers insulated with Nema class 220 degree maximum with a 40 degree centigrade ambient. . . .

Idly he scrolled the file forward and paused, resting his fingers lightly on the keys. By now he'd developed a sense of what he had to remember, of what to ignore, and especially of the fact that the bulk of what was written was not meant to be retained. Once used, the data became waste, like the tie bands and bits of wire, rebar ends, wads of insulation, chunks of wood, bent Dottie plates, empty cans, cardboard boxes, polyurethane containers, plastic bags and cups. It left a wearying residue in the brain, that was all. He better understood what to leave to the foremen, particularly to Lopez, now, the mechanical foreman. Because of the quantity of details to be executed at this stage, the work on the project seemed to have exploded like a flower, casting its seeds willy-nilly outward.

At the same time, Lafleur's supervisory role had become increasingly specific, increasingly localized, dark and compressed like a bud. This was what he desired. He would leave the site in a few days. Lopez would take over.

Iris stood near Lafleur. Her perfume cut through the obscure but pervasive odors of concrete, acoustic tile, and steel. He scrolled the file slowly forward. Iris's attention was caught by something on the screen, something from her sector of this world, and she leaned toward the screen. He stopped the scrolling action for her and straightened up and looked leftward at two men who had just appeared from the loading dock. They were pushing two metal storage cabinets along on rollers. The cabinets boomed softly. The men moved even with the tower and stopped at the elevator. The elevator doors opened and the men went in. The doors sucked shut. The elevator hummed. The man who was hanging up stringers fired his power nailer. The reports echoed through the building. The electric motor of his lift whined as he crossed to the two-foot false wall on the inside. On the lower level, the elevator doors could be heard opening, and then the rumbling sound of the cabinets being rolled across the floor. Other workers could be heard down there, too, their voices, the muffled sounds of heavy articles being moved about. They were installing Sheetrock and insulated ceiling tiles. Their power nailers sounded like gunfire being returned from a distance.

The bottom floor, the pit, the bowels of the building, was complete, and also empty. El Gallo's lawyer had finally got him released, and the rest of the prisoners had been taken away by immigration authorities. During the last days El Gallo had been here, he'd resumed talking to the prisoners. In the evenings his voice could be heard outside the building. It went on at length, rising from the pit and slipping through the open entryways in the upper floors. One evening while he was here in the control tower, Lafleur had heard El Gallo's voice from the pit, speaking in Spanish. The voice echoed softly at first in the bottom and floated up to the tower. Its intensity increased, washing against the walls, then fell almost to a hush. It rose again and kept rising fervently until the entire building vibrated with its power. Lafleur had stood transfixed.

The next morning while he was down in the pit, Lafleur asked El Gallo what he had said to the prisoners. El Gallo said that sometimes he chastised the men and sometimes he encouraged them, that sometimes he spoke to them individually, and at other times he spoke to all of them at once, that he told them stories and jokes. "Sometimes I insult their mothers," he said, chuckling. "That wakes them up." He told Lafleur that he said anything he could think of to make the men remember that most of all they wanted to get out of here, that there was a reason why they'd ended up here. "I failed them as a guide. I'll be out soon. I have to leave them with something. They have to keep their spirits up. And me, too. I have to keep my spirits up. Sounds like there's a crazy sonofabitch down here, huh?"

"Some people might think so." Lafleur had smiled wryly.

"That's my spirit." El Gallo tipped his head back and laughed hollowly. "I got to keep him alive."

Earlier today, Lafleur had ridden the elevator down to check out the pit. As strange as the place had seemed with the prisoners installed in the cells, empty it seemed stranger yet—the lines of electrified cells, the hundreds of electrical outlets, the floodlamps, the high-pressure hosing coiled up in cabinets in the walls, the manacles, the pair of padded rooms that had chairs bolted into the concrete and examination beds with straps, the whole place under harsh fluorescent lighting and everything in line and gleaming, freshly painted, symmetrical, stark and lethal-looking.

So now he knew exactly what the pit had been designed for: interrogation exercises, the extraction of data from the minds of prisoners. He should have figured it out months ago, but even though he'd kept going back to look at the plans for the pit, and then back to the pit itself as it was being constructed—fascinated, obsessed—he had for a long time obstructed the truth from himself. His failing was made striking by the fact that if he was prepared to do anything it was to read blueprints. He'd come to understand that Sabat had succeeded in intimidating him, that as a result he—Lafleur—had from the start somehow closed himself off from what would become obvious only by degrees: first, that Snediker was the same man who had brutalized him in Portland, and then that Snediker had been sent to do it, that the prisoners had been detained here in an incomplete facility illegally, and finally that the pit was an interrogation center.

Iris had known all along what the pit was for. When he had found that out, he had asked why she hadn't told him. She'd said she thought he knew. "There's nothing unusual in that," she'd said. It made him wonder what else she found not unusual, what else he was missing. . . . *An interrogation center for what?* . . . He could actually feel two formidable pulls in himself to ask and to not ask that question. He could still feel himself not wanting to care, to turn his head and go his way. On a certain level he was still afraid.

Iris turned to watch as the man on stilts moved in their direction. Lafleur watched with her. The man bent and with a mechanical wand reached to the floor for a bundle of tie wires. The tie wires came into view, held by the gripping mechanism on the wand, and then the man took them in his free hand and hung the wand from a hook on his tool belt. The tie wires clattered as he placed them in a small shiny bucket attached to the other side of his belt. As he walked away, his body rocked back and forth like a clown's. The stilts made a clicking noise. They had rubber pods on the feet and clasps that went around the lower legs so as to leave the man's hands free. He stopped where he had left off and reached up to fasten a tie wire between the metal gridwork and rough ceiling. From where Lafleur and Iris stood, his hands were not visible, nor was his head, but Lafleur knew that he had a tool for attaching the tie wires, too, a customized pair of pliers with which he could poke the wire through holes, and then twist to cinch up the connection. He moved freely from one position to another.

"So Vic wants to go back to Burns Junction," he said.

"Uh huh."

"Why?"

"He's leaving."

"So?"

"Sentiment?"

"Bull."

"He's finished. Maybe he figures it's time to apologize."

The idea of Sabat apologizing was absurd and Iris knew it as well as he did. "I thought he was throwing a party for the workers tonight."

"That, too."

"All of it?"

"Maybe he figures he's got a lot of bets to cover." She paused, then said, "Look, I'm asking you. It's one last favor. I have to go with him and I don't want to go by myself."

He understood that she wanted him not to press this. He granted her that. They had barriers now beyond which they wouldn't pass. He'd moved back in with Phil the day they'd had the Zeta out. He and Iris were friends. They had claimed this earnestly, their friendship, as a way of deflecting themselves from the ragged edges, from the answers never offered, from questions not even articulated, from the distrust that contained the seeds of rage. He said, "Okay. When?"

"I need to get the mail before five."

The elevator doors opened again on this floor. The two workers emerged and pushed their empty dollies back toward the loading dock. They would unload more furniture from the truck out there—shelving, perhaps, more cabinets, desks, or electronic gear—and take them down to the second floor, where the interior of the command center for the fabrication plant was being assembled. Two other men, the guards, the well-matched pair who had replaced Snediker, were working in the room. Lafleur had seen them down there earlier today, half-hidden behind a column of partially unpacked cartons. Clean, closely cropped, and muscular, they looked like Marines in civilian dress, but he gathered that they'd been sent directly from International Data. Every evening the two jogged down the road toward Rome. Their brown legs and dark heads shone. Their faces seemed perpetually calm. They were the image of self-satisfaction.

"You're not touchy today?" Iris asked.

"Me? Touchy?"

He bent down to the counter and wrote a note on a clipboard, telling Lopez how far he'd gone through the Project Manual, and in his view where the work stood in relation to the manual, where it should stand tomorrow. He straightened up, put his finger on the computer's power switch, and glanced back at Iris, checking to see if she wanted to use it. She shook her head. He shut the computer down and spread a plastic drop cloth over it. The two men returned, pushing the dollies loaded with cartons. The cartons had HEWLETT-PACKARD printed on their sides. Those two men, as well as the two working in the room below, were not under Lafleur's supervision. They, along with ten or so other men, worked from their own set of plans and were installing the cabinetry, filing systems, desks, chairs, and other furniture. Soon they would turn to completing the computer-fabrication system, the factory that had been roughed in by Lopez's mechanical workers. In a few days, a fabrication supervisor was to arrive on the site, but exactly who these workers were reporting to now Lafleur did not know. As well as the work had progressed on the site, there had been a major breach in communication between it and the main offices, because of Sabat. Iris had become the conduit. She received instructions on the computer modem and gave them to the crew.

They walked through the gate and down the ramp. Lafleur watched the trail of red light slice higher and higher up the side of Iris's arm, then he bent his head and watched it climb his body. He felt it flash across his eyes. They crossed to the doorway and stepped out into the brilliant light. Directly before them loomed the two Housing Units, one to their right, one to their left. From each of them emanated a steady racket—carpenters, nailing down plywood subfloors. Four stories high, square but blunted at the corners in a way that made the concrete look like a skin, slotted with reinforced windows, massive, the units cast long shadows and appeared to be precisely what they were—a prison.

Iris and Lafleur headed down toward the river, circled the lower Housing Unit, then entered its shade and cut upward toward the house. To their left was the Support Building and from it came the whine of a drill, the beat of hammers, the scream of a power saw. Lafleur looked down. The earth had been finish graded and compacted. A watering system—another grid—lay under the surface. Soon trucks would bring in big rolls of sod that would be laid out like carpet, and then backstops for the softball fields would arrive, goal posts for football and soccer, basketball hoops. A cinder track would be installed. Trees would be hauled in and inserted into the ground by an automatic planter, and then the fences would go in, fences upon fences, fences sunk into four-foot trenches, fences with razor wire, electrified fences. Everything was on time. By rearranging the work schedule during the past two weeks and by paying the mechanical crew to work overtime, Lafleur had fulfilled his half of the bargain and would receive bonus shares in the company, which, in turn, he would trade to Blaylock for control of the partnership. When he returned to Portland he planned to strip down the partnership to a scale he could manage on his own. It seemed strange.

They walked alongside the stone wall, then turned up in front of the house. Sabat waited next to the pickup truck in front of the animal pens. "The truck?" Lafleur said.

"He wants to pick up those paintings."

On their side of Sabat, in the open space between the house and the first animal pen, a short trough had been dug in the ground. Smythe, the owner of the Owyhee Café, had come by last night and butchered one pig and one sheep, and then taken the remainder of the animals back home with him. He'd returned early this morning and built a fire in the trough, quartered the carcasses, and set them to cooking on a jerry-built grill made out of hog wire. Smythe, an odd one, a wiry man with one ear and a stutter, was hunkering in the shade and using a large paint brush to swab sauce over the meat. It was Sabat's doing. He'd insisted upon going ahead with the party for the workers.

"I don't want to do this," Lafleur said.

Iris looked up at him and whispered, "I know." Her eyes glittered. As she looked down again, she raised one hand and tentatively touched her fingers to his arm.

They moved across the lawn in front of the house. "All right," he said, more to himself than to her. By tonight or tomorrow, he understood, Sabat was to leave. Jackson was gone. The semi-rigs and cranes were gone. The loaders and backhoes were mostly gone. Diane's husband had come after her in the pickup with the dented fender and the front bumper that twisted up like a grin. Lafleur had seen them driving away along the top of the site—Diane, her husband, and one young child in the cab, and three more kids in the back, clinging to the stock rack and swinging to and fro with the motion of the road. After a few moments, their only trace had been the wispy cocoon of dust above the road to Rome.

The circle of campers and trailers up at the crest of the slope had been reconstituted. The stacks of rebars had been replaced with pallets of Sheetrock and insulation. A week ago, Phil had left for Portland, leaving Lafleur alone in the room. Phil had hauled back Lafleur's trailer and dozer on his rig so that all Lafleur had to do was load his backhoe in the dump truck and drive away. Phil was going to work for Lafleur.

The final tailings from the razed silo had been dozed into a hole. The last of the berm pile had been used to backfill the drainfields. The heaps of gravel and sand were gone. In their place was an asphalt parking lot. The toolshed was gone. The pulpit was gone. Snediker was gone without a trace. Before they were done, the police had combed the plateau for him and checked the farms for twenty miles in all directions. Lately, Sabat had been in retreat in the house. The threat that the company would take its revenge on Lafleur had yet to materialize. Lafleur still felt edgy about that, and about Sabat himself, but the man was infrequently seen. He ate alone. Light from the television screen burned through the windows of the house late into the night.

Lafleur and Iris moved onto the lot, where the sand was packed by the incessant turning of vehicles. Sabat watched impassively as they approached. He wore loose-fitting tan trousers and a lightweight white jacket, and was leaning back against the side of the truck bed with his arms crossed. His face seemed masked. Lafleur glanced at Iris. Her face was steeled. The sound of the work in the buildings—clattering hammers, the report of the power nailers, the shriek of saws and drills, the thud of things being moved around—had blended into one distant racket.

Smythe cocked his head as they passed near him. Lafleur nodded. Smythe nodded back. He was crouched just above his smoking trough, holding a coffee can full of sauce in one hand and the paint brush in the other. To his right a large heap of raw meat was piled up on an old fender, and on the makeshift grill slabs of meat sizzled and spat, and filled the air with a sharp odor. Smythe was shirtless under a pair of blue overalls. His arms were dark and sinewy and shiny with sweat, and besides the missing ear he had a deep crease across his forehead. He grinned crookedly at Lafleur. Crouched at his fire in the shade of the animal shed, he looked like a wild thing, a demon. Lafleur felt Iris's hand on his arm, clutching him tightly. He nodded at Smythe again. Smythe nodded back. Lafleur looked up at the skyline above the house and sheds—the buildings of the prison, gray and stark, the angular rooflines, the square guard towers poking through. It looked precisely as he had imagined it would months ago. It gave him an odd feeling to think that the prison he'd built and didn't like was there now and would go on under its own power.

They drove away from the project in silence. Iris sat in the middle with her knees angled toward Lafleur. When they turned onto the gravel road to Rome, they passed a government sign that Lafleur hadn't seen before, and he stuck his head out the window and looked back at it through the dust—OWYHEE DETENTION CENTER. Before that moment he hadn't known the name of the place. He watched the desert go by, then the irrigated farms. The alfalfa was ready for the third cutting.

They stopped at the Rome Café to get the mail. Lafleur slid out of the cab to let Iris by. No one spoke. She went inside the café, which was brilliant in its whiteness. Sabat leaned across the seat and took something out of the glove box, straightened back up, then got out of the pickup. Lafleur watched uneasily as Sabat moved down and leaned against the tailgate. Lafleur stayed where he was near his door. The sun burned through his shirt. Each day the first glint of the sun at dawn was hot, and then searing from morning to dusk.

Lafleur stared across the road at the Owyhee Café, a rundown stucco affair built in a vaguely Spanish style. There Smythe served beer, sold gas, performed mechanical work, pursued a desultory trade in meat animals, and apparently operated an occasional rough-hewn catering service. A brand-new but crudely painted sign had been mounted near the road.

OWYHEE CAFÉ, it said. CIGARETTES, TACKLE, BEER TO GO.

When they'd pulled in, he'd seen that the Rome Café had a new, neatly painted sign on its roof: ROME CAFÉ, GROCERY, BEST EATS.

At the intersection with the gravel road there was another government sign with an arrow pointing north: OWYHEE DETENTION CENTER.

"Look," Sabat said. Lafleur turned his head. Sabat gestured to the south, toward the limestone cliffs on the other side of the river and to a series of low hills. The hills were sandy, cone-shaped, and had dark basalt crowns with regular vertical fissures that made them appear to be embattlements. "A man named Stine thought they looked like the Roman Colosseum," Sabat said.

Lafleur had heard this tale.

"But how did he know?" Sabat said. He moved around the tailgate and came along Lafleur's side of the pickup, stopping several feet away. Lafleur felt himself stiffening. "Maybe he saw a picture of the Colosseum, or one of those what were they?" Sabat asked. As he spoke his lips twisted back from his purple gums. Lafleur had no idea what Sabat wanted him to name, but looking at the man he grew fascinated by the whiteness of his lips, a cream color with a bluish tinge most pronounced at the rim and corners. The bulge was there, too, thin and white. His face was taut as a pimple. "Stereoscopes," Sabat said. He swept the air with his hand. "The Colosseum!"

Lafleur gazed across the river at the cliffs, then at the hills, which were olive drab against the bright sky. The river was not visible, only the top of the cut it made in the earth. Beyond the hills were buttes and mountains. Everywhere one looked, the desert rolled toward mountains that deepened in color the farther away they were. He and Sabat stood in the hollow of a dish and looked out at the distant, jagged rim, the mountains like paper cutouts pasted against the ends of the world. The sky was full of light. The sand reflected light. In the extraordinary light the place appeared dimensionless. Lafleur supposed that it was not unlike the effect of a stereoscope. The mountains appeared closer and smaller than they were. The landscape looked huge, insistent, and exquisite. Most of all it, too, looked precisely like what it was—a magical wilderness through which he was passing—like Beer-sheba, Jeshimon, Shur, Paran, Negeb, like Zin. Across the road, the Owyhee Café with its fuel pumps mounted under an awning and the rickety animal pens in the back looked like a stage set.

"Ruins," Sabat said. Lafleur glanced at him. Sabat was leaning against the truck, gazing at the buttes, then he swung his head toward Lafleur and said, "They look like ruins." His voice deepened with mockery. "It's all a ruin. The world's a ruin. People keep raising one ruin after another to celebrate the ruins they began with."

Lafleur said nothing.

"One ruin begets the next," Sabat said. "And the river, the Owyhee, named after Hawaii." His condescension overt now, he added, "The Hawaiian porters came even cheaper than French-Canadians, I guess. Rome on the Hawaii. Visions of paradise, but what do you do with paradise except wreck it? They used to call the Snake the Sandwich Island River."

Sabat laughed wildly and leaned toward Lafleur. He showed his gums again, and his gray tongue. His laugh was directed at Lafleur, and not at the stew of transplanted nomenclature that the region had: Rome, Basque, Tudor Lake, Frenchglen, Sacramento Hill, Jordan Valley. Most of what Sabat had just told Lafleur was printed on a historical marker not far up the road. Dazzling as Sabat could be with arcane data, it was unlike him to pass material off raw from a road sign. Lafleur supposed that Sabat meant to demean him. It was all theatre, Lafleur guessed, one more queer, elaborately conceived slight that included a degrading innuendo on his French-Canadian origin. "Talk about wishing," Sabat said. "Like you and Iris."

Lafleur's blood jumped with anger. Sabat grinned aggressively. Flecks of spittle hung from the corners of his lips, and then his face hardened and he made an awkward, fluttering motion with his hand toward his belt. The motion, indeterminate though it was, triggered an alarm in Lafleur. Instinctively, he stepped toward Sabat, stopping only when he was close enough to touch the man, near enough to grab him, and his mind raced. He remembered Sabat bending toward the glove box, then straightening and pausing before getting out of the truck. Something had been taken from the glove box. Lafleur stood glaring at Sabat, his limbs tensed. Sabat held his ground and hooked his thumb in a belt loop. He leaned forward ever so slightly, glaring back at Lafleur. His lips twitched and his small, beady eyes glittered with fury.

The door of the Rome Café slapped like a whip and in the corner of his eye Lafleur saw Iris coming toward them. Sabat eased back and said, "You're living in a dream world." He turned sideways and leaned up against the truck bed. Lafleur inhaled deeply and quickly inspected what he could see of Sabat's pockets and belt. For an instant he'd thought Sabat had a weapon. Now he thought not. It was the enmity, he thought, that had built up in the man, the disappointment, the sense of failure, and jealousy, too—still, at this late date. The opposition between them had been deeply impressed into service, kept there, and now it was coming out hot as jealousy of an entirely alien order to Lafleur—wildly costumed, excessively mental, ornate, weird. Lafleur wondered if Sabat knew that he and Iris were no longer sleeping in the same room.

Sabat gazed down the road. Lafleur turned to Iris, who'd come up next to him. The look between them grew portentous. Her eyes glittered, registering his distress, and dug into his head as if to ask him: *What?* And then, as if she understood, she seemed to say: *Steady. Steady.*

And he—if she had actually said that—he would have said: *Clearly.* And she: *It's meaningless. Give him rope. It doesn't matter to you.*

Then why am I here? he thought, or thought he might have asked—but then he corrected himself, thinking, It's her world, her entanglement, not mine.

But she might have answered his question: *I need you with me for the same reason you've needed your friend Phil sometimes, or Blaylock the night we found the old woman, or Abe Kasanian, or me sometimes—not to do anything, necessarily, but just to be here. Help me.*

So he thought. If she needed him in that way, he guessed he didn't mind, but he also had the uneasy feeling that if he and Iris had actually been talking she would have deflected his attention by now—drawn his eye to her brown, silken limbs, or his nose to the odor of perfume and soap that wafted from her body whenever she moved, to some softness that was meant to keep him from seeing the hardness in her that had become as bright as a coin. Lafleur no longer wanted to be seduced.

Sabat moved slowly back around to the other side of the truck. The gravel crunched under his feet. Iris looked at Lafleur. Her eyes were steady. Lafleur looked away from her. He stood still and gazed out across the desert. The sun beat on his head.

They drove. The truck's suspension calibrated the patches and seams in the highway. Iris bent her head down and flipped through the mail. Lafleur glanced behind her at the side of Sabat's round head—the protruding lower lip, the smooth brow, the dark, neatly combed hair that encircled the meat-colored bald spot in the center. He flicked his eyes away and scrutinized the town of Rome's third establishment as they passed it—the place which was a combined junkyard and rock shop. It had distilled commerce to its two essential elements: rocks for the highway trade and parts for the local. The rocks went out. The place had a wrecking truck and a corner on miles of highway collisions. The junk came in.

Its one low building was surrounded by wrecks. It had a new sign, a double-entendre—ROSCOE'S GEMS. Heat shimmered in the air above the junked cars and trucks. Lafleur knew that every establishment around here, every farm and house, had a small junkyard behind it. It was a long haul to Boise and longer to Portland. Spare parts were at a premium, but Roscoe's, no doubt, had the advantage of quantity, maybe four or five versions of certain models, and enough of a variety of Chevrolet transmissions to find one to drop into, say, a '74 Buick. That place and the two cafés behind the car constituted the mercantile world proper of Rome, although the Rome Café—because of the post office and the money orders written there, and the power bills that could be paid there, and the few groceries sold (bread and candy bars, milk, eggs, hamburger, soda pop, and ice cream out of the cooler)—was still what might be called the nerve center of town, if the idea of nerve center applied at all here. The town was more like a brain chopped up into bits, strewn about and connected by long neuropapillae: the telephone cables through which passed the talk about Jack Scofield's Massey-Harris, or about the chance of Edie Wilson's boy, Tom, coming down to the Knoxes' to help buck hay bales, or about Julie Baxter spending the night in McDermitt with the Halverson boy, the voices falling to insistent whispers, or about Ginelle Davis, who was going back east to college; and the gravel roads along which the people drove, waving stoically at each other, and by seeing each other confirming to themselves that they, too, were still here after all; and the natural threads, the trails that the roads sometimes followed, the dry, rocky stream beds that the snakes liked, on which the farmers dug earthen "tanks" to catch spring runoff, along which the young people wandered and met at night. There was a gas station here, a junkyard there, one kind of church (Protestant) ten miles that way and the other kind (Catholic) twenty miles the other way, a school over in the town of Arock and past it in the buttes the ranger station, the holding corral for wild horses, and nestled in the canyon beneath the cliffs, now, the Owyhee Detention Center.

The prison, no doubt, had caused a great deal of telephone talk, both angry and hopeful. The merchants mounted signs in response to it. Maybe some thought the prison would become the new nerve center. It would only be a pretense, though, Lafleur thought—like Sabat himself. International Data's trade routes ran through computer modems, and on these routes the things—secrets, mainly, that junk—would only come in. The light planes or armored vans that carried prisoners in would not stop in Rome, Burns Junction, or Jordan Valley, nor would the trucks that carried the computer systems out. The effect of International Data would be everywhere, like air, like color, like a weight out there by the cliffs that changed the balance, but finally all that would ever go out to the little towns was loose change—junk. Lafleur felt a wave of melancholy wash over him.

Iris set an envelope on his lap. It was from Penny. He picked it up. It was heavy. It probably had information in it about his parents' house. Maybe it had cleared probate and there was an offer to be considered. Jewel should have returned from California by now. Maybe there would be a note from her. He hoped there would be something from Andy and Tricia. Maybe they'd had their school pictures taken already. He would like that, to have new pictures of them. Maybe they'd written to him. Maybe Penny had enclosed some of their schoolwork for him to see. There might be something from Penny herself. He held the envelope between his two hands, gauging its weight. It filled him with expectation, but he didn't want to open it now. He hiked his weight toward Iris and eased it into his hip pocket.

Chapter Twenty-one

Burns Junction came into view and Sabat pulled into the lot. Their new sign was a half-lie: EASTBOUND? LAST GAS TO ROME AND OWYHEE DETENTION. Lafleur opened the door, stuck his legs out, and slid to the pavement. Iris followed him. Lafleur arched his back and stretched out his body. He felt dizzy. "I think this was your idea," he said.

"I know." She stood straight as a pole and didn't look at him. When Sabat came around they walked to the café. Lafleur glanced over at the shed and saw that the large rolling doors were padlocked shut. Abe Kasanian's Buick was parked in the narrow passageway between the shed and café. Entering, they caught people in motion. Ruth stood at the table just inside the door, restacking the Harlequin Romances and Louis L'Amour Westerns. As they passed she nodded faintly. Sally was behind the counter, fumbling underneath it for something. Beside her, Frank pulled a clean apron over his head. Kasanian sat on the far stool to the left of the counter. He swung around to face the new arrivals.

Lafleur moved to sit next to Kasanian, who was dressed up in a black suit, white shirt, and tie. He nodded gravely at Lafleur and curled his lips ever so slightly in a smile. His silver hair was combed back. He looked like a small-town justice of the peace—neat and wise. He held a cup of coffee. Along the counter were three additional cups, one for each of the others. They all were dressed in their Sunday clothes.

Iris sat to Lafleur's right. Sabat sat to her right. Sally took water glasses from under the counter, and set them out, and silverware and cups, and she filled the glasses from a pitcher. She asked if they wanted chili. It came out a rhetorical question, and she smiled at it, but at the same time something in her face was churning. Kasanian sipped his coffee. Frank moved out of sight behind the coolers into the kitchen. Sally told them it would be a few minutes because Frank had to fire up the stove. Sabat told her not to worry. "We're just back from Owyhee Springs," Sally said.

Sabat said, "I am very sorry," and Lafleur felt himself chilled. He glanced at Iris, who had a startled expression. The churning thing in Sally's face was about to fly loose. "He had a wonderful gift," Sabat said.

Sally's face wrenched.

"I didn't realize the funeral was today," Sabat said.

Lafleur stiffened and he thought, *Who?*

Sally stared at Sabat.

Iris inhaled slowly, then let the air out.

Sally smiled. Her eyes were excessively bright.

. . . Jim?

Sabat bent forward and looked down the counter, passing his beady eyes from Iris to Lafleur, and then to Kasanian.

Sally brought them coffee, then moved down the counter and emptied the pot into Kasanian's cup. She started another pot on the coffeemaker. Frank could be heard in the kitchen, scraping violently at the griddle. The odor of warming food drifted through the room. Sally leaned against a cooler and crossed her large, fleshy arms. She stared past the counter out the front windows.

"How's the work?" Kasanian said in a low voice to Lafleur.

"Almost done." Confused, Lafleur stopped and cleared his throat. "We're working on the interiors."

"So you're about to pull out?"

"Me? Yeah."

Kasanian touched the rim of his cup with one blunt finger. Lafleur heard Ruth moving behind them and a tension entered the room like a skin pulled taut. He thought, She's going for the door, she's going out. But she didn't. She walked around Kasanian and behind the counter, and took her chair against the wall. She had her needlepoint. She put it on her lap—hoop, needle, stretched white cloth, and a ball of red thread. She gazed up at Kasanian. Lafleur gazed at her. She was truly an extraordinary beauty, her dark hair and fine skin and gray eyes set off by her gray dress and black beads. She had an air of fragility and in her eyes a deep, irreconcilable sadness. In her nearness to Kasanian, the resemblance between them became apparent. What was raw and thick and dark in him had been refined to its essence in her.

She spoke: "I guess the old place isn't the same, now. Maybe it's not even there anymore." There was a pause in which the room seemed to breathe with relief.

The air went taut again when Sabat spoke. It wasn't what he said, but the oiliness of his tone, the falsity of it: "You should come out for a tour. The ranch buildings are all there."

"Except for the silo, I hear," Ruth said, and this time, her soft, clear voice failed to relieve the tension. She looked up at Sabat, then back to Kasanian. Lafleur watched as something weighty passed between the two cousins. Suddenly Sally pushed away from the coolers and hurtled down along the counter. Lafleur thought she was headed for Ruth, but then her large body, filling a dark-blue sheath, turned to the right and vanished into the kitchen. She could be heard back there, her legs stumping against the floor, and then her voice, whispering to Frank. Ruth looked down, idly fingering her hoop and needle. Lafleur glanced at Iris. Her face was drawn tight.

"Did you find any more artifacts out in the field?" Ruth said.

No one answered at first, and then Kasanian said, "I doubt it. Heavy equipment is awful rough." He glanced at Lafleur and Lafleur nodded.

"That's a shame," Ruth said. She'd begun stitching her cloth. She looked up and said, "We found arrowheads when we were kids, and a Sharps rifle. There was an Indian battle on the river in the 1870s." She looked down again. Hot water gurgled into the pot on the coffeemaker.

"I thought the battle was on the other side of the river," Kasanian said.

"Maybe," Ruth said, looking up. "Daddy said Uncle Cipriano was in that one."

McHugh—Lafleur thought.

"Couldn't be," Kasanian said. "Cipriano didn't get here until the nineties."

"Oh, that one," Ruth said. "I guess I was thinking of the other one. That one was a war."

Lafleur and Iris sat quietly, listening. Sabat had his elbows on the counter. His head hung down. Carefully he tore his napkin in half.

"Right," Kasanian said. "It started way up in La Grande. General Howard. A Bannock chief was killed. Egan."

Sally came out with two bowls of chili. Frank followed with the third bowl and a plate of cornbread. They set the articles down softly in front of Sabat, Iris, and Lafleur. There was a momentary tangle between Sally and Frank, their arms crossing each other as they attempted to be unobtrusive. Frank pulled back, frowning. To Sabat he said, "You wanted to pick up those paintings?"

"If it's not too much trouble," Sabat said in the same false tone.

Frank's frown deepened, then he turned and went back into the kitchen. Sally took her position in front of the cooler and stared out the window at the desert. There was another tense pause. Above the door to their right, the air conditioner hummed. Strips of cloth had been tied to its grille and the fan made them waggle. Lafleur poked at his chili with his spoon. Ruth spoke: "I thought you meant the one when the town of Jordan Valley called out the cavalry because a young woman had been raped."

302

Sabat's head turned toward Ruth. His lips pulled back from his teeth.

"That woman," Kasanian said.

Sabat's eyes bulged. He looked like a weasel.

"She had the baby, too," Ruth said.

Kasanian murmured and sipped his coffee. Ruth poked her needle deftly in and out of her cloth. Already she'd sewn the shape of a petal. Outside, a truck could be heard approaching on the highway. Its whine ascended until it sounded like it was headed right for the café, and Lafleur saw Iris straightening on her stool. Her chin went up ever so slightly as she listened. The truck roared by. Its noise diminished to nothing. Iris's chin came down. Sally glanced over at Ruth, then at Iris, and said, "When they get to talking like this, I feel like a stranger even though I've been here over thirty years." She laughed nervously.

Iris sat poised on her stool and looked back at Sally, and though he couldn't see her eyes Lafleur thought he knew how they appeared— widening, the skin pulling back from the whites and the glitter intensifying in the center, taking Sally in. Sabat hunched over the counter and tore the two halves of his napkin in half again, first one, then the other. He turned his head slightly and looked down at Ruth out of the corners of his eyes.

Ruth drew her needle through the cloth and bent to see as she grasped the thread and tugged lightly on it. She said, "That was back in the nineties." She looked up at Kasanian. "Didn't the old Harkness family over in Jordan Valley take the baby?"

"Yes," Kasanian said. "That's Bill Harkness, the wheat farmer, and Sandra who went to California to be in the movies."

An eager glimmer crept into Sally's eyes. "You mean Sandra Harkness?"

Kasanian nodded. "But that wasn't the baby. The baby was a boy, and Sandra was his daughter, not a Harkness at all except by name, just taken in by them. They were good people."

"Imagine," Sally said.

"And finally everybody knew the woman was lying," Ruth said.

"Yes," Kasanian said. "Cipriano may have been in on that one. I don't know."

"Daddy said he was," Ruth said. "The Indians only retreated so far. They camped down by Grassy Mountain, and ran down the river, then stopped to fight not far from the ranch. They gave up running to fight. Nobody understood it."

Ruth looked up at the people at the counter and Lafleur saw Sally's face grow maternal. Her body shifted in Ruth's direction, ready to move to her. Sabat moved, too, sliding his elbows forward a little on the counter as if he were about to speak. Lafleur wished he wouldn't. Iris sat still, her weight poised on the stool. Ruth went on, "Daddy told me that Cipriano said nobody understood it because everybody doubted the woman and her family, even then. They chased the Indians for show. They called the cavalry, but that was for show, too. Even the cavalry officers knew it. They wanted to chase the Indians, but not to fight them. They wanted the Indians to run. Then everything would have been all right. They could go back and say they'd done their duty," she said, still speaking softly. In her trouble, or in what Lafleur presumed was her trouble—something to do with Jim somehow, his death, his funeral—Ruth seemed to find solace in the troubles of others ninety or more years removed. Lafleur understood that Kasanian meant to get her to talk this way, to draw her out and assert the web of history she inhabited, even if it was talk of rape and killing. Kasanian meant to comfort her and at the same time to keep a steady pressure on the conversation, to hold firm to the distance between her and the object of her grief. "It went bad," Ruth said. "The Indians stood their ground right out in the open, according to Uncle Cipriano." Her voice rose and quavered. "All they had to do was run."

After a moment, Kasanian said, "It was pride. They'd had enough. They didn't want to run."

"Too much pride can be like a death wish," Sabat said. Sally gasped and Lafleur looked up quickly. Iris rocked back on her stool. Sally was gazing beseechingly at Ruth. Everything quickened in the room and directed itself to Ruth. Her face was the same, composed and exquisite, but her eyes were liquid, hurt. Her hands held the hoop and awl frozen in the air, and suddenly Lafleur understood what he guessed Sabat had known all along—how Jim had died. Understanding that, he saw Sabat's conduct as loathsome and sadistic. Or, even more than that, the man was a lunatic. Lafleur was still gazing at Ruth. Her face was the same, and her hands were the same, frozen in place, and then, driven from her by the extraordinary pressure she was under, he looked away, up at the pictures on the walls, Jim's seascapes, wrecked ships, ships tossed on waters that roiled with evil power, waters like wastelands. The paintings were rough, frightfully inward, filled with longing, and Lafleur named it to himself: *A suicide.* And then . . . *What are we doing here?*

From outside, there was a sharp hissing of gravel followed by a spattering noise as a car approached the café and braked. At first Lafleur felt rather than saw Iris's abrupt motion. Then he saw her body half-twisted around and her head turned to look outside. She turned back and looked at him. Her eyes flashed. The others—Kasanian, Sally, Ruth, and Sabat—adjusted to see, and then Iris turned around again and Lafleur saw her face as it went by, seized with fear. He turned to look.

He saw a man in a suit out there, starting toward the café door, and another man getting out of a black car and moving to stand under the shade of the awning. That was all. Iris turned back again. He turned with her. She folded her hands on the counter before her. Her face was pinched. He glanced at Kasanian and Ruth, and across at Sally—their faces outraged. They hadn't seen what Lafleur had seen in Iris's face. They were still back at Sabat's extraordinary insult. Lafleur was there, too, still half-stunned by that, but somewhere else at the same time, with Iris.

. . . *What? What is it?*

Frank emerged from the kitchen, balancing four more bowls of chili. He set two down on the counter, one for Kasanian and one for Ruth, and moved toward Sally with one, but slowed before he reached her, and looked around, sensing the bad air, the confusion. He searched Sally's face, and looked back at Ruth, but before he could speak the door slapped. The man came in, moved to the counter, and sat two stools away from Sabat. He was a big man with curly blond hair, a traveler. His expensive gray sharkskin suit was deeply creased. He wore a pink shirt and a loosely knotted blue tie.

Sally roused herself, and without speaking gave the man a menu and poured water for him. The ice rattled in the plastic jug as she held it. Frank stood still, looking around with a disconcerted expression, holding the chili like an offering. Lafleur felt something on his leg and he looked down and saw Iris's hand there, touching him with her fingertips. It was as if she were balancing herself.

The stranger ordered two hamburgers, two small French fries, and two Cokes to go. Frank moved back into the kitchen. Ruth resumed stitching. A second petal, cupped close to the first one, took shape on the white cloth. Lafleur ate a spoonful of chili, but he'd lost his appetite. He returned his spoon to the bowl and put his elbows up on the counter, and then reversed himself and picked up the spoon again and resumed eating, thinking that he had to finish, that Iris and Sabat had to finish, that as soon as they did that they could leave, that they had to get out of here.

"Heard you lost the big one in the rocks," Kasanian said.

Startled, Lafleur turned to Kasanian.

"It's too bad somebody didn't just nail him up there," Kasanian said. A smile cut across his rugged face. His eyes moved to Sabat, then to Iris, and back to Lafleur. He said, "We had one like that once. Like Bigfoot. A hundred years ago." He turned and looked down at Ruth. "Nampuh?"

"Starr Wilkinson," Ruth said.

"Nampuh was his Indian name," Kasanian said to Lafleur. "Named Nampa, Idaho, after the poor devil."

They paused. Lafleur reached out and drew a cross in the condensation of his water glass, then glanced up at Sabat, who was still playing with his napkin. He had torn it up into tiny pieces. His face was taut. Beyond him, the stranger had turned to listen. He was closely shaven, and had clear, untroubled eyes and a soft roll of fat under his chin. Next to Lafleur, Iris was not looking at anything or anybody except the bowl of chili from which she ate. Woodenly, she lifted and lowered her spoon, and she chewed mechanically. Lafleur bent forward and finished off the last spoonfuls of his chili.

Kasanian reached out and held Lafleur's arm for a moment. The touch was fatherly. It felt different from Iris's touch a moment ago, by which she had balanced herself. This touch balanced Lafleur. He thought that Kasanian also sensed that something was up here, that the strangers—the one at the counter and the one standing outside—hadn't just happened to stop by. Lafleur was grateful for Kasanian's gesture, but then, even as he felt himself steadying, he remembered Sabat's strange behavior back at the Rome Café. He remembered Sabat's previous threat and a horrible possibility entered his mind—that he was the reason the strangers were here, that he was being set up. He straightened on his stool.

Kasanian released his arm and turned to Ruth again. "He was Cherokee, wasn't he?"

"Partly."

Lafleur was looking down at the stranger, who was still listening in on the conversation. The man looked like a former athlete, handsome, sunny, and strong as an ox, and Lafleur was thinking, *But why me? Why here? It can't be.* He heard Kasanian's voice at his back, going on: "Now that was long before Cipriano got here, even before old McHugh or any of our people. People claimed he was six foot ten. They said he could outrun a horse on the flat."

"He fell in love on the way out west . . ." Ruth said. Her voice trailed off. But for the sound of meat sizzling back in the kitchen and the hum of the air conditioner, the room fell quiet. Lafleur turned and saw Kasanian looking tenderly down at Ruth, and then her eyes rising to the wall opposite her. Lafleur followed her eyes. There was a painting of the sea at night. It was bordered on one side by a beach. The sand was white. On the beach was the white skeleton of a ship. In the distance was the moon, full and white, and it cast white highlights over the surface of the water, over the beach, over the ship. It was the moon of this place, Lafleur knew. It had that whiteness, and there was a face in it that looked like Andy Warhol's silkscreen of Marilyn Monroe—a phantasmagoric gilding in which Marilyn's mouth was open as if she were about to scream. ". . . on the way out west," Ruth repeated, "and the woman rejected him. Starr killed a man with his bare hands. Over the woman."

"Then he went back looking for her later," Kasanian said.

"Yes."

Frank came out with the hamburgers and French fries, which he set down on the back counter. He wrapped the hamburgers in white paper. Ice rattled as Sally ladled it into two paper cups. She filled the cups with Coke from the dispensing machine. Frank put lids on the cups. Lafleur watched them, and watched the stranger watching them, and he thought, *It's not me.* He leaned forward and drew a circle around the cross in the condensation on the side of his glass.

"And he found her," Ruth said.

Frank wrapped up the French fries, then searched a tray for the little packets of salt and pepper, ketchup, mustard. Sally walked to the far end of the counter, to the right, and reached up and switched off the air conditioner. The little flags collapsed against the grille. The absence of the humming noise made the room seem to expand. She flipped up the gate, the hinged section of counter down there. The gate banged when she dropped it. She moved around the perimeter of the room, opening windows. It was evening, now. The air outside would have begun to cool. The sharply angled light streamed through the front windows clear to the table of books and the snack rack. It silhouetted Sally's thick figure as she bent and straightened and grunted softly, moving aside the blinds and pitting her weight against each sash. The second stranger was still out there, standing under the awning between the door and the black car. Lafleur studied him for a moment, then turned back.

Frank had an orange bag. He snapped it open with a flick of his wrist and loaded the food into it.

"He killed her and her family and took to the hills," Ruth said. "He was a pariah."

"Easy," Kasanian said to her.

"They said he moved with the speed of a ghost," Ruth said.

"Easy," Kasanian said.

Frank set the orange bag in front of the stranger. "Comes to five eighty-five."

Iris, who'd finished her chili, stared fixedly into the darkness of the kitchen.

The stranger stood and pulled his wallet from his pocket.

Lafleur watched every move. He reached back and touched the envelope in his hip pocket, as if to make sure it was still there.

The stranger took a step toward Sabat.

Frank spoke to Sabat: "We're getting a beer license."

Sabat's head jerked.

Frank looked down at his feet, and up again. He said, "We're going to recondition the motel and add a couple rooms. For the traffic." His

307

dislike for Sabat showed in his face, but so did his cupidity. Sabat had shrunk on his stool. His shoulders were hunched and his head hung down toward the littered counter.

Lafleur thought, *It's him.*

Frank picked up the twenty-dollar bill the stranger had set on the counter and stepped back to the register.

"I'd like a receipt," the stranger said.

The old-fashioned register rang and the change door jumped open when Frank punched in the numbers. He stepped back to the counter with change and a receipt. "I guess there'll be traffic. People coming and going. Visitors, maybe?" he said to Sabat.

It was a point on which Sabat previously would have waxed garrulous. He would have probed Frank and recommended one strategy after another. He said nothing.

The stranger picked up his bag, and stood for a moment. Gradually everyone's attention moved to him, because he was there, waiting. He said, "Iris?"

From the back, Lafleur saw her head looking up, the short hair close to the skull.

The stranger took a step forward. "This is him, right?"

Iris nodded quickly. Lafleur saw Sabat's head jerk to her. His round face was twisted with an ugly loathing. Iris didn't move. The stranger didn't move. The hinged gate banged as Sally came back behind the counter and opened the wooden side door. She hooked the screen door. It was the door Jim had pressed against like an insect the last time they were here. The opening vented the space and suddenly the café filled with air. Outside, a bird, a woodpecker or flicker, tapped at an eave. Sally returned to her station in front of the cooler. Her eyes widened with surprise when they fell on Sabat. The stranger's coat had parted and Lafleur saw the edge of a leather strap that passed over his pink shirt at the shoulder—*a gun*. Lafleur darted his eyes back to the windows and saw the other stranger still out there, but positioned nearer the door now. The skin in Sabat's face was pulled back tight. His lips drew a short, straight line. His eyes looked feverish. Iris didn't move a muscle.

"It's time to go, Vic," the stranger said.

Sally couldn't contain herself. Her frantic-sounding voice cut in: "They're leaving, Frank. You'd better get those pictures out from the shed." Frank grunted with annoyance and moved out by the side doorway. He had to hike himself sideways to get by the Buick out there. Sally hooked the door behind him and turned back to the group. Her eyes danced around nervously. "Flies," she said.

Sabat had slipped off his stool and moved stiffly in the direction of the

308

door. Lafleur saw his hand move. It was the same fluttering motion he'd seen back at the Rome Café. He felt his body tensing, and quietly then, as if in his amazement he had to state it first to himself, he said, "He also might have a gun." No one heard him, and now Sabat had stopped and his hand was fishing underneath the lightweight jacket. Lafleur spun off his stool and said it again, but louder, "He's got a gun," and in the same instant the stranger leaped and grabbed Sabat's arm, pulled it straight and lifted it. A small, steel pistol glinted in Sabat's hand. The stranger twisted the arm backward and down toward the floor, making Sabat's entire body tip. Suddenly and expertly, the stranger overpowered Sabat as if he were nothing, a man of straw. Sabat moaned softly. His face was precisely as before, a rigid mask. The pistol clattered on the floor. The stranger scooped it up and pulled out the clip, then dropped the gun and clip in his coat pocket and grasped Sabat's upper arm. Again Sabat moaned. Faint, it sounded like the coo of a dove. The stranger nodded at Lafleur. "Thanks." Propelled by the stranger, Sabat went through the front doorway without looking back.

Outside, the second stranger met Sabat. The two of them disappeared behind the wall between the door and windows, then appeared again. The second stranger pushed Sabat up against the black car and frisked him. The first stranger had caught the screen door by its edge and looked back into the café. "I'm sorry, folks," he said. He shut the door gently. He disappeared, then reappeared at the back of the car. He opened a rear door. Iris stepped down from her stool and walked to the windows. The two men put Sabat into the car. Iris stood silhouetted in the light, watching as the second stranger slid into the back beside Sabat and the other got behind the wheel. Sabat was an obscure hump in the back seat. The engine started. The first stranger passed a hamburger back to the second one as the car backed away. Gravel crunched under the wheels. The car pulled out of sight. Gravel hissed. The hissing stopped. The tires hummed on the pavement. The whine of the engine rose and then fell.

Lafleur turned back to the counter. The room was filled with a stunned silence. He looked down at Ruth's design. Her hands rested beside her hoop. She'd completed another petal. She had three. She was stitching a red rose. He looked up at Kasanian and said, "I'm sorry, too."

Kasanian raised one hand and shrugged.

"We didn't know about the funeral, none of it," Lafleur said. "I'm sorry."

"I know," Kasanian said.

"And I'm sorry about this," Lafleur said, gesturing vaguely at the room. "Whatever it was." He stood and placed a twenty-dollar bill on the counter and glanced back at Iris, who was still standing at the window, looking up the road. "I'm sorry," he said, leaning toward Ruth. She looked up at him and smiled.

Frank appeared at the side door. Sally had to unhook it for him. Frank squeezed inside and looked around with a bewildered expression, and said, "I put them in the back of the truck."

A voice came across the room, low and vacant-sounding. Iris had turned to them. Her face was white. "We won't need them."

"No," Ruth said. "He paid. Take them."

Iris turned away and walked outside.

"Even though he may not care about them anymore," Sally said.

"Hush," Ruth said. Her eyes were filled with tears. She bowed her head and pulled a handkerchief from her sleeve and dabbed at her eyes, then looked up again.

"He promised he would come back and buy more," Sally said to Lafleur. "He said he'd put Jim in touch with a gallery, and when Jim called he said he didn't have time to come by. Does he have any idea what that did to Jim? Jim didn't care about the money. Whatever Vic Sabat's getting he's got coming so far as I'm concerned."

"That's enough," Kasanian said.

The room fell silent. The bird outside tapped on the eave in short bursts. Frank put his arm around Sally and drew her close. Ruth looked down at her hoop. The proportions of the emerging rose allowed for an inscription at the bottom, like those that hung in a line above her head beneath Jim's paintings—LADIES LOVE OUTLAWS, TAKE NOTHING FOR GRANTED . . .

"I'm sorry," Lafleur said again. Kasanian walked him to the door, and outside. A flicker hurtled out from under the eave and flew off. They paused at the edge of the gravel lot. To their left, Iris was sitting in the pickup cab, waiting.

Softly Kasanian said, "Jim hung himself in the shed. It's not right to blame Sabat like Sally does. Ruth doesn't. Sabat didn't help any, that's for damn sure, but it ain't that simple."

"I know," Lafleur said.

"What galls me is the way he kept pushing."

"He's cracked up," Lafleur said.

"Those two boys just up and carted him away. Were they police?"

Lafleur drew a line in the gravel with his boot toe. "I don't know."

"It's the damnedest thing." Kasanian looked back into the café, then said, "I told Frank not to open up today, but that fool thinks you got to lay your head down on the ground and let folks stomp on it. I'm taking Ruth home with me tonight, by God."

Lafleur touched Kasanian's arm and walked to the pickup. As he stepped up on the runningboard, he glanced into the bed. Two large paintings lay there, swaddled in an old sheet. He slid in behind the wheel. Iris passed a key to him. He started the engine and let it run for a moment.

"I brought him here," Iris said. "It's my fault."

"You mean it was your idea to come here?"

"No, not my idea. They wanted me to arrange it, get him someplace where they could pick him up without trouble."

"So you chose here? That's your idea of no trouble?"

"It was the only way I could get him to agree to be someplace at a certain time. I didn't know about Jim. Vic did. He knew what was going on."

"You didn't tell me any of this."

"No."

"Who were those two?"

"Company security."

"Christ. He had a gun, Iris."

"I know."

"I think he damn near used that gun on me back in Rome."

"On you?"

He pulled the pickup out and started back for the project. He drove intently. After they turned onto the gravel road, he told her what Kasanian had said about Jim hanging himself, how Sally had blamed Sabat, and how Kasanian had said Jim had been close to the edge, anyway.

"God!" Iris moaned. The stones hammered against the undercarriage. She leaned across the seat and said, "But Sally's at least partly right. Don't you see what he did today? He wants to take his revenge on the world, just using those people for that. And I let him." Her voice sounded wild.

She straightened up and rode the rest of the way with her head against the window and her eyes closed. One hand lay stretched out toward him on the seat. A mile yet from the site, the tops of the Housing Units became visible, like wafers floating in the air. It was dusk. As the pickup approached, the Housing Units grew larger and the adjoining roofs of the Gymnasium, Industries Building, and Support Building appeared—a weird geometry of rooftops. Gradually, the whole became visible, the buildings and guard towers gray against the darkening cliffs.

They passed the runway. The black car was parked there by the windsock. "They're flying out tonight?" he asked.

Iris rolled her head and looked out. "Yes. I guess he doesn't even get to pack."

He turned down toward the site, then stopped in front of the house. Between the shed and house the coals of the cooking fire were visible as a glow behind the legs of the twenty or so workers who had gathered there.

A bonfire burned nearer the center of the lot. It sent a spray of sparks into the air. The workers milled around, eating barbecued pig and mutton and drinking beer from the kegs. Lafleur got out of the truck and walked around, stopping near Iris's door. He spoke toward her open window. "Why?"

She opened the door and slid to the ground. "The party?"

"No, but you can answer that if you want."

"He can't let go."

Lafleur grunted.

They moved into the crowd of workers. Someone gave them large glasses of beer. Smythe came up and pressed plates heaped with meat and cole slaw into their hands. He was still in his overalls and he was a little drunk, and excited, it seemed, to be holding court here. He darted back and forth between the fire where the meat was roasting and the table where he piled it up on plates. Despite the chili he'd just eaten, Lafleur found himself suddenly ravenous. He tore the meat from the bone with his teeth. It felt comforting to be in the density of the crowd. Iris stayed near him. Lafleur drank a second beer.

To their left a man was telling a joke. A small group had gathered around him. Lafleur couldn't hear the words, but when the man reached the punchline and the group jumped around and bent with laughter, he could tell that it was a good joke. Lopez came up and said that he'd checked through Lafleur's last batch of notes, that they looked fine to him, that he thought they might actually be ahead of schedule by the time they finished. Lopez was a tall, taciturn man and Lafleur trusted him. For a fleeting moment Lafleur felt grounded. On the other side of the fire, Smythe was tapping the second keg of beer. He vented the keg, then held a pitcher under the cock, and slapped the handle to open. His head bobbed crazily up and down as a stream of pure foam poured out. The men cheered him. The group had shifted ground, so that Lafleur and Iris stood in the midst of it. He leaned toward her ear and said, "Why is Sabat flying out tonight? Where are those guys taking him? I mean, it's been obvious for a couple weeks that he's finished, but why this way? What the hell's going on?"

"I have to talk to you."

They'd come to her room, bringing glasses and a pitcher of beer. She turned on a lamp in the far corner so that the room was dimly illuminated. He sat in a chair next to the old timber that was tipped against the wall. Iris sat cross-legged on the bed, holding an empty glass. She leaned forward and stared down at the bedcovers. To her left, the window looked out on the lot in front of the house. Sparks from the bonfire scattered in the air. The voices of the men could be heard.

"Smythe," she said.

"Smythe?"

"You overheard us talking about him way back when you first got here, but he meant nothing. Just like Jim meant nothing." She looked down and rocked slowly for a moment before resuming. "That's how Vic operates. But he was worried about you from the start, even before you got here. That's why he had you beaten up, I guess. When you did get here he was afraid, but he was bringing Snediker out, knowing you'd recognize him eventually. Or he could make sure you did if he had to, and then he'd have that, somebody you were afraid of, and he'd also have Snediker to use on anybody else he wanted to. That's the kind of frame of mind he was in. I should have known what was coming because I never meant anything to him, either."

"Why didn't he just leave things alone?"

"Things?"

"Me. You. Jim. Afraid of what?"

"Good question."

"Whatever he's getting now he's asked for. That's what Sally said and she's right."

"Do you know what he's getting?"

"No."

"Neither do I, but I don't like to think about it."

He reached up to the bureau for the pitcher of beer, filled his glass, then gestured to Iris with it, offering her some. She shook her head. "What does Smythe have to do with it?" he asked as he stretched to return the pitcher to the bureau.

"The day you arrived, we'd just got the pigs and sheep from Smythe, you see. And after dinner, after you left the house, Vic and I went out to feed them. Vic really liked the pigs." She set her glass aside and picked at the bedspread, then told Lafleur how Sabat liked the way the pigs shoved each other and squealed and bit each other's ears as they struggled over the food. "But Vic didn't know anything about pigs," she said. "I did." She told Lafleur how having the pigs took her straight back to the place in the Imperial Valley where she'd grown up . . . home.

"While we were there, Vic asked me what I thought of you," she said. "I asked him what did it matter what I thought. He said he wanted a woman's opinion, but I knew my opinion was about as much use to him as the three pigs, three sheep, and the two horses on a multi-million construction site. He said that he guessed you'd do. And I said that you probably would, that anyone could see you'd do the work, all right. It was clear as a bell."

She looked straight at Lafleur. "And anyone could, too. You looked a little rough, all right, the day you turned up, with your dirty clothes and

313

bandaged head, but certain of yourself, nevertheless, and probably pretty damn effective, and assuming absolutely nothing. That was the impression you gave—that you assumed nothing. And you had those haunted eyes with the pain in them that roved and took in everything." She hugged her knees and rocked back on the bed, and smiled faintly. "These people carrying pain, you have to give them a wide berth.

"I told Vic that he'd find out soon enough," she said. "He said he thought you had a mind of your own, and I asked him what did he want. He knew you were going to be good. Christ, he already had a file on you thick as a twenty-dollar steak: work records, military records, college transcripts, FBI reports. He had Blaylock in there telling the owners you'd be great, which meant if the project took you on, then Vic would have a lever on Blaylock, one of the owners, for God's sake. He knew what I meant, but he didn't say anything at first. That's when I began to see that he was afraid."

Lafleur said, "You knew all that?"

"That he was afraid?"

"No. The FBI files and all."

"Yes."

"You didn't tell me that."

"No. I know. That's what I'm getting to," she said. "Just wait. It's getting a little easier." She looked up at the ceiling, then continued, "He asked me if I liked you. He meant personally. He was trying to take me into something. That was like him, trying to pitch me against somebody else so he could pry something out for himself. What he wanted was what I hadn't allowed him that afternoon. You heard it while you stood at the door. Sex. He wanted it all the time. It'd got so that every time I turned around he was priming the pump. And then he wanted the other things, too, the advantage, the hold on me. He'd like to turn everybody into a pig so he could watch them fight over the feed.

"I told him I'd just met you. How should I know whether I liked you or not? But something happened when I told him that. Like a spinning thing that rose from the shadows and hurtled at me. The pigs were fighting over the last of the feed. They tangled there, snarling and biting, then they stopped and turned back to the trough. Those pigs are bred to be hungry. Him too, like them, bred to be the hungriest of all. And me, made somehow to like him as long as I did, maybe even to love him. You said it the day we split up, that he was a romance for me. It scares me to death when I think about it now, how much out of control I was. But I knew, just then. Wait," she said, raising her hand.

Lafleur had moved forward on his chair. He'd been about to tell her to go a little easier on herself. As he settled back, the old wooden chair creaked. He crossed his legs, and waited.

314

"I knew," she said. "And Vic even knew, somehow. It began right then. Somehow you know these things are beginning long before you even think them let alone say anything. What's done usually follows what's felt, but that's a hard thing for a man like Vic to accept because he's so busy all the time manipulating and plotting that he's completely out of touch with what he feels. Too much personal power. Too infectious. I got drawn in and ended up almost the same as him, but that was because I needed to find somebody with his kind of power. And then meeting you raised the possibility of another road I could follow. There I was, face to face with something I couldn't even recognize . . . you." She caught her breath and her voice came out huskily. "And not even you yourself, but what you could call out of me. That's what I felt without knowing it yet, and now I'm sorry because I've used you." She stopped and gazed at Lafleur. "Do you understand what I'm trying to tell you?"

He sat still and looked back at her. A trickle of sweat ran from his temple to his chin. Outside the window, the men could be heard laughing. What he understood so far was that she was at war with herself.

"I never got over my father's death. I was just a kid." She looked down at her hands, then up again, and told Lafleur about how her father had driven a truck for the growers in the Imperial Valley, how he and her mother had a place in the foothills where they kept animals and a small orchard. Her father had been a gentle man, she said. He spent long hours away from home trying to string the family finances together. She told Lafleur how she remembered him in knee boots, slopping the pigs, or pitching hay to the pony and the three or four head of cattle they kept, or walking in the orchard, and taking her with him, lifting her up over his head when she was little so that she could reach the fruit.

"I was twelve," she said. "The wrong age to have a parent die. Mother sold the place and we moved to Fresno. With Father gone, I lost my sense of where the control was. I had to invent my own. I became my own father in a way, and as a father I was a sonofabitch. Half of me grew up that way, desperately trying to find the control, driving myself. And in architecture, what I was really good at was bidding, running the inventories, and doing this, the field work. The same thing led me to be fascinated by Vic. He's a wizard. If you're with him in just the right way, when he's a certain way, he's like a drug. It seems like nothing will ever get out of control again.

"But they did, and then you got here, and I did like you. Right away. That was the thing hurtling at me, that and the memories of home the pigs caused, and Vic pressing it by asking about you. From the start I liked the way you approach things with your body, with your hands especially, the delicate way you address things. Sometimes men communicate possibilities that give a woman hope, which in my case was a hope I'd forgotten I could have—for a different kind of man. And maybe Vic sensed something, too, a sexual threat maybe, back then when neither he nor I had hardly any idea who you were. Maybe it was just what he'd been worried about all along—his job here, his fear that he'd blow it, or that he was already blowing it. Maybe that anxiety became real for him when you turned up because deep down he knew you were going to do your job and get everybody else to do theirs, Snediker or no Snediker. Then whatever was left would be up to him."

"No," Lafleur said. "It can't be that simple."

"Wait," she said. "I'm almost done. Your first night here when we were out feeding the pigs, I told Vic I was going back to the house and he asked if I wanted him to come. Solicitous. You need a sign with a man like him. No solicitors. I said I guessed I could find my own way out of the shed and fifty steps back to the house. I went back and waited for him. Can you believe it? In a while I heard him in the hall and then in the room, and his boots dropping, and then his belt slapping through the trouser loops. I felt the bed tipping from him leaning on it. Then I looked and watched him crawl up to me like a dog. I felt nothing for him. I couldn't even work up a lie for him. Do you see? My God, Hank! Like a whore! I've been a whore for years!"

"No," he said.

She stopped.

"It's not right for you to speak of yourself like that."

"I used you."

"You could say that about any two people. There's this kind of use and that kind."

"Yes. But if the use is equal?" she said.

"Equal?"

"If it's truly equal, there's only one kind. Love. You're angry."

It was true. Although he believed she was being too hard on herself and far too easy on him, he was angry. His legs were knotting up with tension.

"I've seen that before in you," she said.

"I'm sorry." He stood. Releasing his body, the chair creaked deeply. He moved across to the window. Iris swung her legs out, and stood beside him. The men were like black cutouts standing around the fire. Sparks floated into the sky. There were fewer workers gathered than before, and their voices had softened.

He turned his head and smiled stiffly. "But what about Smythe?"

Smythe was still out there, sitting now in a folding chair. He had it tipped back and his feet were up on a table. The firelight danced in the beer pitcher as he lifted it and drank. His bare arms glowed. "Looks like he's having a good time," she said.

"He's having a great time."

Down at the house, the yellow buglight on the porch burned, and lights burned in the bedroom, study, and kitchen, although so far as Lafleur knew Sabat was still up at the runway with the two men from the black car. He hadn't heard the Cessna arrive. Iris was looking at him. He felt his forehead beaded with sweat. His eyes felt dry.

"Smythe," she said.

Lafleur said, "Even though he means nothing, I'm curious about why you and Vic were arguing about him the day I arrived."

"I know," she said. "And about the soldier of fortune."

"Snediker."

"The day before you got here we went out to the Owyhee Café to try to get Smythe to deliver fuel to the site, and he took us out back where he has his animals. He has his pens made out of about equal parts wire and posts and old car bodies." She nudged Lafleur lightly in the ribs. "You know. Out of junk."

Lafleur nodded.

"He has sheep and pigs, quail, pheasant, chickens, and a damn jackass. You've seen how Smythe is, with his missing ear, the way he stands crooked and how he talks. He had the idea he could sell worms to Vic. He has a worm farm back there, too. There are twenty-pound catfish in the river, he said. He seemed to have trouble understanding that Vic wanted fuel delivered, that was all. Anybody that comes through here is a fisherman to Smythe, I guess. He's poking around with his shovel and stuttering, trying to talk to Vic.

"Vic gets down with him and fiddles with the worms. He really likes the con Smythe's trying to put over on him. He likes having me there wondering what the hell kind of place this is I've come to. He liked the whole pitch of things, Smythe thinking he was one kind of a fool, a dumbass city slicker, and me standing there thinking he was another kind, a fool for acting like one in front of a fool like Smythe. He liked all that and the complicated, barely coherent barter he got into with Smythe— fuel, pigs, sheep, the worms he kept refusing, and the quail, which he could have dead or alive, or if dead unplucked or plucked. It was too much for Vic to resist. He loves that, the murk. . . ." She paused when Lafleur cocked his head toward the window. "What?"

"There. The Cessna."

Suddenly the plane, alight in the sky and roaring, swooped over the house, then curled up out of sight. Its noise made the bunkhouse vibrate. At the fire, the heads of the workers tipped up toward the sky. They turned as one, watching the plane bank to land. "They'll take him away now," she said.

317

Faintly, the Cessna's wheels could be heard squealing on the asphalt strip. "Where?" Lafleur said.

"I don't know."

"They can just haul a guy away like that?"

"They fired him over two weeks ago. He refused to leave. Technically, I guess he's trespassing."

"Yes, but trespassing is against the law," he said.

"Yes."

"The law," he said.

"They like to take care of their own."

He reached out and picked at the paint on the window sill. "That's the kind of stuff you get over the modem?"

"I get it all over the modem. They've offered me Vic's job. Not just fill in for him. The job."

Lafleur wasn't surprised because it made complete sense. He said, "Are you going to take it?"

"I have taken it. Two weeks ago. If I see this through, they'll send me to Washington, D.C. I'll be in charge of feasibility studies, an executive. I'll be traveling all over the world. This winter I'll spend a month in Brazil preparing a mockup of a new penal system."

"Congratulations," he said, but it came out weakly. Such a prospect chilled him.

"Yes," she said. "I'm ambitious. I do good work and I keep my mouth shut, so I'm moving up. I'm scared, too, but I also like the rush you get from power. I'm a Judas."

"And that makes him what?"

She paused, then understood, and chuckled softly.

"So they're pissed with him," he said.

"Pissed? He brought Snediker in as his own man, which was a mistake. But what really got them was the fact that he couldn't control Snediker, or didn't. There's the press, which hasn't got into us too deeply, yet, but if they work up a head of steam on something like that, it could get very bad. This is a politically sensitive operation, especially in this state, and it was looking like Vic wanted to show everybody just what kind of abuse it was capable of, like he was running up a flag to get the press's attention."

"Those prisoners were here on the quiet, right?" Lafleur said.

"They should never have been sent to an incomplete facility. They were excess from Texas that the company agreed on the spur of the moment to take in temporarily. Everything . . ."

"Wait," Lafleur said. "There's something I want to know. I thought this was a federal pen."

"Yes."

"This place is built to house long-term prisoners, mainly. Like American felonies, right?"

"Yes."

"Not foreigners. I mean, legally, can it do both?"

"Don't ask," she said. She reached for her bag, which was on the bed, took out a Gauloise and lit it. The flash from her lighter briefly swept the ceiling. She turned back to him. As she inhaled, the glow at the end of the tube cast two faint shadows from her nose. Like wings the shadows darted across her eyes to the sides of her forehead. "Yes, it's a federal pen. In most respects it's like any other federal pen, but there are new laws that provide for flexibility in its mission."

He looked at her, frowning. "And the pit's part of that flexibility?"

She shook her head slowly, telling him once more, *Don't ask.* She said, "Let's say it's a training facility."

"Training who?" he said. "And who the hell gets to be the guinea pigs?"

"Even if I knew the answer to those questions, I wouldn't be able to say."

Lafleur turned away and leaned against the window sill. He looked out at Smythe and the few workers who were left there, gathered around the fire. The scent of Iris's cigarette drifted past his nose. He had a hollow feeling in his belly. He felt angry and afraid—for himself, for Iris, for his countrymen. "The pit is the bottom line in this operation."

"For you, maybe," Iris said.

"For whoever gets put in there," he said without looking at her. "For anybody who touches this place."

In the periphery of his vision he saw her head tip back and then the intensifying flare of her cigarette as she dragged on it. The cigarette descended and a cloud of white smoke flattened against the window. "Anyway," she said, "Vic jeopardized the whole damn thing. Everything was going out of control. You bet the company was pissed."

In the distance, the Cessna could be heard taking off, its roar rising, then dwindling. The workers lifted their heads to watch, but the plane couldn't be seen from the bunkhouse. It would take off with the wind and circle westward.

"He's gone," she said.

The last of the workers drifted away. Smythe was left there, sitting with his pitcher of beer. The bonfire had burned down and was visible only as a glowing bed of coals.

"Why did he do that with Snediker?" Lafleur said.

"Mainly his fixation on power, his desperation to keep power."

"But if he's the control freak you say he is, why the hell couldn't he control Snediker?"

"He overreached himself. That's what I'm trying to tell you. What he was very good at got outside of him. It got bigger than he was and it overpowered him. And somehow Snediker seems to have got the idea that he could do whatever he damn pleased. It's psychic symbiosis."

"All right," Lafleur said. That much he could understand. He gazed at Smythe, who looked happy out there with his pitcher of beer. Iris put out her cigarette and took a breath. Lafleur heard the air going in and felt her body poised beside him, holding the air. "So," he said, turning his head to her. He felt his smile on his face almost like a sneer. "Smythe."

"So that came out with Vic buying three pigs and three sheep, no worms, and six plucked quail, which we had for dinner the night you arrived. Remember?" she said. She looked closely at him, too closely. They both turned away and gazed out the window again. She said, "And Smythe didn't deliver the fuel after all and Vic had to go after it himself the next day, then Smythe started delivering, but with the price marked up, and now we've eaten one pig and one lamb and the others Vic's given back to Smythe in exchange for Smythe butchering the two of them and cooking them up and taking the trouble to haul the rest of them out of here, those with several months' worth of feed in them and that bought retail from Smythe. Smythe's got to think it's great."

"Lots of free beer, too," Lafleur said.

"Right. He's got to think he's pulled a fast one. He doesn't understand that Vic never cared, not about that. Vic didn't care about money, especially when it wasn't his money he was squandering. All he really cared about was power. And Smythe probably still doesn't understand that he was conned by Vic, according to Vic's own terms, for the sake of Vic's pleasure, but maybe it doesn't matter with Smythe, you see, because he hasn't been hurt. So maybe it's all right in that case. Maybe the only way to deal with Vic is to not know what he's up to."

"And with International Data, too?" Lafleur said.

Iris paused, then said, "Maybe."

"And Frank?" Lafleur said. "He doesn't know what the hell's going on, but maybe he'll make a few extra bucks off the traffic. Maybe that's okay. Maybe you have to work at being stupid."

"Maybe," Iris said. There was an aggressive edge to her voice.

"And you?" he said, looking at her. "Your plan is to go on here and somehow not know about the pit?"

She didn't respond. Her head was utterly still, backlit by the lamp in the corner and washed faintly white by the light from the window.

"And Jim Basto?" he said.

"All right," she said softly. "He was hurt."

"Hurt?" Lafleur said. "He's dead."

"All right," Iris said, more forcefully. "But I didn't know that. Vic knew. That should tell you something. I arranged to get Vic to Burns Junction like I was told to do. I knew something unpleasant was going to happen. But I didn't know about Jim."

"Unpleasant?" Lafleur said.

"That's what it was," she said, jerking her head toward Lafleur. "Extremely unpleasant. And in Vic's mind he still nailed me, or us. In his mind he's hurt us. And he certainly hurt the old woman that Snediker raped. He hurt Snediker. Maybe he killed Snediker." She looked at the wall, and reached out and touched it, then looked back at Lafleur. "He practically killed you, and he hurt those prisoners who were sent here. Right?" she said, cocking her head. Her eyes flashed.

She went on before he could speak: "And then he went completely out of whack. But he couldn't give up. You have to give him credit for the strength of his will. He still threw this party for the workers, so they'd be grateful, and by not telling us about the funeral he still managed to embarrass us at Burns Junction." She stopped, caught her breath, then said, "Extraordinary! I think he's genuinely mad." She stopped again, took another breath, and said, "And that gun he was carrying? That wasn't for you, or to protect himself with. He was going to shoot himself."

"Are you kidding?" Lafleur said, startled.

"No, I'm not kidding," she said. "I mean I don't know, really, but that'd be my guess. He had nothing left. A mind like his, used to maneuvering through the labyrinth, when it's deranged, takes refuge in the extremes of symmetry. So he thought he could get the last one over on everybody by killing himself right there in Burns Junction. Just like Jim. Don't you see? It's not just you. You can't take everything so personally."

Lafleur's body rocked back slightly and he felt his face blanch.

"Now, I've offended you," she said. "But you're pushing me, Hank. I've never wanted to offend you."

Again she startled him, saying that. It was true that he was offended, or more correctly, mortified. He wasn't convinced that she was right about Sabat—he remembered too vividly the moment on the parking lot in Rome, Sabat's fluttering hand, his venomous expression—but if she was right, then he would be mortified by the continuing distortion of his perception. Whether she was right or wrong, he was mortified, or even galled by the fact that she still knew him well enough to strike that close to the heart of what troubled him most, now—his failure to see clearly. "I don't like being a fool," he said.

"I know," she said. "It hurts to be one. I hurt." Her voice suddenly modulated downward to a moan: "God, I hurt." She bowed her head and lifted her hands to her face. She was about to cry. "I'm sorry," she said. She turned her back to him and moved over by the bed.

He thought he should comfort her, but he couldn't. He looked back out the window. The black car returned and stopped in front of the house. The headlights switched off.

Iris's voice came softly and evenly as if from the far end of the room, as if she were informing herself: "This isn't like me." She stepped back beside Lafleur. Down at the house, a figure emerged from the car: the unmistakable portly outline of Clinton U. "There he is," Iris said.

Lafleur glanced at her. She seemed to be herself again, her composed face fringed by light from the lamp, and her body poised, balanced like a dancer's body. Seeing her so, he felt himself steadying once again in his anger. Outside, the figure moved to the door of the house and went inside. "U," he said.

"He's back."

"The way I see it," Lafleur said, "a guy like Vic is the creation of an outfit like International Data."

"Maybe."

Lafleur said, "The soldier of fortune you two were talking about while I was standing outside the door that first day, the one you called a killer. That was Snediker?"

"Yes."

"So you knew."

"I knew about Snediker. Yes."

"You knew he'd beaten me in Portland."

"Yes. But not that the rest of it would happen, not the raping, not that he would try to kill you. I didn't imagine it would go that far. I suspected that Vic somehow needed to have somebody like Snediker around, but I didn't put it all together until later. That's all. U knew about the beating in Portland, too, and he didn't approve. I knew that. I was sure U would take care of it."

"But he didn't. And what you knew you didn't tell me, not even after you'd figured it out, not until it was done."

"No."

"And you tried to warn me, but only in your own way. Not in a way that would've convinced me. Not with everything you knew."

"Yes."

"And today you got me to go along with you to Burns Junction without warning me."

"Yes. But you wouldn't have come if I'd told you. I wanted to have you with me."

"Okay," he said. "I'll grant you that one for the sake of friendship, but not the others."

"I wanted you to know all of it. But I needed you more than you needed me," she said. "I didn't want to lose you."

"So instead you let me get set up to be killed?"

"I didn't know that!"

He shook his head. He saw that they'd reached what he'd wanted her to name the day they split up, what he himself in his idiocy hadn't been able to grasp. "I don't understand," he said. "I understand what you're saying, but I don't understand you."

"I was disentangling myself from Vic," she said. "When I was with you I wanted to avoid anything that had to do with him."

"And that's all?"

She stood still next to him. He sensed the coldness of her presence. She said, "That isn't enough? Look, I loved him once. It was wrong for me, God knows, but I ended up inside him for a while just like Snediker, inside his charm, and Vic was different back then, too, before we came out here. He was just a little crazy. I was different. But for a while, yes, out here, with you, that was all because I was getting out from under Vic's power, which was more than enough for me to handle, and then even as I was doing that, just when I saw I was going to make it, I saw I was going to lose you. At about the same time I saw I was going to be promoted, and I'd have a company car, and more possibilities for the future, authority, a trip to Brazil. It was something like that, all that mixed in and overlapping, happening almost at once. Now I don't have you, but all those other things will help me bear being alone. Don't you see?"

"No." He looked at her. Her cheek and jaw were drawn. She, too, was angry. Her eyes looked ferocious. Her anger reaffirmed his own and he felt secure in it, and suddenly more certain than he'd felt for months. He said, "When you work for a company like International Data, there are certain things you don't talk about. You've made that very clear."

She kept staring straight at him. "All right."

"Not talking about certain things is a condition of employment."

"All right," she said. Her voice was tight. "So you think it was that, too."

"It's impossible not to think that."

"And you think it was a betrayal."

"Of course," he said. "Even if I were just a friend. I never thought of you as someone who would have done that to me."

As he watched, the hardness and ferocity passed from her face, then she touched his arm lightly. "But deep down I knew you wouldn't keep me. Almost from the same instant I knew you could rescue me."

"And if I would have?" he said. "If you'd believed that I would?"

"I don't know," she said.

"If I'd stayed in love with you, you'd have fucked me over anyway."

"But you didn't. You weren't! I never had a chance with you, even though you were right for me," she said. "Right enough, anyway, but we were on a collision course. We were bound to wreck."

Lafleur shifted his feet. The floor creaked. His entire body felt tense, and almost painfully alert. He stared out the window. The lights were still burning in the ranchhouse. "That's probably true."

She didn't move. "Yes. One way and another you've been saying that all along. It makes my blood run cold."

"It's all right. I obviously never had a chance with you, either."

"So we used each other."

He detected a note of hopefulness in her tone, which increased his anger. "Somehow that doesn't handle it, Iris."

She reached out to the window sill and picked at the same scaling paint he'd picked at. In the arc of its movement her hand moved into the light and stayed there for a moment, whitened, then fell back to the darkness at her side.

"Look," he said. "The way I figure it, people are going to be tortured in that place."

She didn't speak.

"And say your company runs short of them, the felons, or illegals, or whatever? Then what? How does it re-stock? Such possibilities don't bother you?"

She slipped away from him once again, saying, "I've always known you were going back to your wife."

Exasperated, he spoke almost brutally. "She won't take me."

"You don't know that. You haven't even read your letter."

They stared out the window. Smythe had fallen asleep. He still had his legs up on the table. His chair was balanced on two legs and the beer pitcher was perfectly cradled in his lap. The ground was littered with paper cups and plates. The coals from the bonfire played across the side of Smythe's body. His strange creased, one-eared head lolled to the side. In his stupor, he looked contented. He was one of the few persons alive to have ever wrestled Victor Sabat and come out unscathed.

"How are you going to live with it?" Lafleur said.

"What about you? Your hands aren't so clean."

"Exactly. I've never been this close to evil, not even in war, and I've never felt so stupid. I built this horror."

"I've got myself. I'm not Victor Sabat. I can live with myself," she said.

"Just one of you, or the both of you?"

"Both of us," she said. The irony in her voice came out hard as steel. "Iris and me."

Lafleur's body, shuddering like a flame, was consumed by anger. He turned and walked swiftly to the hall and down to his room. He took Penny's letter from his pocket, and paused for a moment, just stood there gazing at the envelope. He stripped and climbed into bed. He lay still on his back, holding the letter. His legs and the back of his neck ached. When he closed his eyes, he saw Ruth's needle, poking in and out of the cloth. The cool air, the huge silence of the desert filled his room. He began to hear sounds in it, a creak of wood, a bird, singing frantically at the night, and a hushed sound, something like trucks passing in the distance. It was the muffled voice of a woman, sobbing uncontrollably.

Chapter Twenty-two

Three mornings later, Lafleur parked his dump truck in front of the bunkhouse. His backhoe was chained down in the bed and his tools and spare cans of lubricant were loaded. He had mounted the tailgate. This equipment of his, which he still did not own exactly, but would someday, and to which he had given so much forethought in the bringing, now seemed an afterthought. He'd loaded it all carefully enough, and had gone around tugging on chain and kicking tires, but it all seemed to be just what it was now, tools, mere accessories to the fact.

He also had four of Jim's paintings in the truck, wrapped in the sheet and wedged gently between the front of the bed and one backhoe tire. He planned to drop them off at Burns Junction. When he'd gone down to the house, the place was empty. The doors were open, including the bedroom with its two double beds. U had slept there. His thin suitcase stood on the floor. Lafleur took the two paintings off the walls of the study, and paused, looking around. The computer was gone, but everything was exactly as it had always been—the books, the drawings by Colnett, the models of ships, the carpet, the furniture. Lafleur looked down at the model of the project, then out the window and over the rock wall at the actual project. Except for the toy prisoners in the model, the little men with rosy cheeks, the two were a match . . . out there what he could see of the big one, and in here the tiny one, foreplay to the complicated act, the three-dimensional map mounted on plexiglass complete with the river on one end and the runway on the other. He felt like a giant looking down at the model. He felt like a corrupt god.

He picked up the two paintings and went out, stopping at the company pickup for the two remaining paintings that still lay in the bed, wrapped in a sheet and untouched since the trip to Burns Junction. He leaned the two paintings he had against a tire, hopped into the bed, and tipped up the others. The sheet was coated with dust. It slipped away from the paintings. The one in front, the smaller, was another seascape, but the visible edges of the second painting immediately asserted something different. The colors were different—beige, soft green, a luminous yellow. Lafleur lifted the front painting up and looked down at the second. It was a picture of this place, the ranch, in the old days. It showed the front of the house, the sheds and pens, the barn, and behind the barn the top of the stone silo, and in the background the lime-green cliffs. A corner of the planted field, a deep green, was visible, and from the edge of the field a file of Guernsey cows moved toward the barn. A man drove a tractor along the front of the barn. A woman waved to him from the porch of the house. Three children, two boys and a girl, ran toward him with outstretched arms. A goat peeped out from one of the pens. It was like a Currier and Ives scene, but western. It was a romance with everything squeezed tightly into itself under a phenomenal soft yellow light. The painting didn't have the same illusory quality of his seascapes. It had accuracy. It was a history. History, Lafleur remembered, was created by the dead. The dead, he thought, had conjured up this picture in the imagination.

He took all four paintings up to the dump truck and packed them in. He went back into the bunkhouse to gather his personal articles. He moved quickly, stuffing things into cartons—clothes and odds and ends all mixed together. He paused when he came to the half-full sack of dog food, then went out and put it in the truck along with the cartons. He returned to the bunkhouse and pulled open the top drawer of the dresser. It was littered with memento-like articles, things he had almost forgotten about, his junk—the clay head, the pictures his children had sent, the pens and pads of paper, the magnifying glass, the cold chisel, the shotgun shell, the triangle with Chinese writing. . . . He put the triangle in his shirt pocket, thinking that he could show it to U. Everything else he dumped into a carton.

He took that out and as he returned again he glanced over at U, who was perched on the top rail of the corral, watching Iris saddle the white horse. U was waiting for him. Iris was going to make herself scarce. He went into Iris's room, and gathered what of his had been left there, the two rifles and the pistol in its case. He picked up the book, the Zeta, that Iris had insisted he keep, then put it down again. He crammed everything he could into the suitcase with the mouse hole in it. He stood the suitcase on its spine and looked around. Several of Iris's dresses hung in the closet. He gazed at them for a moment, imagining her in them, then picked up the suitcase in his left hand and cradled the two rifles in the crook of his right arm and started out, but stopped and turned back for the old post that had the records of harvests penciled into it. He planned to leave that for Kasanian in Burns Junction. He jammed the post under his left arm and went out into the morning light. He thought, I'm going out of the bunkhouse now. For the last time.

He loaded his things and walked up to the corral. When he came to the end of the barn, he saw Iris astride the white horse, rounding the far corner outside the corral. U swung his legs over the top rail, turning to face outward. Iris walked her horse in front of the metal building. Her reflection shimmered behind her. Inside the corral, the black horse walked along beside her, then stopped at the corner and hung its head out. Iris wore dark-blue corduroys, high boots, and a loose white shirt. Her horse snorted and shook its head. The black horse nickered back. Iris looked over once, seeing Lafleur, and he looked back at her. A searching exchange flashed between them, and then he felt his eyes grow hooded. She looked away. They took cover from one another. Her horse sidestepped. Her body rocked, then snapped forward. The horse jerked. Iris appeared hard to him as she had in the beginning, smooth, angular, and bright.

Lafleur stopped beside U, grasped the fence and hiked himself up. U wore a pinstriped western-cut suit, alligator cowboy boots, and snapdown shades over his thick glasses. Lafleur hooked his bootheels over the bottom rung of the fence. At their backs was the project, from which hammering, voices, and power tools could be heard. The work went on. To their right was the alleyway that passed alongside the barn toward the house. Before them was an open view of the desert. To their left was the metal building and just past it, now, Iris, keeping the horse at a walk.

He and U discussed the schedule and their arrangements—how often Lafleur would come back (perhaps no more than twice), when the final phases of the project would be complete, and how Lafleur would be paid his bonus, which he in turn would sign over to Blaylock. They discussed Lopez, who would be in charge in Lafleur's absence. They paused, gazing out at Iris, who had the horse at a trot and was turning it around and around in a tight figure eight. She'd taken to riding again. The horses, she'd said, had become sloppy. Puffs of dust lifted from the hooves and made a slowly lengthening lateral sheet above the ground. Lafleur reached into his pocket, took out the metal triangle, and passed it to U. U flicked up his shades and turned the triangle slowly in his short, pudgy fingers, squinting at it.

"I guess you heard about the body we found," Lafleur said. When U nodded, Lafleur said, "We found that with it. I thought the writing was Chinese."

U looked down at it again. "It is."

"What is it?"

U shrugged. "A medallion." He flicked his shades down and passed the triangle back. "It's from a secret society."

"Secret. Would it tell you something about the boy?"

"Boy?" U said.

"We figured it was a boy."

U turned his head to Lafleur and said, "That he might have been Chinese."

Lafleur looked at the medallion, then down at his dust-coated boots. He sensed that U considered it improper for him to have the triangle, or to ask about it. He didn't know. It didn't matter. Carrying on this conversation with this man, the pleasant proprietor of horror, made everything seem strange, as if all the rules had been suspended. Lafleur felt as though he were dancing on a very thin skin through which he might break at any moment. He returned the triangle to his pocket and thought of Jones bringing him the hand in the night. He thought about the trail in the bank above the body, and of the music left in the grass by those who had passed there. He could see it in his mind, the grass blades waving in different fashions. He thought of Mr. M., who had his power of traveling taken away from him.

He and U discussed Lopez again. They decided that the manager who was installing the computer plant should report to Reno through Iris, that Lopez would continue reporting to Lafleur, and that if there were problems Lafleur could work through Iris. If necessary, Lafleur could make an extra trip out or call U. U eased down from the fence, took out his wallet, and handed Lafleur a business card.

Lafleur stepped down and put the card in his wallet. He bent and unbent his legs. They heard a truck approaching. In a moment, a two-ton van appeared, turned down the drive, then cut across above them to the site, raising a large wedge-shaped fan of dust. He and U turned back and leaned against the fence, facing the desert again. It was midmorning. Lately, it had begun to turn chilly at night, and standing in the seventy-degree sun felt good. Iris was still out there, going around and around. Her head was bowed with the intentness Lafleur knew well as she reined the horse sharply back and forth.

U said that Iris was going to stay on.

"I heard," Lafleur said. "She's replacing Vic."

U turned his head to Lafleur and smiled. The corners of his lips turned up and his dimples deepened. The sunglasses made it impossible to see his eyes.

Lafleur took a chance and asked, "What'd you do with him?"

U stopped smiling. "Victor wasn't reliable."

"I guess not," Lafleur said.

"He was dishonest and unreliable," U said. "So we took him off the job. We nearly lost our contract because of him. He knew far too much to be that unreliable."

"I see," Lafleur said. He gazed out at the desert, and wondered just what "off the job" meant to U. Iris had reined in the horse. It stood still. Iris sat still. She was making the horse obey. Her white shirt fluttered lightly in the breeze. At his back, Lafleur could hear the black horse walking across the corral to the water tank.

"Snediker, too," U said. "He hurt us. We picked him up."

"No kidding," Lafleur said. He looked down and stubbed his boot toe into the sand. He wondered if the police knew, but decided not to ask. The ability of U's organization to drop on a person out of nowhere and the perfunctory way U spoke of it horrified Lafleur. He wasn't getting out of here any too soon, he knew. "I wish somebody had told me you had him," he said. "It could have saved me some worry."

U shrugged. "Sorry." His apology meant nothing.

Lafleur thought about Snediker roaming around up there above the cliffs with the wild horses and snakes. He wondered how long he'd done that before he was picked up. He wondered how they'd found him. He wondered what it would have been like if he hadn't been found, or how it might still be in the talk among the local people with none of them knowing he'd been taken away—the speculative talk that might have him turning up in one place and another and in the spaces in between, the gossip that could make him legendary like Sasquatch, like Starr Wilkinson, like Claude Dallas. In reality, Snediker was just a deluded sonofabitch who'd been picked up, but in the talk he would always be out there, a huge, snakebit survivor, a carrier of trouble, an essential aberration who ran with the speed of a ghost.

"What kind of shape was he in?" Lafleur said.

"Physically? Not bad, I hear. Otherwise, a mess."

Lafleur nodded. Something boomed from the site. The echo bounced around. It was the door of the two-ton van, probably, thrown open in preparation for unloading.

"He's under treatment," U said.

"Treatment for what?"

"Madness," U said. "He's crazy."

"But when he's treated, then what?"

"Who knows?" U said. "It will be a long time."

Unnerved, Lafleur remembered the beating in Portland, the smell of wet wool, Snediker's breath, the fist slamming his head against the window. He said, "Look, I know quite a bit myself. I know the design better than almost anybody."

U stared out into the desert for a moment without speaking. Then he turned his head and said, "But you're reliable."

"I see," Lafleur said, looking at the two images of himself in U's sunglasses. He thought it strange that being assured he was reliable sounded like a threat, and equally strange that U would perceive him so.

"You wouldn't talk," U said.

He turned back and looked out at the desert, galled by the fact that he'd been read that way. Iris had set the horse to a trot. She was moving farther away. Her shirt fluttered behind her. Lafleur looked down at the ground, then along the ground to his left toward the metal building. He saw something moving behind a bush. It came out, slithering . . . a snake, one of those western blacks. Lafleur stared at it.

U went on: "Don't take me wrong. You attend to work, not to talking. You honored your contract. That's all I mean."

"I object to this project," Lafleur said.

"Yes," U said. "We know. But what can you do?"

"I feel compromised by it. I don't like it. I put up with a lot of bullshit here and in Portland. I will talk."

"Even that doesn't matter, now," U said neutrally. "It's too late."

Lafleur watched the snake. It slid in their direction. It acted like it had all the time in the world. He was not alarmed because by now the snakes had become almost a daily matter. He looked out into the desert again. Iris and the horse had grown smaller. He saw the dark head, the white shirt, the white rump of the horse, and the dark hooves kicking up dust.

"So far as security is concerned," U said, "we're much more worried about what goes on in the plant than about somebody knowing how or why it's built. What are you going to do? Organize a raid? With Vic it was mainly his unreliability. You understand that."

Lafleur grunted, and thought that if U meant using secrets and being deceptive, and likely to devalue character at any turn, always making use of people for his own purposes, and of being pathologically manipulative and creating a house of lies, of constructing that for himself and for whoever else could be tricked into living in it, then he guessed he understood that Sabat was unreliable. But what, Lafleur wondered once again, of the house that stands behind us, the towers and secured buildings, the pit buried three stories down, grotesquely equipped with electrified cells and instruments? What of its purpose that Iris told me not to ask about? For training foreign insurrectionists? Housing terrorists? Detaining who? What, for God's sake? What of those secrets, what of the people I am also not to ask about who are to be kept there, subjected to such interrogation? That's the house of lies. And what if Sabat merely became who he was by being involved in such a place, and so was never unreliable, for these purposes, but on the contrary utterly and thoroughly reliable according to U's terms, of a piece with where he was? And what, he thought, if it's for that reliability grown somehow too complete that he had to be junked like a piece of debris? Lafleur remembered liking Victor Sabat, once, briefly. Iris had liked him for a long time, even loved him.

"You're not unreliable," U said. "We admire you."

Lafleur looked at the snake, which had moved half the distance between the metal building and where he and U stood—close enough to require a reaction. He felt cold. To be told by U that he was admired also seemed dangerous. He said the only thing he could think of: "There's a snake."

U turned his head. He wasn't afraid. "Where?"

Lafleur nodded his head to the left and U looked.

"Now we stay still, right?" U said. He smiled faintly. His dimples deepened.

Lafleur thought that he might have liked U, too. "Yes," he said. "But I bet he turns away before he reaches us."

They watched the snake for a moment. It took its time. They could easily have moved away, but they didn't. "We owe you an apology for what happened to you here and in Portland," U said.

"According to Iris, Vic sent Snediker after me in Portland," Lafleur said.

"Of course."

Lafleur looked out into the desert, not speaking. The affirmation told him nothing more, after all. U's apology meant nothing. Iris and the horse had become a vague whiteness, now. That was all. "So what about Vic?" he said. "He's under treatment, too?"

"No," U said.

The snake was clearly visible. It was not an old snake. It was half the size of the one Lafleur had thrown at Snediker, and it was the color of the desert exactly. It had the darkness of desert shadow and the lightness of desert bush, stalk, leaf, sand, and stone. All the colors of the desert were in its skin. Lafleur regarded it as a friend. It marked him as being here. The snake turned away from them, as he had expected. They watched as it disappeared under the bunkhouse. In a moment, a mouse darted out.

U chuckled softly. In the distance the white of Iris's shirt and of the horse's rump were barely visible. The longer he watched the less sure he became of what he was looking at, and then just when he was sure he was looking at nothing out there, just at the desert, the whiteness suddenly popped back into view and increased in size. It was a dust cloud, hurtling across the desert. He saw four white horses, galloping, pulling an open wagon. Above the wagon the dust cloud curled and billowed, and he saw Uncle Spence driving the horses with a whip, and Jim, sitting beside

Spence, both of them swinging heavily to and fro with the motion. In the back was a load of quarried limestone blocks. The dust, the horses, and the limestone were all the same color of white. The wagon was black. The load swayed. The horses strained against their traces and their hooves thundered. The wagon careered toward the hills.

Lafleur glanced at U. He was staring blankly outward, then he bent to adjust his belt buckle. Lafleur looked back out into the desert. The wagon was gone. The dust cloud was gone. It was a vision, that was all, come to break the ground of his horror, the web of the thrall he was under. Lafleur felt quite calm. He had his idiot chained up tightly inside himself. Iris was completely out of sight. A crow flew overhead and cawed. Its black shadow skittered across the ground. That, too, marked him. Iris's absence marked him. The black horse came up beside him, stuck its head over the top of the fence, and looked out into the desert. U, who stood right there, marked him like a negative entity and defined his guilt.

Lafleur had a host of questions he might have liked to ask. He reached up and stroked the black horse's nose, and thought that on the other hand he didn't really want to ask anything. He had enough, now, enough data. It would be all he could manage to hang on to himself with what he had.

But, as if beckoned, he turned and looked at U—pudgy face, freckled cheeks, dimples quick to register humor, black mirrors over his eyes in which Lafleur saw himself twice. . . .

"Sabat's dead," U said.

. . . *a messenger, evil angel* . . .

"Dead?" Lafleur said. He saw the man of iron in U, the very mind of I.D.

"He jumped out of the plane over Nevada."

"What?" Lafleur said, appalled. "Jumped?"

U shrugged and said, "Be careful."

Quickly, Lafleur looked back out into the desert. It was a lie. Sabat hadn't jumped. Behind him, hammers and power nailers reverberated softly. The black horse blew air. In the distance the crow cawed again. Lafleur saw nothing out in the desert, just the exquisite desert itself. He felt cold and empty and afraid. It was surely time to leave this place.

He took the drive away from the site without looking back, through the sandstone formations, past the increasingly frequent jackrabbit bodies, past the alfalfa farms to Rome, and turned onto the highway, heading west. He left the Rome Café, and Smythe's place, the Owyhee Café, and Roscoe's Gems. All those new signs fell behind him.

At Burns Junction he stopped and dropped off the pictures and the post from the barn. Only Sally was inside, setting up for the day, although

Lafleur could hear Frank out back, hammering away at the new motel rooms they were adding. There was a new sign in the window, too—BUDWEISER. Sally was grateful for what he'd brought. Effusive, she assured him that Ruth and Abe would be grateful. She wanted to give him coffee and call Frank in, but Lafleur declined. He came away thinking about death again—Jim's death, and then Sabat's death, the death of old Spencer McHugh, whose ghost he'd seen lifting the stones, Nampuh's death, Mr. M.'s death, the death of his father, Nicole's death, and the death of Jones, whose body had been scattered across the desert and turned into coyote dung, bird dung. He missed Jones in the cab of his truck, leaning against him and slobbering on his leg. He heard Kasanian's parrot crying, *Goodbye! Goodbye! Goodbye!*

He passed a small battleground of newly erected billboards, mounted for the eastbound traffic. He read them inside out in his mirrors. A new and flimsy telemetry, they carried messages about the mythical last gas and food in Oregon.

He passed Princeton, Crane, the satellite receiving station, Lawen, Hines, Riley, Hampton, Brothers, Millican, and Tumalo. The Three Sisters, brilliant, white, and huge, came into view just west of Burns. They disappeared. Then they came back again. They were like a twinkling in the distance, and as he watched them, or watched for them, he thought about where he was headed—back to see Jewel, back to see Tricia and Andy, back to visit his father's grave, back to where Nicole had died, back to talk to Louis about the partnership, back to see Blaylock, back to the new company, which he would keep small. . . .

His mind wrenched on that point, this wish to keep his company small and compact, a lightweight craft of commerce that he would never again allow to nose into another multinational. It struck him suddenly that he was slipping into another false romance. The farther away he drove from Rome, the more ghastly what he was leaving behind seemed to him, all of what had been realized by his effort—the pit deep in the Industries Building, the manacles, the electrified pallets, the cells wired to high voltage, razor wire, guard towers, the control monitors, the people seized by power. It wasn't going to be enough to keep his company small, and not enough to never again treat his work as only a job.

But what? he wondered. *What?*

He was going back to see Penny, whose letter he had in his hip pocket again, keeping it secure there. The letter contained probate papers for the inheritance he and Penny shared—the house on the river, the partnership. He was to sign these, Penny had written, and also to sign the papers that would allot proceeds from the sale of the house to Jewel and the children. There'd already been an offer on the house, which he was to consider. His father's will, he'd observed, gave no credence to his and Penny's separation. That was a web, gathered around a rip. Penny explained all the papers to him in a note, and also said that Jewel was back from San Diego, that she was fine, that the kids were fine, and she closed her letter with this: "When you return, come here."

On the page, the words looked neutral and might have meant anything—come here and drop off the documents, come here and visit the kids. . . . But he also heard her saying the words, and saw her face, the eyes fixing him and the voice rising, meaning him, you come here. Penny did not make such statements lightly.

He knew of one thing he wanted to tell her . . . that in that moment of barbecuing for a picnic their attention had lapsed and Nicole had fallen in, and what had happened and what they had done in their lapse were irrevocable. What they had done wrong next was to take the blame on themselves, each of them exclusively. They held it hard to themselves as if—paradoxically—to keep themselves from being blamed, as if they needed the exclusive blame in order to continue standing up against the world. It was proper to blame themselves, he thought, but once the blame was placed it had to be shared, which he had never done with her.

It was more his fault than hers. It was mainly he who had allowed death itself to come between them. Nicole was out there along with Jim and Nampuh, Gus, Sabat, Jones, Uncle Spence, and Mr. M., waiting for them to do something about death. The blame needed to be passed back and forth and dispersed among the evil and good things that surrounded them. It had to be aired like gossip and woven into history. One had to try to move freely in the terrible thrall, to accept it as a condition of living, and then to be alert. It was only so that one could conduct oneself properly. If he'd learned anything from Sabat, from Iris, and, today, from U, from that menace of the living dead, or from Hector Zeta, from the wisdom of the book which he'd left for Iris in the hope that she would use it, resting where she'd be sure to see it on the upturned milk carton beside her bed—if he had learned anything it was to stop tripping over his own junk and to be alert, to come back to life. That was what he wanted to tell her. He would go there and tell her that to start with, then let it rest and try to stay calm, to accept whatever came, expecting nothing. It was going to be hard, but then maybe he could be friends with himself and keep himself steady in his outrage and, threat or no threat, find a way to struggle against the likes of International Data, to air that horror. There, he thought. Start there. He had a long penance before him. He had no alternative but to go through it.

He went through Bend and the pine trees started in, first the piñon pines, then scraggly ponderosas. He went through Sisters, the little town dandied up for the tourist trade. The mountains loomed before him. The ponderosas presented themselves in earnest and then the white pines, the spruces, the firs. Everything felt steady in his truck. He felt as though he were ascending from Hell, from a scorching wilderness but one also beloved of God. He was weary, as weary as he'd been when he'd first driven out here, but in his weariness he felt himself slowly filling with hope. Soon he would wind through the mountains. Night would fall. He would see the lights of Corvallis in the valley. From there he would turn north.